Praise for
*MAGE HEART*
and the other Dion novels by
**JANE ROUTLEY**

"A mixture of cleverness, subtlety, and emotion."
*Locus*

"A winner . . . High fantasy which doesn't pretend to be
anything else . . . Some fantasy tales are derivative.
This one stands on its own."
*Coastal Maine News*

"Rewarding . . . Characters that engage one's interest
and noteworthy world building."
*Booklist*

"Entertaining . . . a pleasure . . .
Routley keeps the action moving at a brisk pace."
*SF Site*

"Routley's attention to detail and her gift for creating
strong characters make this a good choice."
*Library Journal*

"I've already read Jane Routley's *Mage Heart* twice."
*Philadelphia Weekly Press*

*Other Eos Titles by*
**Jane Routley**

FIRE ANGELS
ARAMAYA

# Mage Heart

## Jane Routley

*An Imprint of HarperCollinsPublishers*

EOS
*An Imprint of* HarperCollins*Publishers*
10 East 53rd Street
New York, New York 10022-5299

Copyright © 1996 by B. J. Routley
Cover art by Donato
Library of Congress Catalog Card Number: 95-47952
ISBN: 0-380-78127-1

First Eos paperback printing: May 2000
First Eos hardcover printing: July 1996

Eos Trademark Reg. U.S. Pat. Off. and in Other Countries,
Marca Registrada, Hecho en U.S.A.
HarperCollins® is a trademark of HarperCollins Publishers Inc.

Printed in the U.S.A.

WCD  10  9  8  7  6  5  4  3  2  1

www.avonbooks.com/eos

*To Terry Cooper and Cherry Wilder*

# Mage Heart

# ONE

The first time I saw the demon was in a vision, a vision brought on by chewing the drug hazia. But it was more than a vision.

I was walking along a beach in cold darkness. I knew, even then, that I was in some place I should not be, and I felt the nervous tenderness between the shoulder blades that comes with such knowledge.

It was easy to see. Cold brilliant stars spiraled slowly and hypnotically in the sky. Did they pulsate as well? Were they eyes? I don't remember now.

The beach was not sand, but millions of tiny, fragile bones that crunched and shattered under my feet. The sea heaved silently as if exhausted. It seemed dappled with starlight. Then I saw it was covered with thousands of little faces, mouths really, which opened and closed with the long, slow roll of the waves and shrieked like seabirds as they broke against the shore. I think I stood for some time looking out across the languid expanse. Suddenly my eye was caught by a different movement, a quick movement. What I had thought to be a rock just offshore stretched in the dark light and resettled its bat wings. Some kind of creature sat on that rock.

I suspected what it was. Desperately. I wanted desperately to see that creature closer. I paced up and down the shore in frustration.

There was a pounding.

The rock was so close; my desire was a torment. Recklessly I stepped into the sea and began to wade. It was not cold and wet as I'd expected, but warm and viscous, like jelly. It held me up, smoothly and firmly. The little gaping maws seemed to move aside for me. As I got deeper in, I noticed little pink tongues lashing out of them as I passed. It tickled deliciously where they touched the skin. There was a sickly scent, rotting and sweet, like nothing I had ever smelled. So strong that it was nauseating. Like roses—pustulant, rotting roses.

By the time I had waded in up to my waist, I knew that the being on the rock was, as I'd prayed, indeed a demon. It crouched there, betoothed and beclawed, its scaly wings spread out as if to dry, its face to the swirling stars.

A pounding on the door warned me to go no closer.

I had never seen a real demon before, but all my waking life I had been fascinated by the chaotic, winged denizens of nightmare. Now one of these awesome and dangerous beings was before me. I did not have the sense to feel more than the tiniest delicious tingle of fear. Instead, I devoured it with my eyes. It must have felt my gaze, for slowly, like a lizard, it turned its head and looked at me.

Someone was yelling and banging on the door.

Its red reptile eyes were heavy-lidded. It smiled charmingly, urbanely, and held out its spiky hand in greeting. I felt an intense desire to put my tiny, shatterable hand into that hand and feel the rough, horny skin.

Then, suddenly, the compulsion was terrifying. I pulled back violently, lost my footing, and fell backwards into the firm and sucking sea.

And off the bed. I was encased in a white, sticky womb, struggling to be born, my arms pinned to my sides, my head just sticking out. There was a great crashing in my head. Or was it at the door? Suddenly the sheets ripped apart and I tumbled onto the cold floor and lay there panting and twitching, covered in blood and jelly like a newborn worm. I was on a plain covered with huge boulders as the world whirled around and was filled with the most terrible pounding. I covered my head. The pounding was like the blows of a hammer crushing down on a walnut; I had a sticky vision of my brain oozing out like grey stew.

The room turned another circle. The vision peeled away. I broke the surface, and suddenly I was in my own familiar ordinary room, and everything was unbelievably small, quiet, and colorless.

Someone was banging on the door.

"Dion!" yelled an irritable voice. "Oh! By the Seven! Dion, answer the door."

My mouth tasted of sour phlegm. My vision was blurry and seemed ready to whirl again at any moment. I opened the door slightly and saw a pimple-faced second year boy.

"Lord of all," he said. "What took you?"

I didn't feel up to standing on my dignity.

"What's going on?" I croaked.

"The Dean wants to see you."

Oh, God and Angels! No!

"I can't ..."

"He says its urgent."

He craned his skinny neck forward curiously and moved closer to the door. His spots were fiery red on his bluish morning skin. He smelled of body oil and grit. He suspected something. I could tell.

"Tell him I'm sick," I said. "I'll come as soon as I can."

I slammed the door shut. It was only then, as I stood behind it, that I realized I was covered in warm slime. Warm slime smelling of pus and roses. It had not been just a vision. Oh, God and Angels! My neck tingled as the hair on the back of it stood up. The room spun around dizzyingly, filling me with such vertigo that I sank to the floor, still clutching at the door handle.

How could I have entered the world of demons, a plane so remote, so unreachable from our own, that only the strongest mages and the strongest magics could touch it? Was that where the beach of bones had been? Had I actually journeyed there physically? It was as if I had just peered gingerly into a magnetic abyss. I had been to an unknowable world filled with the most malevolent and destructive beings imaginable. If it hadn't been for that revolting boy, I might have touched the demon.

That pulled me up. What the hell was I thinking of? How could I, a mere student mage, accidentally go to that impossibly dangerous place—a place which only the strongest touched, and nobody had ever entered? There had to be some other explanation for the rapidly cooling slime covering me, an explanation that I was too inexperienced to know.

And to reach out to touch a demon! The fact that I had come into contact with such a being should have filled me with horror, not fascination. How could I be fascinated by such an evil being? How could I have even thought of touching it? That was the way into necromancy, the obscene magic of death and destruction. Was I going to add that to my other sins?

"Demons are always watching, waiting to tempt unwary mages into necromancy."

This was the warning my foster father, Michael, had given me when I was about fourteen. His face had taken on the rather pompous look that always made me want to hit him on the head with a pillow and say something flippant. Though, of course, I had never actually dared to do it.

Not that there was anything wrong with his advice.

"No self-respecting mage even thinks about demons," he told me. "They are always out there, waiting, ever hungry for life, drawn especially to those of us who touch the world of magic, ever ready to tempt the unwary into magical pacts that they might be allowed to feed their hunger on the life of our plane.

"Demons have amazing power. No one can withstand them in their own place, and, even from the misty distance of another plane, they are lethal. Irresistible. Throughout the ages evil men have sought pacts with them. Under such a pact a weak mage can bring demon power across heavy barriers, between their plane and ours, and become a mighty necromancer. But a terrible price is always exacted in return, for these demon familiars hunger always and must be fed.

"The hand of every sane mage, nay every sane human being, must always be turned against necromancy, for necromancers are a bane upon the land. Mysterious disappearances plague any place in their vicinity, until great tracts of land are denuded of animal life to feed the immense appetites of the demon.

They flourish only in borderlands and places torn by civil strife, for no ruler can suffer his people to be used up in such a way.

"For demon familiars, say rather demon masters. The pacts demons offer are never honorable. They seek always to enslave, to trick. They are inhuman, without conscience or compassion. They are pure evil, insatiable appetite incarnate, a sink which sucks in all life. Obscenely. Their greatest desire is to find a mage powerful enough to bring them through into our world and one whom, at the same time, they can trick into setting them free, so that they can satisfy their dreadful appetites at will. Thank God, that has only happened twice in our world. A demon let loose could lay waste to whole countries within days."

We both knew the truth of what he said. Almost a century before, our homeland of Moria had been the victim of one of these disasters. The demon Smazor had consumed the life out of thousands of miles of Moria and killed half its population in the few hours it took the United White College of Mages to cooperate in a dispelling ritual. Smazor was the reason Moria was now a poor, backward, sparsely populated country on the lunatic fringes of peninsula politics. Even though some of the land he laid waste had slowly recovered, there was still a great flattened wasteland called the Plain of Despair, a hundred miles deep in places, cutting off most of Moria from the sea to the east. Michael once showed it to me in a Bowl of Seeing. It was a terrible place, populated only by the white skeletons of trees and storms of grit and bone dust. Even caravans of merchants would not cross it. They said the air was thick with the spirits of the agonized dead, and that their cries would send a man mad.

"Smazor's Run" had been caused by the United White Colleges in the first place. Unaware of his existence, they had killed his master, the brutal necromancer Jubilato, leaving Smazor free to ravage at will.

I once asked Michael how on earth the United Colleges could have made such a mistake. It was the only question I ever dared ask him about demons.

"Such an oversight is easily made, child. We detect demon magic because of the human magic that must be used to get it. If a demon slave is on this plane, his master has no need to use further magic to force the demon to do his bidding. And the actions of demons themselves are completely undetectable to our magic. Aristo postulates that this is because demons are supernatural rather than magical. I hope," he continued sternly, "that you are not allowing yourself to become unwisely interested in this subject."

Like so many things Michael said, his lecture on demons had the opposite effect to what was intended. Necromancy held no appeal for me. I had no taste for violence. But demons . . . that was different! That night I lay awake in the darkness, seduced by a longing to comprehend them. Their soaring power and guiltless freedom of action was intoxicating to one who had so little of either.

From then on I sought out every scrap of information I could about demons. I did not take Michael's warnings very seriously. You can't get into trouble just by reading books, and that was all I was doing. I wasn't stupid enough to try to communicate with demons; I was quite content to study them from afar. There was not much to know. Necromantic magics like demon summoning could no longer be performed on the Oesteradd Peninsula since the white mages had formed the Anti-Necromantic Pact shortly after Smazor's attack.

But I had not just read books. I had also thought about demons a great deal. I had pondered at length over their nature, trying to imagine their lives on their own plane. Did they all live on different planes or on the same plane? And if on the same plane, how did they live with each other? As humans did? Or as predators and prey? What was the nature of the barrier between our worlds? How had it come into being? If demons could send their powers through it, why was it so hard for them to cross it? And so on and so forth. It had crossed my mind at the time that I might be being unwise, but I comforted myself with the thought that I was hardly important enough for them to bother with.

Now back in my little room at the college I wasn't so sure. As I stripped off and destroyed my slimy nightdress, scoured myself all over with icy water, and swore off hazia for life, I wondered if all those thoughts and researches back then had been as harmless as I'd thought. A sense of horror and a sheepish feeling of shame filled me. I had not thought much about demons since we'd left Moria, yet the fascination must have been lurking in my mind all the time, waiting to be set free. . . . Had it taken me to the demon? Or had I got there by the demon's will? Had it been waiting all this time . . . ? God and Angels! I peered over my shoulder quickly, and the shadows behind the desk and under the bed seemed to take substance. A demon had seen me now. There was a link, and who could tell were that might lead.

If I wasn't careful. I pushed anxiety off resolutely. No matter how it had seemed in the hazia dream, it was in its world and I was safe in mine. Logically, what could it do to me? Necromancy held no attraction for me. I would put up the runes of distraction and protection and it would lose interest in me. It was not as if I were strong enough to bring it into this world.

I was just finishing dressing when another knock came.

*Just my luck*, I thought as I went to the door. Usually no one visited me and now, just when I really didn't want it . . .

It was the college healer, a neat, quiet woman dressed in brown.

"Hello," I said. I could not remember her name.

"The Dean sent me," she said, firmly pushing open the door and coming into the room. "I believe you are sick."

"I'm fine," I said. Now I was in trouble. The minute she examined me she'd recognize the symptoms of hazia use. "I had a headache, but it's gone. I was sleeping when the messenger came."

She stiffened. I followed her gaze. The rest of my lump of hazia sat, small but as obvious as a beacon, on the worktable. She stared hard at me. I could not meet her eyes. Then she reached out, picked up the hazia, and put it in her pocket.

I made a sound of protest.

"I think," she said deliberately, "I will tell the Dean that you have a headache and need to lie down for a few hours. I imagine you will be feeling more yourself by, shall we say, three o'clock. I will tell the Dean you will see him then."

She walked to the door.

"That's mine!" I said, forgetting I'd just sworn off.

"I'm surprised you admit to it. You might like to spend the time till three meditating on the unwisdom of indulging in forbidden substances, especially during the school day."

She closed the door with a snap.

*Pompous bitch,* I thought. Michael said it was typical of such women to take the opportunity to lord it over those of us with greater powers. He was usually right about such things.

Still, she had a point. I did need to lie down till the effects of the drug wore off. Though I'd come out of the vision, the world was still showing a distressing tendency to change color and whirl about. I seemed to have lost all concentration, too, for after I'd placed the runes of protection and distraction around the room, instead of continuing to worry about the demon, I did indeed spend the intervening time meditating on my unwisdom. If the Dean found out, I was in serious trouble. The use of hazia was banned in the college, and several students, including Mylon, the fellow who'd sold it to me, had recently been expelled for using it. They, at least, had somewhere else to go. If I was expelled, where could I go?

That morning, a few hours before dawn, unable to sleep, I had committed the indiscretion of taking some hazia, knowing full well I would have to spend the day hiding out in my room till the visions stopped. Boredom, however, is the worst part of insomnia. I'd assumed nobody would notice my absence. Looking back now, I couldn't believe how stupid I'd been.

I would never have dreamed of using hazia while Michael was alive. It was popular among students of magic, and even some communities of mages used its visions as an occult enhancer, but Michael had always said that if you had sufficient powers, you shouldn't need to use other things to enhance them.

Then he died. And I was alone, a Morian refugee

in a strange land, the only woman in a college full of men. I quickly lost all interest in the studies and disciplines that had previously filled my day. If the truth be told, magic is basically a dull business—the endless grinding rote learning of true names and spells, the endless repetition of small rituals. I tried to continue Michael's research into the secret names of stones, but that failed to absorb me. I tried to keep up with my studies, but it was no use. I was so far ahead of the other students that there was no need for me to keep on with the boring grind. I was already qualified to become a mage. All I needed was the three years that would make me old enough.

Nothing it seemed could distract me from my despair at Michael's loss and my overwhelming sense of being all alone in the world. Until I discovered hazia.

I'd always avoided the other magic students. Michael had warned me against the friendly overtures of male students so often that I was cold and suspicious to them, and they left me completely alone. Nonetheless, during the desolate time after Michael's death, I did make a kind of friend. This was Mylon, whose room was near my own. He was two years younger than I and, moreover, such a vague and gentle soul that I found him completely unthreatening. It was he who told me of the wonderful dreams that were to be had from chewing the drug and who sold me my first lump of it. I had always loved to dream. I was too cautious to attend student hazia parties, but I experimented with the drug alone in my room.

Oh, the marvelous, sometimes terrifying, visions and dreams I had while chewing hazia. They blocked out loneliness and fear and took me to a world far outside the gritty rooms of the college. Once I'd discovered it, I spent many nights in the four months after Michael's death in a drug-induced haze or in related meditations. I'd even kept a detailed diary recording my experiences. It was the kind of thing I could get interested in. Michael would not have been surprised.

But I hadn't realized that those wonderful dreams existed anywhere outside myself. The possibility worried me now as I lay on my narrow, lumpy bed. I struggled not to think about it, but it ran round and round in my head till it felt as if it had carved out a dusty little path. Eventually I hypnotized myself into a mindless trance just to get some peace and quiet. At last, the college clock struck three and it was time to go and see the Dean.

It was the tired, grey end of winter. A searing cold wind whipped down the open cloisters and blew my woolen robe scratchily against my legs as I walked quickly to the Dean's office, head down, hands in sleeves, a demeanor which not only kept me warm but disguised any signs of hazia use as well. I felt better, more "normal" by then, although the students I passed on my way down the clammy corridors seemed to stare at me pointedly. Did they know? Was it obvious? Would the Dean notice? He was one of the few masters in the college who seemed to like me, and I hated the thought of disappointing him. I remembered having this nervous, suspicious feeling after other hazia episodes, but that didn't make it any better.

The Dean sat behind a desk that today seemed miles wide. Though his room was very grand, all dark wood paneling and carving as suited the head of such an important college, even in summer it was clammy cold and smelled of rot and damp. I always wondered how such an old man stood the chill, but then, most of the college rooms were like that.

When I entered, the Student Supervisor, Master John, was leaning over the Dean, looking at some papers on the desk. Unfortunately, Master John was the most attractive of the academic staff, still quite young. He was tall, with dark hair and a serious demeanor, but I knew that, like most mages, he disapproved of women. This made me uncomfortable with him, made me worry about everything I said in front of him. Uselessly, because it always seemed to be the wrong thing no matter how much I tried. The fact that I'd sometimes daydreamed of turning the disapproval in his eyes into adoration didn't make the situation any more comfortable either.

The Dean rolled up the papers, and his mild elderly face creased in a reassuring smile. His face always took on a blind, questing look when he smiled. Such an old man must be quite shortsighted.

"I'm sorry I could not come earlier, sir. I was unwell."

"Yes, so Maya told me. I hope you are better now."

Maya. That was the healer's name. Had she told him about the hazia? I searched his face for signs of disapproval. But no, he seemed his usual calm and kind self.

He motioned me to sit down, so I took a seat on one of the hard chairs in front of the desk. To my secret dismay, Master John did not leave the room but stayed, leaning against the stone windowsill, his arms crossed. It was his right to stay, of course. As Student Supervisor, what concerned me, concerned him. But his sullenly attractive face seemed more than usually grim, his rather full lips clamped together in a hard line.

It had not occurred to me before to wonder why the Dean had sent for me, but I now did so and found I was trembling with anxiety. It *had* to be something to do with hazia.

"Dion," said the Dean, "I have sent for you because I have decided that it is time to talk about your future. It was a question that worried your foster father deeply in his last days. He was sorely troubled by what would become of you after his death. He told me once that he feared he had done a terribly cruel thing to you by training you to be a mage and making you unfit for the only livelihoods open to a girl."

Michael had said this to me, too. He had always assumed that I would be able to take over his private practice. His clients knew me and had become used to being served by a woman, and I would have inherited his house and the small patch of land that came with it. With luck I could have made a living out of it. But that was before the Revolution of Souls forced us to flee Moria. After we came to Gallia, he worried a great deal about what would happen to me after he died. Positions open to students of the College of Magic, teaching positions or postings with the great families or city-states, had never been filled by women, and nobody would trust a female mage enough for her to set up a private practice. The only branch of magic normally open to women was healing, a task for which my years of training as a mage made me badly qualified and, moreover, one for which Michael felt I was temperamentally unsuited.

"Your foster father entrusted me with the task of finding you some livelihood, and since his death I have been casting around for openings. I have not liked to speak of it before now. I felt it was too soon.

But circumstances have arisen which make it imperative."

Oh God, I thought, I knew it. They've found out about the hazia. They're going to throw me out.

"You are well aware that because of your foster father's teaching, you are one of the most advanced pupils in this college. Everything but your age qualifies you to be a Magus. Now a position has come up for which you, as a girl, would be uniquely suited. In fact the Duke has asked for you."

Relief. Excitement. Amazement.

"The Duke?"

"Yes, Dion," said the Dean. He looked pointedly over his shoulder at Master John.

"What is this position, sir?"

"We'll come to that in a moment. In view of your foster father's advanced teaching, you are well able to handle the position magically even though you are still very young. But it is also a situation that requires tact and discretion. It is that which has made me hesitate in accepting on your behalf."

He sighed.

"But in view of your difficult situation, I feel it is too great a chance for you to miss. I think that if you are careful and restrained, you should be able to negotiate any political difficulties which must be inherent in working for a ruler."

How like Michael the Dean sounded. Spoiling everything with warnings. It always worked, too. I was beginning to dread hearing the position's name.

"As it is, you will not be leaving the college, and thus you will have my guidance every step of the way." His face as he said this was half-turned toward Master John, as if reassuring him rather than me. Master John's mouth became even grimmer, and he turned and faced the window.

The Dean's face was more earnest than usual.

"So, despite reservations, I urge you to accept this position. It is an opportunity to gain the notice and the gratitude of the powerful, and as such it may be the answer to our prayers."

"What is the position, sir?" I asked again.

The Dean looked uncomfortable.

"Guardian-mage to Madame Avignon. The Duke believes her to be in some kind of magical danger."

I stared at him openmouthed. Kitten Avignon. The most notorious whore on the Peninsula and the Duke of Gallia's openly acknowledged mistress.

Even Michael and I, living quietly in the Morian countryside, had heard of this scandalous woman and her liaison with the Duke. Rulers had mistresses and Gallian rulers had always been more flagrant in this respect. Their mistresses usually had the bluest of bloods, however. Not so Kitten Avignon. She was an actress and a courtesan, a woman whose background was unknown, who was surely nothing more than a common prostitute. At home people had talked of such great courtesans with a kind of greedy pleasure—their faces mean with contempt, their mouths pursed, sucking on the delicious sweetmeat of Gallian decadence.

I had once seen Kitten Avignon. It was on the very day that Michael and I, covered with grit from our long walk east from Moria, had entered Gallia.

She was the most beautiful woman I had ever set eyes on. All around us enthusiastic people waved and cheered as she rode by on a huge white horse surrounded by darkly clad servants. She sat with straight-backed dignity, smiling and gently waving her fine-boned hand. She was dressed in deep red, and everything about her, from her pure white skin to the red rose in the hat that covered her fair hair, seemed to glow vividly. Even at that distance she looked soft and touchable.

We had walked a long way that day. My foster father swore and grumbled about parades. But I was fascinated by the beautiful lady, so fascinated that I asked the friendly-looking woman beside me if that was the Duchess.

She laughed.

"Oh no, that's Kitten Avignon, the Duke's mistress. Our Lady of Roses they call her."

Michael smiled his cynical smile and said softly in my ear, "Welcome to Gallia, my dear! Where whores ride through the streets like queens. Look at all these poor people under her spell."

In my memory the woman's glowing beauty became spoiled and sinister.

It was as if the Dean, that fragile and avuncular old man, had made an obscene proposition. Maybe he had. Suddenly I felt terribly afraid. Maybe they were just trying to get rid of me. Was this the fate of useless women? Prostitution?

"No." I whispered. "No."

"Dion?"

"How can I? How can you ask me . . . ? She's a whore . . ."

"Dion! Hush! I know that as a Morian you might have some problem with this . . ."

"Sir, you're asking me to associate with a woman who's . . . Michael would have been horrified."

"Dion, please. Listen . . ."

"My lord," said Master John. "The child has said no. And who can blame her? Surely it is unfair to press her to take such an obviously distasteful position."

"Keep out of this, John." The Dean's vague, gentle face had suddenly become astonishingly hard and forceful. "Dion, you must see reason."

"My lord, she does see reason. It's you. Can't you see yourself . . . Pushing an innocent child into the arms of such a creature."

"John!"

"How can you do this?" Master John was beginning to yell. "How can you even take it seriously? Magical danger! It's ridiculous! What mage on earth would bother with a common drab?"

"Master John!"

"And what college on earth would even dignify such a request from such a woman?"

"May I remind you that this is the Duke's request?" The Dean's voice was soft. But it cut.

"Oh yes! A man completely under her control. A man ruled by the honey sisterhood. Government by the worst in the land! Does this accord with the dignity due to this college?"

"And how does it accord with our dignity to have members of staff brawling in front of the students?"

Master John scowled.

The Dean stared at him. Gone was the kindly old man. Before me sat an austere man, harsh and dignified and bristling with power.

"You're being a fool, John. Disapproval of the Duke's intimates can only be interpreted as disapproval of the Duke. In different company you'd be thrown in the Fortress for what you've said."

He turned to me, and his face softened again.

"Now, Dion. Believe me, I understand how distasteful this is to you. I understand that a respectable young girl must be reluctant to associate with a courtesan. But you must remember this is not a request from this sad and abandoned creature, but from the Duke. From our ruler, and a man to whom, I might add, you and your foster father owe a great deal. He did not have to give you asylum in Gallia. You must realize it would be ungracious, not to mention unwise, to refuse this quite simple task out of disapproval. Madame Avignon is the Duke's favorite, and because of this, it must be an honor for anyone to serve her. That is the way it works in Gallia. I would be surprised if it is different anywhere in the world."

Suddenly I was very frightened. I could not do this thing. How could I? I struggled to put my reasons into words.

"But, sir. Will it not ruin my reputation? How will I ever find a respectable position afterward? Who will have me then?"

"Yes, my lord," said Master John. "Have you thought of that? Have you considered how people might treat her once her association with this woman is known?" He struck the desk. "Have you considered that you might leave her with no prospects? Have you really considered her future, my lord Dean?"

The Dean closed his eyes with a pained expression. Master John fell silent.

"Finished, John?" His voice was heavy with sarcasm. "Kindly allow me to point out to you both that Dion has no future. Honestly, John, have you not said this yourself? Who in the world would grant a position to a female mage? Dion is not trained for healing, and I doubt if anyone would consider a dowerless woman with magical powers a suitable wife. What is this future you are talking of? There is no one to provide for her unless we at this college do it. And this is what I am attempting to do. Here is a situation which makes her very disability an asset. Think how much more unsuitable it would be to bring a young man into contact with one of the honey sisterhood. The Duke must naturally prefer a woman for this kind of thing."

Everything he said was true. I already knew it to be so. But it was bitter to hear it said all the same. I bowed my head lest they see the tears in my eyes, but I could not miss the pitying look Master John gave me and the discouraged way his shoulders sank.

"I'm sorry, Dion," said the Dean. "It is a cruel thing to have said even if it is the truth. Believe me, I do understand that a besmirched reputation is a heavy burden for any woman to bear. But I have taken steps to protect you from your association with Madame Avignon. Protection is hardly a very intimate spell, so you are unlikely to meet with her more than twice at the most. The Duke tells me that only a few trusted advisers know of the situation. Very likely nobody much will ever know of your position. You will be staying safely at the college and will have us to guide and protect you. Above all, you must remember that this is an opportunity to win the favor of the Duke. *That* can only lead to good things."

I was not reassured, and yet I could think of no other objections in the face of the Dean's calm certainty. I just stared at him dismayed, frightened, thinking if I had not clouded my brain with hazia, the objections to undertaking this task would be clear to me and everyone else.

The Dean sighed. "Dion, if the worst comes to the worst . . . I have planned for that, too. I have negotiated a life pension and a small farm for you on top of a very considerable money fee. You can always retire to the country till people forget. Don't you see that whatever the risks in this position, you can only gain from it? This may be the only position that will ever be offered to you. For no other reason than that, I would urge you to take it."

I could only think of the contemptuous faces of the villagers at home when they spoke of women like Madame Avignon and the sad stories our housekeeper had told of ruined girls and their fates. I was afraid.

"Dion, you will have myself and Master John beside you all the way, and we will do our very best to protect you. What will you have if you say no? You must consider your future."

I had considered that prospect. Often when I sat alone in my room. Too often. It was one reason I'd started taking hazia.

I looked at Master John, but he'd gone back to staring out the window.

I looked at the Dean. I could see him willing me to say yes.

I had every reason to trust his judgment. If he said it would be all right, then surely it must be. I would have money, a little farm, a chance to get away from this hole of a college, where every night I sat alone in my room and listened to the students in the corridor outside calling to each other in friendly voices.

"Very well," I said.

Looking back, I find it hard to believe the extent of my fear of Kitten Avignon. But then, I was a young woman from a small village in a country famed throughout the Peninsula for its prudery. I had never actually met anyone who openly deviated from conventional morality. I only knew of such people from the all-too-believable talk of our housekeeper. Even Michael warned me about "fallen" women. He was

well known in Moria, and sometimes city courtesans
would send to him for salves or love potions. He
would send the messengers to other, less discerning
mages.

"Involving yourself with whores will only lead to
trouble," he warned me. "They are vicious and bitter
women, who, because they lack any control over their
own lusts, have ruined their lives. They use men's
weaknesses to achieve their own ends, which are always corrupt and self-seeking."

If everything they said about such women was true,
Kitten Avignon would automatically hate me. What
if she tried to make use of me or harm me? How was
I to guard against that?

I did have another reason for fearing contact with
Kitten Avignon. As Michael once reminded me when
he'd caught me talking with a village boy, I had reason to be especially careful of my morals. My mother
had been a servingwoman at an inn, a woman with
several children, who had never had a husband.

I approached Madame Avignon with the feeling you
usually reserve for particularly contagious diseases.

The following evening, as the sun set over the towers of Gallia and the bells had begun ringing for evening mass, Master John and I walked obediently
through the narrow streets to the Ducal Palace. The
sky was golden with the setting sun, and the huge
flock of crows that nested in the cathedral steeple
were swirling around it in a raucous black cloud.

I had never seen the Ducal Palace so close before,
and its grandeur did nothing to ease my nerves. It
was nothing like the ancient stone castles I'd seen in
Moria. Instead it was square, with a long facade of

white marble columns and a huge gilded staircase
leading up to vast iron doors.

"The Duke's father began it. It's built in the very
latest style," said Master John, who was a native Gallian, proudly. He was being unusually chatty for Master John, pointing out all the finer features of the
palace and telling me that the gilded staircase was a
gift from the Ishtaki merchant-princes. I suspected he
was trying to put me at ease. As we climbed the staircase between the lines of marble saints, I kept my
hands firmly clasped behind my back so that Master
John could not see how much they were shaking.

We were met inside the doors by a bowing major-
domo, who directed us to follow him. Stalking stiff-
legged ahead of us, he led us through a dazzling
series of rooms, each more hectically decorated than
the next. In each, the walls were a blast of color and
movement, writhing with figures—animals and angels all intertwined—twisting in huge draperies. The
ceilings were great chunks of oak, carved with gilt
banquets of fruits and flowers or violins and pipes.
Huge stone dragons swirled up the balustrades of a
white marble staircase. Brilliantly shining confections
of crystal and candles hung like fantastic clusters of
grapes from each ceiling. We passed through one gallery whose walls were dangerous with the mounted
antlers of deer and another lined with soft, golden
brocades. It was gluttony for the eye and, thank God,
completely distracting. Even Master John stared. I had
never seen such richness, such grandeur before in my
life. I wondered what it must be like to live in all this
splendor and could not picture any actual living going on at all.

At last we passed into a huge, silvery chamber
which seemed full of men in whispering robes of

sumptuous velvet, moving, leaning, and nodding among themselves as if in some courtly dance. They all seemed to watch us, and yet I couldn't see them looking. At second glance I realized that the walls were covered in mirrors so that each figure in the room stretched away to a crowded infinity of space and that, in fact, there were only four or five people in the chamber. The throne at the end of the chamber was empty. Our guide did not hesitate, but led us across the room, pulled aside the soft velvet behind the throne, and motioned us within.

Lolling on a brocade chair in the middle of the shadowy anteroom beyond sat the pivot on which all this splendor turned; Duke Leon Sahr, a small, neat man with nondescript brown hair and a soft, pointed beard, eating cherries and spitting the pits into his hands.

So this was the Duke—the man who had executed his own cousin at eighteen, the man who had won the battle of Lamia at twenty-one and, in winning it, had united the city-states of Ishtak and Gallia under his rule to form the most powerful state on the Peninsula. This was our ruler, who had power of life and death over us all.

Somehow I had expected someone bigger, someone physically greater, yet as I watched him making small talk with Master John, something in that soft face with its thin cynical smile inspired true fear. It was easy to believe that this slight man was capable of the things they said of him. He looked capable of any necessity.

His dress was no disappointment. His robes were sumptuous red silk worked with gold in the Sahr crest. The feather on his cap was pinned with a huge ducal brooch in ruby and gold and his thin fingers were positively weighted down with enormous gems.

"Well," said the Duke after a few moments. "So this is the student we spoke of. Come forward, student."

Master John nudged me. I managed to curtsy.

"Ah, yes. So this is Michael of Moria's little daughter. The prodigy."

His eyes narrowed.

"She is young."

"But I assure you quite capable of the task you have set for her," said Master John. "Michael trained her beyond her years. Only her age prevents her from being a fully qualified mage. She has passed all the exams very well. I assure Your Grace, you will not be disappointed . . ."

There was an uncomfortable silence broken only by the dull chink of cherry pits as the Duke dropped them into the small golden bowl beside him. He picked up a linen napkin of such perfect whiteness that it seemed to shine in the shadowy room, shook it out delicately, and began to wipe each jewel-laden finger.

I stood, head bowed, feeling like a naughty child. In that long silence I stole a look at Master John and saw to my secret pleasure that he looked much the same as I felt.

"Yes," said the Duke in a quiet voice which somehow expressed disbelief. "I'm sure the college would never disappoint me."

He leaned back and elegantly crossed his legs.

"Come forward, child!"

I moved forward, stopped, and curtsied again for good measure.

"Your foster father was a great favorite of ours. We met him when we were in Mangalore visiting the late Duke. Such a sensible, plain-spoken man. A sad loss to Moria we would have said, though, for some rea-

son, the Morians do not agree with us. We were sorry
to hear of his death."

I bobbed my head and murmured my thanks. There
was something in the way he spoke which made me
feel it was a deep honor that such a great man should
speak well of Michael.

"You were very lucky to have such a fine teacher.
I would have every faith in any student of his. Do
you think that I am right, child? Look at me. Do you
feel able for the task before you?"

He peered with hard narrow eyes into my face. I
felt as if I'd been blinded by the sun and dropped my
eyes.

"Yes, my lord."

"Make sure you are right, Mademoiselle. I would
not be pleased if you failed."

"Your Grace, we would not allow an unworthy
mage to come before you," said Master John.

Silence.

Suddenly the Duke smiled. Then he laughed. He
stood up and clapped Master John on the shoulder.
At once the room seemed lighter, was lighter.

"Of course you would not. Worthy Master John.
You must forgive your ruler a momentary uncer-
tainty. The thought that this charming young girl
could be versed in magic is hard to believe, that is all.
It is so strange to see a woman mage. Though I believe
it is common in the old empires of the West." He
laughed. "A disturbing thought. Considering the be-
witchments of which women are capable without
magic, I wonder our poor Western brothers hold their
own. Take my dear Madame Avignon for instance."

He turned his head, and suddenly I realized that
there was a slim shadow standing in the darkness by
the door.

The Duke beckoned. "Kitten, stop lurking about in the darkness. Come and meet these people."

As she came forward, Master John and I both gasped. I would like to think that it was merely the fabulous peacock blue velvet gown she wore. But I know that it was her breasts that I was looking at. How could I help it? That dress was intended to draw all eyes to those firm, white globes, crammed so tightly into her bodice that it was a miracle they didn't fall out. Her fair hair was piled up on top of her head so that her long, white neck was bare, framed only with a ruff of dark feathers. The space between her face and her nipples seemed an endless expanse of nakedness; she was more naked than if she had worn nothing at all. She was so luminescent, so soft, so touchable that it made the hands itch to feel her skin. I blushed and dropped my eyes. The sight of her made me uncomfortably aware that all of us were naked under our clothes.

"Ah yes," purred the Duke. He was obviously delighted by the effect his mistress had had on us. "One could almost believe her to be an enchantress, could one not? Come, Kitten, my love, sit by me."

She curtsied to us (which made her cleavage even ruder if that was possible), smiling and murmuring a soft greeting. Then she moved gracefully past us, slowly and languidly, her hips swaying, the cloth of the dress whispering against the ground as she went.

The back of her gown was even worse, for there was, in fact, no back, just another expanse of bare flesh. Again I was transfixed, this time by the long, smooth line of her spine. Her skin shone like soft silk against the deep midnight blue and gold peacock feathers of the gown. It had to be the most indecent dress I had ever seen.

She curtsied before the Duke, and he bade her sit on a brocade footstool beside the throne. She looked graceful even in this pose, the train of her gown trailing across the steps of the dais. In one hand she carried a huge fan of peacock feathers which she draped across her knees. I stared at the floor, determined not to stare at her yet constantly aware of her on the periphery of my vision.

"Mademoiselle Dion," said the Duke, "you must realize that the safety of our dear Madame Avignon is of paramount importance to us. I'm sure I do not need to impress upon you the significance of that. Or the extent of our displeasure should any magical harm befall her. It would be an irreparable loss to our court were such a precious jewel to be harmed."

He smiled at Madame Avignon and kissed her soft, white hand (her arms were bare, too; was there anything that dress covered?), and she smiled back at him, sensuously. Then he turned his hard, bright glance back at us.

"Of course, we expect total discretion. We do not wish it to be known that you are protecting Madame Avignon. For it to become generally known might involve you both in . . . unpleasantness. If anyone asks, you must say that you are merely performing healing magic. That perhaps is the beauty of your being a woman."

I nodded and curtsied, not knowing quite what to say.

The Duke leaned forward and smiled. It was a smile to die for. The thought of disappointing him was too dreadful to contemplate.

"I'm sure you will not let us down. Is there anything else you need to undertake this spell of protection?"

"Master John must draw certain symbols on the ground. Madame . . . the lady must stand inside them. Then I must look upon the lady for a few minutes in order to weave the protective magics around her."

"A pleasant task no doubt."

He and Madame Avignon exchanged smiles again.

"Do you two need to be alone for this?"

"No, my lord. It is not necessary."

Thank God, I thought. There was no need to be flustered. Yet Madame Avignon and that damned dress made me so nervous. It was so hard not to stare at her cleavage and yet . . . What normal woman stares at another woman's bosom? *For God's sake, Dion. You are a mage. Be dignified.*

"If the lady would just come forward."

"Of course," murmured Madame Avignon. Even her voice was seductive, low and soft, with a slight foreign accent.

She smiled at me. It was the first time I'd noticed her face. It was beautiful but . . . knowing—eyes heavy with kohl, lips firm and an unnatural, brilliant red. The smile seemed wrong for it. It confused me. It was so warm and friendly, somehow comforting. I felt suspicious all of a sudden. What business had she being so warm to me? She didn't know me from the next man, and yet here she was smiling at me as if I were her favorite sister.

Master John crawled around her, a little awkward in his long robes, chalking symbols on the floor. It was an odd feeling. Usually it was someone like me who did such menial tasks. He expounded on protection spells to the interested Duke as he went, explaining how they were simple to maintain by renewing the ritual four times a day, how they wrapped a person in a kind of magical cocoon, making it impossible for any other mage to fix another spell on them and how I would be able to maintain it without ever having to trouble Madame Avignon again.

"Do I turn?" she asked me.

"I will tell you."

I needed to fix a picture of her in my mind, but it was hard to picture her. I didn't want that kind of intimacy with such a woman. At least my suspicion made her seem real, made it easier to concentrate on the task at hand and not on her disturbing cleavage.

Master John stood up and nodded at me.

I closed my eyes, found my own center, and began to recite the incantation under my breath. Concentrating, I opened my eyes and, for the first time, looked full at her.

Magic has a strange effect on the practitioner. It pulls you away from the everyday world, the world of people, of dust under the bed and the scent of sweat, and makes it all seem flat and unreal, as if it were a picture in a book. It is this that makes mages so cold. Feelings don't touch us while we perform magic. The only thing we ever feel is the logical realization that we would probably be distressed by what we saw if we weren't performing magic. What I mean is, that in that moment I could have watched Kitten Avignon and the Duke writhing on the floor in the act of love and have felt nothing except the dispassionate realization that I would be embarrassed remembering this. So it was now easy for me to look at Kitten Avignon and concentrate on winding the incantation round her like a ribbon. I think if it were possible, most mages would spend their lives in such a state. It brings such peace and freedom from pain. But, sadly, most magic is too exhausting to practice for more than a few hours a day.

I connected that ribbon of incantation to myself, weaving it firmly into my being so that I was the weakest point in the strand. I was tired when I finished, but the magic had brought, as it always did, a residual calm with it.

I stood quietly as the two men discussed fees and other practicalities. Madame Avignon, too, sat quietly on the footstool beside the throne, her eyes downcast, as if, like me, she was merely waiting for the men to finish their business.

Master John was silent during the walk back to the college. I had an overwhelming desire to ask him what he thought of it all, how he thought things had gone, what he had thought of *her*. I wished deeply for Michael in that moment, for I knew he would have told me what to think. All Master John said was, "The correct way to address a duke is Your Grace, Dion."

We reported to the Dean and I had been dismissed, but before the Dean's door had closed fully after me, I heard Master John say irritably, "As usual That Woman was prancing around half-naked and the Duke was bedding her with his eyes the whole time we were there. Honestly my lord I cannot like . . ."

The door clicked shut.

## TWO

I poured the water into the bowl and cast a spell of
seeing on its surface. The water went black. Sparkling, multicolored dots of light began to appear
in it. This is not always the result when you cast a
spell of seeing. The spell shows all magical activity in
a particular area, so that sometimes it can be quite
empty. When centered on a big city like Gallia, however, where people buy all kinds of spells for all kinds
of reasons, the view is more crowded than the most
brilliant part of the heavens. With the help of a pack
of Prophecy Cards, I began to search the bowl carefully for signs of a magical threat to Kitten Avignon.
It is standard practice to do this daily when using a
protection spell, so I was doing it, even though I was
convinced that it was a waste of time. Michael had
always had contempt for useless people, and it ran-
kled me that I was wasting my power soothing this
woman merely because she was immoral enough to
share the Duke's bed, and he was fool enough to listen to her because of it.

But before I had got very far with the search, there was a knock at the door. To my astonishment it was Garthan Redon.

Garthan was one of those students every school seems to have—one of the leaders of the college, smart, charming, and good-looking. The Redons were rumored to be close to the Ducal family. Whether they were or not, Garthan had success written all over him in big, strong, clean letters. What on earth was he doing visiting me?

"My mother sent me a honey cake," he said. "Thought you might like some."

"Oh," I said. "Um... Thank you." I'd never even spoken to him before. Somehow it was hard to imagine such a hero having a mother, especially one who sent him honey cake. Suddenly I realized that I was standing there staring at him.

"Please come in," I said, hoping I wasn't committing some serious breach of propriety. "Would you like some tea? Please sit down."

I pulled some books off one of the chairs and tossed them on my bed. He looked around the room and caught sight of the Bowl of Seeing in the corner.

"Hmm. What are you looking at?" he said, peering into it. He fingered the Cards of Prophecy lying beside it. Cards of Prophecy are used to help determine the identities of particular points of light in the bowl.

"Oh. Nothing in particular," I said as calmly as I could. I ran my hand quickly over the surface of the bowl to clear it. He probably couldn't have seen anything anyway, but it was better to be safe than sorry.

"Are you doing a protection spell?"

"Oh, no! No! Of course not. I just like to watch what's going on sometimes. You know. The magic and countermagic. Jasmine tea?"

"Fine," he said. He stretched out in the chair and began to ask questions about my studies and how I liked Gallia. I fussed around finding clean beakers and boiling water on my little oil stove. It was pleasant to have a visitor, although I would have preferred someone less daunting than Garthan.

The time I'd been protecting Kitten Avignon had been more than usually difficult. Oh, the spell was easy enough. Protection is one of the first spells a young mage learns. Any mage can do it, and, being a defensive spell, as long as it is regularly maintained even weak mages can hold it against quite strong opponents. The problem was that it was one of those tasks, so common in magic, which require a constant low level of attention without being interesting enough to absorb you. There was no way, for instance, I could continue with my hazia dreams. Of course, I had already sworn off, and, logically, I knew it was a good thing that the temptation was closed to me. I'd have been a fool to continue after my last experience.

But though I had used enough magic when casting the spell to be emotionally affected by it, maintaining it was such a low-level task that the coldness of magic did not operate and I was once again prey to boredom and self-pity. I tried to stave off the boredom by going on with Michael's work on stones and by doing the mathematical problems that Master John had kindly offered to set me. Naturally I failed.

Garthan gave me a slice of honey cake and accepted a beaker of tea in return.

"So," he said. "Rumor has it that you've had an audience with the Duke."

I almost choked on my honey cake.

"How . . . ? Who told you?"

"So you did then?"

I was trapped now. I'd as good as said yes. What a fool. The Duke had said it was a secret. Tell them you are doing healing he'd said. But Garthan was a mage. He was never going to accept a story like that.

"Yes," I admitted.

"By the Seven! That's not a thing to keep to yourself. What was it like?"

"Good. Yes. Good."

"Good?" echoed Garthan a little derisively. "Tell me about it. How is Duke Leon these days? Who else was there? Did you get to see Kitten Avignon?"

Oh angel! How much did he know? How much did everyone know?

I tried not to panic.

"Yes," I said carefully, staring into my tea. "She was there."

"Tanza. I've seen her riding in the city. She's the most beautiful woman I've ever seen. None of the ladies at court will speak to her, but everyone copies her dresses. Did you get to meet her? They say she can charm the birds off the trees."

"No," I said, risking a lie which was almost a truth. "The Duke didn't introduce us."

"Well lucky you anyway. Where did you go? Were you in the Peacock Room or the Throne Room?"

He plied me with questions which I did my best to answer as noncommittally as possible. I got no pleasure out of the conversation. All the time I was wondering what I would say when he asked me why I had gone there.

But Garthan was subtler than that.

"Did you see Lady Jassie there?" he asked.

I stared at him in surprise. Lady Jacinta Ren-Sahr

was the Duke's six-year-old daughter, the oldest of his three illegitimate children.

"No. Why . . . ?"

"Oh! Just thought you might have. Some of the chaps have been saying that the Duke's hired you to protect her."

I laughed with relief.

"Oh no. Heavens! No! Nothing like that. He just wanted to talk to me about my foster father, Michael of Moria."

"Perhaps there's someone else he wants protected. I couldn't help noticing the Bowl of Seeing . . ."

Relief had given me confidence. He was on the wrong track. I was safe.

"Well, he didn't mention it if he did. No, I think he wants to extend Michael's pension to me. After all, I haven't got many other prospects, have I?"

I was pleased with this explanation. The remark about my prospects had the ring of irrefutable fact. I had believed it myself till a few weeks ago, and I could see from Garthan's uneasy face that he did, too.

He stayed a little longer, trying to prod me into making a confession about Lady Jassie, but my heart was lightened by my escape and I held firm to my explanation with little trouble. He left disappointed. I closed the door behind him with a sigh of relief. If this was what socializing with the other students was going to be like, it would be better for my peace of mind to keep well away from them.

I could understand why Garthan had thought of Lady Jassie. If one were to hire a woman mage at all, it might well be as guardian-mage to a six-year-old girl. But the usual male mage would do just as well and provoke much less of an outcry. I'd wondered several times in this light why the Duke had hired me to protect his beloved mistress.

My position in the world of magery was a very peculiar one. There were rumored to be powerful female mages in the faraway West, but in Gallia and the familiar countries of the Peninsula, women did not study advanced magic as I had done. Healing was women's magic. There was a powerful belief that women were not intelligent enough to grasp advanced magics and that even if they were, they were not reliable enough to use the magic of power responsibly. They were, after all, ruled by the illogical promptings of the womb.

My foster father, Michael, had adopted and educated me with the specific intention of exploring this belief.

The earliest memory I have of him (almost the earliest memory I have at all) concerns a colored ball. It was one of those little balls made out of strips of colored felt, in this case red, blue, and white, and stuffed with clean rags. I think I remember my mother sitting by the kitchen fire one winter evening sewing it up, but it most definitely belonged to the innkeeper's daughter, Sonia.

I discovered to my delight that I could make that ball dance above my head, out of the reach of even the bigger children, simply by willing it so. I was four at the time. I must have made it float more than once, for I seem to have many memories of rushing up and down the dim wooden balconies of the inn, surrounded by a pack of screaming, laughing children, all leaping and trying to bat at the ball above my head.

But I remember clearly one time when I came around a corner and rushed past a tall, grey man who was leaning on the balcony rail. As we passed, he reached out and plucked the ball out of the air. It lay lifeless in his hand as he asked in the sudden silence, "Who did this?"

The man's face was huge as he bent toward us and it had that forbidding look on it that often came before punishment. Most of my companions fled, but Sonia stayed beside me, wide-eyed and clutching her little brother by the hand. I realize now that he must have cast a spell on them. His eyes were very compelling, although they did not hold my gaze the way they held Sonia's and Mouse's. My resistance to Michael's spell must have been one of the many tests I passed that day. He would have taken it as a measure of my innate power.

I didn't run away, my usual and wise response when a stranger at the inn tried to handle me. I was too fascinated. Suddenly I could hear his voice speaking to me in my head and, to my fear and delight, could answer in the same way. I can't remember what he asked me, but while he questioned me, he took my face between his hands and, though I flinched and wriggled, looked deep into my eyes, tilting my face to and fro and up and down.

The examination was cut short when Old Hallie the innkeeper came hurrying up the stairs. I remember the man turning as if in slow motion and as he spoke with the innkeeper, the innkeeper's anxious expression changed to one of awe.

Later I belonged to Michael. He had persuaded my mother with a sum of money to let him take me away to be educated near Mangalore. Sometimes I used to wonder how my mother could have done it, could have sold me to a stranger. Michael told me by way of explanation that my mother, who was only a servingwoman at the inn, had more children than she knew what to do with. He implied that one child more or less meant nothing to her. I suppose one could not expect a woman who had been so imprudent in the getting of her children to be any more careful in their disposal. I remember very little about her myself and would be hard put ever to find that inn again. My life before leaving it is like some well-remembered dream. Reality started with Michael.

Sometimes when I had failed in some way and he was very angry with me, he would tell me that it had been a great waste of good money. I think he regretted it more often than he said. He had chosen me to be his foster daughter because he wanted to explore the theory that women were capable of advanced magery. That was why he had been so taken with me that day at the inn. It took exceptional natural ability to be able to levitate a ball without the aid of spells.

He wrote his doctoral thesis on my education. He pointed out in this thesis that natural ability was not everything. From the very beginning he suspected that I would have problems in temperament that would always flaw my magic. I was flighty, unwilling to concentrate, slapdash, frivolous; there was an irresponsibility in me that had been there at the start and that he feared I would never be able to change. The thesis remained inconclusive on that point. He pointed out that all girls could not be judged by the study of one example. I don't remember if he ever told this to anyone, but I think he feared privately that I might just be the child of my husbandless mother with her large brood of children.

For twelve years of my life, I lived as his daughter in a small village outside Mangalore, the capital of the Duchy and later the Archbishopric of Moria. For ten hours a day, seven days a week, I studied all the magic he could teach me. Mages from all over the Peninsula, and sometimes even farther, visited us to put me through my paces. If I failed to measure up, Michael would drill me even harder. I suppose I was a sort of dancing bear. Certainly like a dancing bear, I had no real function in the scheme of things.

Then when I was sixteen that life ended. When I was sixteen, the new Morian Church of the Burning Light took over the throne in the Revolution of Souls. The Burning Light intended to bring forward the Day of Melding by creating the City of Tanza on earth. A series of bishops rose to and fell from the throne as the country went through paroxysms of purging. All morally dubious persons were persecuted. Whores were whipped through the streets and driven from the towns. Other criminals were executed or maimed.

Outrageously, mages were treated no better. "Thou shalt not suffer a witch to live," intoned the Burning Light priests. Within two years there were no healers or non-clerical mages left in Moria. Many of Michael's friends had been chained in witch manacles and burned at the stake before he decided to flee the country.

Michael believed that the Church wanted a monopoly on magical power and could not suffer a group of freethinkers like mages to exercise it outside their control. He blamed Smazor's Run as well. Smazor's freedom had, after all, been the result of a mistake by mages, and the bitter resentment many Morians still felt over this mistake found its voice in the Church's current outlawing of all nonclerical magic and the subsequent persecution of its practitioners.

But Michael also said, "It's been so long since those fools have seen a necromancer that they've come to believe that they can do without non-clerical mages."

So Michael and I fled Moria. We traveled on foot for over a month and came by a roundabout route to the neighboring state of Gallia, a rich and powerful country whose dynamic young ruler, Duke Leon Sahr, was known to be a friend of mages. Michael was by now a famous educator, so it was easy for him to join the Gallian College of Magic, the Alma Mater of magery on the Peninsula. He settled easily into college life. I did not.

There were other women in the college it is true, the wives and daughters of the few staff who had families and the cleaners and servingwomen. There was even a college of healers affiliated with it, who used the college's classrooms. The wives and daughters of the staff should have been the natural companions to the foster daughter of one of the masters. But like most normal women, they were interested in children or cookery or sewing; they knew no Aramayan or Ancient Soprian and cared nothing for magic. Being with them made me feel odd—skinny and clumsy. My wispy hair was always coming out from under my cap, and I was small-breasted, built more like a boy than a girl. I was stupid at all the things that mattered to them. I did my best to avoid them. And as for the healers ... Michael told me never to trust healers. "They're hard women," he said. "Arrogant and competitive, jealous of a mage's power."

I was the only woman anywhere studying advanced magic, and all my years of special teaching from Michael put me far ahead of most of the other students. When I was almost seventeen, I sat my final exams three years early and passed ahead of students even ten years my senior. Michael was both gratified and worried. He would not let my results be publicly displayed. As he explained to me, it was not wise for a woman to humiliate the male students by outstripping them too obviously. It would only anger them and lead to trouble. There was no need to be too proud of my results. They were merely the result of all those years of special teaching. I was not troubled by this. These were the kinds of considerations that had always concerned Michael. For myself I was bored by the classes and happy when Michael decided I should return to private study and to helping him with research. Life continued in Gallia in much the same way as it had in Mangalore. If I was restless, it was no more than I had ever been.

Until suddenly Michael had a heart attack and within two days was dead.

I was in limbo. The college staff, most of them old men like the Dean, were supportive, but embarrassed by the weeping of a young girl. They quickly left me to my own devices. I was completely at a loss. For almost thirteen years Michael had filled my days with lessons and research. I did not know what my own devices were.

I was very lonely. I did not have the knack of making friends. I'd never really talked to anyone except Michael. I was not good at trusting people, being suspicious of their motives in the case of young men and uncomfortable in the company of women.

Night after night I would sit in the dingy college dining room at the high table, for I sat with the staff and their families, watching the students at the tables laughing and playfully cuffing one another and feeling conspicuously alone. I was always on the outside, and no matter how much I told myself it didn't matter, I couldn't stop myself from wanting to be part of things.

These were the feelings that the hazia had blotted out, and they had returned even more strongly now that I had stopped taking it. I had been convinced that once I had employment things would be better. Of course they were not. I was back to lying on my bed and thinking maudlin thoughts.

I thought constantly of Michael. I wished so much that he was still alive so that I might have a chance to make up for all the mistakes that had so angered him in the past. I remembered his being particularly disappointed over my clumsy rendering of a spell only a few days before he died. I could imagine what he would make of my present sordid employment.

Sometimes, though, I found myself shaking with anger because he, who could never be pleased, had finally abandoned me as he had so often threatened. Then I would remember his many kindnesses to his disappointing daughter and how sometimes he had been pleased even though it was not his nature to show it. Then I would feel deeply guilty for being angry.

Now I was quite alone in the world and I was going to be incapable of finding a place in it. Nobody knew or cared if I lived or died, and I had no gift for making new people like me. Like someone fascinated with a needle who cannot resist touching it to feel its point, I could not stop picking over memories that hurt me. I was a mess of guilt and self-pity.

Then, after almost a month of this, there came a diversion. One afternoon as I was crossing the courtyard with Master John, a carriage came sweeping through the gates. It was a beautiful equipage of gleaming, dark wood sprung high across thin wheels, drawn by a pair of high-stepping white horses with pink roses plaited into their manes. Where most carriages had coats of arms, this had a twining rose carved and painted on the door. The blinds were pulled down, making the occupant invisible, but Master John acted as if it were the chariot of Smazor himself. He rushed forward, flapping his hands as if he were driving birds off a field.

One of the two tall footmen who had been clinging to the back of the carriage, descended and stalked decorously toward him. Master John grabbed his arm and tried to hustle him back toward the carriage, but he might as well have tried to hustle a stone or a tree. The footman merely stood there speaking to him with delicate politeness, impervious of the way Master John was pulling his arm across his body and almost spinning him round. I kept walking toward them. I was going in that direction anyway. Master John called over his shoulder,

"Dion! Stay where you are."

At the sound of my name the footman turned, skillfully shrugged Master John off and bowed toward me.

"Mademoiselle Dion," he said, "Madame Avignon seeks an audience with you."

The sound of her name sent a horrified thrill down my spine.

"Stay where you are, Dion," repeated Master John.

He said something to the footman and went determinedly toward the carriage. The footman, his face still showing nothing, turned and stalked unhurriedly along behind him. Master John was also stalking, but his was a stiff outraged stalk, a slamming of feet against the unfortunate ground. Suddenly he stopped short and looked up at the windows of the college.

They were crowded with the faces and arms of the young second and third year boys who were shouting and waving at the carriage.

"Stop that," he shouted. "Go back to your work this instant."

His voice, magically enhanced, filled the courtyard in a deep distorted yowl. He must have sent a charge of magic along the window frames then because the tardy boys yelped. The windows quickly became faceless.

Another footman stood holding open the carriage door.

Master John stood for some time, having a stiff, but heated conversation with the shadowy form of a woman in the dim interior.

Finally the footman closed the carriage door and the high-stepping horses drew it slowly out through the gateway.

"That was Madame Avignon," said Master John, pronouncing the Madame with sarcastic emphasis. "She wishes to have speech with you. I told her you did not wish this, but she insisted. That Woman implied that she'd go to the Duke if I didn't cooperate."

"But she has gone now."

"No," he said leading me into the college hall. "She is merely waiting down the street. I asked her to at least show some care for the reputation of an innocent, young girl, and she saw my point. I fear we cannot stop people from knowing that she has a connection with this college, but we can at least prevent too many people from seeing you have contact with each other. We shall go out the front door to avoid being too obvious."

The carriage was waiting for us around corner of the street.

Master John gripped my arm.

"Dion," he said, "you must do your best to be diplomatic. You must not offend this woman. Humor her, but be firm with her. Don't agree to do anything. Never forget that no matter how charming she may be, The Avignon is a courtesan and without morals. She will try to manipulate you. Don't put yourself in her power no matter what. Now go and take care."

He pushed me toward the carriage. One of the footmen let down the step and opened the door.

I approached the carriage as one approaches a lion—mostly with fear but with excitement and curiosity as well.

I expected its interior to smell of something dirty, like stale sweat, but in fact it was filled with the most delicious perfume. Sweet without being cloying, sharp without being bitter. It was warm, too, after the brisk spring wind that had been blowing down the street.

Madame Avignon sat in the farthest corner of the carriage, but the huge, green silk skirts of her gown seemed to fill it. She looked almost as if she were a goddess emerging out of the sea, for the top half of the gown hugged her body like a second skin. I was relieved to see that today it went all the way up to her neck, though the effect of this clinging bodice was not much more modest than the last.

She smiled warmly and motioned one elegant gloved hand.

"Please. Sit down. May I offer you refreshment? Sherry? Sparkling wine? Or lemonade perhaps?"

I thought it advisable to decline.

With a sudden movement, she leaned forward and banged the top of her parasol against the roof of the carriage. I felt a momentary panic as it lurched off.

Where was she taking me? I reminded myself that I was a mage, and nobody could harm me unless I allowed them to, and felt calmer. The blinds were still drawn most of the way down, I supposed to protect my reputation. It was a pity really. I'd never ridden in a carriage before.

Madame Avignon took off her gloves and smoothed them between her small white hands. I had expected her face to be a heavy mask of cosmetics, like the faces of the prostitutes in the town, but in the dimness of the carriage, it was hard to tell if the flush across her cheekbones was real or applied. Really she was quite lovely, with her soft, shining hair swept up beneath a huge graceful hat covered in feathers, and just the right amount of lace at her slender neck and the wrists of her long fine hands.

She sat draped across the seat opposite, regarding me from under her eyelashes. The attitude was languid, but her movements were quick and forceful, and whenever she lifted her heavy lashes (false?) her eyes were lively and sparkling.

"I hope I have not taken you away from your studies," she said. Even her voice was charming, with its warm tones and slight foreign accent.

"No."

"Indeed I am sorry to have waylaid you like this. I have been trying for some time to speak to you privately, but there seems to be some resistance among your colleagues to my doing so. So! Here I am!"

Her words startled me. I knew nothing of any attempts to contact me.

"I came because you know nothing of the man from whom you are protecting me. This could be dangerous. I felt that we must speak of these things."

I nodded, carefully noncommittal. Was this the beginnings of a manipulation?

She lifted her eyes and looked hard at my face. Though I could detect no sign of magery in her, there was something in her look, so bare and serious, that seemed to read me, everything about me. Despite my best intentions, I dropped my eyes and blushed. I felt suddenly dishonest.

"You have looked in the Bowl of Seeing."

"Yes." I was surprised she should know about it.

"I have had other people look also," she said. "I know you can see nothing there. That is one reason why I asked to see you. I feared you must underestimate your opponent, who is a very clever and dangerous man. His name is Norval. He is a necromancer. An Aramayan."

I gaped at her.

A necromancer and an Aramayan! Death magic, and from one of the great old empires of the West. I was excited. Then I became doubtful. What she was saying was ludicrous. Surely mages and necromancers had better things to do than persecute courtesans. Master John had had no doubts about that. Here was a woman who was overreacting, overdramatizing in the way one might expect from her kind. I tried to answer as politely as I could under the circumstances.

"Please don't be anxious. I do have the situation under control. I foresee no difficulties."

"No," she said ruefully. "I don't suppose you would. We both know how powerful you are. I'm sure you would have no difficulty in a battle of magic with Norval. And I'm sure the Duke and I can rely on you to do your duty, however much you underestimate your opponent."

She began to pull her little lemon gloves back onto her hands. Sharply.

I bristled at her remark. Was the woman threatening me? Yet she had paid me a compliment. I began to have some inkling of what Master John had meant by manipulation. The extent of it, the huge vistas that opened up, frightened me.

I took my courage in both hands.

"I do assure you that I have the situation under control."

She put her hand over her eyes for a moment and her figure, which a moment ago had been upright, drooped. She sighed. I almost felt sorry for her. Till I realized that this must just be a play for sympathy. But she surprised me.

"I realize that people here cannot believe a mage would bother himself with a whore. Mages here are so . . . separate from ordinary humans . . . I think they forget sometimes how much people . . . can hate each other. Aramayan mages are not so separated from everyday life. And Norval was once my lover. It makes a difference, you know."

I was shocked, but tried not to show it. God and angels! Things were beginning to look very sordid indeed. I wanted to tell Madame Avignon that I had no wish to be involved in her private life. I said nothing. For a few moments the tension in the carriage was unbearable.

"Mademoiselle Dion, I have no doubts in you as a mage. It is Norval I fear. He is cunning. He will have realized by now that I have magical protection. Have you considered the physical danger to which you might be exposed? Have you considered that Norval might launch some kind of conventional attack on you? That is the way he works. Have you taken steps to make yourself safe in that sense?"

Dignity, Dion. Dignity. I was beginning to get hardened to her. I pretended I was Master John.

"Madame, I live in a college of mages. We take steps to protect ourselves from intruders."

"Yes, magical intruders. But what about more conventional assailants?"

"We have wardings against those with evil intentions. Anyway, how should anyone know to attack me? The Duke himself said that nothing is known of our association."

"I fear that is not the case. Very little is secret at the court. My informants tell me that our association is already known in certain circles."

She frightened me there. Who knew? Or was this just another part of the whole fantasy. I was unsure what to do. I wished Master John was dealing with her. "Agree to nothing, Dion," said his voice in my head.

"Mademoiselle Dion, any good assassin knows methods for disguising his intentions. It might interest you to know that the captain of my bodyguard has twice entered the college, even to your own door. No one challenged him; no one stopped him. This is why I have come to see you today. If he can do it, so can an assassin."

I could not help feeling frightened and a little outraged. What a liberty the woman had taken!

"If anything happens to you, the way would be immediately open for an attack on me. I have many enemies in this city. It's not inconceivable that one of them may be in contact with Norval and will send an assassin against you."

Now I was sure she was overdramatizing.

"I am a mage, Madame Avignon. No ordinary assassin can harm me."

"You are not invincible, Mademoiselle. A good assassin knows how to get round a mage. Have you never heard of witch manacles?"

She couldn't have guessed how much that question would distress me. I knew all about witch manacles. They're the only way to disable a mage. An iron neck manacle breaks our circle of power and renders us helpless. Once I saw witchfinders in Moria come to take the village healer away. How could I forget that cold iron manacle? I had felt the evil of it even from where I had been hiding. The healer's drained old face was white above it.

Once, too, Michael and I had hidden among the chimneys of Mangalore from a huge angry crowd, unable to escape without using magic, yet not daring to use magic because we could feel the questing minds of the witchfinders reaching out for us. We hid there while they burned other mages in the square below, mages chained helpless to the stake with witch manacles. It was almost as if my nostrils could still smell the bitter scent of singeing hair and the sweet smell of burning flesh. It had smelled like nothing so much as roasting meat. As we lay there forced to listen, the soft old faces of the mages Michael had known came like possibilities into my mind, and I wondered which ones . . . The awful screams . . . I wanted to kill her for that remembrance.

"I have heard enough," I snapped. "If you would kindly take me home now."

"Mademoiselle?" She stared at me.

"I do not wish to discuss this foolishness anymore," I snapped. I jumped up and staggered against the movement of the carriage.

Her face was stricken. "Mademoiselle Dion, please."

"Please take me home." I said through clenched teeth.

"Of course. But please sit down."

She banged the roof of the carriage with her parasol.

Silence.

"Mademoiselle, I did not mean to upset you. Please accept my apologies."

I was silent, too angry to accept anything.

"Mademoiselle, I merely wished to make a point," she said suddenly, beseechingly. "You would be much safer if you let me offer you protection."

"What do you mean?" I snapped.

"If you were living in my house, you would be safe from attack. The house is well guarded, and my bodyguards would watch over you as well as me."

She was trying to get control over me just as Master John had said! And then? What other favors might she feel free to ask?

"That could never happen," I said with what I thought seemed admirable restraint. "What about my reputation? What you are suggesting is ridiculous."

"Mademoiselle Dion, please," she cried. Her look was beseeching, and for an awful moment I thought she was going to throw herself down on her knees.

"I understand perfectly. I do not believe it would be . . . right for me to stay in your house. A mage must remain a free agent."

Her face hardened.

"You must believe as you see fit," she said coldly (with enviable dignity). "I am thinking of my own safety and, therefore, of yours. I can tell you for certain that you are in danger. I offer you the services of my captain to guard you in the college. He is well versed in the ways of assassins and will be at your command. I beg of you to take my offer."

The carriage stopped. We were back where we had started.

"Thank you, Madame," I snapped. "But I can look after myself perfectly well. Good day."

I did not look at her again.

Master John asked me what had transpired, and I told him about Madame Avignon's fears. He took them no more seriously than I had.

"I was afraid of something like this from the start. I just hope it goes no further."

I told him I had been polite, but firm in my rejection of her offer.

"Yes!" he said. "You have done well."

I couldn't help feeling a little uneasy about how I had dealt with the situation, however. The woman had seemed terribly afraid. It would have been kinder to have soothed her fears more. In other moments I knew that I had done the right thing. My pity for her was obviously a sign that she had manipulated my feelings. Whores made their own beds. It was their own fault if they had to lie on them. I would have liked to have been able to talk about her with someone. Anyone. The thing was, she didn't seem like a bad woman. She didn't seem dirty. Mind you, I knew evil was not always unattractive. But up close she had seemed so . . . normal.

I just wished there was someone who was able to explain things to me. Like how she could do what she did for money and why?

But though I had a bad conscience about her, it didn't once occur to me to take her seriously.

\* \* \*

I dreamed of witch manacles.

I have always been a nervous sleeper, inclined to wake up rigid with terror in the middle of the night. Does studying magic make this worse, I wonder. You certainly learn that there are terrible things in the universe to be afraid of, things more terrible than other human beings. The fact that a mage is unlikely to come into contact with these evil powers unless he goes looking for trouble is small comfort in the dark. When, as a child, I cried out in the night, frightened by some strange noise or unrecognizable shape in my room, Michael would try to calm my fears by taking me through the spells for dealing with supernatural attack.

"I, too, am sometimes nervous in the dark," he would explain, patiently at first, but with increasing irritation as time went on, "but I reason with my fears and thus defeat them. You must learn to conquer this irrational fear."

Then he would go away, taking the light with him, leaving me alone in the dark again. His pearls of wisdom gave off insufficient illumination to comfort me, but fearing his irritation, I ceased to call out to him.

Instead, whenever I was afraid, I taught myself to cast a brilliant light into the room. It is a habit I have never grown out of. Eventually it became so automatic, I could do it even before I was properly awake. Once or twice at inns on the road to Gallia I had seriously embarrassed myself, and Michael, by lighting up a room full of sleepers before I realized what I was doing.

Now, in my dream, the huge cast-iron manacle hung on a charred stake. It seemed to snarl like a mastiff and reach out hungrily at me.

I started awake in a cold sweat, with a terrible burning feeling at my throat, blasted a light into the room, and sat up.

And knocked the arm of the man in black, who had been bending over me in the darkness. I screamed. He dropped his thin, spiked club, but his other hand thrust a huge, open witch manacle at me. My skin burned with the fear of that dreadful thing. With all my being I wanted it away from me. He put his hand over my mouth as he tried to force the manacle through the crackling air. I clawed at him, and suddenly magical energy surged through me. Manacle and assailant hurtled across the room and smacked hard against the stone wall opposite. The man collapsed limply on the floor.

The door flew open. Another man rushed in with a drawn sword. I stood up on the bed. Tried to scream for help. My voice came out feebly. The man at the door looked at me and the bundle by the wall. Then he darted away. Someone began yelling.

After years and seconds, the room filled with people. They all seemed to be staring at me. Eyes and upturned faces. Maya made me sit on the edge of the bed with my head between my legs and wrapped a blanket around me. I could not stop shivering. She led me away through a crowd of staring faces, a babble of voices. She gave me hot, sweet tea and put me in a strange, cold bed which I could not make comfortable.

But although Maya spent the night sitting beside me, and though I could see for myself the guard outside the window and the shadow of the one outside the door, I did not sleep again until it became light.

"You are quite safe," she said. But I could not believe her.

Even when dawn came and I slept, I dreamed endlessly of cold iron and the crack of the body as it hit the wall.

I awoke properly midmorning, feeling sore and dry and stretched to the limit. Maya was still sitting beside me.

"How are you feeling?" she asked kindly. Embarrassed and uncomfortable was how I was feeling.

"All right," I said, and then, with a prickling horror, "Oh no! The ritual."

I leaped out of bed.

"Hush," soothed Maya. "Someone else is taking care of your work. If you are rested, the Dean is asking for you."

"Then I will go to him," I said. "I can't rest any longer."

I'd never much liked Maya before. I'd thought her pushy and abrupt, but I was grateful to her that morning. She helped me dress, an intimacy I could not like, but afterward she rubbed soothing oil into my neck and temples. Then she gently brushed and plaited my hair.

"You have a visitor," she said. "I want you to look nice for her."

I was so touched by this my eyes filled with tears, and I submitted without a word. I rarely paid much attention to my appearance, and it was the first time I could ever remember having my hair brushed.

An atmosphere of deep dismay filled the Dean's office. The Dean and Master John looked ravaged. But the first person I noticed was a woman sitting with a straight back amidst a swirl of silk skirt. I could not see her head for the enormous befeathered hat she wore, but I knew it was Kitten Avignon. I recognized the cloud of delicious perfume that filled the room.

Her hand rested emphatically on a gold-topped cane. It was hard to connect her appearance with what I knew her to be. She looked nothing short of regal. It occurred to me to wonder what the Dean felt about having a courtesan within the sober precincts of the college.

After the greetings there was silence in the room. I sat uncomfortably on my chair, staring at my hands, knowing myself to be the center of attention. Suddenly the Dean and Master John both spoke at once. They stopped, each motioned the other to go on, and then the Dean spoke.

"We have been discussing what happened last night. It is shocking to think that your life is not safe even here, and it is obvious to me and Master John, indeed all the staff, that steps must be taken to prevent a repetition of this dreadful incident."

I nodded.

"Madame Avignon here has reiterated her claim that you are not safe in the college, and that you would be best to reside with her where she says she can have you guarded properly. Indeed, while we cannot approve of her methods, were it not for her forethought in placing one of her own guards in the college, who knows what might have happened."

"Not at all!" said a voice from the corner of the room. A short, stocky man dressed in black stood there, his feet apart, hands behind his back. I was startled that I had not noticed him. Later, when I got to know Captain Simonetti better, I realized that it was usual not to notice him in a room.

"Give credit where credit's due," he went on. "I did nothing. By the time I got there she had already disposed of the bugger. Very nicely, too."

"This is Captain Simonetti. He is the man who

raised the alarm last night," said the Dean.

A terrible fear had gripped me.

"Where is the man who attacked me?" I asked.

The two mages cast down their eyes. Captain Simonetti looked surprised.

"Why dead, of course," he said. "Didn't I just tell you so?"

I had killed a man. I was a killer. And I felt nothing much. Nothing at all, except shame at my numbness.

The Dean cleared his throat.

"Captain Simonetti has been explaining to us the enormous difficulty of making the college safe, Dion. There is even a chance that your very presence here would put the other students in danger. This," he said, looking apologetically at Master John, "is what weighs heaviest with me. The man who attacked you was a Soprian assassin. The people who hired him are obviously prepared to go to great lengths."

I still felt numb. Soprian assassins were famed for their skill and deadliness. And price. They were creatures of legend, not reality.

"I was dreaming about the witch manacle when I woke," I said. "I was frightened . . . The rest just followed. I didn't mean . . ."

The Dean looked sympathetically at me.

"My dear, I do believe that you might be safer living in Madame Avignon's house."

I nodded. At that moment Madame Avignon, with her big gold cane and her queenly bearing, seemed to offer the only safety. I was filled with a desire to get away from the college, from the scene of last night's terror.

Master John did not agree.

"Enough of this!" he shouted, banging his fist on the table. "You're allowing yourselves to be manipulated by fear. It would not be impossible to guard the child here. Surely that is better than . . ."

"Master John," said Madame Avignon, "it would be far simpler for her to live in my house, which is already well guarded by Captain Simonetti and my other bodyguards."

"Dion can defend herself. She has already shown that."

"Of course she can. But she is not a soldier. She is not used to being constantly vigilant. And how can you place her in a position where she might have to kill and kill again? Isn't killing against all the precepts of magery?"

I felt almost grateful to her. It was as if she read my mind. I knew I could never feel safe in my room, or even in this college, again.

"You think of Dion as nothing more than a mage. You forget she is an innocent young girl. How can we expose her to the lifestyle of a, a . . ."

The Dean placed a warning hand on his arm.

". . . woman like yourself?" he ended lamely.

"Whore is what you no doubt meant to say," said Kitten silkily. "Let us leave this uplifting discussion of my past for a moment and consider the present. As the Duke's mistress, I can assure you, my activities must always be above reproach. I live quietly with a woman companion. I can promise you that Mademoiselle Dion would witness nothing in my house that she would not see here. But it is Mademoiselle Dion's decision to make. As you say, she is an innocent young girl. You seem to want to make her into an assassin. Perhaps we should ask her what she wants to do."

She turned to me. "Mademoiselle, which do you prefer? Master John's plan or mine?"

All I wanted now was escape.

"Your plan, Madame," I said. I expected her to look triumphant. She merely looked enormously relieved.

"Dion!" cried Master John. "How can you? My lord, you cannot allow this."

"Master John," said Madame Avignon, "you are making a complicated matter out of something very simple. All I wish to do is survive. And to do that I must make sure that Mademoiselle Dion survives." She stood up and pulled on her gloves. "Good day, gentlemen. I will send a carriage for Mademoiselle Dion this evening."

"Very good," said the Dean. He put his hand on Master John's arm.

She swept out, followed by Captain Simonetti.

The Dean sat down and mopped his face.

"My lord . . ."

"Hush, John. Dion, go and pack. And take one of the guards with you."

Later, as I watched the passing houses from the window of Madame Avignon's carriage, I felt a terrible fear. Had I indeed ruined my reputation and my life? Despite what Madame Avignon had said, I felt sure I would have to be constantly vigilant to prevent myself from being drawn into distasteful situations.

Master John had been angry and disappointed at me. Only the Dean came down to the college steps to say good-bye to me. It was all I could do as the carriage pulled up not to cling to him and beg him to let me stay. I had never before been away from the college on my own. But his firm assumption that I was going was more persuasive than words.

"Dion," he said, "I feel that you are doing the best thing for us all. Try to remember . . . Many things are forgiven one whom a ruler favors. If you can win the

Duke's patronage, you will have no need to worry about your future.''

He helped me firmly into the carriage. I felt cast adrift. He must be glad to be rid of such a misfit, such a nuisance.

Yet just before the carriage drew away he stuck his head in the window.

''I promised Michael I would protect you from . . . moral corruption. If you have any of that kind of difficulty, send me a message, and I will bring you back to the college.''

I was comforted. My resolve firmed. It was time I grew up and went out on my own. I would learn to deal with and transcend my environment. Only the terrible knowledge that I had killed someone haunted me. Even after knowing this for a whole day, I still felt nothing more than a vague dismay. I wondered if there was something wrong with me. But I knew I did not ever want to have to hear that sickening crack of bones again.

# THREE

A courtesan living quietly with a woman companion. How did that look? I imagined a florid
mansion, full of red velvet and silk and huge
gilt mirrors, cacophonous with the secretive sounds
of lovemaking. Grunts and groans. Creaking bed-
springs. Dirty. Full of the close, fishy smell of
women's private parts and the servants an ugly,
grubby pack of individuals. Millie, our housekeeper
back in Moria, used to be full of stories about the
scandalous lifestyles of fallen women. Though, come
to think of it, she'd been a bit short on details.

In fact, from the outside, Madame Avignon's house
looked quite innocent. It was in a respectable part of
town, across from the park, a quiet area full of big
leafy trees. It was a graceful white house, quite plain
on the outside except for black wrought-iron lace,
sticking up like a crown, around its grey slate roof.
How appropriate for a Ducal mistress I thought.

The house was protected by a heavy stone wall
topped with black iron spikes, but the green shutters

on the big windows gave it a pleasant, homey appearance, and there were pots of early daffodils on the front steps.

The door was answered by an immaculately dressed butler. There was nothing smarmy or knowing about his manner or that of the neat woman who met me in the front hall and proclaimed herself to be Madame Donati, the housekeeper. They seemed . . . nice. Clean.

The housekeeper explained the security arrangements of the house, showed me how to open outside windows without setting off the warding spells placed on them, and even introduced me to the two guards who were patrolling the ground floor. I had to admit it put my mind to rest. Maybe I had done the right thing. Even I could see how much easier this house would be to guard than the college, which was a huge building with many doors.

There was not even a single scrap of red silk inside that house, at least not in the rooms I was shown. Instead it was full of softly polished wood, warm fabrics, bowls of hothouse fruit and roses and the scent of lemon. Carpets from the West lay like warm, jeweled mosaics on the shining floor. There was some dark red velvet. It was used to upholster a graceful set of gilt chairs in the drawing room. But they did not seem the right shape for the receiving of lovers. Everything was so beautiful, so delicate and comfortable, so unbelievably clean, untainted by the woman who lived here. It looked like the house of a wealthy aristocrat. I picked an apple out of a bowl, expecting it to be rotten on the inside or to have a bite taken out of it, but it was perfect, glowing red, smelling deliciously of sweet apple.

Sin, I reflected, was subtler than I had thought.

*    *    *

Later the housekeeper took me to my room. It was
an attic room with a sloping ceiling, but it was much
bigger than my room back at the college. My things,
a bag of clothes and case of books, which had over-
crowded my college room made a dusty little pile on
the blue rug. Standing in one corner, almost like a
symbol of maturity, was the large Gallian magic mirror that I had inherited from Michael, and which had
been lying in storage since his death.

There was a wide bed covered in a soft, pink quilt,
a worktable by the window, even two comfortable
chairs. And the room was warm. There was a little
blue-and-white-tiled stove in the corner. I remembered how clammy the rooms at the college had been,
especially in winter, and how they had smelled of un-
washed students and old, old dust. This room smelled
faintly of lavender. Despite my mistrust, I felt something inside me uncurl and relax, especially after I
saw that there was a lock on the door and a key in
the lock.

After the housekeeper had gone, I let myself go. I
ran my hand across the smooth fabric of the quilt,
inhaled the lavender smell of the sheets, took off my
shoes and wriggled my toes into the thick pile of the
rug. This room was positively luxurious. And so
pretty. I had never lived anywhere so pretty before.

I drew aside the fine, white curtain and opened the
window. I was high above the ground, so high that I
could see the tower of the cathedral and the spires of
the city through the trees. I could almost imagine myself up in a castle like a princess. I could see now that
the wrought-iron lace around the roof made it very
hard for anyone to climb up to my window. I leaned
against the windowsill for some time, dreaming and

feeling the cool evening breeze blowing on my face, till the soft chiming of bells made me jump. It was quarter to eight by the cathedral clock.

I scrabbled round in my luggage for the magical apparatus. Praise God it was all there. Hastily I set up the candlestands and drew out the chalk symbols, smudging them in my hurry. I cursed myself for having left it all so late. I could imagine what Michael would have said to my dreaming instead of setting up the spell. Magery is an ascetic art. As Michael was always pointing out, a mage cannot afford to become too involved in his surroundings lest he be distracted by them. It seemed as though I had just proved this point. I had been seduced by the luxury of my new room and almost forgotten about the ritual. I resolved to be more on my guard.

After the incantation, I sat on my bed wondering what to do next. It was way past my dinnertime, and I was hungry. At this time of night the corridor outside my room would be echoing with the sounds of students coming back from dinner, sounds that had always made me feel so lonely. Here all was still. The silence wasn't much better than the noise had been. I was just trying to get up the courage to ring the bell for a servant when there was a knock on the door.

It was a crisp little woman dressed in the brown robes of a healer. She held out her hand and I shook it, a little mystified. It was a small hand, but surprisingly hard and callused.

"I'm Genevieve Appellez, Madame Avignon's personal healer. She sent me to welcome you to her house. She apologizes for not being here herself. She attends upon the Duke most evenings."

This, then, must be Madame Avignon's woman companion. I had not heard she was a healer. Oh dear. Here was trouble. Mages and healers traditionally got along very badly.

She looked very serious, in the way healers always did. Her light brown hair was scraped severely back from her thin face under the usual brown cap. I was sure her hair never escaped in little wispy pieces like mine did. She didn't look the type. Her face was quiet and watchful, not unfriendly, but her quick definite movements suggested a forceful personality. She was the sort of person who was certain to disapprove of me. Michael's housekeeper had been just such a one. The best way to deal with such people was to avoid them.

I bobbed my head awkwardly and murmured my thanks.

"May I come in?"

I nodded.

"Do you like the room? Do you have everything you need?"

She looked about her with sharp eyes as I mumbled my thanks.

"So this is the protection spell," she said, going over to the table. "Do the candles have to be constantly alight?"

"No," I said. "They merely serve as a focus." Here was a healing woman prying into my magic just as Michael had said they did; I blew the candles out quickly, before she could learn anything.

We looked at each other across the table for a moment.

She looked wholesome. Not at all as if she lived in the house of a courtesan. This relentless wholesomeness everywhere was beginning to unnerve me.

"I will call you Dion and you must call me Genny,"

she informed me. "Come. You must be hungry. Let's go and have dinner."

As she led me down the stairs Genevieve explained that it would just be the two of us at dinner most evenings.

"Kitten usually dines at the palace."

The food was wonderful. Instead of watery stew, there was fish in a delicious sauce and crisp, bright vegetables arranged on elegant white platters in beautiful combinations of color and shape. After I had eaten, I realized that I had probably gobbled and sat embarrassed in front of my empty plate, watching Genevieve eating carefully. Guiltily I refused a second helping.

It was a strained meal. Since I was bent on not revealing too much, conversation did not flourish, though Genevieve did her best to keep it going. The big dining room with the sound of the clock echoing in the silence and the impassive butler didn't help. For the first time, I missed the noisy, smelly dining room at the college.

Genevieve asked me about my studies, how I had liked the college and the various masters. Apparently she knew some of the healers there, but since mages tend to keep themselves separate from healers, this line of questioning didn't get us very far.

Then she asked me if I was at all interested in healing.

"I have studied it a little," I said, "but I've no vocation for it."

"I spend most of my days at St. Belkis' nunnery, where Kitten maintains a charity clinic."

I was astonished. It was such a peculiar thing to say. Why should Madame Avignon keep up a clinic and at a nunnery, too?

"A clinic?"

"Yes, a free clinic for the poor."

She must believe that it would cancel out her sins. It seemed a ludicrous superstition to an agnostic such as myself, but probably very common here as it had been in Moria, especially among uneducated people. Perhaps it was not so surprising in a courtesan after all. One of the well-known facts about Madame Avignon was her popularity with the lower classes. Michael and I had seen it for ourselves when we'd first come to Gallia. Rumor had it that Gallia's aristocracy feared Madame Avignon for this reason.

"That must make her popular," I said.

Genevieve looked at me sharply.

"With the poor," I said.

There was silence for a moment, and then she said, carefully, "The clinic is always in need of more people to do healing. I don't wish to offend you, but I thought to ask if you would be interested in assisting me there."

"I don't think so," I said as politely as I could, embarrassed by her asking and guilty for saying no. It was unheard of for a mage to lower himself to being a healer, a gross loss of dignity, almost like being a servant and cleaning up after people. Michael would have been horrified to think of me working in a clinic. In fact, why should I feel guilty? I'd done well to say no. Maybe I should have been ruder and put her in her place.

But no seemed to be the answer she'd expected, so I did not get the opportunity to be rude to her. I was secretly relieved and then annoyed at myself for being relieved. "For Seven's sake, stand up for yourself, Dion," said Michael's voice in my head.

After dinner Genevieve asked me if I would like to

see her still room, but I could see it was just a politeness. I made my excuses and went back upstairs.

I opened the window of my room and stood at it, breathing the chill night air and looking at the lights of the town through the treetops. The incident with Genevieve had depressed me and left me once again thinking sadly about my inability to make friends. Up here in the attic, the whole world seemed to be only me and my candle. Was it some failing in me that meant I was all alone in the world? Yet nobody could claim that Kitten Avignon was a virtuous woman, and all kinds of people seemed to be concerned over her.

It wasn't fair. I closed the window quickly and began unpacking my books. Maybe I should have said yes to the healer, I thought. It hardly mattered what they thought of me in this house, and it would have been something new to do.

At the bottom of the book box I found my diary of hazia dreams. I began to flip through it, dreaming back to some of those dreams. I had not written up that one on the beach of bones. I would have liked to have explored it more. I began reliving it in my mind, the crunching of bones, the sticky flaccid feel of that sea.

And the being on the rock, its leather wings and scaly hands. I could almost see it, red eyes gleaming in the light of those cold, swirling stars. Fascination returned. If only we could have talked, if only I could have asked it . . .

The candle went out.

My scalp tingled and I groped quickly about for the matches. I hated total darkness. Simultaneously with that thought, I heard heavy breathing somewhere in the room behind me. Heavy, rasping breathing.

I whirled around and filled the room with the

blinding white of magelight. There was nothing there, nothing.

Yet still I could hear the breathing. Resting the magelight on my fingertips, I crept slowly around the room, trying to find the source of the breathing. I looked quickly under the bed and opened the wardrobe.

God and angels! It was coming from the corner, behind the mirror. No. From under the cloth that covered the mirror. I stood there not daring to touch it for a moment and then, in what seemed like the longest moment of my life, I reached out and twitched the cloth away.

Nothing. It was only my reflection. And still the breathing.

I leaned over cautiously to look behind the mirror.

Bang! The whole mirror shuddered as a wave smashed hard against the glass. I jumped back. The wave seemed to suck the glass back and then, slimy and clinging, it slid slowly away. I caught a glimpse of little mouths, puckered, sucking the glass and little, flashing pink tongues. Behind was darkness, the cold, whirling stars, the heaving mass of the jelly sea and a rock. On the rock was the dark outline of bat wings and a huge craggy head with red lizard eyes that stared straight at me.

A hand, huge and spiky, reached out. A terrible voice that sounded like the voices of a multitude rolled into one said, "TAKE MY HAND."

Oh Angels, the pull of that voice.

My hand reached out, was dragged toward that hand.

No. I must not.

I shook my head, snapped out of it, pulled my hand back to my side. A terrible power was pulling me into the mirror. It was making my hair and my dress stir as if in the wind. But, like a wind, it was superficial now and could be resisted.

The demon's craggy head moved, straightened. For a moment I almost thought I had surprised it. The cold stars were the only light inside the mirror. The magelight in my hand made it even darker in there. I held it behind me, so I could see better.

There was no way it could get out of there. It would require enormous magics to bring it through, magics that I had no idea how to perform. Yet I was frightened. It really felt as if there was only a thin glass wall between me and its almost-limitless power, and there was that terrible magnetic pull toward the mirror. It couldn't get through itself, but what if it could pull me through? It really felt as if it could. Could I have taken its hand? What would have happened if I had? My knees went weak just thinking of it.

Pull yourself together, Dion. Dignity. That was what was needed. That was how Michael had taught me to deal with supernatural beings. Make it respect you. Like a horse, let it know you are in control. I quickly suppressed the memory of what a terrible rider I was.

I was a mage. I stood up straight and demanded in my best haughty mage's voice, "Who are you?"

"I am Bedazzer." The voice was deep and terrible and textured. And it pulled.

"What do you want here?"

It had become lighter inside the mirror. I could see the demon crouched, enshrouded almost completely by its huge bat wings, except for the thick sinewy arms resting lightly on its knees. I could see clearly as it smiled, drawing its lips across a fanged mouth. A firm pink tongue appeared between those lips. It ran it slowly down its finger. It was as if it licked my own flesh.

"Why don't you come in here and find out, little girl?"

I shivered. Its expression changed. It frowned.

"What were you doing walking on my beach, little girl? TELL ME!"

I jumped. "I don't know," I said before I could stop myself.

"You don't know," it repeated. It seemed to roll this round in its mind for a moment.

"I followed you back, little girl. I like the look of your moist little world. I want to come through and explore."

It lashed out suddenly with its huge claws. Brought them slowly screechingly down the glass. The mirror shuddered.

I screamed out the words of dispelling. It snatched its hand back under its wings. Definitely disconcerted this time.

It hunched over and its eyes narrowed.

"You like demons don't you, little girl? What sort of wicked little girl likes demons? But you do, don't you? I know. I can see into your little mind. You came because you were curious."

It seemed best to say nothing. We both knew it was right.

"I'm . . . curious, too," it said. "An alliance, little girl. You could help me. And I could please you."

I didn't know what to say.

Suddenly it reared up and flung open its wings so that its strong, perfectly formed body was fully displayed. It swayed its hips from side to side, lifted its head, and cried to the sky.

"I am Bedazzer. Lord of Pleasure. Render of Virgins . . ."

Lord of All. His . . . thing. It was huge. And spiky. I musn't look. I couldn't pull my eyes away. I'd never actually seen a real one before. I was so embarrassed, I blushed all over. I couldn't help it. I giggled, horrified, my hand over my mouth.

"What?" he screamed. "You laugh at ME? You stupid little virgin." He flung himself at the glass, fists out. The mirror shuddered with the impact, tottered, keeled over.

I leaped back screaming.

There was a smash of breaking glass as the mirror hit the floor. Glass flew everywhere. Then silence. I stood shaking, staring stupidly at the shattered glass, clean and silver and flat on the floor. I poked it tentatively with my foot and was oddly amazed that there was no sign of the demon. No slime, nothing.

The door slammed open. A figure rushed in like a wave. I threw myself back against the wall screaming and cast a light spell again.

It was Kitten Avignon carrying a drawn sword.

"What's going on?" she yelled "Are you all right?" Her eyes darted from side to side in the brilliant white flare of the witchlight. She held that sword as confidently as any swordsman.

I stared amazed, and she stared back at me.

"Oh," I said. "Yes of course. I'm fine."

"What happened?"

"Oh . . . nothing really. I . . . broke my mirror."

"So I see. Well." She breathed out heavily "Phew! You gave me one hell of a fright. I was expecting a band of rampaging Soprians at least." She poked the glass with her foot. "What a mess!"

She was wearing a frothy white gown. It looked like

a cloud of swansdown. I was transfixed by the sword in her hand.

"Nice sword, isn't it?" she said with a grin.

Suddenly another figure barreled in through the door. There was a flash of steel. It was Simonetti. Sword drawn, wearing only his leather breeches. He was dripping wet and the witchlight gave his skin a ghastly pallor.

"False alarm," said Kitten. "She's safe."

"Shit," said Simonetti. "Took years off my life. What's been going on?"

"Dion broke her mirror."

"Sweet Tansa, how'd you do that?"

"Trouble?" asked Genny, poking her head round the door. She, at least, was not carrying a sword. Her head was covered with a frilly, white nightcap tied like a bonnet under her chin. She wore a long nightdress and a printed cotton wrap over it.

"Aye," said Simonetti. "Our little mage just broke her mirror. That'll be seven years bad luck, girl, and you know who's going to have to protect you from it, don't you?"

He and Kitten grinned at each other. I could sense their relief.

"Caught you with your pants down, did we? Or are you just showing off your muscles?"

Simonetti snorted. "Well, you're hardly battle ready either . . . MADAME."

"What happened?" said Genny. Her face was serious. "How'd you break the mirror?"

Now was the time of reckoning, the time for a convincing lie.

"I . . . was trying to move it," I said limply. I felt myself blushing.

Fortunately Simonetti took the blush as embarrassment.

"Well. By the Seven, I'd blush too if I'd scared the life out of everybody. . . . Hey," he said, blinking in the magelight, "can we have some normal light in here instead of this bloody flare? It's beginning to hurt my eyes."

Genny put her finger to the candlewick and lit it. It was a nice trick. I'd never thought to do it like that. But she looked at me as if something was wrong. I didn't think she believed me about the mirror.

I put out the magelight.

"Why don't you both go back to bed? I'll finish up here," said Kitten.

The other two went—Simonetti muttering, Genny with a single worried glance.

"We must get one of the servants up here to clean this up. You can't spend the night with glass on the floor."

Kitten reached for the bell rope and pulled it before I could protest.

"No," I said, "I can clean it up. Really." I blew a spell through it and the glass rose in a whirling, tinkling mass which carried it to the corner and left it in a neat heap.

"Well. Well. Look at you. You know, it never occurred to me that you could use magic for such a small thing." She ran her foot over the carpet. "Yes, that's got it all I think. What a great way of cleaning house." She smiled at me.

But suddenly I wasn't in the mood for pleasantries. Suddenly my knees were turning to water. What had I done? I sat down at my worktable and put my face in my hands.

"Dion?"

"Yes. I'll be right. Just the crash made me jump."

Silence for a moment and then, "Are these mirrors special, or will any old one do?"

"What?"

"We can get you a new looking glass."

An open window for the demon to enter . . . I couldn't help shuddering.

"No, thanks."

She came up behind me and touched me on the shoulder. I felt myself flinch. She took the hand away. Her voice wasn't particularly offended.

"You've had quite a shock, haven't you?"

"I'm all right," I said, rubbing my face and hoping she didn't see how my hands were shaking.

"What really happened with that mirror? Did you . . . er . . . see something?"

"I was moving it," I said.

"I see."

Silence.

"There's Maria," she said. "I'll be back in a minute."

I wished she would go away. I was uncomfortable with her here. On the other hand, I didn't really want to be alone just now.

When she came back into the room again, I looked at her through my hands. She reposed gracefully in a chair, one delicate hand hanging loosely over the end of the armrest. She looked incredibly fragile and feminine sitting there, as if she'd never handled anything as brutal as a sword.

I wondered if I had imagined it. It seemed to have disappeared.

"You had a sword," I said.

"When I heard the crash, I thought someone was trying to get at you. I came up to help you." There was a pause. "I do know how to use it," she said.

I must have looked disbelieving, for she laughed and said, "Ah. You're making assumptions. People shouldn't make assumptions, you know."

"What have you done with it?"

"I gave it to Maria to put away. A proper sword's follower is supposed to take care of her own weapons, but ... Well, to hell with tradition. I was taught swordplay by one of those who tried to get you last night. A Soprian assassin. They're very practical people. They believe that they can best protect those they love by teaching them to protect themselves, so they have a whole method of swordplay for women and another for children. It has been very useful one way or another."

I was silent, not knowing how to respond or what to say. It was so hard to believe any of this. Was she really telling the truth?

"You see, you are safe here. There are always men on guard here, and on the off chance that someone did manage to get in, Simonetti and I are well able to protect you. Though I'm not sure you need us. You did a good job on that fellow in your room last night all by yourself."

It brought back bad memories, bad feelings.

"I didn't mean to kill him," I whispered.

"I'm sorry," she said. "It is a horrible feeling. But you were defending your life."

"Yes." It seemed a little better in that light.

There was a knock at the door.

Kitten took a tray from the woman outside.

"That will be all, Maria. Go to bed now."

I listened as she poured out the hot liquid. There was a homely clatter of cups and the delicate ring of spoons on china.

"Here," she said, "get this into you. You'll feel much better."

I took a sip. There was something odd about the flavor.

"What's in this?" I asked.

"Brandy," she said. "I thought it would relax . . . Oh dear, perhaps you don't drink."

"I don't mind," I said, not wanting to appear unsophisticated. It wasn't actually too bad. It was nice and warming. I was glad of it.

"Does everyone at court need to protect themselves?"

"Not everyone, no. But courts are dangerous places, and my position as ruler's favorite . . . that's especially dangerous. An aristocrat has patrons and family for protection. Someone like me though, without family, a foreigner . . . I'm like a goat in a tiger cage. I don't belong, and a number of people have found me inconvenient. Everyone wants my position, you see."

We sipped our chocolate in silence. I scoured my mind for something to say. There were a lot of questions I wanted to ask her. The main one, of course, was how she could live her kind of life? Was it possible she loved the Duke? But there were other questions. Some of them were just standard for undertaking protection. Some of them I should have asked that first night at the Ducal Palace, but I hadn't wanted the contact with her. I knew I should know more about this supposed opponent of mine, Norval the necromancer. He still seemed a shadow, a mere hypothesis. Michael would have found my behavior unprofessional, but then he would have found it difficult to take Madame Avignon seriously, too. And he would have been disgusted (but probably unsurprised) by the curiosity I was beginning to feel toward this woman who sat delicately sipping hot chocolate out of a bone china cup and claiming to have been trained in the art of swordplay. *There is too much you don't know*, I reminded myself. *Stop making assumptions.*

I tried a question. "Why is he so interested in you?"

She looked surprised. "Who? The Duke?"

"No. Norval. Mages don't usually bother themselves with women."

She laughed. "A mage is a man like any other. Except you, of course"

I must have frowned at this glib reply, for she went on more politely, "Western mages are a little more venal than you Easterners. I'm always surprised at the high emphasis placed on asceticism here on the Peninsula. In my country, the greatest mages take part in political affairs and live like princes, with huge estates and many slaves. Anyway Norval wasn't a necromancer when I first knew him. He was just a well-bred gentleman of the court. He was my first... protector. It was from him that I learned many of the arts of the courtesan. I'm afraid he came to think he owned me. Such people become very angry when they discover it is otherwise. I'm not the first woman to be pursued by her ex-protector. I'm just unlucky that he is what he is."

So what this really was, was a fight between a whore and an "offended" protector. If the stories of our housekeeper were to be believed, she had only herself to blame. The court of Gallia must be a corrupt place when a woman could enlist the aid of the college of mages to help her escape some sordid imbroglio, just because she happened to share the Duke's bed. My thoughts must have shown on my face again, for now she said, "It's an imperfect world, Dion. I suppose my life is a sordid life. But I like being alive, and I want to stay that way. That was why I left Norval in the first place."

I felt embarrassed that she had guessed my thoughts.

She said, more gently, "Norval didn't own me, you know. There was no reason in the world why I had to stay with him. In the end it seemed more wrong to go open-eyed to destruction than to be disloyal to a lover who was already playing with my life. Norval was involved in a plot to overthrow the ruler of Aramaya. The plotters decided to use my particular gifts in this game. Of course they told me nothing. All I knew was that I was supposed to 'be nice' to a man Norval wanted to help him. In fact they were using me as a go-between. If the plot was discovered or Masud betrayed him, Norval would be able to claim ignorance of the whole thing."

She sighed.

"He was a charming man. When it dawned on me what was happening, I couldn't believe he would do such a thing to me. But it became obvious that I was no more than a pawn to him. Then I was very, very angry. So I thought, damn him, damn them all. I didn't share the political views of Norval and his friends, anyway. Emperor Jerzack, for all his faults, is a better ruler than their puppet Emperor would have been. So I ran for it. I changed my name and disappeared. I joined a traveling theater company which was leaving Aramaya. Within a week I was a hundred miles from Norval."

I managed to keep my face bland. The way she talked was seductive. I almost found myself agreeing with her point of view. Even in my sheltered life, I remembered wondering at the stupid things women sometimes did for those they loved. There had been a scandal in our village when one of the maids at the inn had let her lover in the back door one night so that he could rob it. Poor Hannie was sent to jail, but they never caught the robbers. I'd wondered then what had possessed her to be so stupid. I could sympathize with what Kitten Avignon had done. If it was indeed the truth. On the other hand I could still hear Michael's voice saying of such women, "They make their own beds, and they must lie on them." She'd never have been in this situation if she hadn't become a courtesan in the first place.

Kitten was staring into space. The candlelight made her face soft and delicate.

"Of course shortly after I left him the plot did collapse. Perhaps the man whose silence my favors were meant to buy ceased to be silent. I don't know. I heard that Norval had been thrown into prison on suspicion and tortured and that it had left him scarred. That would have hurt him. He was always a very vain man."

Her face had the same unreadable expression I'd seen in the carriage. It was impossible to tell what she was thinking.

Courtesans and necromancers. Fine company I was keeping.

"So Norval didn't practice death magic when you knew him?" I prompted.

"I think he may have dabbled, yes. Yes, there was definitely some unpleasant magic going on in his house. I made a point in those days of remaining ignorant of anything that wasn't nice about Norval. He was a beautiful man. So witty and clever. Powerful. The power was exciting. Except when you were on the receiving end of it. He liked power. He was that kind of man, the kind of man who, if he knew you had a soft spot on your foot, would step on it deliberately, just so he could be the one to make you jump. I'm not surprised that he took up necromancy."

The magic of pain and death. It did seem appropriate for the kind of man she was describing.

"I left Sopria because of him. Came here to the Peninsula. Changed my name again. There are quite a few of us who have offended mages hiding out here. The Eastern Colleges of Magic have done a great thing for people like me. Once we are here, evil magic cannot reach us. But I didn't hide enough. Well why the hell should I, anyway? Am I going to let Norval ruin my life? Now I'm too well known. And someone back in the West has put two and two together.

"A month ago I received a package. With compliments from Norval. I don't know whose finger was in it, but the ring belonged to an old friend from the Sopria days. I only hope the ring was stolen or that he was already dead."

So did I. Since necromancers gain their power from the slow, painful deaths of their victims, falling into one's hands was not a fate I'd wish on anybody, no matter how wicked.

She began striding up and down the room. Her face was tight and almost scowling. She no longer looked fairylike, but dangerous, powerful like some great warrior.

"Damn Norval. Damn his black soul to hell. He likes people to be scared. He likes to see them run. But I'm not going to. I've got a life here in Gallia; lands, wealth, money to buy the freedom to please myself. With your help I'm going to fight him. Fight him and win and show him I don't give a damn for his mean heart."

She whirled to face me, gripped my arm.

The sheer cold-blooded determination of her face was shocking, but thrilling, too. Her words electrified me. My muscles tensed, ready to battle anything. And to win.

"Dion, you are a very powerful mage. You can beat Norval, show him . . . strike a blow for good over evil. You can do it. But you have to take it seriously. You can't underestimate Norval. Necromancy uses allies. That makes it stronger than white magic. And even without magic, he is cunning. He learned cunning at the court of Aramaya. You must be on the lookout for tricks. Always, always be on your guard."

I realized that she was leaning toward me, glaring fiercely into my eyes. Suddenly I needed to keep her out. I pulled back before I could stop myself and jumped out of my chair.

"I'm sure everything will be all right," I said.

She stared at the ground for a moment.

"Forgive me," she said. "I get a little . . . excited when I talk about Norval."

"Of course," I said breathlessly.

She turned and walked away from me.

"Tell me, Dion, is there any chance Norval could send anything else against us?"

"Anything . . ." I stopped. She meant a demon of course. A demon slave. The coincidence of this conversation made my hair stand on end.

"I mean something like a demon," she said into my sudden silence. She turned and smiled ruefully. "I suppose you're going to say I'm being ridiculous."

"It is very unlikely," I said carefully. "He will probably be using demon magic in any spells he brings against us, but bringing an enslaved demon onto this plane . . . I believe it's very difficult to obtain a demon slave. You have to know its true name, and you have to sacrifice an enormous number of people in the enslavement ritual. And you have to start by having enough innate power to do it."

I stopped, embarrassed by the authoritative sound of my own voice. "At least I think that's how it works. Only a handful of mages in the history of the world have managed to do it. I really doubt that Norval could be powerful enough. If he were powerful enough, he could probably make mincemeat of me without needing to go to the trouble of sending a demon." The most persuasive argument, of course, was that any mage that powerful was not going to waste his time creeping up on Kitten Avignon. I doubted that that would be a tactful thing to say at this point in time.

Kitten looked relieved. She sighed and smiled and looked utterly charming again.

"Yes. I doubt it, too." She laughed. "If it's so difficult to enslave a demon, I'll stop worrying about it. You're right, too. If he was that powerful, I'm sure I'd be finished by now.

"Tell me," she continued, "is there anything I can do to make your stay here more enjoyable?"

"No thank you," I said. After what I had discovered, I wanted her to go as quickly as possible.

"I sometimes hold salons in the afternoon. Many people from the court and the city, very respectable people, come. I hope to see you there, too."

I was on the point of refusing. Then I thought about the lonely days that had just passed. Better to keep my options open.

"Thank you," I said.

She stood up to go. "Perhaps I should leave you to rest now."

She wished me good-night and left, left me with my head buzzing. As I scurried around placing the invisible runes of protection and distraction on the walls and over the openings to the room, I hardly thought of the demon who had caused everything. Instead my head was full of thoughts of her. On one hand, I congratulated myself on resisting her manipulations. How strong they had been in that frightening moment. But I had noticed and pulled back in time. On the other hand, I was drawn to her by an enormous curiosity. So that was Kitten Avignon. Would I ever understand such a woman? I had to admit she was a very attractive person.

When I awoke next morning and heard the chirping of the little birds in the trees outside my window I was filled with joy. After the eight o'clock ritual I got back into bed and lay there watching the tips of the trees moving in the wind. A maid brought me breakfast. She seemed to assume I would eat it in bed. The food was delicious—crusty rolls and incredibly strong hot chocolate. I must have been a little hazy from lack of sleep for it was not until the maid returned with a brush and bucket that I remembered the demon.

Then I was disgusted with myself. Michael had been right when he had said I was flighty. Last night I'd had a brush with death magic and I'd gone to bed with my head full of childish thoughts about the life of courtesans. Oh, I was a fool. There was no doubt about it. I had caught the attention of this demon, and I hadn't the wit to worry about it.

I started to worry then, to wonder what on earth to do. I knew I should go to the Dean and confess the whole thing. And yet ... Runes of protection and distraction were the only method for driving off unwelcome attentions. I couldn't think of anything else the Dean could do, except never forgive me or trust me again. Except always suspect me of having death magic leanings. One mistake, and in their eyes I would be damned. It had been an accident, for God's sake.

I was rationalizing. I had almost touched the demon's hand that first time. I could almost hear Michael telling me that one was never an innocent victim. He would have made me go to the Dean. "Take your punishment," he would have said. "You deserve it. You did wrong." I knew that was what I should do. But I shuddered at the thought of the Dean's anger and disappointment.

No. There was nothing to be gained from telling the Dean. I was sure I had done the only things possible. I had dispelled the demon and taken steps to hide myself from him.

"Yes, girl, eventually you dispelled him. But first you listened to him. And you were tempted, weren't you?" said Michael's voice in my head.

No, not tempted. Merely curious. Merely fascinated by this creature, this evil, amoral creature.

He could not enter this plane. He probably would not even have appeared had I not been thinking about my hazia dream with such longing. So if I didn't think about him, he wouldn't come. Maybe he'd already lost interest in me in the chaotic way of demons. Somehow I doubted it was that simple. That meant that he would return, and that meant that telling the Dean would be my wisest course.

My thoughts kept on like this for the rest of the morning. I tried to settle down to some trigonometry, but I couldn't stop arguing with myself.

By the early afternoon I'd begun thinking about

what Michael would have said and how I'd let him down. *This is ridiculous,* I thought. *Come on. You're going for a walk. You can't sit here and mope over Michael all day. Not again.*

I put on my cloak and went downstairs.

The house seemed empty except for the distant clatter of the dishes in the kitchen. The rooms downstairs were big and light and white. My feet clomped across the polished floors in a very satisfying way.

It would have been better if I had gone down for lunch. It would have given me a rest from my worries. But I'd been afraid Kitten Avignon would be there, and I'd decided, now I'd recognized how curious I was about her, that it would be wisest to keep away from her. Why did I have to be curious about such unsuitable things? Courtesans and demons. Why couldn't I be interested in something worthwhile, like Michael's secret names of rocks? I could see my curiosity over Kitten Avignon getting me into as much trouble as my curiosity over demons had.

There were some sweet-smelling roses in the front hallway. I took a deep sniff of them. Already my heart felt lighter. I was managing to avoid Kitten Avignon well enough, and I had done everything I could to get rid of the demon. Bright, early spring sunlight was coming in the windows. It looked like a beautiful day outside. I was suddenly sure everything would turn out right. I opened the door and went out into the garden.

# FOUR

It was a beautiful day outside; one of those days when it feels as if winter might really be over. The air was still fresh, but soft now and warmed by the sun. It was good to be able to walk among plants and trees. Our house in Moria had been in the country. Sometimes, when Michael was busy with other things, I'd escaped my studies to run about in the fields and forest nearby. Even though this was just a garden, it was a great improvement on the bleak yards surrounding the college.

The garden was cunningly designed to seem bigger than it was. Trees and shrubs were planted seemingly at random, so that to walk among them was a tour of mystery and discovery. Daffodils and some other outrageously bright flower dotted the smooth lawn. Roses were already blooming, far earlier than they would have been at home in Moria. The freshly turned earth round their roots was rich and brown. I came upon a stand of fir trees and stood among them for a while, enjoying their spicy smell and the sound of their branches in the wind. The happiness I'd felt that morning when I'd awoken returned.

The wind made a constant low roar through the fir needles so that I was not aware until I was almost upon them that there were other people in the garden with me. I heard laughter as I came out from under the trees and saw two people rolling on the grass in a flurry of white petticoats. I froze. Then I realized that both of the people on the ground were women. It was all right then. For a moment I'd been afraid I had walked into something improper.

Now I could see there were several other people sitting around a white wrought-iron table at the edge of the clearing, rocking back and forth with laughter. As I watched, one of the women straddled the other and began stuffing leaves down her bodice. Relieved that it was all so innocent, I turned to beat a swift retreat. But it was too late.

"Dion!" called a voice across the clearing.

I considered running away, but Madame Avignon had already leaned over and said a few words to a young man standing beside her, and now he came toward me.

He bowed.

"Good afternoon," he said. "I am Erasmus Tinctus. Madame Avignon has sent me to escort you over to the party."

"Er . . . Thank you."

"So you are Madame's new helper, Dion, the mage. Please."

He took my hand and drew it easily through his arm, and suddenly we were walking across the grass. I could not say I enjoyed being so close to a man, but he seemed harmless enough. I was uncomfortably aware that the hem of my robe was muddy from the garden. I hoped Erasmus had not noticed it. Then I saw that his long sleeves were marked with dabs of color; red, blue, and yellow, and a large dab of green on his hand.

"Good afternoon, Dion."

"Good afternoon, Madame." I hoped I sounded dignified. I resented being trapped in this way.

She smiled cheerily up from under the jaunty little pink parasol she was holding. Her eyes were dancing as if she had been laughing and was about to laugh again. Her cheerfulness made my dignity feel stiff. "Isn't it a beautiful day?" she cried. "I'm having an early garden party. Would you like some tea?"

I nodded.

"Erasmus. Tea for us both."

The young man smiled and bowed mockingly, with a huge flourish.

"What more could a faithful knight ask, but to do the bidding of such charming ladies? Any other feats of bravery you want done while I'm about it? Shall I fight a dragon as well?"

"Not over tea, dear boy. So bad for the digestion."

Erasmus flourished again and moved away.

"Allow me to introduce you to everyone."

They were mostly women, all of them beautiful and richly dressed. Judging by the fact that they wore makeup, they were all courtesans, and from the expensiveness of their dress, leading lights of the honey sisterhood. In trying to avoid Kitten Avignon, I had stumbled into a whole nest of them. The atmosphere of the party was not dark and vicious as I would have expected, however, but lighthearted. They were all giggling, smacking each other, putting bits of stick down each others' backs, and trying to flip sugar lumps into each others' teacups. Later, when I remembered it, the garden party reminded me of nothing so much as the groups of students you saw larking about the college courtyard on sunny days.

Two of the group were men, the young man Erasmus and an older man in shabby black, with huge gnarled hands, called Bordino. The women were Sateen, very young and gaudy; Demoiselle, mature and elegant; and Lucia, who looked a little out of place with the others in her dark plain gown and with her hair elegantly in a bun.

". . . And those two disporting themselves in such an unladylike manner are Rapunzel and Lisa."

Rapunzel was now sitting on one of the white chairs, pulling leaves out of her velvet bodice and her hair.

"Damn you, Lisa, you've destroyed my hair," she said. "Anyone got a comb?"

Lisa pulled an ivory-handled brush out of her reticule.

"Here, let me."

She began pulling down and combing out Rapunzel's long black hair.

"You have beautiful hair, Rap. I love brushing it."

The woman did have beautiful hair. It was thick and silky and must have reached almost to her knees when she stood up. It looked so soft to touch. Such softness seemed out of place against her low-cut red dress and exotic dark face.

Suddenly the young man was beside me again.

"Please have this chair," he said. "I apologize. I should have offered you one before."

He motioned me to a chair and, as I sat, he placed a little tray containing two cups of tea and a plate of cakes on the cane table beside me. To my dismay he settled himself on a nearby chair.

"Madame Avignon tells me you are from Moria,"
he said to me in perfect Morian.

"Yes."

"So am I. I'm delighted to meet a countrywoman."

I should have realized his nationality the moment
he spoke, though I had not. I had a fleeting moment
of fear. How did he feel about mages?

"I have come to Gallia to study the New Learning,"
he said. "And you?"

"We left because of the witch-burnings," I said.

"Oh." He looked embarrassed. "Yes. Of course.
That must have been very painful for you."

Silence. I wished Kitten had not seen me. I was
bound to disappoint this poor young man. I'd never
been a great talker, and this conversation felt like I
was pushing a rock uphill.

"What part of Moria are you from?" he asked.

"Near Mangalore," I replied. "My foster father
taught at one of the colleges there."

"Really. And what was his name?"

He seemed genuinely interested in my answer.

"Michael," I replied.

"Oh yes!" he said delighted. "I've heard of him.
You must be the little girl he adopted in order to
prove that women can be mages. Well not little anymore of course. I have always wanted to meet the pair
of you."

"I'm afraid my father died five months ago."

"Oh, I'm sorry. I hope you have other relatives and
friends in Gallia."

"No. I've no one." Then, in case this sounded too
pathetic, I added, "But the teachers at the college have
been very kind. They have offered to let me stay there
until I graduate."

"And when is that?"

"In two and a half years' time," I said.

"I've heard that they are very impressed by your abilities."

He was just being polite. It certainly wasn't what I'd heard. But I blushed at the compliment anyway.

"My foster father was a very good teacher."

"You must miss him," he observed.

"Yes, I do." It was the first time in all those months I'd said such a thing to anyone. The natural way he asked the question made my grief seem quite reasonable and normal and not at all as neurotic and undisciplined as I had begun to think. I could not have asked someone such a question myself. It would have seemed too intrusive. Yet he spoke quite comfortably about it. This I found, along with his genuine interest in what you said, was Erasmus' great gift.

We fell to talking of Moria then, for it transpired that Erasmus was from a district near ours. He spoke longingly of Moria now the spring was coming, and we both remembered the snow trees in bloom and how little sunny flowers would be appearing in the silky mountain grass at this time of year. We talked of the local beauty spots—of Flameflower Gorge and the White mountains. The conversation became relaxed and easy, and I surprised myself at the questions I asked. I scarcely noticed the others.

Except once when Lisa let out a yowl.

"Ooch! Why'd you do that?"

"Shush, Lisa," said Rapunzel.

"But Kitty kicked me. That hurt, you bitch."

"Lisa, behave yourself."

"Why on earth . . ."

Rapunzel nudged her and looked meaningfully at me.

"Oh!" Lisa grinned and dropped her eyes and went back to brushing Rapunzel's hair.

I knew something was going on, but I couldn't imagine what it was. I watched them for a moment to see if they were making fun of me. Then Erasmus asked me if I'd ever been to the Morian High Plains, and I forgot about them for asking him about a place I'd always wanted to see.

The next thing I knew the servants had come to clear up the tables. I looked around me feeling as if I had just awoken from a long sleep. Bordino was headed toward the house with Sateen and Lucia on either arm, and the others were following in a chattering group.

Kitten came over to us.

"Well look at you two. Talking about the old country? Erasmus, would you like to come into the house for a drink?"

But Erasmus decided that it must be time for him to leave, so we accompanied him to the garden gate. I stood at the gate and watched him walk away. I had probably bored him by talking too much, but it had been a wonderful conversation for me.

"You enjoyed talking to Erasmus?" Kitten asked. "He's a charming young man, isn't he?"

It occurred to me that she, of course, would put quite a foolish construction on a man and a woman talking to each other all afternoon.

"It was good to talk of home," I said firmly.

"Exactly."

She led me back toward the house.

"I hope you will take afternoon tea with us some other time."

The gathering had seemed harmless enough. On the

other hand it wouldn't do to become too intimate with courtesans.

"I wonder . . ." she said thoughtfully. "I wonder if you would mind . . . I have a favor to ask of you."

Oh dear. Now I would have to refuse her, and that would lead to unpleasantness.

It was as if she read my thoughts for she said, "It's nothing improper. It's just . . . well . . . I had a pageboy who used to read to me in the afternoons. Recently he had to leave my service. I miss his reading very much. I wondered . . . if you would be kind enough to come some afternoons and read to me. I should try to choose works that you would enjoy. I could pay you extra. It would be a great service to me."

Of course I should say no. That was too much contact, and what on earth would she want me to read. Yet it was such an inoffensive request. Was she manipulating me? If I agreed this time, who knew what it would lead to. At the same time she made me so very curious.

"Why do you not read to yourself, Madame?"

"I do not read very well," she said, and actually blushed. I had asked an insensitive question. Quite likely Madame Avignon, the courtesan, could not read at all. How awful to have to admit that.

"I-I'd be pleased to read to you," I burst out, full of contrition.

Thus it was that the following afternoon I found myself following a maid down into Madame Avignon's private apartments on the second floor of the house. The maid opened a door and motioned me inside.

It was a large, light apartment. Huge white curtains billowed gently at the open window. Madame Avignon was standing among them, eyes closed, lips parted, face turned toward the soft afternoon breeze. Her long fair hair was loose and fell in waves about her shoulders. A tendril of it lifted delicately in the breeze and blew silkily across her face. She shook it away and, with a soft, lazy laugh, reached out, shut the window, and turned toward me.

"Mademoiselle Dion," she cried. "You've come! I'm so glad."

She was wearing a deep ruby red silk wrap over white. Apparently she had not dressed for me. Should I be insulted? I decided not to decide about that yet. Would she have dressed had I been a man?

You could feel an energy flowing from her, a sense of excitement, of things happening. I had felt it before. It was unnerving, but hard to resist.

She spread her arms.

"Welcome to my boudoir, my private domain. This is where I cease to be a courtesan and please only myself."

If anything in this house was going to look like a brothel, I had felt Madame Avignon's apartments would, but once again the room was disappointingly free of red silk. It was full of fat, comfortable chairs upholstered in soft leaf greens and pinks. A multitude of little pictures were clustered on the walls, the open desk was crammed with papers, and a pile of books lay on a table. The room was not cluttered, just pleasantly full. Homely. Vases full of flowers, mostly roses, were everywhere. Their delicious scent mingled with the freshness of the breeze. It was warm, too. I could not remember feeling cold since I had come to this house.

"Now," she said, touching my arm lightly and quickly, "here are the books I need to read. Have a look through them and see what you think. I must just tell Maria one or two things."

She disappeared through one of the white doors leading off the room.

Fascinated I peered in after her. The room was full of row after row of dresses, a mass of soft and shining jewellike colors. It was as if a throng of court ladies stood enchanted, wanting only the right spell to make them dance and swirl again. Madame Avignon and the maid were looking through the dresses, discussing what she was going to wear that night.

I turned my attention to the books. There were a surprising lot of them.

The first was bound in black leather and untitled. I opened it. A satyr with a huge purple erection was chasing a naked nymph through a meadow.

I gasped and closed the book with a bang.

"What?" said a voice behind me.

Before I could answer Madame Avignon had taken the book and was leafing through the pages.

"Hmm. I'm sure he catches her—yes, as I thought. Oh I know whose this is." She looked at me. "Oh dear. Now you are shocked. This isn't mine. Somebody left it here. Hoping to win my favor, I imagine."

Did I believe her?

She laughed and shut the book with a snap. "Well I suppose everyone has different tastes. You know I'm sure the owner of this too charming book must be missing it terribly. I think we should return it to him."

She rang the bell for the maid.

I wanted to tell her that even though I might be very young and inexperienced, I knew all about sex. Michael had very carefully told me all about it when I was fourteen. He explained everything, all about reproduction and intercourse, even down to a woman's menses. Actually I wish he'd mentioned those a bit earlier. He would have saved me from a terrible fright. Nor did he neglect to tell me about what he called degraded forms of sexuality, intercourse between those of the same sex or between man and beast. Sexuality, Michael said, was a form of energy, and so had a place in the practice of magic, but it was a degenerate magical practice, like the practice of taking drugs. Both were much out of favor among mages on the Peninsula, and rightly so. If you had sufficient discipline and fostered your power correctly, you had no need to resort to such distasteful activities. I must always avoid those who tried to draw me into sexual magic, for their motives were unlikely to be pure.

"Virginity, too, has its power," he said. "For you especially, Dion. A woman's honor rests in her virginity. All people respect that, whether they admit it or not."

Indeed what little I had seen of the world showed this to be very true. Secretly I felt sure it was so of Kitten Avignon.

That was why I suspected her now of making fun of that power in an envious attempt to belittle it. I burned to tell her that her dirty book had not shocked me because, though I might not be a worldly as she, I knew quite enough, thank you.

"Now what would you like to read?" she asked.

Then she stopped and looked at me. "Mademoiselle, please don't be angry at me. It really is not my book. I would not have such a book in my private rooms. It's business to me, you see, and I do not like to let business in here. I'm sorry you had to see such a thing."

She did not seem to be lying.

She smiled at me. "Now let us have a little revenge on the owner."

She went over to the desk and took out a small pair of silver scissors. Then she flipped open the book and deftly cut the threads binding the pages together.

"What . . . ?!"

A maid appeared.

"Netta. How did this book get in my room?"

"Bishop Albenz sent it, Madame."

"Why am I not surprised by that? Netta, my love, you have my express permission to look in all the books I am sent from now on. It would be best to send back books like these. Yes?"

She showed the open book to the maid, who pulled a wry face.

"Oh, Madame. I am sorry."

"Never mind," said Kitten Avignon. "Take this book to Giovanni and ask him to give it to some street urchin, someone trustworthy, and get him to take it back to the Bishop in the cathedral square."

She winked at me. "Now, as you can see, Netta, it's terribly badly bound. Look how the pages have come loose. Think of the scandal if the boy were to drop the Bishop's book and the pages were to blow all over the square in this wind. Especially if some of those horrible grey Morians were hanging about . . . Tell Giovanni to let the boy know that if there's enough of an uproar for me to hear of it, it's worth a ducat to him."

Netta nodded. We could hear her laughing in the hall as she went away.

Even though students of magic wear grey, I knew that it was not us Kitten was referring to when she spoke of horrible grey Morians. She was referring to Morian Church of the Burning Light worshipers, who also wore grey. Gallia was full of Burning Light refugees, people who'd followed the wrong archbishop or believed the wrong thing about the Godhead of Lord Tansa or the Feast of Aumaz. It was ironic and a great source of disgust to them that they had wound up in the same position as the whores and witches they'd previously persecuted. They weren't comfortable fellow refugees. They still hissed at mages and called us names just as they had done at home. The thought of one of these mean-minded prudes being faced with one of the Bishop's pictures; the outrage, the wailing and gnashing of teeth . . . I could not help laughing.

Kitten's eyes were sparkling.

"I'm tempted to drive down there just to see the fun. But you can't really rely on these things to come off. Anyway, we must work. I'm getting very behind. Have you decided on a book? May I then?"

I was happy to let her. A quick look at the spines had shown them to be on serious subjects like optics and architecture and philosophy. None of them seemed suitable for a courtesan.

"I think this green book is the one on optics." She showed me the spine. "Am I right?"

It was. So she couldn't even read enough to make out the titles.

"And then there is another one there called the *Romance of the Lily*. It's by a darling little man called Dolce. His last book was wonderful. Funny. I think you will enjoy it. But business before pleasure. I propose we read the optics treatise for an hour first, and then we have the *Lily*. Agreed?"

I nodded my assent, and we sat down.

"It's in Ancient Soprian?" I asked. I found it hard to believe that a woman who could not read would understand the international language of learning. She motioned to me to go on. Was this some kind of peculiar game she was playing? Was she trying to impress me?

Yet it seemed she did understand the Ancient Soprian, for she stopped me once or twice when I pronounced a word wrongly. She seemed to make sense out of the contents, too, which was more than I could. The writer, a Monsieur Alberti, claimed that light was made up of a whole spectrum of colors. It was the most fanciful thing I'd ever heard. I told Madame Avignon so when the hour had finished, and Maria had come in with tea and cakes.

She laughed.

"Nonetheless it is true. I've seen it proved. So could you if you cared to attend a little soiree I'm giving in Monsieur Alberti's honor in a few weeks."

This kind of talk made me feel very off-balance. I wondered if she had intended this effect. Soirees for scientists! Things were not as they should be here.

I was still troubled by that other book, too. Everyone knew that the Church of Gallia was corrupt, but would one of its Bishops really own such a book? And send it to such a woman?

"Madame," I began, "does Bishop Albenz really own that book?"

"That's what Jeanetta said. I thought he might. Its the kind of thing he would own. We call him Old Fumbler in the trade. He collects salacious picture books as aids to seduction. He's persistent, too. I can't imagine why he thinks I'd risk the scaffold just for the pleasure of lifting my . . . on his account."

She halted suddenly and then continued in a gentler tone. "Oh well, churchmen are men like any other," and changed the subject.

What had she meant about the scaffold? I plucked up my courage and asked her.

"Dion, you know, I am the Duke's favorite. And being the Duke's favorite carries certain responsibilities with it."

"Like bodyguards."

"Yes, that too. But a ruler's mistress is a little like a ruler's wife in that she must be above reproach."

I felt confused.

"Duke Leon doesn't share his women with anyone. Lots of men feel the same, of course. But the Duke could send me to the scaffold if I offended him. If I were unfaithful to him, he would find it necessary to punish me very severely. Our lives are too public. If a ruler's mistress is unfaithful to him, it means a serious loss of face. People say that if he can't control his womenfolk, perhaps he's unfit to control his country. They might start to see him as a weak ruler. So. A charge of treason and off with my head. Or hanging since I'm a commoner. That is why the Duke is so careful of my reputation; why he persuaded me to leave the stage, why he dismissed my page, why now I live so respectably. Respectably enough for Genny and even you to be associated with me. I never thought I'd be so respectable."

How cold she was about it all. How could she talk so matter-of-factly about the Duke cutting off her head? As if he would do such a thing. He . . . loved her. Or did he? Why else would he give her money and lands? Even if he didn't love her, he must have some tenderness for her. But then I was thinking of this relationship as normal and it wasn't and Kitten Avignon was not a normal woman.

"Of course, the theory is that anyone who can stop a courtesan leaping on anything that moves must be a hell of a man. A very powerful person. That's the theory, anyway." She smiled a little wryly.

"So if I'm a good girl, I'm quite an asset to him. And I shall be good, because why on earth should I upset a situation so much to my advantage. Respectability is a bit dull, but I contrive to amuse myself. And now, my love, it's time for the *Lily*."

I had been taught to despise novels even though I'd never actually read one before. I now learned my mistake. By the tenth page of the *Romance of the Lily*, I was enthralled, and several times Madame Avignon had to ask me to slow down. The story plunged a knight into the most amazing and delightful adventures as he tried to outwit an evil mage. The writer had such a way of describing things that Madame Avignon and I were soon in stitches with laughter. I was still reading when Maria poked her head into the room.

"Madame, the carriage will be here in three-quarters of an hour."

"Damn! Is that the time? Will you stay and read to me while I dress?"

I wanted badly to find out the end of the knight's particular adventure, so I agreed, though I knew I should not. But the dressing was harmless enough. I sat outside the dressing room and read loudly while there was a flurry of cloth inside. When she came out again, she was wearing a white linen coverall over her gown.

"Now for the face," she said. "Come."

I followed her to the end of the room.

"This is my bedroom," she said, opening the door.

It took me completely by surprise, though I should have been satisfied. Here was the longed-for red silk room.

It was festooned with swaths of red silk, and the walls were covered in gilt-edged mirrors. I had a frightening momentary thought of the demon leering out of all those mirrors and repressed it quickly. A huge bed stood in the middle, again curtained and hung with red silk draperies. On its canopy gilt cherubs writhed and sported, while the bedposts were golden mermaids, their faces upturned and lips parted in a look of ecstasy, their golden hair streaming down their backs and their hands grasping their breasts in a counterfeit of modesty.

Everything about it cried out "Whore," except the bed was made up with crisp white linen and covered with a thick white quilt that looked quite out of place with the rest of it.

Madame Avignon motioned me to sit on a couch beside the dressing table with twinkling eyes. I suspected her of being amused by my obvious discomfort, so I sat up as straight as I could and concentrated on reading.

I could not help being fascinated by the deft way she applied the delicate ointments and powders to her face with soft little brushes. It looked as if it might feel nice. It looked hard to get right. It was not that she had not been beautiful before she had begun to paint her face, but somehow as she applied the makeup, her looks were enhanced. She became more vivid, brighter. Once or twice she smiled at me in the mirror and I realized I was staring. I definitely kept my eyes to myself when she took off her coverall and began to powder her cleavage. The bodice of that dress was far too low and too tight, and the white lace trimming just emphasized it.

Shortly after, she rose from the chair. She twirled in front of the mirror, looked herself over with a critical eye, and said, "I think we must finish now. The coach will have arrived."

She looked around the room and sighed. "All this red. It's like being inside a stomach."

"Why do you keep it?" I asked.

"The Duke likes it," she said. The thought of the Duke, our ruler, lying in that bed, perhaps naked . . . All memory of what she was and all the dirty things that must mean came back to me in a rush.

"I must go, Madame," I said.

"Tomorrow afternoon, then?" she called after me.

"Yes, Madame."

"Dion?"

"Yes, Madame?"

"You might as well call me Kitten. Madame Avignon is much too formal."

I let myself out quickly, vowing never to go into that heavy red room again. Perhaps I should have refused to read again, but I didn't really know how. Anyway, it had been an interesting afternoon and not, as far as I could tell, a harmful one. Besides, I wanted to see how the book turned out.

At least that was the reason I gave myself the following afternoon as I waited anxiously for the maid to come for me. In fact, we did not continue with the knight's adventures that afternoon, and I did not feel the lack of it. Instead we read the optics treatise for longer and then, when Maria brought in the tea and cakes, she also brought with her a tall and garrulous man with long auburn curls and a big hat with the most enormous purple feathers I had ever seen. This was Archimedes Brown, actor, theatrical impresario and, said Kitten, "My business partner."

This sounded a little farfetched. Everyone knew it was against the law for women to buy and sell property. How on earth could she be in business with anyone?

I watched them closely. The way he kissed her cheek and called her Kitten darling put me in mind of what she had said about the Duke's jealousy the day before. At least she had got dressed that day. Perhaps I had added chaperone to my other roles. I was not best pleased by this, but stayed for tea when she pressed me.

I was soon glad I had. Monsieur Brown was the most wonderful talker. He had a wonderful rich voice, a fascinating Holy States accent, and a hilarious way of caricaturing people. He did not forget my existence, either. As he recounted all the latest gossip, he added funny little asides and faces to explain to me who he was talking about. Best of all, he was brimming over with news of a scandalous happening in the Cathedral Close the day before. It seemed that while Bishop Albenz was walking there with a group of Burning Light elders, he had been jostled by a gang of street urchins, causing him to drop the "artistic" book he happened to be carrying at the time and spreading loose pages, covered with the most "anatomical" paintings, all over the square. The way Brown imitated the icy expression of the head elder as he peeled a page depicting a couple in a "most companionable" position off his face and the protestations of "the good Bishop" that he knew nothing of such things and he couldn't imagine what had happened, had us almost weeping with laughter.

Tea finished, Kitten opened her desk and took out a huge leather-bound book, and the two of them began poring over it. Kitten gave me another novel to read, but although I found it interesting, I could not help keeping an apprehensive eye on them, both afraid and convinced that there must be some kind of impropriety going on. Archimedes was merely writing figures in the book, however, and explaining them to Kitten; regaling her with such facts as how he had bought ten feathers for two shillings, "gross highway robbery," and how Lord Petari had donated four jackets and a pair of hose to the company. It all seemed innocent enough.

"We own a theater company together," she explained to me after he had gone. "The Ducal Players. Perhaps you have heard of them."

"But how can you . . . ?"

"What? Oh, own a theater company? You mean because I am a woman?"

I nodded.

"Well, Archimedes gave it to me. A woman can't buy and sell, but she can accept gifts."

She laughed at my embarrassment, but it was kind laughter.

"This is the way many women get around the law. I gave Archimedes a gift of money, and he very kindly made me a gift of half his company in return. There was no buying and selling involved. Just an exchange of gifts between trusted friends."

"Is that legal?"

"It's not illegal. Anyway it's a stupid law when half the world is forced to break it just to put food in their mouths. Why shouldn't women buy and sell property in their own right?"

"My foster father always said women weren't responsible enough . . ."

"Rubbish. That's what they all say. Really, Dion, how can that be true?" She continued more mildly. "Look at yourself. A fully-fledged mage. Surely you don't think of yourself as irresponsible."

"No," I whispered, more to end the discussion than because I really believed it. It frightened me that she had suddenly become so passionate. Perhaps it was this tendency to become passionate that explained the life she led. And to dismiss the law as silly just like that . . . It did show a certain recklessness.

Such incidents, though uncomfortable, made me feel that I was getting to the center of her mystery. I continued to go to her boudoir most afternoons. I had plenty of opportunities to observe her in the company of other people, for Kitten often had visitors at that time of day, and she always asked me to stay. Perhaps she guessed how much I enjoyed these teatime gatherings. It was her way to know what pleased a person. I usually stayed despite my better judgment and the remembered warnings of the Dean against being seen in public with Kitten Avignon.

Kitten's boudoir was hardly a public place, I rationalized, and indeed most of her visitors hardly noticed me. No doubt they dismissed me as some kind of high-class servant.

All manner of fascinating people came—groups of actors ("watch how they jostle for the limelight, Dion"); titled gentlemen of the court ("those people have all the tenderness of a mating of cats"); artists with paintings to show; a sea captain who told wonderful stories of the twin empires of Aramaya and Sopria and their endless war; and once even a skinny herd of scholars who ate all the cakes in gigantic bites and were ludicrously put out to realize that Kitten spoke both Ancient Soprian and Ancient Aramayan and could top them in a battle of quotations. But her most frequent visitors were Archimedes Brown, with his facts and figures, and the courtesans I had met on that first day.

I did try to keep out of the way of the honey sisters. It wasn't always easy. The thing was that even though they must have felt my disapproval, they ignored it. Perhaps it was force of habit on their part. Since I couldn't bring myself to be actually rude, they treated me as a friend, smiled warmly, greeted me, included me in the conversation, added their insistence to stay to Kitten's and seemed to mean it. They could talk like Archimedes Brown could talk, talk to keep you laughing and enthralled, witty, slightly wicked talk. Sometimes I couldn't help lingering. I especially liked Demoiselle, who was one of Kitten's best friends and almost never vulgar. She had the driest sense of humor and a matter-of-fact way with her.

It was she who said to me once, "Do you think they pay us so much for mere sex, my love? Oh no! You can get good gallop from a street drab. It's the laughter that keeps the gold rolling in."

In fact the only courtesan I really avoided was Rapunzel Calvino. She was Kitten's other close friend and visited far too often in my opinion. She had a very reprehensible effect on Kitten, who normally behaved with such dignity and good taste.

While Kitten had managed to assume an air of breeding, which admirably suited her to being the mistress of a ruler, Rapunzel looked every inch a whore, from the top of her fabulous coiffure to the toes of her flashy shoes, with their pointy toes and outrageous bows. She wore bright scarlet lip rouge, lots of kohl round her dark flashing eyes, and her vividly colored dresses were always cut very low, even when she was just visiting Kitten and might have been assumed to be "off duty." She talked and laughed loudly, gesticulating all the time with her long hands. The epitome of a woman of passion.

"I like Rapunzel," said Kitten to me once in those early days. "She's so zesty. She always makes me laugh."

Which was all very well, but did it always have to be about such vulgar things? Once I made the mistake of lingering when she was visiting by herself. Only once. After Kitten admired the new jewels that Lord Rashmon had bestowed upon Rapunzel, the conversation turned to Rashmon's aunt, the Lady Amarillo, and degenerated into something like this.

"My dear Pussycat, she's absolutely my idol. If I've managed as well by the time I'm her age, well then I won't mind too much being her age, will I? They say she persuaded Amarillo to leave all his money in her name so even though the family don't like her being unmarried, there's not a thing they can do about it. She has a lovely big house, all the servants she wants, and does exactly what she wants all the time with no husband to interfere. And you know what I heard. The cleverest thing of all. She's solved the problem of sex, and so cunningly."

"Tell. Tell."

"She has the loveliest little page, and he *is* quite mouthwatering. I've seen him carrying her parcels in the high street. Sweet sixteen and such a nice little bottom. Anyway, anytime she's feeling a little heated, all she has to do is lift up her skirts and under he goes!" She whispered something into Kitten's ear.

They both screamed with delighted laughter.

I stood up and, muttering my excuses, made quickly for the door.

"I tell you it true," shrieked Rapunzel. "Rashmon's seen them at it. He wants me to get a page so he can watch."

"Lord of all! What a clever trick!" cried Kitten, clapping her hands.

Another ribald shout of laughter. I could still hear them even though I had snapped the door firmly shut behind me.

To top the whole thing off, who should I see coming up the stairs but Erasmus Tinctus.

"Joyous greetings, Mademoiselle Dion. How are you today?"

"I'm well, Monsieur," I said, both wanting and not wanting to get drawn into conversation.

"My lord Duke has sent me with a commission to Madame Avignon."

A scream of laughter burst from down the hall.

"Ah! I see she is at home. Hmm. Should I be correct in deducing that the delightful Madame Calvino is with her?"

"Yes," I said, though delightful was hardly the word I would have used.

"Ah," he said, "I'd know that laugh anywhere. Perhaps it's not an opportune moment to call. If I know those two, they're telling each other rude stories at the expense of my sex. Enough to bring a blush to a young man's cheek."

"Yes," I replied. I found that he was grinning at me. It was hard not to grin back.

"Well," he said, placing one hand on his heart and flinging the other out in a heroic gesture, "my lord Duke has entrusted me with a mission, and I shall not fail. You behold me the hero. I shall brave the lions' den."

He took off his hat and, with a flourish, bowed deeply. I chuckled. He knocked on the door and, as he was bidden enter, waved his hand at me and cried,

"Farewell, Mademoiselle. If I die, tell them I died bravely."

Somehow he put things back in proportion. The incident was just foolish talk among foolish women and not something to be troubled about.

"That's the nunnery of St. Belkis," said Genny, pointing to a muddle of grey stone buildings and small spires up against the cathedral walls. "And the clinic's that old warehouse building over there."

It looked pretty shabby to me, low and grey-brown and chilly. Cold as charity, Michael would have said. He'd never had much good to say about charity. "What does it achieve in the long run?" he'd ask. "Better to make sure there's enough crops in the fields and work in the town. Then the poor can better themselves."

Though I'd done my best to remain detached from Kitten, I felt a little lost on the days when she was required to attend upon the Duke, and there was no reading. Then the hours stretched away forever. But that was only one of the reasons that I finally asked Kitten if I could help out at the clinic. For, although I'd told Genny point-blank that I didn't want to work in the clinic, and I'd known it to be the correct answer, I thought about it a great deal and often regretted saying no. The months spent alone in the college had left me demoralized. I could still hear the Dean telling me that as a female I had no future as a mage. I believed him. It was consistent with everything I myself had experienced. Though one part of me was reluctant to give in, my more sensible side knew that healing was a profession that a woman could practice. It seemed stupid not to take the opportunity to learn something that might, in the end, put bread in my mouth.

Still I felt it was important for Kitten and Genny to know what a concession I was making in helping out at the clinic, so I'd made up all kinds of dignified excuses for changing my mind. However, Kitten was so delighted that she almost embraced me, and I had no chance to tell her my reasons.

Genny, thank goodness, was less demonstrative, but had got down to business immediately, quizzing me on what I could actually do and asking me if I had a strong stomach. She'd made me feel a little daunted by what I'd taken on and frustrated that she had not acknowledged how I was lowering myself.

Now I stood beside her at the top of the street, panting a little. I was glad she'd stopped. She'd set such a brisk pace through the streets I'd had to adopt a sort of quick half-running skip to keep up with her. My shoulder blades were damp with sweat, which was turning cold in the sharp morning breeze. Even our two bodyguards, big men both of them, had had to hurry to keep up.

She pointed to a motley group of figures lined up against the wall, most of whom looked like piles of rags with legs.

"We'd better get to it. It's going to be a busy morning." She strode forward again, continuing the explanation she'd been giving me all the way here. I scurried after her.

It seemed that the clinic had been Kitten's idea. "Kitten was one of the first of the Grand Courtesans to come here after the unification of Gallia and Ishtak. She was lucky and won several rich patrons. Suddenly, after trying all her life, she'd made her fortune. So she wanted to thank Gallia in some way, give something back. She'd always noticed how many beggars there were in the streets here, people crippled by quite small things. She was shocked to find there was no kind of hospital for the poor, nowhere people could be healed without having to pay enormous fees. Honestly, I've never heard of such a thing. All the religious houses in Ishtak have some kind of healing clinic. It's the same in the Twin Empires. It seems the Gallians have some idea that being poor involves some kind of fault or sin or something. Have you ever heard anything so stupid?"

Actually I had. I'd heard it all my life. Morians had the same attitude to poverty, only harsher. I thought I'd keep that to myself, however. I'd never questioned it before, but it did seem stupid when she put it like that. Mages like us had no business believing in sin anyway. I had a feeling she wouldn't have thought much of Michael's ideas on charity either. Not that he would have worried what a mere healer thought of him.

Genny pulled open the door of the clinic and pushed me through. "Soon," she yelled over her shoulder to the people round the door who were beginning to mill about and beseech her.

She shut the door and pulled the bolt home behind us. We were in a dim hallway.

"The clinic's through here," she said. "Kitten donated this building to the convent and organized a group of eminent merchants to fund it. I think she took me into account when she had this idea. She's like that. She knew I was bored being her personal healer. I worked in several charity clinics even when I was working as a guild healer. So she asked me to be resident healer, and I was delighted. There still aren't many of these clinics about, so it gets very busy here. That's why I'm grateful you've offered to help."

She showed me the examination room, a bare white room with floorboards scrubbed almost white, and nothing inside but a table and some chairs.

"This is the room for operations, and through here"—she flung open a door and bustled through it—"is the treatment room."

It was bigger than I had envisaged, with a table in the middle and the walls covered with shelves and shelves of serious-looking jars and bottles, all bulbous and shiny, some full of dried herbs or odd-colored salves and others empty. Those must be the jars where they put the diseases to die. There were even the usual pickled snakes that you always see in healers' shops. Why do healers always have pickled snakes? I've never seen one use one.

"Now, to start with we will do some of the examinations together, and then you can do the simpler treatments in here. Are you happy with that?"

I nodded. Michael would have been disgusted with me for taking such a humble position. You're a much better mage than she is, he would have hissed. But I was completely daunted. I knew the theory—spells to bind bones, some elementary bandaging, the use of the pipette, even some of the spells to call diseases, but I'd never done any of them. I stared glumly at the long glass pipette on the table. No doubt it would be my job to use it.

The way a pipette works is this: a disease is a group of beings, the ignorant call them spirits, who invade the body and make it sick. A healer uses a spell to call the disease into a certain part of the body and then, using another spell, sucks it into the long glass tube known as a pipette and traps it there by putting the end of her finger on the top of the tube. Then she releases the disease into a glass jar, where it is trapped and quickly starves to death. Simple enough, and yet the idea of sucking diseases up through an open-ended tube . . . Revolting!

Theoretically the tip of the tube in your mouth is covered by another little spell, but there was always the possibility that it might fail against a particularly large disease and you might find yourself with a mouthful of, say, cholera.

Genny now confirmed all my worst fears by telling me the emergency procedures in case you got contaminated with the disease yourself.

"I'll help you for the first little while," she promised, but I wasn't much comforted. She was sure to be too busy. She was already impatient to get to her patients. Now she pulled open another door.

"This is the hospital ward," she said.

The ward took up most of the warehouse. It was a large, drab room filled with rows and rows of beds. The white sheets and institutional grey blankets reminded me of the college. But the room was light and warm after the chill outside. Nuns clad in black-and-white floated gracefully among the beds, bending over the patients, straightening sheets.

"The nuns are responsible for the nursing. You'll find them very amenable to your orders. Mother Theodosia!"

Inwardly I cringed. I hadn't considered the possibility of actual nuns. In Moria if a mage got too close to a nun, he was likely to be spat on. I knew it was supposed to be different in Gallia, though I'd never been game to test it out.

Mother Theodosia seemed nice. She had a calm unlined face. Her skin was darker than that of most Gallians and she had shining dark eyes. She introduced

me to the other sisters, who nodded and smiled. Nobody drew back and crossed herself. Some even shook
my hand.

The idea of nuns cooperating with courtesans had
struck me as unusual to say the least. I'd asked Genny
as tactfully as I could about it the night before.

She'd grinned. "Mother Theodosia had wanted to
set up such a clinic for some time before Kitten sent
me to her. She knows better than to ask where donations come from. She's an Ishtaki, you know."

This was more of an explanation then it might
seem. The inhabitants of the great merchant city-state
of Ishtak were as famous for their surpassing love of
money and the resulting flexible morality, as the Gallians were for their sensuality and we Morians were
for our strange religious movements.

I did not expect to enjoy working at the clinic, but
after feeling very inadequate for the first couple of
days, I began to find it enthralling. I enjoyed learning
something new. While I was at the clinic, I was so
busy, I didn't think about anything but the work. The
nuns remained pleasant, and Mother Theodosia often
stopped to chat with me and praise my work. My
tasks boiled down to dressing and dosing the less important cases, drawing out diseases, and making up
potions for the nuns to give to the hospital cases. Contrary to expectation, I didn't have any horrible accidents with the pipette, and I enjoyed working with
Genny. She was an excellent and very tolerant
teacher. She did not get frustrated with me even when
I had to ask her the same thing three or four times.
Once I apologized for my stupidity, and she said,
"That's all right. It takes a lot of learning and a lot of

memory. You mustn't make the mistake of thinking otherwise. You're doing very well."

She did not hesitate to praise me. Nor did she hesitate to tell me if I could have done better. But the first made the second more bearable, since my first few days had plenty of successes to balance out a couple of real mess-ups. She rarely spoke to me personally, however. I could tell she was a reserved person. It was relaxing after having always to be on my guard with Kitten Avignon.

She was not reserved with the patients, however. I was impressed with the way she handled them. She knew who was who and would ask the beggars how other beggars fared, the wool workers about their children and how the price and quality of wool was, the peddlers about the news and personalities of the countryside, and everybody what they thought about things like the return of the Duke's brother Dane from exile or the high price of wheat this spring.

It was fascinating to listen to them talk. I had always looked at people in the street and wondered what their lives were like. Now I realized that, for most of them, life was a frightening struggle to keep warm, find enough food, and, especially, to stay healthy. Small disasters were large ones for them. A broken ankle for a peddler could mean loss of customers and livelihood to another healthy peddler. The loss of a limb or an eye, a common work accident amongst the masons and carpenters, could mean the loss of one's livelihood and the rest of a short life spent huddled under a pile of rags on some street corner or in some noisome hovel.

It quickly became clear why Kitten was so popular that people cheered her in the streets as if she were a member of the Ducal family. That very first day at the clinic one woman suddenly burst into tears under Genny's gentle inquiries. Her family's sack of flour had been stolen and they would not have enough to eat for the next fortnight. The following day Genny gave her a new sack of flour. The woman wept again and called down blessings upon Genny and upon Our Lady of Roses.

Genny turned nobody away. She treated the lowest of the low. I was shocked to see the confident way the street prostitutes, mere common dirty drabs, most of them too low to be even considered members of the honey sisterhood, walked into the treatment room and expected and got treatment for venereal disease and botched abortions. The child of my Morian upbringing argued that this should not be so, that such women had no place in a respectable house of healing, much less a nunnery, that their very presence bought disrepute on it and the healers working there. A prostitute's illnesses were hers to bear, the just return for a life misspent.

After a few weeks I began to wonder if the popular opinion of our village in Moria was not a little oversimplified. The women at the clinic were not evil. Some of them had a certain defensive bravado, but most of them were just pathetic—plain, often middleaged women whose joy in life seemed to have worn away. I watched them with the same fascination I seemed to have for all sordid things, the usual question of "How could they?" echoing in my head. I quickly realized the real question was "How could they not?" Many of them were so very poor. More than once Genny treated a woman for venereal disease, and I would see her later in the day sitting by the bed of one of the crippled male patients with small children at her side.

I had not been in the habit of questioning popular opinions, at least not ones Michael concurred with. Had I realized where my thoughts were leading, I would have been horrified and put it down to the pernicious influence of Kitten Avignon. Instead I just felt worried. In a roundabout way I asked Genny what she thought of such women.

She seemed to understand what I was asking about. "What should I think?" she asked. "You know this is one thing in which we Westerners differ from you Peninsula folk. Where I come from, what with the war and everything, the worst thing a woman can be is barren. Even healers like me, who are traditionally chaste and unmarried, come under pressure to have children. Even illegitimate children. They're not approved of, but a blind eye is turned because it's considered better then having none at all."

"Where do you come from?" I said, momentarily distracted. I'd always assumed she was some kind of Ishtaki.

"Sopria," she said shortly, and began to bustle about in a way that forbade more questions. Which I was suddenly full of. Sopria was the Twin Empire of Aramaya, the two of them inextricably entwined in an intermittent war which had lasted a thousand years but which, so it was claimed, did not prevent considerable associations between the common peoples of both countries. It had not surprised me that Kitten had spent time living in Sopria. What surprised me now was that Genny came from so far away. Sopria and Aramaya were thirty days dangerous sailing across the Western ocean. Why had she come here? Had she actually come with Kitten? Why should anyone, least of all a healer with a respectable profession of her own, follow a courtesan so far from home and family? Did she have some dark secret? Was she barren and despised in her own country? I wanted to ask, I wanted to know, but the moment for questions was past. I would have to bide my time.

Watching Genny closely, I noticed that she was gathering information from the patients, especially from the prostitutes. Some people seemed to come in just to give her news. Were these the sources Kitten had once talked of? Was this information gathering the whole point of this clinic business? Or was it a bald attempt to curry favor with the common people? I found it hard to accept the simple reasons that Genny had given me for Kitten's sponsoring this hospital and searched for more real, more sinister motives. Nothing about Kitten Avignon should be taken at face value. The lives of all prostitutes were based on deception, upon a counterfeit of caring. But though I thought about it long and hard, I could not figure out what the "real" reasons were. So Genny told Kitten the news she got from her patients. Even I knew that there were easier and cheaper ways of gathering information. And as for popularity, I could not see how it would serve Kitten to be popular with those who were too poor even to pay for their own healing.

Another surprising group of people frequented the clinic, very different indeed from the street whores. These were beautifully dressed and aristocratic ladies. I asked Sister Bertrida, the most friendly of the nuns, who they were.

"It has become very fashionable in the last few years to come here and help nurse the poor," she said, pulling a wry face.

There was something ridiculous about the ladies. They would arrive about midmorning in small groups, often with one or two servants in tow, and would float round the hospital room, sniffing their pomanders, gossiping with one another, and getting their huge silk skirts caught in the furniture. There was, however, a small core of more quietly dressed ladies who did indeed read and sometimes even pray with the patients. One in particular, an attractive blond woman dressed always in black, was there so often that she began to nod and smile at me.

Mostly, however, the ladies were a nuisance. They seemed to be constantly wandering into the clinic and trying to engage Genny in conversation. She would answer briskly and call in some particularly smelly beggar for treatment, which usually chased them out.

I remember especially one morning when Lady Cora Morfelda, daughter of the very powerful Lord Zenon Morfelda, visited us in the clinic and spent almost three-quarters of an hour telling us how concerned her family was for the poor. Genny was scrupulously polite, but I could tell she disliked Cora intensely. It was something to do with the way she asked her to hold the basin, while she cleaned and cauterized the huge suppurating sore on the thigh of an ancient wool carder.

Even I wouldn't have liked the task, but Lady Cora was made of stern stuff, and though she blanched at the putrid matter in the bowl, she did not retch and she did not leave. She was just telling us how much more she liked the city than the country, because there were so many more poor people to help, when she was the victim of a terrible accident. The heavy pestle that Genny was carrying slipped and fell on Lady Cora's foot. There was an audible crunch of bone. The lady doubled up, screaming in agony. Genny was all sugar-sweet contrition, giving the poor creature a painkilling potion and binding up her foot with a healing spell, but her very sweetness made me suspect that she had dropped that pestle on purpose. Lady Cora suspected it, too, for she seemed about to utter accusations, when her mother, Lady Ulla, who had rushed into the room at the sound of Cora's screams, silenced her with a "My dear, you are being unwise."

The two gentlewomen were bundled into a waiting carriage by a blunt and capable nun.

Genny bolted the door shut behind them, went over to a cupboard, took out a bottle, pulled out the cork, put the neck to her lips, and drank a long draught of it.

I watched her, not knowing what to say. Poor Lady Cora. I could still hear her screams. She was silly, but she meant well. How could Genny, who'd always seemed so kind, have done such an awful thing?

She put down the bottle, breathed out, wiped her mouth.

"Don't look at me like that! I didn't mean to break that silly girl's foot. Just wanted to get rid of her. I lost my temper."

Her voice was hard and angry.

"Aumaz! I hate those hypocritical bitches. Before Kitten was Leon's mistress, they never put one foot in here, they never lifted a finger to help anyone. Not one finger." She slammed her fist down on the table. "Now the great families send their women here with instructions to curry favor, through me, with Kitten. In reality they hate and despise her, write poisonous poems about her, and whisper behind her back. She shrugs it off, says it's to be expected—but I . . ." She snatched savagely at a piece of leaf on the table.

"I see their treacherous smiles and it makes my blood boil."

She sat down at the table and put her head in her hands. Suddenly all the tension went out of her with a great sigh.

She looked up at me. "I'm sorry, Dion. I have a terrible temper. By the Seven, I didn't really mean to break her toe, poor silly thing. That must've really hurt."

"She seemed sort of harmless," I said.

Genny's face darkened. "Oh, Dion. You're really not cut out for this life, you know. Court people are never harmless. They're snakes. The Morfeldas have had it in for Kitten for some time. When she came on the scene, they were all set to launch poor little Lady Cora into the Duke's bed."

"But she's only a girl."

"That's right. She was only fourteen at the time, but you're never too young to serve your family. They sent Kitten a pair of gloves with a disease spell sewn into the lining—smallpox to kill or disfigure her. These courtiers will stop at nothing. The favor of the Duke is life and death to them, and Kitten is their rival."

Something sinister did happen during those first few weeks, but it had nothing to do with Kitten Avignon.

One midnight early in my stay in Kitten's house I felt a presence in my room, that soft spine feeling of eyes behind me, watching me. The demon. Who else could it be?

I searched the room, checking all my invisible protection runes—under the bed, in the wardrobe, under the rug, the corner where the mirror had been. I could find nothing. Not a shard of mirror, not a patch of slime. And yet still this hard predatory staring behind my back. Even if I lay down on my bed, it was there behind me.

I was frightened. Obviously the runes of distraction and protection I had put up to prevent myself from attracting the demon's attention again had proved useless. I did my normal protection ritual with shaking hands and thin concentration and immediately afterward cast a spell of distraction. Distraction is a white magic spell aimed at turning away the gaze of such beings once it has been directed. It is reputed to be ineffective, too, but it was the best I could hope for. I didn't even bother casting a Bowl of Seeing. Demons were supernatural, not magical, and thus not detectable in the bowl.

After an hour the feeling subsided, but it was there the next night and for several nights thereafter. I told nobody what was happening, for there was no way I could tell anybody without revealing my guilt. Instead I cast and recast the Distraction spell and spent some shivering nights trying to gain comfort from the fact that nothing worse was happening. *It cannot come through unless I bring it through*, I reminded myself. This didn't make the watching any better. Finally I even cast a Bowl of Seeing, in the vain hope that there might be something to see in the water. Oddly enough this seemed to drive the watching eyes away, so I continued to use it.

And then, suddenly, the watching stopped. Though I was still fearful over the evening ritual, I no longer felt the eyes. The nights became as benign as the days.

# FIVE

I stood alone in the hallway. In the Green Salon to one side of me a group of serious-minded people, among them the Duke himself, sat elegantly on thin-legged gilt chairs watching with rapt attention, while a little man in a dusty-looking robe held prisms of glass up into the sunlight and made rainbows on the wall behind. This "refraction of light," as he called it, had been throwing the company into ecstasies.

In the Red Drawing Room on the other side of the hall, a larger host of the less serious were playing cards with an air of life-and-death struggle. Considering the amounts of money and jewelry lying on the tables, I was not surprised at their intensity. Their elegant white hands held delicate fluted wineglasses, and their enormous lace cuffs dragged across the green cloth as cards clicked and fortunes changed hands. These magnificent men and women were the hard-edged wits and rakes of the court, the intimates of the Duke. I'd peeped through the half-open door and watched them. I'd heard that Lord Dane and

Lord Pell, the Duke's brothers recently back from exile, had accompanied him here today and I was curious. However I saw nothing of them except a couple of soberly dressed men standing at the farther side of the room who must have been their bodyguards.

It was the first time I had been to one of Kitten's soirees. She had persuaded me downstairs by finding me a place where I could stand behind the big white folding doors between the drawing room and the refreshment room and see without being seen by any of the company. It had been fun until Monsieur Alberti had started refracting light. Before him there had been a clown singing a series of hilarious songs. A merchant-venturer had spoken of his travels in the Spice Islands and told the chilling story of the recent unexplained disappearance of the whole population, some 450 souls, from one of them. Once Monsieur Alberti began his boring dissertation, however, I had slipped out into the hall.

I supposed I should slip back upstairs, but I was tempted to take tea with the others. I'd just spent the last hour in the same room with the luscious spread of food that had been set out for the tea. Erasmus had come in to steal a little cake while the sea captain had been talking and had told me I was to have tea with him after all the talking had finished. I was sorely tempted to do so. I figured that if I blended in with the crowd, people would continue to assume that I was some kind of servant.

I was still undecided when Rapunzel and Demoiselle came rushing down the stairs. They were breathless and giggling and Rapunzel was holding something close to her chest.

"Dion, here," said Rapunzel. She thrust something silky into my hand.

"Wha . . . ?"

"Quickly! Quickly!" hissed Demoiselle, pushing my hands behind my back and thrusting me into the corner by the staircase.

"She's coming." She put a finger on my lips. "Not a word."

She and Rapunzel arranged themselves against the opposite wall, hands behind their backs and unconvincing looks of wide-eyed innocence on their faces.

"You trollops. What have you done with it?" Sateen came limping down the stairs, clutching a lump of her skirt with one hand.

"Who? Us?" said Rapunzel.

"Come on. Give it back."

"I haven't got it," said Rapunzel holding out her hands.

"Demi. Please."

"What are you talking about?" inquired Demoiselle, keeping her hands behind her back.

I stole a look at what I was holding. It was a white satin garter. No wonder Sateen was walking so oddly. She was having to hold up her stocking.

Meanwhile . . .

"Look, we haven't got it," cried Demoiselle and Rapunzel, dancing around her, wiggling their fingers in her face.

"You tarts! Where have you put it?" hissed Sateen, looking nervously over her shoulder.

"Sateen!" I said. "Here it is."

She snatched the garter gratefully out of my hand.

"Thanks, Dion. Glad to see someone's being sensible."

She scowled at the other two, boldly hitched up her skirt, slipped on the garter, and swept away into the drawing room.

"Well! You were a big help, weren't you. Tell-tale. 'Here it is Sateen.' " Demoiselle mimicked. She came toward me, grinning. I shrank back.

"Tell-tales have to be punished, don't they Demi?" said Rapunzel.

"That's right."

I made a run for the stairs.

"Get her!" they cried, and leapt at me.

Suddenly I was being tickled unmercifully.

In a moment I was rolling on the floor, helpless with laughter surrounded by a suffocating cloud of silk and lace, perfume and powder.

"No, no! Stop! Stop!"

Then suddenly they did stop. Suddenly Demoiselle and Rapunzel were looking away up the hallway. I gasped and sat up, wiping tears out of my eyes.

And saw him.

A tall, dark man was leaning against the wall and looking down at us, at me as I lay sprawled across Rapunzel's lap, legs all awry, hair coming down.

He was the most magnificent and startling creature I'd ever seen. His pale face was lean and hard and beautiful, surrounded by a mane of long black curls. A wicked little half smile played on his full red lips and his large, dark and, God and Angels!, kohl-lined eyes regarded us caressingly.

He nodded.

"Ladies," he said softly.

He unfurled himself from the wall and sauntered slowly past us. As he passed, he looked at me from under his lashes, eyes widening for a moment. I was suddenly aware that my dress had ridden above my knees. I pulled it down quickly and sat up straight, but he had disappeared into the card room.

"You handsome bastard!" breathed Rapunzel. "Shall we go after him?"

Demoiselle got up and began dusting off her gown. "Behave yourself, Rapunzel."

"A woman's got to have some pleasures in life. Well, look at you, Miss." Rapunzel pushed me off her lap. "Lolling about like the Empress of Aramaya, letting men admire your legs."

The pair of them hauled me up off the floor and began straightening me out and pushing my hair back into place.

Not a moment too soon, for just then there was clapping in the lecture room and a moment later the doors were thrown open and people surged out into the hall. Rapunzel winked at me and the two of them disappeared into the crowd, leaving me feeling hot and ashamed.

Erasmus appeared at my elbow.

"Dion, did you enjoy the talk? Come on. Let's get to the refreshments before all these greedy pigs eat all those nice little cakes."

He was as homely and friendly as a favorite dog after the magnificent dark lord.

We sat down in quiet little corner and drank spiced wine cordial, and I told him that I'd enjoyed most of it, but not the talk on optics.

"An interesting subject, but Alberti's not much of a speaker."

"It's not just that. Surely if people wanted rainbows, they should ask a mage to make them. I could make much better rainbows than Monsieur Alberti."

Erasmus laughed.

"You're missing the point of the New Learning. Don't you realize how much those of us born without powers envy you mages? Many of us would like to be able to do those kinds of things for ourselves. These new sciences give us the hope that one day we may be able to use science to perform feats only now possible through magic."

I sipped my tea and digested this.

"By learning more about the natural order of things, we learn how to control it and change it. Many people hope that New Learning will give us the same control over nature as mages have."

I couldn't think of a polite way to say how foolish this idea seemed to me. Balance is one of the first lessons a mage learns. All humanity's acts change the balance of the natural world, and a mage must always keep this in mind when he performs an act of magic. Mages often make a mess of nature's balance, but at least there are only a few of them. The idea of thousands of ordinary people altering nature at will seemed a recipe for disaster. I changed the subject.

"I never expected this to be the kind of party Madame Avignon would give."

His normally mild blue eyes narrowed.

"Why?" he snapped. "Madame Avignon is the most cultured woman I know. And good, not just stuffily respectable. She is more like one of the Amourettes of old Sopria than an ordinary courtesan."

There was an uncomfortable silence between us. Then I thought Erasmus might leave soon if I didn't think of something to say so I asked,

"What is an Amourette?"

"Amourettes were Soprian courtesans as much sought for their intellects and their witty conversation as for their physical charms. I think this is the secret of Madame Avignon's popularity, too."

What a naive thing to say, I thought a little vengefully. Who ever heard of men going to prostitutes for conversation? But I was curious to hear more about Kitten Avignon, so I nodded encouragingly.

Erasmus' expression became intense.

"This New Learning I was speaking of. Do you know anything about it?"

I shook my head reluctantly.

"Well, it's ... You know how tradition and the Church law define how we think about everything?"

"Except magery."

"That's true. Except magery. But my profession now. Painting. That's always been completely defined by the age-old traditions handed down from father to son. Take figures for instance. As you know, traditionally the size of figures in a painting is dictated by their holiness or importance."

Actually I hadn't known, but I nodded sagely anyway.

"When you think about it, its a ridiculous way of thinking. It has no relation to reality. The New Learning takes reality, the reality we experience with our physical senses, into account. It's a movement of ... knowledge I suppose, that questions established traditions in the Arts and Sciences. New Learning has existed in the Western empires for some time, and that is how Kitten knows so much about it. But in the last ten years we on the Peninsula have been discovering it and, according to her, making it into something all our own. You can't imagine how exciting ... It could revolutionize everything we do. I came to Gallia to study this New Learning way of painting with Bordino, but it wasn't till Kitten Avignon came here that New Learning really took off in Gallia. It was she who first commissioned the translation of some of the most important texts of Western New

Learning and she who influences the Duke to take interest in it. That's why she's so unpopular in certain court circles. The Reform Church people hate her. It is she who is the center of New Learning here in Gallia. Why, she has even written a very fine treatise on the new theory of art."

"But she can't even read," I protested.

"Yes. I know that. She told me that when she and Bordino were together. They had quite a long liaison, you know. That's how I know her so well. She told me that she had fallen foul of a necromancer back in the West, and he'd robbed her of her power to read and write. She says she's never been able to get it back."

A necromancer. It could only be Norval. So that was how Kitten could understand Ancient Soprian and still could not read a word. It was a moment of deep satisfaction for me, for I'd found the answer to a mystery. The way Erasmus was talking about art treatises sounded strange though—ludicrous to think that a woman of pleasure could write anything so intellectual.

"Many people think it is Bordino who wrote that treatise," said Erasmus, unnervingly echoing my thoughts. "That makes me so angry. Everything she does . . . People say, 'What would a whore know?' But I know. I studied under Bordino. I was there. Before she was Ducal mistress, she would come to the house with her latest piece of work and order her page to read to us, and then she and Bordino would dispute various points. Bordino's ideas about art are very different from hers." He laughed. "Bordino once told me of their first meeting back in Ishtak. Here was this foreign courtesan come to see him. Of course, he refused to let her in. But she just came in anyway and before he knew it, they were arguing about perspective. And she was changing his mind. Now scholars come from all over the Peninsula to study the New Learning. Gallia has become a center of it, and the Duke is called one of the most enlightened rulers of the age. But some of those scholars accept her patronage and still call her Whore behind her back. That's why I snapped at you before."

He turned and put his hand on mine.

"I hope you will forgive me. But the ingratitude of some people. Everywhere I go . . . I hear her dismissed, dismissed because she is a public woman and credit for all her ideas given to men like the Duke and Bordino. It makes me furious. I wish there was some way I could make people realize the truth."

I had despised Madame Avignon myself, but now I felt an odd certainty that what he was saying made sense. He was describing the charming and intelligent woman with whom I spent my afternoons.

To cover my confusion I asked, "Is the Duke really interested in the New Learning?"

"Duke Leon has little time for study," replied Erasmus carefully. "Remember, he has two states to run now Gallia and Ishtak have joined."

All at once his attention was claimed by a large man in a squashy purple velvet hat who insisted he come away with him. Erasmus excused himself and left.

Alone, I soon became bored with the soiree. Kitten nodded encouragingly at me once or twice, but she was sitting beside the Duke, and I did not feel I could approach her.

I saw the dark man from the hall again. The bad man. I had no doubts about that. He was standing in the doorway of the room with a wine flute in his long fingers, watching me from under his eyelashes. I looked about for a way of escape. The problem was that he was placed so that even if I went out of the room by another door, I would have to pass close to him to go upstairs. He looked like the kind of man who would be sure to say something as I went past. There was something so penetrating about his stare. He tapped his full bottom lip with one long white finger as he looked, and when I checked to see if he was still looking, he lifted his head and smiled quite openly at me and in such a friendly way, that I almost smiled back. I flushed and looked away quickly, but worse was to come. When I peeped back again, he heaved himself away from the doorframe and lazily began to make his way through the crowd toward me.

I turned and slipped behind the curtain at my back into the window embrasure. The window was open and large enough for me to jump quite easily over the sill and down into the garden. I ran across the lawn and was quickly hidden in the bushes.

I decided to stay out here till I could be sure most of the guests had left. Though it was still only spring, the sun had a warm sleepy quality, and I wandered among the pine trees and stood for a while, happily watching a flock of bright parrots squawking noisily and chewing the pine cones with neat little bites.

I blotted out all thought of the man. Instead I began to think about all I'd learned about Kitten Avignon. What a strange woman she was. A major patron of intellectual life! And yet sometimes she had a wicked twinkle in her eyes, a knowingness which was entirely courtesan. I imagined men must find her hard to resist. But the image of her that came automatically to my mind was of her alone against the books and the fresh white curtains of her boudoir, elegant, luxurious, beautiful.

I could almost hear Michael's voice warning me that her seeming beauty was the very sign of the depths of her evil, but I could not believe Kitten Avignon was evil. Perhaps there were extenuating circumstances that excused her life. Like Norval, for instance. Perhaps like those women I saw at the clinic, she did not enjoy doing what she did but was trapped into it by her need to protect herself from him. If he was not around, perhaps she would be able to give up her immoral life. Perhaps I would be able to help her give it up.

I wished I had someone to talk these things over with. Not Michael, for I cringed at the thought of the harsh way he would have spoken of Kitten, but someone new, someone gentler who would not pooh-pooh my ideas as quickly.

"Hello. You must be Mademoiselle Dion."

A panicky image of the tall, dark man sprang into my mind, but it was a woman who addressed me, an attractive fair-haired woman in sober black, who had come up behind me along the path.

I nodded shyly.

She was smiling in a very friendly way. She seemed vaguely familiar.

"My name is Rosalinda Quarttaro," she said. "I was walking in this beautiful garden and saw you were doing the same, so I thought I would say hello. I hope I'm not intruding."

I shook my head.

She began to praise the garden to me. There was something very likable about her. In a few moments I found myself telling her of its best features and offering to show them to her. We strolled up and down the pathways. She was a widow, she told me, living under the patronage of a bedridden elderly relative

who was very interested in the New Learning and
liked her to come to these kinds of soirees.

"At first I was very anxious about coming to this
house. But I find the most respectable people come
here. The very cream of Gallian society."

Her frankness was so appealing and it echoed so
much what I had thought myself, that shortly I found
myself confiding some of my thoughts about Kitten
to her. I told her of my confusion in judging her and
my theory that necessity may have forced her to become a courtesan. To my delight she did not seem
shocked or even critical. She merely listened and nodded.

"You know," she said, "I have never considered it
before, but I do believe you may be right."

It was wonderful. She seemed just the kind of person I'd been longing for. For almost an hour we wandered in the warm spring garden, and by the end of
it I felt completely at home with her. In fact I was
overjoyed to have made her acquaintance. Here was
someone safely outside the peculiar honey sisterhood
world, someone with whom I could discuss how
strange that world actually was. I even asked her inside to drink a cup of tea with me, a thing I had never
done with anybody else before. I realized almost immediately that it was a foolish thing to do. How could
I expect a respectable widow to come into a courtesan's house for a private visit? My request broke the
spell. She realized what the time was and decided that
she must leave. Was it possible to go out the garden
gate? she asked, showing what seemed to me an understandable reluctance to go back into the house at
this late stage. I found the guard, who was happy to
unlock the gate for us. She turned and shook my hand
before she left.

"I have enjoyed talking to you. I hope we will meet again. Perhaps at the clinic."

I realized suddenly where I had seen her before. She was one of the quiet ladies who did actually read and pray with the patients, the one who often smiled at me.

"Yes, of course," I said, delighted.

I felt a warm glow of pleasure at the idea of seeing her again as I walked back into the house.

I had been living at Kitten's over a month by the time I met Rosalinda. By then my life had become so full I had little time or energy to think of demons or to fall into the kinds of despairing thoughts which had filled me at the college.

I would arise at seven-thirty, gobble down some breakfast, and perform my morning protection ritual. Then, shortly after eight-fifteen, I would accompany Genny and the bodyguard to the clinic. The morning would pass quickly until, just after eleven-thirty, another bodyguard would arrive to take me back to the house, where I would perform the midday ritual and have lunch. Then I would sit quietly in my room, reading or studying, until, after an hour or so, Kitten's maid came to fetch me to read to her. I would read to her until the late afternoon ritual, after which I took tea, sometimes alone with her or, more often, while sitting quietly in the corner of her room and listening to the talk of her guests. On afternoons when Kitten was called to go hunting with the Duke, I would spend the afternoon walking in the garden or doing the study necessary to keep spells fresh in my memory.

Any other spare time I spent with my nose in a book. Kitten had a considerable library tucked away in the attic. I would like to say I read the great philosophers, but the most intellectual things I read were histories and travelers' tales. Mostly I indulged in my new vice of novel reading. Now I had discovered the pleasures of novel reading, I'd developed an unquenchable thirst for them.

I learned plenty of philosophy like science from reading to Kitten, and I was certainly getting an education hearing her discuss the city politics and Church reform with her afternoon callers. Everything in Gallia seemed so much more complex than I could possibly have imagined, and she seemed to understand all of it. Sometimes she would try to discuss our reading or court politics with me, but I resisted such intimacies.

I usually ate dinner alone with Genny, and we would gossip about the patients of the day. At first I was left to my own devices after dinner, and I would feel a little worried sitting in my room alone. Night was when the demon had made his appearance, and my thoughts still sometimes turned worryingly toward him at those times.

Then Genny suggested I come down to the still room in the house and help her grind up and prepare powders and potions. I accepted at once though, in itself, it was boring work. Often Madame Donati, the housekeeper, or Kitten's maid, Maria, would come in and chat to Genny as we worked. They were full of juicy gossip. They always had the latest on the feuds between the Duke and his brother Dane or his sister Matilda, and they knew all about the love affairs of the great.

One especially good evening Genny persuaded Madame Donati to get out her lute and sing us some Gallian folksongs.

Though I was often confused and sometimes frightened, I knew I was happier living in the house of Gallia's Great Whore than I had been for some time. Sometimes in my few spare moments I worried about it. Was it some instability of character, my mother's taint showing through, that made it so easy for me to accept this life? Most of the time I was well aware that this happiness was just the result of being busy and interested. I was even thinking about Michael less. Sometimes unnervingly I would find myself thinking of him only to realize that I disagreed with his judgments.

True to his word, the Dean kept an eye on me. He invited me twice to visit the college and take tea with him, and he was encouraging when he found that I was working as a healer. Both times I felt relieved that I was able to assure him that everything was as respectable as could be at Kitten's house. The college oppressed me with its dreary greyness and its institutional smell of dust. I had no desire to return there.

My newfound respect for Kitten Avignon did not prevent me from portraying her as an anxious woman in order to get some information about demons out of the Dean.

"My, my, she is a nervous creature," he said leaning back in his chair, hands lightly pressed together at the fingertips.

"Have you any reasons to suspect this Norval to be a mage of such power? Have you felt this of him?"

"I've felt very little of Norval. He has barely brushed against my barrier."

"Nothing, eh? That would seem to indicate that you have brought him to a full stop. On the other hand I suppose he could be marshaling his strength . . ."

"That was what she feared, my lord," I lied, hoping to hear more.

"It seems very unlikely. It takes enormous strength to enable a demon to extrude itself into our world. All the old books are agreed on this. Not only must the necromancer know the secret name of the demon concerned, but enormous amounts of power must be expended to keep it from slipping back into its own world, and it must be regularly fed with some of the mage's substance. Very few mages can keep that up for long."

"Is that how a demon gets free? Like during the Cleansing?"

"No! An enslaved demon will only seep back into his own world if not maintained. Part of them is left on that plane when they come here, and apparently it exerts an enormous pull on them. A demon gets free when the enslaving mage is killed, as Jubilato was killed during the Cleansing and then . . . Well I imagine you've seen the Wasteland of Moria. Thank God it has only happened twice."

"The other time . . ." I asked.

"Was a mage called Ballan. Almost a thousand years ago in Aramaya. I believe the demon tricked him into drinking a poisoned drink. Apparently this is ever their way. You must always give a demon very precise instructions, or he will find a way to twist your orders and use them against you. If I had enough power to bring a demon across, surely I could easily sweep you and Madame Avignon away without resorting to such a dangerous and difficult tool. You should tell your Madame Avignon that. I'm sure it will reassure her."

He'd obviously read some books I had not. For a

moment I was tempted to ask . . . The old fascination again. I suppressed it.

"If a person finds himself confronted by a demon on this plane, how can he fight him?"

"He can't. Surely you've read Aristo. Don't you remember how he describes Smazor consuming a living human being so quickly that he was gone before his screaming had died away? These are vastly destructive beings. Never, never imagine you could ever be a match for one. On the other hand, if you are asking me, how we white mages go about fighting one . . . ?"

I nodded.

"I imagine you know the Great Chant for expelling demons."

"Yes."

"Well, a circle of mages chanting this ritual can encircle a demon, forming a ring out of which he cannot break to feed and which, moreover, cuts him off from that part of himself which is still on his own plane. Cut off from his own plane he quickly dwindles away, eaten up inside, I imagine, by his own terrible hungers. It leads one to speculate, doesn't it? Theoretically it should be possible to cut such a being off from its own plane simply by severing that connection, using an ordinary magical knife wielded by a priest or a virgin or some other such holy being."

He had forgotten I was there. His face was blank with thoughtfulness.

"But how to find the connection . . . Given the chaotic nature of demons, I doubt if it is consistent between demons. It probably changes constantly even on the same demon."

His face lightened.

"Well enough of this idle speculation. What have you been learning from Madame Appellez?"

\* \* \*

After I met Rosalinda Quarttaro at the soiree I often saw her at the clinic. She seldom spoke to me inside the building, not liking, she said, to distract me from my work. I didn't see her at any of the later soirees I attended, either. Often, however, she would be sitting reading in the garden of a church along our route home and the bodyguard would allow me to stop and talk to her, or she would walk part of the way home with me. Early on I discovered to my dismay that she was devoutly religious. I was afraid this would put a dampener on our friendship, but on the contrary she seemed to see a mage like myself as an ally.

Rosalinda was very worried about the New Learning.

"Many people are very concerned by its growing popularity, especially at court. I'm sure this is not so with your Madame Avignon, but it does seem to attract the very worst people; disreputable elements of the Church, those who dabble in magic without being mages, buccaneers, artists . . . Do you know that some New Learning thinkers even question the existence of Aumaz and of the spiritual plane? They claim that the spiritual plane is just invented by mages and priests to keep the respect of the ordinary people."

"But I've seen it," I said.

"You've seen Aumaz!" she cried, looking half-shocked.

"No, but I've seen spirits. Every mage has." I was nervous and reluctant to talk about the subject anymore. This kind of remark used to cause dangerous outrage in Moria, even before the Revolution of Souls. The Church of the Burning Light insisted that only priests could see spirits. Anything a mage saw was a demon, and therefore evil. I changed the subject.

"How ridiculous to say the spirit world doesn't exist."

"Quite," she said more calmly. "But that is typical of them. It is true that the Gallian Church is in desperate need of reform, but these New Learning people ... They question everything, they seek to overturn everything, and by doing so they will end up destroying the Church completely. The Church needs careful cleansing, not this terrible sweeping away of everything."

She was so passionate about everything she said, sometimes I got carried away with it and agreed enthusiastically with her. It was only afterward that I would see flaws in her argument and start to wonder how a questioning frame of mind could be incompatible with Church reform.

To Rosalinda, however, it was so.

"The worst of it is that these New Learning people have the Duke's ear, and while he dabbles with them, he is deaf to all other advisers. Even great spiritual leaders, like Prelate Newsanhausen, who is desperate to bring some sort of reform to our poor abused church, are ignored. I fear, I greatly fear, that they will win him over. You should ask Madame Avignon if you dare. I'm sure she would tell you without shame that their aim is to break the Church's authority. You know, Dion, you are not the only mage to be worried by this happening ..."

"Mages?"

"Yes, Dion, mages. There are many people high up in the College of Magic who are just as worried by the New Learning as we Church people. Yes, well may you look surprised, but think about it sensibly. If the Duke forces the New Learning on the people of Gallia, if the Church is discredited in their eyes, where will they turn for spiritual guidance? Not to the New Learning. Oh no. That is a completely material philosophy, the philosophy of cynics and courtiers. It has no spiritual food to offer simple people in trouble. Oh no, if the Orthodox Church falls, as it well may, people will turn to extremists. There will be a terrible backlash as there was in Moria. That's right! This country is full of Burning Light people just waiting like wolves. And when they take over we shall all burn."

The way she described it made me shiver with frightening memories. Could what happened in Moria, really happen among the easygoing pleasure-loving Gallians? Could harsh fanatical Tansism spread to take hold of the populace here as it had there? Yet ten years ago who would have expected the Revolution of Souls and the Spiritual Cleansing that had caused so much suffering in Moria?

"I tell you I really fear for our poor country." She caught sight of my haunted face. "I'm sorry," she said. "I've upset you."

She clasped my hand warmly.

"No!" I lied.

But she had upset me, so much so that when I got back to the house, I ran up to my room and huddled for some time under the quilt, overwhelmed by terrible memories of fires, angry mobs, and the smell of burning flesh.

When at last I managed to think about it sensibly, however, I decided the situations were different. The Morians had never had any interest in anything like the New Learning. On the contrary, the Spiritual Cleansing had been brought on by a series of bad harvests, the tragic death of Duke Argon and his oldest son in a hunting accident, and the ascension to the throne of his crazy religious cousin Lord Ayola, who'd handed over power to the Burning Light Bishops.

The Dean did not seem at all worried about the New Learning.

"A fad," he said when I questioned him. "Some people in the college worry, but I see no reason for it. It will be a long time before their science is advanced enough to emulate magic. Though if the New Learning breaks the hold of the Church on state policy, it will be a very good thing." He laughed reassuringly when I told him of the rumors I had heard of the New Learning leading to a Moria-like situation. "What rubbish! The New Learning is an anticlerical movement based on Non-Tansite traditions of the West. I can think of no better antidote for religious extremism."

But since Rosalinda was the only person to whom I could express my remaining doubts about Kitten Avignon and my still-strong anxieties about what our association would mean for me in the future, I took care not to alienate her by openly disagreeing with her. Though I did not actively deceive her, I always looked serious and nodded enthusiastically when she shared her doubts about the New Learning. She in her turn would always nod and agree with me in the most tactful way that Kitten didn't seem an evil woman, but . . . It was a great relief for me to have someone I could talk to.

One morning several weeks after the soiree, when I was talking to her in the little garden and the bodyguard was standing at a discreet distance, she said, "I want to ask you something, but I'm afraid it will be something of an imposition. I hope you will forgive me if it is."

"Of course," I said.

"My kind relative has expressed a wish to make your acquaintance. I wondered if you would come to visit her with me."

I felt uneasy, but there didn't seem any real reason to say no. "Yes, I suppose I could. Who is she?"

"She is the Countess of Frieburg."

The name meant nothing to me.

"Perhaps I should not ask you. Your patron Madame Avignon does not like her at all, and perhaps she would not allow it. I would not want to make her angry with you."

"It's none of her business," I said crossly. "And anyway, she's not my patron. She is just my employer. I am free to choose my own friends if I wish."

She had hit a raw nerve. Just a few days before, one of the aristocratic clinic visitors had realized my connection with Kitten. Since then they had all been doing their tiresome best to endear themselves to me. Several of them had referred to Madame Avignon as my patron. I worried about how being seen as her client was going to reflect on me.

"Then you will come," said Rosalinda delighted. "My friend will be so pleased. When should you be able to?"

The following afternoon Rapunzel was coming to visit, and I knew I would be free after the afternoon ritual.

I arranged to slip out and meet Rosalinda then. Of course I would have to go out without my bodyguard. It would have looked foolish to insist otherwise after all my protestations of independence. Anyway, if the Countess of Frieburg was someone Kitten didn't like, it would be better if there was no way for her to find out about the visit.

I had faith in my ability to protect myself against a

daytime attack. I could cast spells to protect myself from harm, and, if things got really difficult, I could change shape or turn invisible. The only thing I needed to fear was witch manacles, and I seemed to be able to sense the presence of those.

I very much wanted to please Rosalinda, who had been so kind to me. I trusted her, though I did wonder at this Countess's wanting to meet me. I feared some embarrassing attempt to convert me to their religion.

Since I knew Captain Simonetti would not allow me out without a guard, the following afternoon, I took the back gate key, let myself out, and hurried down the street to meet Rosalinda.

She quite won my heart by telling me she felt guilty for putting me in danger like this. I told her that I could take care of myself and recounted some of the feats of magic I could perform if attacked. She seemed very impressed and drew me out with all kinds of questions about myself and my abilities.

She led me through a gate in the town wall and out onto the sheep paddocks on the east side of the town. The paddocks were green and lush from the spring rains, but it was a lonely area. Much of it was Ducal land, so not many people lived there. Occasionally we saw a shepherd's hut by the roadside. I assumed we were heading for one of the stately houses that dotted the distant hills.

Chattering all the while, Rosalinda led me along a dusty road that wound away into the hills for a mile or so until we came to small cart track. A man in black with a crossbow in his hand, some kind of guard, was standing beside it. Rosalinda patted my arm at my anxious inquiry and nodded at him as we passed. He nodded back.

Then we topped the rise. Before us was a shallow

green valley sparsely dotted with trees, and in the center of it stood an open carriage. Its traces lay empty on the ground and a groom was walking two highly bred black horses up and down along the hill. In the carriage sat two people, one of them heavily veiled. Around it were three or four guards. Another stood on the hill behind also holding a crossbow. I had expected we might go to this Countess's house and have tea and biscuits. Instead, here was this secretive meeting in a lonely valley. It looked like some kind of conspiracy.

Anxious now, I put out thoughts to detect magically the intentions of those in the valley. I got one hell of a fright when I found that I could not discover any of them. The men were all wearing iron helms. The veiled figure in the carriage seemed to be wearing some kind of circlet of cold iron under the veil, and the other person, who was dressed in the red robes of a priest, had the ability to veil his mind in the way that priest-mages can learn.

I turned to Rosalinda, quickly probing for her mind, a thing I would never have ordinarily done, for it is considered the height of rudeness and usually leaves the object with a headache. She, too, was wearing a thin iron circlet under her wimple. It was such a heavy thing for everyday wear. I stopped and stared at her.

"What is the matter?"

"What is going on here?" I cried. "Why have all these people veiled their minds? Have they got something to hide? Have you?"

She took my arm firmly and began pushing me gently toward the carriage.

"They wish to keep their own counsel," she said soothingly. "These are people of affairs. Great ones.

They cannot afford to have you roaming free in their minds or in those of their trusted servants. Surely there is nothing unusual about that. It's common practice." She smiled her kind smile.

"Do not be afraid, Dion. I would not bring you to harm."

I, who had lived all my life among mages, did not know if she was speaking the truth, but I wanted very much to keep trusting her. I saw nothing but mildness in her grey eyes.

The soft grass swished around our feet as we went down the hill.

Rosalinda opened the carriage door and curtsied.

"Mademoiselle Dion Michaeline," she said. "My Lord Prelate Newsanhausen."

The Prelate extended a gloved hand adorned with a huge gold signet ring. He evidently expected me to kiss it, but since I was a mage and an unbeliever, I merely curtsied.

Despite this, his smile remained fulsome. He was a big man, with a certain hard charm of manner, solidly built without being fat, and dressed in the red robes of his office. His lips were full, but firm, and the flinty skin of his face was slightly blue around the jowls where his beard had been scraped away. He looked a force to be reckoned with.

"Mademoiselle Dion. I'm delighted to make your acquaintance." He gestured at the veiled figure beside him.

"My companion wishes to remain anonymous, though I have been asked to express the greatest goodwill and sympathy toward you."

The figure beside him inclined its head. The heavy black veil fell all the way to its lap, completely disguising its face and upper torso, and, beneath the veil, it wore a nondescript black robe. Even the hands in the lap were covered, with black gloves and enormous gold rings, the only clue to its elevated station. In fact it was impossible to tell much at all about this veiled figure.

I curtsied, wondering if this might not perhaps be the Countess of Frieburg.

"Please," said the Prelate. "Enter the carriage and sit with us. We have much to say to you."

Rosalinda withdrew to a distance as I climbed into the carriage and seated myself opposite them.

"My child, when my friends told me there was a young mage close to Madame Avignon who felt as we did about the pernicious influence of this spiritually bankrupt philosophy popularly known as the New Learning, I said, 'We must strive to meet her,' and thus our meeting today. Everywhere I look now, I see these dreadful ideas taking root, growing in the darkness of men's minds, threatening Holy Mother Church from every side. Perhaps you will not have noticed it, living quietly as you do in Madame Avignon's shadow, but I see it everywhere: at court among men of affairs, even, God have mercy, in the Church. The situation is reaching crisis point. It is time for all like-minded people, people like us and yourself, Mademoiselle Dion, to come together to oppose these dreadful, dreadful ideas. Do you not agree?"

"Oh, yes, of course," I said.

Was this priest seeking an alliance with a MAGE? And what on earth did he want with this mage. Something was odd here. My survival instincts told me to blend as much as possible into the background, to agree with what he said until his meaning became clear or, even better, I got an opportunity to withdraw gracefully.

"Mademoiselle, if you had seen the things I have seen. Here in Gallia ... The Duke is a wise and good man, but he has fallen under the influence of wrong-minded people. The Gallian Church is in a dreadful state—riddled with corruption, immorality, nepotism. How can ordinary Gallians respect such an organization? Ordinary people are not fools. They are not blind to the terrible abuses. The Countess and I have been urging the Duke to do something about this situation, but he is deaf to our pleas. He listens only to his New Learning advisers, and they refuse to do anything to reform the Church. It is my belief that they wish to see it fall into disrepute, that they wish to see an atheistic order arise." He clenched his fist.

"Oh God, that I should live to see Holy Mother Church under such attack and no one willing to defend her!"

He looked at me.

I nodded, mystified. He knew I was a mage. He didn't really expect me to be moved by this, did he?

He seemed to recognize my mystification.

"I know, Mademoiselle, that as a Morian, you probably regard the Church as an enemy. This is understandable, but regrettable. It is different here in Gallia, indeed on the whole of the rest of the Peninsula. Here we have always been allies with mages, if not always the best of friends. Why, the Patriarch himself has said how regrettable, how wasteful, the Morians' attitude to mages was!"

This was rubbish! In that moment my anxiety changed to anger. Whom did he think he was fooling? I had never yet met a churchman, any churchman, who did not regard mages as the single greatest threat to the health of Holy Mother Church. And as for the Patriarch ... That pious hypocrite, who had mur-

mured platitudinous criticisms while turning a blind
eye to the Morian witch-burnings. "Oh yes, most
tragic," he had said. "But they are Morian citizens and
must be subject to Morian law." The Patriarch indeed.
My desire to blend in turned hotly to a desire to actively deceive.

"Mages have an important role to play in the
scheme of things. Their work is invaluable to the order of society as we know it. To undermine them is
to undermine that order. Yet that is precisely what the
New Learning is doing. What happened in Moria was
a tragedy, and you know full well, indeed Madame
Rosalinda has told me of your concern, that we teeter
on the brink of the same abyss here. If the Duke continues to undermine the Church and to thwart all
moderate attempts at reform, the people must rise up.
They are crying out already against the abuses they
see every day. With the New Learning undermining
the traditional Church like this, the other way, the
only other way, is into the terrible extremes of the
Burning Light, extremes which have destroyed both
the moderate Church and magery in your poor homeland. Faced with such a crisis, a crisis which is loom-
ing daily nearer, we must put aside our differences
and ally against these New Learning traitors."

"Oh, yes, yes," I nodded enthusiastically, trying to
keep irony out of my voice. This man thought I was
a complete fool. Why would a Prelate of the Gallian
Church give a damn about the possibility of the ex-
pulsion of mages from Gallia?

Now he began to look thoughtful.

"Yet I fear you are instrumental in bringing about
your own destruction. Does that not concern you?"

I sensed we were approaching the nub of the matter.

"How is that, Your Eminence?"

"Madame Avignon. She is a staunch supporter of the New Learning, and you are her bodyguard. Oh yes, that is well-known, I am afraid. Your links with her are well-known. I imagine that must be a cause for concern to you?"

"I would prefer they not be known, that is true," I said carefully.

"My child, I was horrified when the Countess told me of your position. What can the Dean of the college have been thinking of? To allow a sweet young creature to reside in the house of such a woman."

The figure beside him shook its head and now the Prelate began to dwell at great length on the evils of my situation and the terrible results of the ruination of my reputation.

"I fear, my poor child, you are already ruined. Who now will ever let you work again even as a healer, now you are tainted with your association to this abandoned woman? It is all very well while she needs you, but after that . . . I assure you, loyalty is not to be looked for in that quarter. The whole nature of the courtesan is to use as suits them and toss aside their victims when they are finished. And even were that not so, Madame Avignon's power is based on her pleasing the Duke, and she cannot continue to do so forever. His fancy must pass, and with its passing will come her ruination and I fear, my child, I very much fear that if your association continues as it is, her ruination will be yours. Her descent into poverty and ignominy will be yours as well. It seems a tragedy to me."

For some time he continued in this vein. He spoke eloquently. He spoke persuasively. He touched on every fear I ever had about Kitten, touched on them so well that I began to feel some of the panic he was trying to arouse. But through it all a small, hard voice kept repeating—What does he care? What does he really want? A true believer or even a Gallian mage might have taken his words for truth, but I was a Morian, a refugee from such men, and I could not believe in him.

At last he leaned forward and touched my knee.

"We could not sit aside and let such a terrible thing happen. We felt it our duty to save you from this dreadful fate. As Tansites we cannot stand by and see such a promising young woman ruined by the thoughtlessness of these men. The Countess has relatives in the Tyronic Duchies, who are in need of a mage to guard and teach their little girls. Out of the goodness of her heart, she has commissioned me to offer this position to you. A new name, Mademoiselle Dion. A new name and a new clean life."

I was astonished. But why . . . Leave Kitten Avignon! Leave Gallia and take a new name!

"I would have to discuss it with Madame . . ."

"My dear, you cannot discuss this with Madame Avignon. She would never let you go. You must not underestimate the vindictiveness of such a woman, though I am sure she has hidden it from you. Do you think she would allow you to go now she has her claws in you? Do you think the Duke would allow it? No, child. His anger would find you even in the Tyronic Duchies. It would be better if you just disappeared. Or better still if there was an accident, and it was believed that you had died."

The hair stood up along the back of my neck.

"An accident?"

A knowing look appeared on the face that had a moment ago been so earnest.

"If the protection barrier were to be breached, for instance. It would be assumed you had died in the breaching . . ."

As Kitten Avignon would also die. Horribly.

"You're asking me to betray Madame Avignon. Aren't you?"

"Discretion, my child," he said benignly. I saw that there was no doubt in his mind that I had swallowed his story and would do this terrible thing for him. A jet of hot anger at him and all his ruthless, treacherous kind shot into my brain.

"Aren't you?" I screamed, springing to my feet. "You want me to bring about her death."

The carriage lurched, and I had to grab the side to steady myself.

"Do you think I'm a fool," I yelled. "You treacherous, heartless . . ." I was inarticulate with rage.

"I take it this means you are not interested in our little proposal."

"You are exactly right."

He lifted his hand and gripped the veil of the figure beside him.

"As God is my witness, I have done my best to save you. May God have mercy on your soul."

With a quick twitch of its hand, the other figure in the carriage reached up and pulled its headdress off.

And there he was. Oh my God. It was not the Countess beneath that veil. It was not even a woman. It was a face that had been burned into my brain in nightmare after nightmare. The relentless face of the Morian Burning Light incarnate. Ryart Dashalle. Chief Inquisitor and Witchfinder General.

His narrow face was twisted with hatred. As I fell back against the seat, terrified at the very sight of him, he sprang to his feet, thrust out his hands and spoke the Words in a thunderous voice. The Words of Silencing. The witchfinder words every Morian mage had dreaded since they made who ever listened momentarily unable to speak spells. A moment was usually enough.

He was a very powerful priest-mage. The power of those words hit me like a physical blow, threw me back against the carriage seat. In that moment he ripped the iron circlet in his hand free of the veil and pulled it open, wide-open, and I saw that what I had thought was just an iron circlet was in fact a witch manacle.

In a swirl of black robes he came at me.

"No!" I screamed thrusting out my hand to stop, to push him away.

Power surged out of me, burning agonizingly down my nerves, out of my hands. Away! I wanted him away!

In a blazing yellow explosion, the carriage shattered. Bits of wood, wheels, traces, all flew out into the air, and with them the occupants, kicking, screaming, flailing the air. Away! Away! Get away!

They were away, all of them, Dashalle, the Prelate, the guards, Rosalinda, the horses and their groom, the few trees that had dotted the valley, thumped flat on the ground, skidding swiftly away in a mass of black-and-red cloth and flailing limbs and branches and the ecstasy of golden power streaming out like the release of aching muscles, holding me suspended in the crackling air.

Then suddenly I remembered another time when someone had flown away. People might be killed. I pulled back, nerves tingling and tension cramping my muscles as I did. The mad flurry around me slowed, stopped, dropped, and lay still on the ground. My feet thudded onto the grass as I dropped gently out of the air.

As the coldness of magic left me I felt frightened. Had anyone been hurt? Had anyone . . . Rosalinda!

The valley looked as though a great wind had swept through it. All around me trees were uprooted and lumps of grass pulled up and thrown about. A great circle of debris radiated out from where I stood, shattered pieces of carriage strewn everywhere, and among them what looked like piles of rags, but what must be or have been human beings.

"Rosalinda!" I called. I twirled around. There was a black pile there and another there. In that one I could see a flash of fair hair. I ran toward it.

Even as I ran the sprawled figure on the grass groaned and pushed itself feebly up from the ground.

"Rosalinda!" I cried. "Are you all right?"

She turned her pale, dirt-smeared face to me. A bright red trickle of blood was running down her cheek.

"Rosalinda!"

Her face creased into a look of horror.

"Witch! Witch!" she screamed. She scrambled away from me tripping and falling backward over her robe, crawling desperately, like an animal. "No! Get away from me! Witch! Witch!"

How often before had I heard that cry? Seen that look of horror and disgust.

"My lord! Help me!"

I saw myself in her eyes. I knew she hated me.

I didn't want to be there then. I just wanted to disappear. So I did, leaving her screaming into thin air.

Invisible, I picked my way slowly up and around the valley side. Rosalinda was still screaming, a hys-

terical sob in her voice. All around figures were moving, sitting up.

At the top of the hill I was relieved to pass two of
the guards, one binding the other's bleeding arm.

"No one's been killed," said the uninjured one,
"but unless Old Newie's prepared to have a healer to
them, I reckon those horses'll have to be put down."

As quickly as I could I made my way home.


"Just a minute, girl," said Captain Simonetti behind
me. "I want to have a word with you."

"I have to go upstairs," I said. "It's almost time for
the ritual. I have to . . ."

"Not before I've had a word with you." He grabbed
my wrist and pulled my hand off the banister.

"But the ritual . . ."

"Come on," he said. "Madame Avignon and I want
to speak with you in the drawing room."

"Captain!"

He would brook no opposition. Instead he hustled
me into the drawing room.

I could not understand his actions. I did not try to.
The coldness of magic had left me outside the house
when I had thrown off the invisibility spell, and now
I was a confused mess of miserable feelings. I was as
sure as if she had told me, that Rosalinda had meant
from the start to betray me. She had never been my
friend. What she really felt for me had been written
on her face when she had turned away from me
screaming "Witch!" All I wanted was to get back into
my room and hide, so that I could give way to my
feelings. And the ritual. I needed to do the ritual. I'd
been away much longer than I'd expected, and it was
time.

The Captain slammed the drawing room door behind him. The room was full of people. Three of the bodyguards were there, and Genny was standing by the window. Madame Avignon sat in a deep chair as if enthroned, dressed in ivory silk, a small heap of pink rosebuds on her lap.

She looked up as we came in.

"Ah, Dion. Please sit down."

"I can't, Madame. I must do the ritual."

"Sit down!" shouted Simonetti.

I cringed away from him, turning to Madame Avignon.

"Please, Madame Avignon. Its past four o'clock. Madame! I must do it quickly or the barrier will be broken. Madame! Please!"

"Of course you must. Genny has your things all ready for you down here. See."

Genny moved aside, and I saw indeed that she had set up my candle on the table by the window. I ran over to it. She had brought all my bits and pieces down, even some extra chalk. I was so anxious to get the spell started that I did not question why she had done so. I simply began chanting and drawing the symbols.

It was not until the last words had died away in the silence of the room that it occurred to me that they were all behaving strangely.

I turned and faced Madame Avignon.

"Genny," she said. "Is all well?"

"Yes. The barrier has been replenished."

"Madame?" I asked. "What is going on?"

She did not look at me. Her head bowed and she took one of the rosebuds from her lap and began to play with it, caressing its petals with the tips of her fingers.

"Perhaps it is for you to answer that question, Mademoiselle," snapped Captain Simonetti. His head was tilted back so that he looked down his nose at me. His face was stern. He stood legs apart, arms behind his back, his compact body stiff with anger.

"What?"

"Perhaps you could tell us where you've been this afternoon."

"I . . ."

"Perhaps you could tell us who you were with."

"I . . . I . . ."

Everything fell into place—the reason they were acting so strangely, this armed interview, the reason Kitten wouldn't look at me. I had just spent the afternoon secretly in the company of Kitten's enemies. They must have found out somehow. I looked at Kitten's bowed head, at Genny's expressionless face, and at Simonetti's angry one. I must look very guilty to them. Angels knew I felt guilty enough, standing here like a fool stammering and twisting my hands together. But what was I going to tell them? How was I going to make them believe . . .

"I went to visit a friend."

"A friend? What friend?"

"Someone I met at the clinic. One of the ladies who works there."

"Madame Rosalinda Quarttaro."

"Yes."

"Don't bother lying to us. We know everything. I saw you meet Madame Quarttaro and leave the city in her company. You'd better tell us where you went and whom you saw."

First Rosalinda and now this. They had made up their minds about me already. There was no way I could convince them of my innocence.

"Who did you meet?"

"No one . . . I . . ."

"Don't give me that, girl. You went to meet someone. Who was it?"

"I . . ."

"You met someone and they asked you to betray Madame Avignon. Didn't they?" he shouted.

I had a lump in my throat. If I said anything, I would cry, and I didn't want these sudden enemies to see me weak.

Simonetti's voice dropped.

"What did they offer you to betray Madame Avignon?"

"Come on!" he yelled. "Tell me."

"Nothing!" I said.

"Don't give me that, Mademoiselle. What did they offer you?"

He grabbed my arm. His fist was clenched.

"You will tell me," he said with frightening assurance.

I quailed before him.

Kitten shot out a hand and grabbed his wrist.

"Captain," she said, and he was suddenly still, head bent toward her.

She took his fist in her hands and said softly, "Leave this to me."

He snorted and, without looking at me, turned on his heel and went over to glare out the window.

"Sit!" said Kitten, patting the chair beside her.

I sat.

"Mademoiselle Dion, you must realize that Captain Simonetti has seen you several times in conversation with Madame Quarttaro, who, while very charming, is a Reformist and in the employ of one who is my avowed enemy. Naturally he became anxious. Today he followed you when you left the house. You went alone despite all our advice to the contrary. He saw you meet Madame Quarttaro and leave the city in her company. There is a logical conclusion to be drawn from all this, and he has drawn it. You must tell us your side of the story."

I was silent. The lump in my throat would not allow me to speak.

"You met some other people in the hills."

I nodded.

"Did they ask you to betray me?"

I nodded.

"And what did you say?"

I was crying anyway. I was too upset even to cover my face or try to hide my sobs. Captain Simonetti snorted.

An elegant hand offered me a linen handkerchief.

"Calm yourself, Mademoiselle. There is nothing to fear. The Captain shouts because he is anxious. We are all anxious. Did you agree to betray me?"

I shook my head.

"Tell me what happened."

"They tried to kill me, Madame. They . . . Oh God, Madame! They had Ryart Dashalle there, and he tried to manacle me."

"Ryart Dashalle. He's one of the Morians, isn't he?"

"He was the Great Inquisitor before the Twin Suns Scandal. He . . . he organized the burnings. He burned our . . . He's a terrible man. Evil. I never thought to see that face so close and live."

"So what is he doing in Gallia?"

"He's in disgrace. I told you the Twin Suns Scandal . . ."

"Twin Suns Scandal? Calm yourself, my love. Explain slowly."

I took a deep breath, trying to still the sobs that kept rising in me.

"The leaders of the Revolution of Souls disagreed about the nature of God, you know, the Duality. Bishop Scorpio held one view and Bishop Ordo another. Scorpio's view prevailed with the Council. Ordo was burned and his followers purged. Ryart Dashalle was one of those followers. We were glad when we heard of it. We hoped he'd burn on his own pyre. I didn't ever think to see him here."

"He must have great powers to have been Grand Inquisitor."

"He did. Oh Angels. That silencing! It was like a blow from a rock, and then he came at me. I . . . I was so frightened. I lost control of my power. Like that other time. At the college . . ."

To my surprise, Kitten chuckled.

"Very good, my little Dion. They did not expect you, did they?"

Simonetti snorted from the window.

"If Dion did what she did at the college, Captain, I imagine there will be debris for you to look at, perhaps even casualties. Am I not right, my dear?"

"Nobody was killed," I said quickly. "At least . . ."

Kitten patted my arm.

"Start from the beginning, Dion. Tell me exactly what happened."

She seemed to believe me. I was comforted by that feeling. I wiped my face and blew my nose and told her everything. I told her of how I had met Rosalinda, something of my conversations with her, about the Prelate, and finally, in much more detail, about my confrontation with Dashalle. I found it a relief to be able to tell her about Rosalinda's betrayal, though telling it made me realize how stupid I had been.

All was calm and serious. Even the Captain ceased to make snorting noises. Kitten did not seem surprised by anything I told her, not even the names of my tempters.

Afterward she sat silent for a while, rubbing the velvety rosebud thoughtfully against her cheek. I felt no doubt that her judgment would be just.

"Prelate Newsanhausen. The same old names," she said. "And I have no doubt that the Countess Matilda is behind this. The Quarttaro is one of her agents. The Countess of Frieburg," she explained, "is one of the titles of the Dowager Countess of Betzoni, Duke Leon's sister Matilda."

I stared at her aghast.

"Yes," she said. "You've been playing with the grown-ups today. These people are part of a court faction that wants the reform of the Church of Gallia. Part of this is the eradication of the New Learning, which they seem to see as weakening it. The Dowager Countess would also like the Duke to marry to secure the succession, mostly from Lord Dane, whom she dislikes even more than Leon. For some reason she sees me as preventing this, though I don't understand why. She has been seeking my 'dismissal' for some time, and she obviously saw you as a means to this end. You have been very foolish, Dion. And very lucky. You know that, don't you?"

"Yes, Madame."

"I hope in future you will know better than to trust respectable-seeming strangers. It will not do in court circles. It is best always to be suspicious of friendly advances, especially now it has become known that you stand between me and . . . annihilation. You represent a splendid opportunity for those to whom I am an inconvenience to be rid of me without getting their hands dirty. I doubt if anyone will try to bribe you again. No doubt there will be other attempts to kill you. You must never leave the house without an escort again."

"Then you believe this ... story," said Captain Simonetti.

"Yes," said Kitten. "I think Dion has too much honor to betray me."

She smiled at me in a way that made me want to cry again, and that was that.

I returned to my room, filled with a shaky pride that she believed in me so much and feeling embarrassed and vulnerable because I had been weak and cried in front of all of them. Genny followed me.

"Will you be all right?"

"Yes."

"You've had a shock," she said. "I'll ring for some spiced milk."

She helped me off with my robe, made me get into bed, and tucked the covers around me. I realized she was trying to say sorry for doubting me and tried to thank her, but she would have none of it and bustled away briskly.

Lying there thinking things over, I realized that dismissal and a return to the college in disgrace should have been the logical outcome of my foolishness. I was grateful to Kitten, though it was worrying to think she might one day ask for a return of the favor.

"Don't get too cosy," said Michael's warning voice. "She's using you."

Yes, but unlike the so-devout Rosalinda, at least Kitten was doing it openly. It was as she said that first time. My survival meant her survival. That realization was a relief to me. It meant I had some standing in the relationship when all along I had thought I had none. It meant that she would protect me, that she might not mean to harm me after all. It was all quite simple. I knew where I stood with her.

# SIX

Sword blades flashed in the golden sunlight streaming through the cellar windows. Steel clashed upon steel and the two figures swayed together, their feet moving in tiny deft steps beneath them. I stared in amazement. After a few moments I remembered to close my mouth. It was not just the sight of Kitten Avignon attired in breeches and wearing a leather armor jerkin that surprised me, but the fact that here she was sword fighting with Captain Simonetti like any man. The sight of her doing any kind of exercise shocked me, for, though I already knew that she rode every morning, I was used to thinking of her as the epitome of soft, useless femininity. Watching the muscular thrusts of her arms and the nimble movements of her slender figure as she avoided Simonetti's sword strokes necessitated considerable reappraisal.

She knew what she was doing, too. Her style of fighting was very different from Simonetti's. It was much more athletic. She spent a lot of time jumping out of the way of his blade, but she was forcing him backwards just as often as he did her. Suddenly she let out a gasp, the blades screeched across each other, and Simonetti's sword fell out of his hand and slid across the floor. The bodyguard beside me let out a "Hooray" and then subsided into blushing silence as Kitten turned and bowed ironically toward us.

Both fighters were breathing heavily and soaked with sweat. Simonetti picked up a pair of towels and passed one to her. He did not seem concerned at having been disarmed by a woman, even though it was in front of one of his men. As he dismissed the guard his weather-beaten face was as calm as usual, and even before the man had left the room he had turned to her and said, "That little twist of yours is a killer. I saw it coming this time, but too late to do anything about it."

She laughed and punched him good-naturedly in the arm. "Thanks for a good fight. I enjoyed that."

"Huh. I bet you did."

She draped the towel around her neck and turned to me.

"Well, young Dion. And how are you this morning?"

It was the morning after Rosalinda's assassination attempt. I told her I was well enough. I felt some praise of her swordsmanship was in order, but while I fumbled unsurely for the words she went on.

"I received a note from His Grace, the Duke, this morning. Much has happened at the court overnight. It seems Countess Matilda has suddenly fallen ill and is retiring to a convent in the Adalani hills to recover. Her dear friend Madame Quarttaro goes with her to nurse her apparently. And Prelate Newsanhausen has been sent on a mission to Mazdan." She chuckled.

"That's the best bit of all. His mission is to negotiate a new marriage for Countess Matilda. I hope her new husband has bad breath and a potbelly."

She grinned at me. "I fear their absence will be a sad loss to the Reformist movement. I wonder how they will go on without their two most eminent members."

"Was anybody hurt?" I asked anxiously.

"The Prelate has a broken arm, which I hope will make his journey very unpleasant." She looked at me seriously. "They would have killed you without a second thought, Dion."

"I know. And Ryart Dashalle?"

"He's in the Fortress. The Duke can't decide what to charge him with. "Well," she continued briskly, "Captain Simonetti and I have been discussing what happened yesterday, and we have come to the conclusion it would be better in future if he acted as your bodyguard."

"But he's your bodyguard," I said.

"That's as may be," snapped Simonetti. "But she knows who not to talk to. You can hardly be blamed for falling into Rosalinda Quarttaro's trap, since you know nothing about politics. So we decided that you'd be better off with me around to tell you which friendly arse-licker is likely to be the one to stab you in the back."

I looked dubiously at Kitten.

"I think you will find Captain Simonetti very helpful. Listen to his advice always. And don't leave the house without him."

I wasn't sure how much I believed them. At the time I couldn't help thinking that they didn't trust me anymore after all, and they wanted Simonetti around to keep watch on what I did. I was frightened of him after his anger of the night before and couldn't believe that he, the complete professional, would forgive me for my carelessness.

Evidently he had forgiven me, though. He told me he had ridden out to see the place where I had met the Prelate. He seemed as pleased about the destruction I had wreaked, as he had been about my killing the assassin at the college. I could not share his pleasure, for I remembered too well how petrified with fear I'd been when I'd first faced Dashalle, and it seemed to me that the ability to lose control of myself and smash things up was no ability at all.

I quickly grew to like Simonetti, however. His grim good humor put me at ease. Only occasionally would I remember with a jolt how he had been the night of the assassination attempt, that he was a professional killer and should be treated with care. Although he stood only an inch or so taller than me, I never doubted that his wiry limbs were more dangerous than a prizefighter's.

I learned a lot from him. He knew the names and histories of most of the people we met during the day. As we walked through the streets, he would often break his watchful silence, to point out the kind of little alleyways I should be careful walking past and the "kinds of seedy bastards" I should be watchful of.

"By the Seven, keep your eyes open. Just imagine that Ryart Dashalle is around every corner."

After a week spent locked in the Fortress, Ryart Dashalle had mysteriously managed to escape and had disappeared without a trace. It wasn't hard for me to picture him vengefully stalking the city. His very name inspired me to be vigilant and careful. It never seemed to be enough for Simonetti, though. He was constantly nagging. But he was a patient teacher, and I found myself striving to please him.

Simonetti also shook me out of the placid attitude that I was doing all that could be done about Norval.

"What's your ultimate plan with Old Norval?" he asked one day after we had just come home from the clinic. It was shortly after he had become my bodyguard.

"You'll have to face it out with him eventually. The man's never going to leave you alone. Or are you just going to let him hunt Kitten till one of you dies of old age?"

"I don't know. I never thought about it before." Protection spells seemed to be based on the idea that your opponent would eventually get bored and go away. "What could I do about him?"

"You could seek him out and put a stop to him."

My blood curdled.

"You mean kill him? But I couldn't."

"Well, I don't see why not. He'd kill you in half a minute. Is there nothing else you can do? Nothing but wait? As long as Norval is around, you and me and especially Kitten are all in danger. People will keep trying to kill you. Even the best defenses can be breached if the siege goes on long enough. Can't you do anything?"

"How could I?"

"Well you should think about it, girl. There must be a way. He's a real cruel bastard. He's not going to let you get away with helping Kitten. And he won't have a clean death planned for either of you. It'll be something a lot worse."

A slow torturous death. I remembered the witch burnings and shuddered.

"Come with me for a moment, girl." He led me down the cellar stairs and into the little room where the guards kept their armor and equipment. He motioned me to sit down on a rickety wooden stool.

"I was in Sopria with Kitten when Norval first caught up to her. I wasn't working for her then, but I saw her often."

This opened up interesting possibilities. Had Kitten and Simonetti ever . . .

"Anyway she was acting in the theater there. Suddenly Norval started appearing in the audience of an evening. He's like that. He likes to make people good and frightened. So he'd just appear long enough to scare her, make her forget her lines, that sort of thing. Then she started seeing him in the street, too, standing at corners or walking ahead of her, but when she'd go to look he'd be gone. Or she'd wake up in the middle of the night and he'd be standing at the end of her bed, a big evil grin on his face. It was a haunting, see. After about a month of this he stopped appearing. Then Kitten was really afraid. She figured he was marshaling his power.

"A few days later when she was onstage, this huge bolt of light struck her down. In front of everyone. There was this Godalmighty flash and there she lay. Still. Her eyes moving and all and still breathing. But she couldn't move or speak. She just lay there. She said later she could feel everything. Every touch was magnified so that it was agony for her. You can imagine the things that might have happened to a woman alone and helpless like that. Norval must have hoped for all those possibilities."

I could see it all clearly in my mind; the great searing flash of light and, afterward, the body lying still on the floor. Helpless. Eyes flickering desperately back and forth in a slack, dead face. I shivered.

"What Norval didn't realize was that Kitten had

people who cared to look after her. People think that because a woman's a whore, nobody can care about her. Ain't necessarily so. You'd think Norval'd know Kitten's nature like she knew his. He should've known she had the way of making loyal friends and that they'd see her right.

"She was lucky she'd told us about Norval. Secretly Genny had done her best to put some kind of shield of protection around her. Not much available to a healer of course, but what she set up cushioned the blow when it came. It was such a strong blow that Genny was knocked unconscious by it as well and she couldn't use magic for some time afterward. I got them both back to my house and the wife and I looked after them till Genny was better. Then I put all of us on a boat to the Peninsula. I'm a local, you see, born and bred in Ishtak, and I knew that this was the safest place for someone running from a necromancer. If Norval had found out that we were her friends, the wife and I would have been dead meat anyway. He works like that.

"We reckon he'd used a mindblast spell on Kitten. Normally there's no cure for a mindblast, but because of that bit of protection Genny'd put on her, it hadn't worked fully. In time and with lots of healing Kitten was able to recover. Took a lot for her to remember things, and some things she was never able to relearn. Like reading and writing."

"How long have you known Kitten?" I said curiously. I was trying to picture the three of them as close friends.

"I've known her some time, girl. I owe her a lot." He held up his finger at me.

"I didn't tell you this story just for your curiosity. I want you to wrap that talent of yours around the problem of Norval. It's stupid just to sit here letting him prowl around you like some old wolf. You wanna spend your whole life guarding against him? You wanna just do nothing and leave him with all the choices?"

"Did Kitten put you up to this?" I snapped, stung by his remarks. "Isn't she happy with what I'm doing? Is that it?"

"Touchy. Touchy. No, girl. That ain't it. It's all me. I don't like the inaction. I can feel him out there, and I know he's up to something."

Silence. I wanted to tell Simonetti that I wasn't a killer, but he had already guessed my problem.

"It's not as if you have to kill him yourself. Can't you get rid of him some other way? Can't you strip him of his powers somehow?"

"No," I said, seizing on this new tack. Maybe I could persuade Simonetti that the whole thing was impossible. "Only a really good mindblast could do that. And I'm not allied to the right powers. That's a necromancy spell. A different kind of magic. Even if I could find him and get through his defenses, I can't use a mindblast spell."

"Seems to me necromancy's a real powerful kind of magic."

"It is," I said. I began to explain to him how white magic and necromancy worked and why necromancy was sometimes the more powerful even though necromancers were usually the weaker mages.

But Simonetti was thinking his own thoughts.

"Tell me, if the White Colleges find somebody using necromancy, what do they do?"

"It's been almost a century since that happened. I suppose they'd do what they did back then. Send out a group of mages to overpower the necromancer and capture him using a witch manacle. Then he'd be tried by the Ducal courts like any other criminal and burned.''

Simonetti slapped his thigh. ''There's your answer.''

''What?''

''All we've got to do is find him and turn him over the authorities.''

''But he's back in Aramaya.''

''Oh, I really doubt that. He's not one to keep his distance. Think about it. Mages can send little spells like hauntings a long way, but they've got to get up close for things like mindblasts. If he really wants to get at Kitten, and, I'm telling you, that one does, he's got to get up close. I have a feeling he's already here hiding out, watching and taking his time till you're out of the way. He knows he can't use necromancy on the Peninsula, so he'll be waiting for the right moment. Then it'll be one big spell and away with him before he gets caught. All you've got to do is find him and turn him in. Simple.''

I'd been fooled. Of course Simonetti knew all about necromancers and the situation on the Peninsula. That was why he'd bought them all here in the first place. Nothing I'd said would have been new to him. He'd just been leading me along the right path.

Simonetti caught my look. His black eyes twinkled. He grinned and shrugged. ''Well you could do it, couldn't you?''

It was hard to get really mad at Simonetti. In his own way, he was as charming as Kitten.

I told him it wasn't easy. Even presuming Norval was in Gallia I had to find him first. Some mages could use psychic abilities to pinpoint a person's whereabouts from one of their possessions, but I wasn't one of them.

"Don't be so negative, girl. Surely you can give it a try. Or find someone who can."

"Have you found him?" I asked nastily.

"Nah! I've had people looking out for him for ages, but there's no sign. But, he as good as told us he was coming. He sent Kit a nasty package. He even gave her some bad dreams. All part of the fun for him. But all that had to stop when you came along. He's had plenty of time to get here from Aramaya since then, even if he just came by boat."

Something horrible suddenly occurred to me. The watching I had felt when I had first come here over two months ago. Mightn't that have been Norval and not the demon at all? Angels! I'd just missed . . . If I'd had a Bowl of Seeing ready I could have . . . Damn!

"What's the matter?"

"Oh. Nothing." I could hardly tell Simonetti about it now.

His dark eyes looked at me searchingly for a moment, but left it at that.

"So listen, girl. He might well be close enough to be worth finding. You can't pinpoint his whereabouts, but there's got to be someone at the college who can."

"We need to have something of his."

"Yep. I thought of that." He opened a small chest and pulled out a small cloth-wrapped bundle. Inside it was a charred piece of brown paper and a small carved oblong box. It, too, was charred, and the lid was broken in two pieces. Inside were several small pieces of brown stained cloth. I shuddered when I realized what the brown was and shoved the cloth back in the box.

"It's a finger box," said Simonetti. "The nobles in Aramaya and Sopria use them when they're ransoming each other. I suppose she told you of the little present Norval sent her?"

I nodded. I remembered her telling me about it the first time in the carriage. It hadn't seemed real till now.

"She was real upset and threw it in the fire, but I pulled it out. I figured it might be useful to us in this way. Maybe Norval won't have thought as how we could trace him through it. But if this doesn't work, Kitten might have something of his."

"All right," I said. "I suppose I can take it in to the college tomorrow."

I was daunted by the idea of asking the college to do anything, but the Dean would probably be cooperative enough.

"Does the College of Magic know that we're looking for a necromancer?" asked Simonetti.

"I don't know."

"Well, you'd better make sure they do, hadn't you?"

I nodded dubiously. I knew what the college thought of Kitten's necromancer.

Simonetti leaned forward, took both my hands in his, and shook them.

"Listen, girl. You gotta be more enthusiastic about this. Remember it's you he'll be out to get first. It's you or him."

"All right," I said, irritated and embarrassed. "All right."

He grinned and rubbed his hands together.

"By the Seven, I'm looking forward to getting hold of that old shit. When they burn him, I'm planning to dance around the fire."

*        *        *

That second assassination attempt made an enormous difference to my relationship with Kitten.

I had always found her easy to talk to, but previously when we had sat and drunk tea after reading a book, and she had tried to draw me into a discussion of it, I had spoken every word with care and suspicion. Now I feared the intimacy less and allowed myself to relax and enjoy talking.

Michael and I had never talked in that way. He was much more of an instructor. It was better never to disagree with him. Generally if he didn't like my ideas, he would get angry, expose the faults in my logic and say, "I expected better of you, Dion."

I quickly realized that Kitten didn't mind what I said. I had taken it as a sign of lack of intellect. Then I realized that though she usually heard me out, she had very definite opinions of her own. She had a very gentle way of expressing disagreement, however. We had the most polite arguments; a gentle series of 'But don't you think . . . 's or 'But how can that logically follow from . . . 's; nothing like the enraged shouting matches I'd occasionally had with Michael. Suddenly I would find that my position was completely insupportable logically, or that I simply agreed with Kitten's opinions more. It happened most when I was unthinkingly defending Michael's judgments. It was just in small issues like the value of flowers or the necessity of beauty, but occasionally it made me wonder about Michael. I began to realize he had been very puritanical and ascetic, perhaps needlessly so. Well, no one could be right about everything, I consoled myself. Of course my foster father was as fallible as the next man. But what else had he been wrong about?

Was Kitten purposely trying to corrupt me and turn

me against my foster father? Sometimes I still worried about that and tried to be more careful. But then the book we were reading would be interesting, or someone fascinating would come to tea, and, sooner or later, I would find myself in an animated conversation with her, cutting her off before she'd finished a sentence, disagreeing with her as I pleased and, occasionally, unnerving myself by pronouncing that I believed something to be so.

It was disturbing. It was wonderful. I was beginning to realize that there was much more to life than spells and study, more kinds of people than mages and their patrons, that the alternatives went on forever and ever.

I couldn't help liking Kitten Avignon, but the moment I'd start to think of her as just a wealthy intellectual aristocrat, as someone clean, something would happen to remind me that she was a courtesan, a shameless, even joyful, whore. For instance, there was the time she revealed that she had once gone to bed with the Ishtaki Vice Chancellor and that he had paid five hundred ducats for the privilege.

The cold, hard things she said showed her as the courtesan more than any sordid story could have, however.

One day she asked me to look over a ledger for her. When I pointed out several glaring mistakes in adding up the figures, she sighed, closed the book and said, "It is as I suspected. I shall have to sack him. It's a pity. He was a good steward, and I pity his wife and children, but I cannot allow him to make away with my money like this."

Suddenly she turned, gripped my wrist and said as if it was gospel, "Money is the most important thing in the world for a woman, Dion, and she must be tough in keeping hold of it. It doesn't need to be a lot of money, but it is more important than love, more important than anything. Without money a woman is at the mercy of others. She has no say in what she does. You must remember this, Dion. You, of all women, can make your own money. With it you can make your own choices."

It was the voice of a hard scheming woman, a woman who had no faith.

Yet this was also the woman who had started the first hospital for the poor in Gallia and whom I often saw give gold to down and out prostitutes begging at the door of her carriage. One day she could be so hard and the next, order a musician come to play for us because it was "such a soft rainy day and the cello is so delicious with the sound of rain." How could two such different women live together in the same skin?

There was another, more disturbing, change. I had always thought of myself as some kind of mutant boy, but in Kitten's house, my previously small and finicky appetite was so well tempted with all kinds of good foods that I began to put on weight. Suddenly my small bosom became worth considering. The bodice of my robe, designed for a more boyish figure, became tight.

I would catch myself looking in Kitten's mirror, sticking out my chest, and patting down my stomach and wondering if I was nice-looking. They weren't big breasts, but at least it was all in proportion. My eyes were a nice green and my skin was passable, but I didn't like my nose and ...

These were not thoughts for a mage. Nor were the thoughts that sometimes came to me early in the soft grey mornings. I would wake with my own hand cupped around my breast or feeling the smoothness of the sheets against my bare legs and lie there in sleepy sensuality, dreaming that someone lay there with me and held me and loved me. In those moments I was as full of love as a ripe fruit is full of juice, and the thought that I should never have anyone to give all this love to filled me with vague melancholy. I could not imagine ever attracting anyone. Anyway, Michael had always told me that I must at all costs retain my purity. Magic was best pursued by celibates.

As I sat in my room after talking to Simonetti, I felt annoyed with myself. I should have thought of looking for Norval myself. The problem was that I wasted all my curiosity on Kitten Avignon. Indeed, I felt immense satisfaction now because pieces of the puzzle that was Kitten Avignon were falling elegantly into place. There was something so unexpected and yet so real about Simonetti's story. He and Kitten as friends? Perhaps they had been more than just friends once? But then why would the Duke tolerate an ex-lover living in this house? Everyone knew how jealous he was. And what about Simonetti's wife? I'd never met anyone as married as Simonetti. He was always talking about "the wife." He was obviously devoted to her. They lived together in a long low cottage at the back of the house. She was a dark sweet-faced woman, but Genny said she had the bodyguards completely under her thumb. Would he make her live in the same house with a past romance of his? I couldn't see him doing that, debt or no debt.

It was only when the maid came to take me down to Kitten that I realized I'd done it again. I'd spent the whole time wondering about Kitten and none of it thinking about getting rid of Norval.

To my dismay, Rapunzel was in Kitten's room. It was extraordinarily early for her to be visiting.

"Good morning, sweetie," she said cheerily. She was standing peering out the open window, resplendent in scarlet velvet and a huge black hat with a veil. I could hear Kitten rustling round in the dressing room.

"It's afternoon," I said primly.

Rapunzel grinned. "That's because you're not a tart. If you were a tart, you'd have just had breakfast like me, so it would be morning. No?"

She poked her head out the window again, peered about a little, and pulled it back in, catching her hat on the windowsill.

"St. Belkis!" She untangled herself with quick irritated movements.

"God, Pussycat! Can't you open this door?"

"Hello, Dion," said Kitten, bustling out of the dressing room. "Yes, you can open it. The key's about somewhere. In that box over there, I think. Yes that's it."

"I don't understand you, Pussycat. If I had a balcony overlooking the park, I'd sit on it all the time." She grunted as she tried to turn the key. "Look at this. Stiffer than a customer's stiff bits. I bet you haven't used it in twelve months."

I'd never realized it before, but the big window at the front of Kitten's room opened like a door, and outside was a little wrought-iron balcony covered in pots of flowers. I peered out at Rapunzel.

"Bloody geraniums. Lord of All, why waste a good balcony on bloody geraniums?" She turned and saw me standing in the doorway. "She's ignoring me, isn't she?"

Kitten was leafing through a book of flower pictures. She seemed completely engrossed in her own thoughts.

"Seems to be."

"Come on out, Pussy. The weather's quite harmless." She grabbed my wrist and pulled me onto the balcony. "You too."

It was a nice afternoon. Sunny and warm with a soft breeze.

"Look. What a view."

You could see most of the park from the balcony, and at this time of day it was full of people, riding and driving and even just walking. Colorful people in beautiful clothing.

"Nice," said Rapunzel. "Hey! Look! There's Sateen."

She cantered past on a big black horse. She even looked as if she knew what she was doing.

"I didn't know she could ride," I said a little enviously. I'd never imagined Sateen doing anything half so useful.

"Oh yes, all whores ride. It's one of the required skills. You know. Woman astride a piece of flesh. Makes the gentlemen's eyes gleam, I can tell you."

"Are you corrupting poor Dion, Rap?" said Kitten behind us.

"Well . . . I'm just making her hair curl a bit. Why not? A woman's got to do something to pass the time. Come on out here."

Kitten stepped out onto the balcony, and we shuffled about with the pots of geraniums until we were all comfortable.

"What are you so restless for?" asked Kitten.

"Nothing," said Rapunzel. She was leaning over the balcony and peering up and down the street. "I just thought it was a nice balcony day. And I want to see Demoiselle when she comes around. We're going shopping."

Kitten looked at me and rolled her eyes, but said nothing more.

Instead she began pointing out people to me: Lord Verona, the Duke's military adviser, the Duke of Sanza, the Duke's cousin, Lady Sharana, a great patron of the arts . . .

"Hey, there's Hippolyta," cried Rapunzel. A huge woman with pale white skin and fair hair drove past in a carriage. Obviously one of the honey sisterhood.

"Apparently they call her Hippolyta because she's such a rough rider," she whispered to me.

Kitten shouted with laughter.

*Oh dear. Here they go again*, I thought. Kitten blocked my easy escape. I would just have to wait and hope for the best.

Maria came to the window behind us.

"Madame. The packages have come."

"Good. Finally. Rapunzel, you've upset everything coming here like this. You know I don't have visitors till later." She waggled her finger at Rapunzel. "Now be nice to Dion while I'm gone. Don't make her hair curl any more."

"Your wish is my command, Highness."

Kitten smiled at me and was gone. I didn't feel right about leaving now. I'd wait a few minutes and then go in.

"I can't help thinking Pussy's neglecting your education," said Rapunzel. "She's pointing out all the boring people. Now look. There's Bishop Albenz. Now he's worth knowing about. If ever you find yourself alone in a room with him, leave immediately."

He was a fat old man in Bishop's black. He looked exactly as I'd expected.

"Hmm. Now here's somebody interesting."

She sneaked a look over her shoulder. Kitten was nowhere to be seen. "There's Lord and Lady Castille. Lady Castille is the Duke's mistress."

"But I thought Kitten was . . ."

"No, silly. She's just his favorite mistress. Our lord is a man of, one might say, Aramayan habit. He likes to have a few ladies in reserve."

Lady Castille was a proud redhead. She was good-looking, but every inch a lady.

"Do you remember the woman in the carriage with Lady Sharana. That was Viscountess Clemence. She and Lady Castille are currently engaged in a fight to the death for the favors of the Duke. Most amusing to watch. And they'd both love to get their claws into our little Kitten, if she'd only bother to engage them."

"Doesn't Kitten mind all this?"

"No. Of course not, you little innocent. She's a courtesan. It's not her business to mind. Her business is to laugh and wish the man well. And she's no family to see favored, no power base to support. Not like the other two. For them it's life and death. Makes me glad I'm just a whore. Look there's Demi. And look who's with her."

"Who?" said Kitten, sticking her head back out through the window. "Oh. Andre Gregorov. Figures."

It was the tall dark man from the soiree. He was astride a huge coal black horse riding beside Demoiselle's carriage with another man. I'd seen him at other soirees since, but I'd been careful not to let him see me. There was something disturbing about him. He always seemed more vivid than anyone else in the room. And there was something about the way he moved, that long lithe walk of his, even the way he sat astride his horse now . . .

Rapunzel called out and waved.

The group had stopped outside the house. The man looked up at the balcony, straight at me. His gaze was as palpable as a touch. He smiled a little crooked smile and nodded. At me.

I turned my face away. He could not possibly be looking at me. Not with Rapunzel making the noise she was making. And yet, though I didn't look back, I could feel his eyes on me.

Rapunzel waved enthusiastically. "Angels," she hissed, "he is soooo nice."

Now she wanted to get off the balcony, which meant we all had to go back through the window.

"Hurry up," she said impatiently pushing us. "I've got to get downstairs. Demi won't wait."

Inside, Kitten's boudoir had been transformed. Maria was unpacking bolts of cloth from two large hampers and spreading them in piles on all the available surfaces. To my astonishment Genny was home. She was standing in front of a big mirror in the center of the room, a bolt of cloth draped across her shoulders. She turned and smiled as we were bundled back into the room.

"See ya later, Pussy," said Rapunzel, and then stopped and looked around the room. "What's all this?"

Kitten draped herself grinning across Rapunzel's shoulders.

"The clothiers got a consignment of new cloth today and they've sent me a sample. Don't you want to stay and help us look through it?"

Temptation played across Rapunzel's face.

"No," she said, "I must go."

She bade us all farewell and left in a flurry of red velvet skirts.

"No?" said Genny. "Good God! Who would have thought it? What's up with Rapunzel?"

"Hunting," replied Kitten. "She's got one of her things."

"Who's the lucky man?"

"Lord Andre Gregorov."

"Who the hell's that?"

"Foreigner. Tall, dark, and handsome."

"Ishtaki?"

"They say he's Aramayan. I've seen him with the Ambassador. Hope he's not the beginning of some kind of invasion."

"He's not the one who seduced all three Asani sisters?"

"That's him. Anyway, enough of this. Time for . . . NEW CLOTHES!"

She grabbed a roll of tawny brown velvet, flung it out in the air, and whirled about the room with it crying, "Whee!"

"Oh, Madame," said Maria mock reproachfully as one of the piles of cloth began sliding to the floor. Genny grabbed the edge of the now-rocking mirror.

Kitten collapsed in a chair swathed in the velvet.

"They always send me the first samples because I'm such a credit to their fabrics," she said, draping the velvet against her face and fluttering her eyelashes exaggeratedly.

"Humph!" said Genny. "Not in that color you're not."

"You think not?" she said, jumping up and peering into the mirror.

"Hmm, you could be right. It's not the best. Pity. It's a lovely color." She caught my eye in the mirror.

"Aha." She grabbed my wrist and pulled me up to it. "Now young Dion here. This'd be just right for her coloring, don't you think." She draped the velvet over my shoulder and pulled it up under my chin. Maria clapped her hands and Genny said gruffly, "You're right. So it is."

I pulled away from the mirror, but Kitten was merciless.

"Do mages have to wear grey?"

"No," said Genny. "Only students of the college."

"Well we aren't at the college now," said Kitten. "I think it's time our Dion had a new dress. Grey is such a wintery color, Dion, and it's the middle of spring now. How about something new?"

"No, Madame. I don't want . . ."

"Now don't be such a mouse. And don't 'Madame' me. You do need a new dress. You're growing out of that one." She poked me in the chest. "One day you'll burst out of this, and then you'll be sorry. Now how about a nicer color? One that flatters you a little."

Tawny velvet? This felt like the thin end of the wedge.

"Um, I don't want . . ."

"Well perhaps not tawny velvet," she said, guessing the source of my dismay with her usual uncanny accuracy. "It's not very practical for everyday wear. How about this nice dark green?" She draped a wholesome cotton over my shoulders.

"See, it matches your eyes. Makes them look really green."

I dared to look in the mirror.

It was sort of nice.

"Or black perhaps. That suits your pale skin. Don't you think? And we could put a little lace on it. On the cuffs." She draped some slippery black silk over my shoulder. "Oh yes. Very mage. A few sparkly bits perhaps."

I ventured a little turn.

"Or there is red."

I turned on her. Red was a prostitute's color. She grinned and wriggled her eyebrows.

"We corrupters of youth have to keep trying," she said.

Genny laughed and threw her length of material at her.

"You're incorrigible. Don't listen to her, Dion. She's a rotten tease."

Kitten struggled out from under the swath of silk.

"Wouldn't it be wonderful to have a room filled with lengths of silk and satin and velvet? You could go in there and roll about in it all day. And lace, that lovely soft lace, the really expensive stuff." The way she said it I could just picture it. All soft and silky and comfortable. I fingered the shiny black material.

Genny plumped down in a chair, grinning. "She's off now," she said. "Off into cloud Kitten land."

Kitten pulled a face at her. "Stick in the mud."

She turned to me.

"Well, what does Mademoiselle like? The black silk perhaps?"

"Yes, but isn't it very expensive?"

"Hah! Expense! If a courtesan isn't expensive, people start to think she's a failure. What's money? If I run out of money, I'll just ask the Duke for extra."

Kitten danced exhilarated around the room as she said this. It was infectious.

Suddenly she started looking at me intently.

"Right! Now! A gown of highest fashion for Mademoiselle."

She clapped her hands.

"Maria. Mademoiselle's robe. Genevieve Appellez front and center."

"Aye, aye, Captain." Genny jumped up and saluted her.

"You're as big a ham as I am," said Kitten, and nudged her. They both giggled.

"But not as big a pork," grinned Genny.

"You . . . crude thing." Kitten smacked her playfully.

They were very close friends after all. Previously I'd found it hard to picture.

Meanwhile Maria was undoing my robe. The air in the room felt nice and cool on my bare arms.

Kitten wrinkled her nose.

"Heavens, child! What is that you're wearing underneath?"

"It's a petticoat."

"It's . . . calico. Angels! That must be scratchy."

"A little at first."

"It's college issue," piped up Genny.

"Gah. You mages really are ascetic. I can see I should have taken you in hand earlier, young Dion. Calico underwear in my house. The shame."

She spread out the black silk.

"Now. Dion as the epitome of fashion. Ready, Sergeant Appellez."

"Ready and able, Captain."

Kitten threw the silk over my head. It came down over me with a delicious tickly softness.

It began to move.

I cried out.

"Don't worry," called out Kitten. "Genny's just doing a little dressmaking spell. Just stand still."

I could feel the spell. A sort of fizzing tingling sensation on my skin. What a wasteful, frivolous use of magic! And this from Genevieve Appellez, who'd always seemed so sensible. Was this what happened after years of exposure to Kitten Avignon?

The cool silk slid itself smoothly over my skin like some big friendly animal. It felt quite delicious.

"Now a collar," cried Kitten, and the silk parted in the middle and began to mold itself round my neck.

"Boat neck?" said Kitten. "Hmm, let's try ordinary."

"Ordinary is nicer on her I think, Madame," said Maria.

Meanwhile Genny said nothing, her forehead wrinkled with the concentration of the spell.

"A little shape in the bodice. That's right. Yes, that's nice. And the sleeves. Long I think. Maybe elbow length. No. Long."

This went on for some time. To be truthful, I enjoyed it. I was curious to see how I looked, but every time I craned round to look in the mirror Kitten would cry, "Stand still, girl!"

At last she said, "Finished." Genny sighed, and slumped back in her chair.

"Now you can have a look." She put her hands on my shoulders and spun me around. "See, don't you look nice. What an elegant figure you have."

She was right. I was transformed. The dress made me look long and thin, but not too thin. Sort of graceful. I couldn't resist doing a little twirl.

"A lower neckline would really suit," whispered Maria.

I looked at Kitten dismayed just in time to catch her reproving look at Maria.

"No, I don't think so," said Kitten. "This is a dress to be comfortable in, not for showing off the goods.

Now Genny, if you will cut it up, Maria and Netta can sew it together."

Maria began pulling the dress off me. It came away in pieces. She arranged them on the floor in a corner of the room and taking some pins, began to put the pieces together. Kitten rang the bell and ordered tea.

"I think Genny needs some reviving after that effort."

Genny smiled. "I'm passable. It was fun."

But she did look tired. It must have been a hard spell to maintain. I'd certainly never seen a healer do anything so complicated before, but then Genny seemed to have all kinds of extra little spells at her command. Of course, she'd been trained in Sopria. Perhaps the gap between healing and magecraft was not so great there.

Had Kitten actually planned to make me a new dress? It had looked like an accident at the time, but now I thought of it she must have known she was getting the materials and she'd organized for Genny to come home early. Yet it seemed an innocent sort of a plan. As far as I could see its only aim had been to provide me with a new dress, which I did need. I wouldn't have taken the dress if I had been asked beforehand. I felt sorry for that. Kitten had not done me any harm in the months I'd been with her, and I had no business being so suspicious.

We sat drinking tea. Genny seemed relaxed and happy in a way I'd seldom seen her. She was looking through the brown materials, so it seemed she must be going to have a new dress, too. Kitten kept on dancing around, flinging cloth over herself just to feel it sliding off. She'd run her hands over it ("Here, feel this, Genny. Isn't it soft."), sniff deep gulps of its scent ("Doesn't silk smell wonderful?"), and plunge her fingers into the pile of loose pieces which Maria had made on the table.

She must be a very physical person. She was always touching things, the velvety petals of roses, the brocade of the couch, always holding out things to me as she kept doing now, saying, "Doesn't this feel lovely?" or "Smell this!" I supposed I encouraged her. I would nod, instead of laughing at her the way Genny was doing now. She made me aware of a whole world of the senses that I'd only half noticed before.

I had thought that this sensuality was a logical part of a courtesan's life. Now I thought again. If she was so sensitive to sensations, it might only make her life harder. She would feel the repellent stinks of flaccid and unwanted bodies all the more. Surely such a life would deaden your senses to beauty, not awaken them. Perhaps she'd always had clean and handsome lovers like the Duke. From what she had let slip, I doubted it. It would be a good thing if she were able to give up being a courtesan.

There was a knock at the door.

"Madame Sorria, Lord Lucienne, Lord De Angelo to see you," intoned a servant.

"Wonderful! Show them up."

Lord Francis Lucienne was, and had been for several years, Demoiselle Sorria's only lover. Kitten claimed they were like an old married couple. Though Lord Francis was actually married to someone else, they certainly gave the impression of being the most complete allies against the rest of the world. I'd met him before. He was a lazy, good-humored man, who had little to say and thought only of clothes and fashion. He luxuriated in the lively company of the honey sisterhood. The others told me that he was a great and wealthy nobleman. My favorite thing about him was that he always wore the most delicious perfume. Lord Dominic De Angelo I knew less well, but I knew enough of him to know that he was the kind of man who went to the honey sisterhood for companionship only.

Rapunzel had told them of Kitten's shipment and the three of them quickly settled down to admire the fabrics. It was not until the flurry of admiration died down that Kitten asked them where Rapunzel was.

"Does this mean she's had luck with her hunting?"

"Francis. The note. The note," said Demoiselle, smacking Lord Francis' arm.

"I cannot tell you of Rapunzel," intoned Lord De Angelo. "When we left her she was in hot pursuit, but I fear she will not be lucky today. Lord Gregorov has been kind enough to accept my supper invitation and I have the greatest hopes . . ."

"Well as if that means anything, Dominic. He might want something before supper. But he gave us a note for you, Kitten. What have you done with it, Francis?"

"Here it is."

Kitten took it and looked dubiously at it and then at me.

"Lord Francis, why don't you read it out to us? I'm sure it will be just compliments or something."

He opened it, cleared his throat, ran his eyes over the contents, blinked, and began to laugh.

"Go on," cried Demoiselle. "What does it say?"

"Lord Andre Gregorov sends his compliments and his heartfelt admiration to the charming Madame Avignon and begs leave to call upon her tomorrow to discuss the cost of a night with the little one in grey."

I was the only one in the room wearing grey. Dem-

oiselle and Lord Lucienne burst out laughing. Lord
De Angelo screamed in mock horror.

"You wretch," he cried. "You've broken my heart.
I shall never forgive you."

Demoiselle smacked my thigh with her fan.

"Well, well, little one, you've stolen a march on
them all. Oh, Rapunzel will be cross! You have an
admirer."

But Kitten's face was hard. She snatched the letter
out of Lord Francis' hands and ripped it into pieces.

"How dare he? How dare he send us this insulting
note? How dare he make such a proposal to Mademoiselle Dion. Who does he think she is? Does he
think I'm some kind of procurer?"

"Here," she said, thrusting the pieces at Lord Francis, "you can give him this and tell him that he is
never welcome to call on me. Ever."

Oh God! This is what having a ruined reputation
meant. This was my punishment for letting myself be
intimate with these women. This was my punishment
for letting people see me here and with Rapunzel. Oh
God! I should never have . . .

"Dion," said Kitten, "I am sorry . . . Don't let it . . ."

"That's all right, Madame," I said mechanically. "I
should go now. Excuse me."

"Dion . . ." she called after me.

I ran upstairs as fast as I could and locked the door.
As I should always have done. I should never have
let myself be drawn in . . . But it had happened so easily. I'd been lulled into thinking it was all right. Oh
God! Oh God! Now I was ruined. Everybody thought
I was a whore. And it was my fault. I deserved that
they should.

I wrapped myself in my quilt and lay on the bed
shivering. Horrible visions appeared in my head. In-

sults, the people of my village talking about me with that mean contemptuous look on their faces that they had when they spoke of Kitten and her ilk.

There was a knock on the door.

"Dion," said Kitten, "let me in."

I must have been really rattled. I did not even think about telling her to go away. Without getting up from the bed, I used a spell to turn the key in the lock, a wasteful thing I never did.

She came over to me and sat on the bed.

"Are you upset?"

"No."

"Why are you shivering then?"

She put her arms around me. For once I did not mind her touching me. I found I was weeping.

"Oh, my love," she said. "I am sorry. But you must not be afraid. It's only one rude man. Nothing will happen. Nobody knows. The others won't say anything. It will soon be forgotten."

She held me till I was quiet again. It was hard to tell her everything I felt. How could I complain of being thought a whore to one who was? But her murmured words were comforting, persuading me that my life was not completely ruined.

"I shall never allow that man to cross my threshold ever again," she cried. "You will never have to meet him again."

"That would be best," I murmured.

"We will make sure that he is under no illusion. Fancy assuming you were for sale. Do I sell my maids into prostitution? Or Genny? Dion, you must not let it affect you too much. You cannot allow the actions of one rude man to spoil your pleasure."

"No, Kitten," I murmured, but I could not believe I would ever really feel comfortable again among the honey sisterhood. I should have been more careful about being seen in her company. I resolved to be more careful.

Her obvious anger comforted me even if I could not believe the things she said. At least I was not alone in this. She would take care of me and help me in any way she could.

I went to the clinic with Genny the following morning, searching everyone's face for contempt, but common sense and hopefulness quickly prevailed. People were the same as ever, the patients just as respectful, the nuns as quiet, the ladies as foolish and complimentary as ever. I realized my horror of the day before had been an overreaction, and my resolutions about Kitten weakened.

When Simonetti and I returned home later, Kitten met us in the hallway, still wearing her riding habit. Her arms were full of white roses. She handed me the note that had been delivered with them. I read the spiky black handwriting apprehensively, but it was inoffensive enough. It merely offered me the roses as an apology for "My ill-bred behavior of the previous day, stemming from a complete misunderstanding of the circumstances."

"Very polite," said Kitten. "A misunderstanding of circumstances." She looked thoughtful for a moment. "Well, white roses. Virginal. Very appropriate." She pinched my cheek lightly when I pulled a face at her. "I wonder if we will hear from him again or if he will subside into embarrassed silence. Personally I favor the embarrassed silence. He sends nice flowers, but he didn't seem a very nice man."

We did not discuss Andre Gregorov again, but he continued to be on my mind. I could not help wondering that he was interested enough to send an apology of flowers. Had he really wanted me? Perhaps he had written that note in a moment of irresistible passion. It was an oddly appealing thought, though I dismissed it as ridiculous.

It seemed he was on Kitten's mind, too. Erasmus came to begin work on the portrait the Duke wanted of Kitten that very same day. She had insisted I sit with them while he painted.

"Who else will keep us from being dull together?" she said.

I was delighted to be included, but dismayed when she asked casually, "Do you know the Lord Andre Gregorov, Ras?"

"What? In the carnal sense? No, I don't. But I must be the only one in Gallia who doesn't. A man of appetite if rumor doesn't lie, although I suspect it must."

"What does rumor say?"

"That he's been in Gallia less than a month and already has the reputation of being a considerable sexual athlete."

"Girls only?"

"Boys, too, so I hear." He looked sharply at us. "Why do you ask?"

I could not help blushing and turning away.

"What's up?" said Erasmus He was always too perceptive for anybody's good.

Kitten sighed. "He sent our little Dion roses this morning."

"Dion! Lord of All!"

He frowned at me from over the canvas and waved his brush.

"You be careful of him, Dion. Nobody is that much of a rake without being a real bastard. I wouldn't take anything he said too seriously."

I felt unaccountably disappointed. It had always

worried me that Erasmus might start to think of me as a woman and that that would interfere with our friendship. But it was annoying that he didn't even think anybody else could. And it was annoying to think that the man would have sent notes to anyone, the more so because it was probably true.

"Don't be silly you two," I snapped. "You know I've got no interest in that sort of thing."

Yet as I stood in my nightgown that night looking out of the open window, I was disturbed by just how deeply disappointed I was. I held one of the white roses in my hand and stroked its petals, soft and silky smooth. They weren't pure white. Their lips were faintly tinged with pink.

I found that I was stroking my lips with the rose. Its touch was so soft like a kiss, like the feel of a soft touch on my face, my neck, my shoulders, my breasts . . .

I shook myself. That stupid Andre Gregorov. What had happened was bound to be disturbing to anyone. But I must rise above it if I was to do my duty toward my profession and Kitten. I lay down to sleep determined to be sensible.

That night my dreams were strange, full of satin and twining limbs, of painful longing and terrifying release. I awoke to the silky smooth touch of rose petals and found that some had dropped from the roses and fallen on my pillow in the night.

# SEVEN

I saw Andre Gregorov again a few days later as Captain Simonetti and I walked through the town. A man in servant's livery fell into step with Simonetti and whispered something into his ear.

Simonetti stopped short.

"Be off with you," he roared, waving his fist at the man. "D'you think I'm a procurer?"

He took my arm and marched me quickly away. The man smirked and disappeared into the crowd. As we passed the opening of the next street, I saw him running to the side of a tall, dark man astride a big black horse. It was Andre Gregorov. He leaned lithely out of his saddle as the servant whispered in his ear and in that moment caught my eye. I looked away quickly, but not before I had seen him smile over the tossing head of the suddenly restless horse. It seemed to me that that smile was not mocking, but warm.

"Him!" scowled Simonetti "By the Seven, now I'm a chaperone, too."

"What happened?" I asked breathlessly, for we

were still marching along at quite a pace. "What did the man say?"

"Bugger said his master would give me two guineas if I brought you round to meet him. What I don't understand is why he can't just write you a letter?"

I wondered that, too. Then again, if such a man sent me a letter, the correct and logical thing for me to do would have been to send it back unopened. I could have no interest in Lord Andre Gregorov.

Yet I was interested.

As Simonetti said, laughing and digging me in the ribs, "Man must be keen. Two guineas is a lot of money, girl."

For a long time after, whenever we walked in the streets I kept seeing, or imagining I saw, a tall, dark figure on a big black horse. Sometimes he would appear disturbingly in my dreams as well.

He continued to send flowers to the house, too, always white roses, their petals stained with pink. There was never a card with them. Only the roses. I liked them, and for almost two weeks I kept some of them in my room.

Then one day as I sat reading to Kitten, Rapunzel burst in on us, breathless and excited. From the story she launched into it seemed she had achieved her ambitions with Lord Andre.

"My dear!" she said. "Virile! You've no idea. There were three of us . . ."

Rapunzel must have heard about the note, for when she saw me slipping away, she frowned and dropped her voice though she continued talking in an excited undertone. I had heard enough. I told the maid not to put the roses in my room anymore.

*     *     *

The college acted much more quickly than I had thought they would. Only a week after I'd gone to him with Norval's package, I received a letter from the Mage in Charge of Seeking telling me that they'd not been able to find out anything from it.

"All those connected with the paper and the box are now dead," read the letter. "Moreover, one of them placed a backfire spell on the box. Our psychic searcher was lucky to escape with only a light concussion. The spell indicates genuine necromantic connections. We are keen to track down the responsible person with some other artifact, if you can provide one."

"They sound almost enthusiastic," laughed Simonetti when I showed him the letter. "But I don't know that we can give them another artifact. You'll have to ask Kit about that."

Kitten had an important visitor that afternoon, the Duke of Sanza, Duke Leon's cousin and currently his principal adviser, so we did not read. As soon as he left the house, however, I ran upstairs to see her. She wasn't surprised at my request for something of Norval's. Simonetti had already told her we were looking for him and warned her that we might be needing some kind of object.

"I have found something that he did sort of give me," she said. "The thing was it never really belonged to him. It was a gift he had made for someone else. Do you think . . . It's the best I can do, I'm afraid."

I followed her into her dressing room. On the small table in the center was a large, battered, leather folder. She unstrapped it and opened it out. Inside were several leather folders and boxes.

"What's in these?" I asked.

Carefully she pulled out each one and opened it.

They all contained pictures—portraits of Kitten Avignon.

One folder held a collection of wonderful theatrical posters "from the days in Sopria." I'd recognized the names of some of the plays. *To Love and Love Not*, *The Countess of Faro*, and *The Assassin's Tragedy* and also the face of Kitten Avignon in the scenes depicted beneath. There was a small canvas in oils of Kitten as a very young girl in a white dress and another much more recent one of her naked but wreathed in vines as one of the classical goddesses.

Finally Kitten opened a little velvet-covered box and brought out a miniature in a small gilt frame. It showed the top half of her body naked except for a few flimsy draperies. There was something lascivious about the way it dealt with her ivory skin and juicy pink nipples. What was the College of Magic going to make of it?

"It's as much an advertisement as those posters," she said. "Norval had it done for Masud, the man he wanted me to be sweet to. Masud liked me and gave it back to me. Blondes like me are rare in the Western empires. We're believed to be the descendants of Crusaders from the Holy States. My fairness in a land of dark people made me popular. That's why I'm on so many of these theatrical posters, too. The owner knew what sold." She held one of them up and studied it.

"The artist was a special friend of mine and let me have the originals. You know, sometimes I really do take these out to look at myself and wonder if I really am as beautiful as men say."

She caught my eye and winked. "Then I remember that men are so much cleverer than women. So it would be presumptuous of me to disagree, wouldn't it?"

She began packing the other pictures away.

"Why did you give it up? The theater, I mean."

"Leon made me. He didn't feel it was respectable for the Duke's mistress to be treading the boards. I miss it sometimes. Life is much less interesting, but . . . Oh well, being financially secure, that's more than a consolation. I contrive to keep myself amused."

It wasn't the answer I'd wanted. The question I'd really been asking was how she could have stooped to selling her body for money when she was, by all accounts, a perfectly successful actress. Money, though. I supposed the Duke had made her richer than any theater could. It didn't explain the others, the earlier lovers. I knew she'd had a string of them both here in Gallia and back in Ishtak. Every time she spoke of her past I discovered another to add to the total. I suspected that there had never been a time when she'd been just an actress. Some of them could have been genuine love affairs. Did that count as whoring?

I studied the miniature in my hand. What must it be like to have someone you love throw you into someone else's bed? It would be horrible. Had she felt it like a normal person would? Then I realized that I was staring at the picture of a half-naked woman and looked away quickly in case she saw me and thought I was a bit strange. It seemed she thought nothing of it. She took the picture out of my hands quite calmly.

"My other pictures bring back pleasant memories. But not this one. I kept it to remind me not to meddle in politics. Mind you, I'm no angel. I've asked Duke Leon for money, for property, I've influenced him in favor of the New Learning, encouraged him to patronize certain scholars. That's won me no friends. But I've never used my power to influence state policy, and I could have easily. What is it Kramer says? 'A ruler's woman, be she wife or mistress, is the most powerful woman in the land.' "

She laughed and held out her hand to me.

"Look at this nice little trinket."

A bracelet of diamonds and emeralds set in gold was clasped round her wrist. Kitten had the simplest of tastes in jewelry, and this seemed very flashy for her.

"Is it new?" I asked.

"Yes, the Duke of Sanza gave it to me. You'd think he'd know me better by now, wouldn't you?"

"Is he . . . I mean he isn't . . ."

"Oh no! He's not trying to steal me away from Leon. No, not that. He's merely trying to keep 'the most powerful woman in the land' sweet. I suspect it's to do with this alliance with Borgen he's trying to push through. It involves the possibility of the Duke's marriage to Lucretzia Scarleone, and Sanza is naturally afraid I might take a dislike to it. He's been assuring me all afternoon that she is the soul of discretion and can be relied upon to look the other way."

"The Duke's marriage! What will you do?"

"What I always do, my love! Absolutely nothing. You would have thought Sanza would have realized now that I never meddle in policy. I've got no taste for deciding what to do with other people's lives. A good thing, too. Leon has no desire to be anyone's puppet, and if I'd wished to play puppet master, he would have kissed me farewell long ago. But he plays this little game with his ministers. When they suggest something he doesn't like, he says, 'I do not think Madame Avignon would care for that.' You'd think only a fool would believe it, but they come running

round here seeking my support for this or that. Unfortunately for them, when Leon first took me up I
had no idea whom to help, so I adopted a strategy of
helping nobody. And when I found it served, I stuck
with it. So now one of the main outlets of the Duke's
power is a dead place. A person who will have none
of them. Poor silly creatures, spending their lives
groveling and clawing for position. No wonder they
hate me so!"

"But the Duke! Getting married."

"Well, why not," she snapped. "The poor man
must marry someone, and it's never going to be me."

"But . . ."

She smiled sadly and squeezed my arm. "I'm sorry,
my love. It does make one think, doesn't it? It would
be awful to be a new bride in a new country only to
come face-to-face with your husband's mistress." She
sighed. "Perhaps the time is coming for an exit. Exit
the other woman. Conclude with a scene of domestic
felicity."

"What would you do?"

"There is no need for me to do anything. In two
years I have accumulated enough property that I will
never need to take another lover again."

"So if it ended now, you would retire."

Her face took on a naughty look. She flicked my
cheek with her finger.

"Let's not get carried away now," she said. "One
likes to keep one's options open."

It was typical of her. She discussed her situation
with almost-shocking coldness, while at the same time
expressing laudable opinions. Then just as I was coming to see her as a victim of necessity, she would say
something to overturn everything.

\*   \*   \*

The Duke wanted Erasmus' portrait of Kitten to be finished by early autumn when rulers from all over the Peninsula would gather in Gallia for the Princes' Conclave. It was to hang in the Gallery where it could be admired by rival rulers, among the portraits of the other court beauties, many of whom, I later discovered, had also been his mistresses. It was very much Duke Leon's production. He dictated what she wore, how she sat, and even specified that she hold a pink rose in her lap. Kitten snorted at that, if a delicate and beautiful woman can be said to snort.

"The imagery of that doesn't bear looking into," she said, but she submitted calmly to the directions.

She did grumble about the necessity of having to spend two or three afternoons a week sitting still and told Erasmus and me that our companionship was the only thing that made it bearable. Myself I thoroughly enjoyed the sittings or rather I thoroughly enjoyed seeing more of Erasmus, who had become just about my favorite companion in the world.

Perhaps Kitten realized this, for, looking back, she, who had always been the very soul of efficiency up till then, was always running late for her sittings and always sending me to amuse Erasmus till she was ready. Perhaps she was throwing us together. If so, it was a good thing I didn't realize it, for I would have suspected her of matchmaking, and that would have spoiled everything.

Talking to Erasmus was just like I imagined talking to a big brother would be. Somehow I could tell him all the small experiences and anxieties of my day. He was such a good listener that I put up with his occasionally patronizing attitude.

He in his turn would share his fears and travails over what he called his "great masterwork," an altarpiece he was working on for the Church of St. Vitalie, informally known as the church of the New Learning. He would explain to me about religious symbolism in painting or tell me how he was having trouble getting the Tansa's Mother to look gentle without making her look bland.

The thing that really cemented our friendship, however, was our discovery of a shared fascination with the sordid side of life, and especially with the life of Kitten Avignon. You would never have guessed from looking at his blue eyes and clean-cut good looks that this altarpiece painter spent a great deal of time observing and drawing the honey sisterhood of courtesans and other entertainers.

He was tantalized by the riddle of Kitten's past. Where had she come from? What dark secrets had driven such a woman into a life of prostitution? We quickly formed an alliance to find out as much as we could and spent a lot of time speculating and arguing about her. I held to the theory that Kitten was an unhappy courtesan who merely did what was necessary to gain money to flee her savage ex-lover. Erasmus, on the other hand, maintained that there was a large element of choice in her profession.

I felt comfortable saying things to Erasmus I would have felt embarrassed saying to anyone else. It was not surprising that I felt at home with him. We were both Morians from typically strict Morian backgrounds and from a very prudish part of Moria's history. Erasmus' father was a Hierach, an orthodox Church official near Mangalore and had been even more straitlaced than Michael. Erasmus had attended one of the most conservative Church schools in the city. He was only a few years older than me, and for all the superficial polish three years in Gallia had given him, he was secretly just as prudish as I was. But then that was the best thing about Erasmus. He wasn't a courtesan or a Gallian, one of the barely trusted *them*, but a Morian, one of the familiar and understandable *us*.

Though theoretically my role was to read to Kitten while Erasmus painted, what actually happened was that they gossiped, while I, all ears, listened. I felt no ill will at not being a part of the conversation. I'd already found that if you just sat back and listened when Kitten talked to someone, you learned all kinds of juicy things without having to embarrass yourself by joining in.

Erasmus showed a more sophisticated face to Kitten than he did to me and could be relied upon to know all the spicy gossip. Kitten made the most of his knowledge and always asked him lots of questions. Sometimes Erasmus would decide that the talk was too racy for me and shoot her a warning look. Kitten was always amused by this. As she once said, "Darling 'Ras, I think Dion is quite old enough to decide for herself what is suitable for her to hear or not to hear. She'll leave the room when things get too saucy."

During the painting sessions Erasmus worked hard and, I'm sure he thought, subtly to draw Kitten out, "to unravel her mystery," as he once put it. Often she would reward him with an amusing anecdote about her life in the theater or her travels. A few times she made personal remarks about previous protectors ("He had a penchant for the smell of sweat which I never understood") although she could never be brought to name names. Once she even talked briefly about working in a brothel ("Just the once when I was down on my luck, for more boring and slimy work you could never hope to find.'').

Apart from a few stories, we didn't manage to find out anything about her origins. All we knew was that she came from one of the Twin Empires of Aramaya and Sopria. She neatly turned aside any question that she did not want to answer. No matter how much Erasmus planned his campaigns, she always threw his line of questioning into disarray. In fact sometimes from the sparkle in her eyes, I would have sworn she enjoyed fencing with him. It amused her when she shocked him, too.

For instance, once he asked her if Rapunzel was Rapunzel's real name.

She laughed. ''No, it's a sobriquet. None of us use our real names. Think of our poor families. Rapunzel chose Rapunzel because of her wonderful hair. Men love a woman's hair long and loose. In the house where she worked, the owner used to put Rapunzel in the salon with her hair down. Everybody would want to know if she was wearing anything under it, but she wouldn't tell them unless they went upstairs with her. A theater manager saw her there and had the idea of putting her in a pantomime as Rapunzel. He must have been crazy for her. Rapunzel was the title role, but not a very large part. When word got out where she came from, it caught the imagination of the students of the town and they used to fill the pit at night crying 'Rapunzel, Rapunzel let down your . . . ' well, I'll leave it to your imagination to decide what sort of variations they made up. Great for business at the theater, though it was an unusual crowd for a children's pantomime. It got Rapunzel her first private patron, too, so it made her.''

''Why did you choose Kitten?''

"My name is Catherine so people used to call me Kitty when I was a child. Kitten seemed appropriate for a courtesan. So delightful and fluffy and of course such fortunate resonances with the word pussy."

She grinned wickedly at Erasmus, who ducked back behind his canvas to hide his blush. Even I knew what she was on about.

Erasmus almost got something out of her once though.

They had been talking about future projects for Erasmus when he said with studied casualness, "You know, Madame, I'm not sure that doing this painting is so good for my career after all."

"Indeed?" said Kitten. Her tone was indifferent, but I could tell by the twinkle in her eye that she'd recognized the signs. Erasmus was about to ask one of his probing questions.

"Yes. I was to do a portrait of the wife of the Ambassador of Aramaya, but yesterday when I was negotiating the fee with him, I happened to mention that I was painting your portrait and he went all silent and sent me away. And this morning I received a letter telling me my services are not required and enclosing two sovereigns."

"Indeed," said Kitten

"Why do you suppose he did that?"

"I can't imagine. Why don't you ask him?"

Erasmus concentrated on a particularly intricate piece of brushwork.

"They say in the markets that you're his long-lost daughter."

"Do they indeed? How very complimentary to me! Or very rude to him!"

"Well he must know you from somewhere. Otherwise, why would he have looked so startled when he saw you at the opera that time. His wife actually fainted."

"That woman always was a fool."

This was too much for Erasmus.

"Kitten! My dear, you must tell me. I scent some fabulous story attached to this. Romance, babies exchanged in cribs, disgraced children being cast out, long-lost sisters . . ."

"Oh Erasmus. Did it occur to you that perhaps he is just an old flame? The whole thing is quite dull."

"But," he persisted, "if he were merely an ex-lover, why would his wife get so upset at seeing you? No there's more to it than that."

Kitten made a face and said, "Yes, Erasmus, that's right. In fact he is my long-lost brother, and I am the scion of a great noble family, attached even to royalty. Happy now?"

Since this was a ridiculous claim courtesans regularly made, it was clear that he was not going to find out anything more.

Erasmus wisely turned the conversation to more general topics, and they spent a happy hour discussing the sexual predilections of the Duke's brothers.

A few days later I discovered that there had actually been some truth in what she'd said.

It was one of the days Erasmus did not come. It was a dark cold afternoon, promising rain, and we were sitting cosily in her boudoir. I was reading to her from a book called *A Discourse on Unholy Noise*, which for several days had been amusing us mightily with its views on the ungodliness of music.

That day, however, Kitten was pensive. She sat at the window staring out at the garden. Several times I stopped reading to see if she was still listening, but each time she noticed after a moment and nodded me on.

The reason for her distraction arrived midafternoon.

"Prince Pyotr Deserov, the Ambassador of Aramaya, has called," said Maria. "Are you at home to see him?"

Kitten's body stiffened visibly as she answered.

"Yes, send him up. And Maria, is he alone?"

"His secretary Lord Krazhan is with him."

It sounded like the kind of official visit that I would not be wanted at, but, to my surprise, as I rose to withdraw she stopped me.

"Stay, Dion. Please. You must however," she continued in a lower voice, "promise not to reveal any of what you hear in this room this afternoon. Especially not to Erasmus."

Fascinated now, I nodded my head.

"The Ambassador of Aramaya and Lord Krazhan," announced Maria.

Kitten whirled around in a susurration of silk. She was wearing one of her most magnificent gowns this afternoon—all crisp white lace and rose pink flounces—a court gown.

The Ambassador was a tall, fair man. He wore the flowing robes of his country—black and magnificently embroidered with red and gold. His companion was much more interesting-looking. He was also tall, but dark, with the high cheekbones and watchful dark eyes that were supposedly typical of Aramayans. He was much more quietly dressed, but a huge gold diadem, no doubt a badge of office, hung at his neck. The bland smile on the faces of both men, however, was exactly the same.

"Katerina," cried the Ambassador, holding out his

hands. "How good it is to see you. Ah, but I see we are not alone," he said, looking pointedly at me.

Kitten kept her hands firmly clasped in front of her. "You have brought your mage, so I think I should be allowed to keep mine by me."

An Aramayan sorcerer! But why was he not showing the fact by wearing mage's robes?

"And since they will both only listen in through the walls, I think we can dispense with the charade of making them wait outside."

"Katya, Katya, you have learned such plain speaking here among the barbarians. Now come. Are you not pleased to see your countryman after so long? Will you not offer us some refreshments? I have news of our families."

"Of course I am delighted to see you, Pyotr. It's so sweet of you to come and see me. Please do sit down and tell me all the news of home. And you too, Sergei. I see you, at least, do have news. Lord Krazhan. You have been doing well for yourself. Very well for a client family."

The mage bowed, but his bland smile slipped slightly at that last remark. Kitten directed him to a straight-backed chair directly opposite mine and we all sat arrayed as if we were opponents. Kitten rang for refreshments.

"Well, and how is my mother? I heard of Father's death while I was in Sopria."

"Yes, alas poor man. Already so ill and so many shocks . . . But your dear mother is still well and living in the convent of St. Namestaki."

"And Shree Tarko?"

"Passed to Vassily of course. But you would be pleased to see it now. He has done great things with it. The model estate, and the house has become quite beautiful with a few repairs."

"I hope Vassily remembers that it is still legally my estate."

"But in Vassily's wardenship, my dear Katya, during your exile. By the way, I'm sure Vassily would send his love if he knew I had seen you."

"You seem to have been sadly ill informed, Pyotr. I believe there are other Aramayans who have known for some time that I was here. You must take a close look at your sources of information."

"I feel sure you are right, my dear. By the way, I have the delightful pleasure to tell you that Vassily is now the father of five fine sons."

"How nice for him. And how is . . ."

My attention was suddenly torn away from this verbal fencing match. Lord Krazhan's mind was attempting to probe into my own. To do so without asking was a serious breach of magely etiquette, on a par with measuring a woman's breasts by just grabbing them. Outraged, my mind pushed his away so roughly, that his chair tilted back and he grabbed the table to steady himself.

"Dion?" said Kitten quickly.

"I beg your pardon, Mademoiselle," said the mage.

At that moment Maria came in with the refreshments and apart from the usual hospitable inquiries, silence fell on the party until she had gone.

"Well, Katya," said the Ambassador pinging the fine crystal of the wineglass with his finger, "you seem to have done very well for yourself among the barbarians. Who would have thought it? No doubt you have lands?"

"Yes, four considerable estates now, owned in my own name. I consider my fortune to have been made."

"That must be some consolation. I'm surprised His Lordship hasn't offered you one of his little titles."

"His Grace did. But I judged it wiser not to accept. I'm surprised to see you here, Pyotr," she continued, rising from her chair and beginning to pace the room. "I hardly know how to judge your presence. Is it a sign you are in favor with the Emperor or disfavor? What business can the mighty Aramayan Empire possibly have with the 'barbarians' of the Peninsula?"

The Ambassador was sprawled casually back in his chair, his ankles crossed in front of him.

"You need have no fear on that score, Katya. The Emperor still holds our family in the highest esteem, despite . . . Well, it was Vassily's idea to invoke the old ties between our land and these outlanders."

"What is it exactly that you mean by old ties, Pyotr?"

"Why Katya, the ties that have always existed between Aramaya and the countries of the Peninsula since Aramayan missionaries brought civilization and Tansism to the barbarians who lived here. The same ties that existed generations ago when Crusaders came from the Peninsula to protect the borders of the Holy Motherland from the Soprian infidels."

"Which you wish to evoke again for exactly the same reasons? I think you may find those ties are a little too old to be reinvoked, Pyotr."

"So you say, yet everywhere I go I am told of the popularity of the New Learning, New Learning which stems from Aramaya, and which, I'm told, you, sweet coz, have been instrumental in promoting. It seems to me that the relationship between Aramaya and the Peninsula might still in reality be that of mother and child."

A slight frown flickered across Kitten's face at the mention of the New Learning.

"If the New Learning of the Peninsula does draw on the Aramayan tradition, it draws equally on that of the Soprian 'infidels.' And it has characteristics all its own which both the old empires would do well to study. Oh no, the Peninsula has outgrown its childhood, I assure you. How else can you explain the fact that the Holy States have sided with Sopria in your latest quarrel over Marzorna?"

"Precisely, dear cousin. The Soprians have been typically cunning in exploiting the Patriarch's fears of Aramayan domination and have gained a terrible advantage over us. Aramaya must try to right that imbalance if she is to regain her rightful lands."

"So you look to exploit the natural competition between Gallia and the Patriarchy by coming here. You are wasting your time. The Duke has no interest in wasting men and money in foreign wars."

"So he has informed me. But I feel sure that I could persuade him to change his mind. With your help, dear cousin."

Kitten stared out the window. "With my help?"

"Indeed. While I admit to have been taken aback to have met you here so unexpectedly, Katya, you must see that God has given us a tremendous opportunity, in placing you in such an . . . influential position."

She turned to face him.

"And why should I influence the Duke to come to your aid against Sopria? What possible advantage could there be in his sending men and money to a war which can bring him no conceivable advantage and, indeed, will upset the Ishtakis who trade extensively with Sopria? And why would I want to jeopardize my position with the Duke by attempting to push him into a course of action which he has already told me he is adamant against?"

"Because, my darling Katerina, you are an Aramayan. And however much you may love these charming little countries of the Peninsula, you cannot wish to end your days among barbarians. If you were known to have given such help to your country, I'm sure the Emperor would forgive all. And if that were so, your return would be possible."

"That is certainly a tempting thought. But no. I do not think I would wish to give up my lands, four estates—remember, Pyotr, four good estates—just for a chance to return home and languish for the rest of my life in some convent, even if it had the advantage of being an Aramayan convent."

"Katya, Katya. The Emperor can recognize good service just as well as any petty Peninsula princeling. I'm sure he would not be ungenerous to one who helped him so."

"Even to the point of returning Shree Tarko, for instance?"

A look of vague discomfort crossed the Ambassador's face.

"Who can say? Really, Katerina. These kinds of negotiations were better left till later."

"But even with my lands, Pyotr, I would still be in disgrace."

"I'm sure my mother would be happy to oversee your reentry into Aramayan society. A good marriage, perhaps."

Kitten's face showed amusement.

"Really Pyotr! Now that would be worth seeing."

"Katya! This is a serious matter. Even at this moment Patriarchal troops are embarking for Sopria. Can you not see the matter is desperate?"

"I don't see what I can do about that, Pyotr."

"All you need to do is to persuade the Duke that his support now would result in our support later should he wish to expand his own realm."

"I believe the Duke is aware of that offer. He really did not seem interested in it. Aramaya has such a poor reputation when it comes to honoring treaties with small allies, you see. So I don't see that I can change his mind on this matter."

The Ambassador's face, still smiling, took on a mean look.

"Still I think you would be wise to try."

"Would I? I've no wish to see Gallia used up in your endless stupid war with Sopria. How can the Emperor be so foolish as to want Marzorna? Those people are nothing but trouble to anyone who conquers them. Why don't you go home and advise the Emperor to let the Soprians have it? Then they can waste men and money on keeping it under control."

The Ambassador stood up. He made no effort to disguise his anger now.

"You are wasting my time, Katerina. An amusing opinion, but hardly very practicable. I suggest you leave the policy to men and concentrate on your own special skills of persuasion. And since your loyalty to your country is, as ever, insufficient to make you support us, I must tell you that I am quite prepared to go to the Duke and tell him all about your treasonous activities with Norval back in Aramaya. I feel sure he would be interested to find what kind of snake he is nurturing in his bosom. Come, Lord Krazhan."

"Then you would be wasting your time, Pyotr. The Duke already knows all about Norval. I've always found the truth to be the best policy. He knows all about my past. He even knows about how you and

Vassily threw me into the arms of the Empress all those years ago. So you can imagine he has a very fair idea of your sincerity."

"What?" Shock was written all over the Ambassador's face.

"Yes, dear cousin. Shall I ring for a maid to show you out? I might add that although I am a loyal enough Aramayan not to repeat some of the very unwise things you have said here today, should I find you are telling tales about me, I shall quite cheerfully tell the Duke how you referred to him as a barbarian and a, what was it, 'petty princeling.' "

"You treacherous bitch," yelled the Ambassador. His hand lashed out to grab Kitten's wrist.

"No!" I cried. I thrust out a hand. There was a flash, and a prickly sting of power surged out of me.

The Ambassador yelped and staggered back.

"Witch," he screamed at me. "Sorceress."

Kitten grabbed my hands in hers.

"Dion! No!" she yelled. Her hands were trembling.

"It's all right," she went on more calmly. "He's just throwing one of his little tantrums."

The Ambassador lifted his hand again, but this time Lord Krazhan caught it.

"My Lord. Don't!"

"Now, Pyotr," said Kitten. "You've upset my little friend, which is a very unwise thing to do. I think it's time you left us. Don't you?"

"Quickly, my lord," hissed Lord Krazhan. He had grabbed the Ambassador's other arm. He was holding his staff protectively in front of them. There was panic on his face. I was astonished to see how frightened he was. Frightened? Of me?

"Don't think I'm going to let you get away with

this, slut," screamed the Ambassador, as the mage dragged him quickly toward the door.

"Don't worry, my dear. I would never dream of underestimating you."

No one could have been more surprised than me at the way I had defended Kitten. The bolt of heat had slipped out in a moment of intensity as I raised my hand to fend the Ambassador off. I had not consciously sent out my power. Once again I had lost control like some silly child.

"Thank you for coming to my defense like that," Kitten said.

"I didn't mean to," I said then realized how that sounded. "I mean I didn't mean to hurt anyone. I hope I did nothing wrong."

"Of course not." She smiled. She didn't seem in the least disapproving. She took her hands off mine and shook herself. "Well that was an unpleasant interlude. Let's have a fresh cup of tea."

She picked up the teapot and began to pour. I just stood staring at my hands and thinking of the blind terror that had been on Krazhan's face.

"Dion?"

"Mmm."

"I'm sorry to go on about this, but you really must not tell Erasmus about what happened today. It might be dangerous for him to have such knowledge. Do you understand?"

I did understand. The Ambassador had shown his nature very clearly. But I couldn't help being curious.

"Was that man . . . your brother?"

"My brother-in-law. We're cousins, too," she said. "I suppose I owe you an explanation."

"Your brother-in-law. Then his wife is your sister. The woman who fainted."

"Nothing as innocent as that. Now promise me you won't tell Erasmus any of this."

I nodded.

"He's my ex-husband's brother."

I stared at her aghast. "You were married!"

"Yes. But I'm barren, you see. There is no worse sin for an Aramayan woman."

"Barren?"

"A riding accident. Oh, I was wild and stupid in those days. I was the favorite of the Empress. I thought the world belonged to me. I should have been more careful, shouldn't have jumped that fence. Shouldn't have been riding at all. When I came off and lost the baby . . . It would have been a son. Vassily never forgave me for 'killing his child' and when he found I couldn't have another he divorced me without a second thought. And remarried as is usual. I couldn't believe how quickly he stopped loving me . . ." She sighed.

I felt so sorry for her all of a sudden. I put my hand on her arm. She smiled ruefully and patted it.

"I was only a little older than you, Dion, and there I was on the scrap heap. A divorced woman cannot remarry. I was sent in disgrace to live with two of my husband's devout elderly aunts. Also on the scrap heap. So when Norval came along . . . Lord of All. That house was a living hell. Nothing but knitting and praying, knitting and praying. And I was never going to be able to leave it as long as I lived. Even if Norval had been a fat old lecher, even if he'd been Bishop Albenz, I would have run away with him."

She was the courtesan again. She stood up.

"So now Pyotr's here as Ambassador. Perhaps I should be more sympathetic if my country is in such danger that it's prepared to lower itself to sending an

Ambassador. But it seems insane to involve Gallia in Western politics. Especially with the Aramayans. I mean you can see how they regard the Peninsula. I was very glad you were there. And it was a pleasure to see horrible Sergei so terrified."

She bought back all the confused feelings I'd had before.

"But why was he so scared?"

She was startled.

"No doubt he'd not realized the extent of your power. He comes in thinking he'd just got to face some junior mage and he suddenly discovers that you can annihilate him if you wish." She laughed. "That's the beauty with you. You don't look like a great mage."

"But I'm not a great mage."

"Yes, you are. Of course you are!"

She was looking at me sharply.

"You're a modest soul, aren't you. Or could it be that you really don't realize . . . ? Dion, why do you think I asked for you to protect me?"

"Because I am a girl and because I am a mage and that's a rare thing."

She laughed. "Only on the Peninsula, Dion. You silly thing. It's because you were the most powerful mage I could find."

What on earth did she mean? Was she trying to fool me?

"When I knew Norval was coming, I had a diviner look in the Bowl of Seeing for all the most powerful mages in the country. And he came upon you. You were a surprise. I sent an agent to the college to question the Dean about you. And he agreed with what the diviner had said. You really are extremely powerful. More than a match for Norval."

I just stared at her. One part of me realized with a kind of blinding light that everything she had said was true. I was very strong. I could do things. It was just that I had never realized it before. Suddenly it seemed so ridiculous. The thing was, it was very difficult to get any idea of how your own power compared with that of others, without either rudely probing their mind as Lord Krazhan had tried to do today, or directly competing with them. Michael had never allowed me to compete with others.

"All our discipline must be aimed at competing against ourselves," he had said. "There is no point in making comparisons. Mages' gifts are too varied."

Of course at the college the students had been very competitive. The quadrangle would blossom with illusions as the young mages sought to impress each other. Michael would always snort at these demonstrations and say something sarcastic about young men.

"They'll learn," he said. "They'll learn."

I was too shy to take part in those informal competitions, so I'd never known, indeed never particularly cared to know, how my abilities compared with theirs. But now I remembered them. They'd never done anything I couldn't do. Nobody, not even the tutors ever had. And I remembered what had happened with Prelate Newsanhausen and Ryart Dashalle. That had been easy. I was probably very good at magic. Very good indeed.

I was suddenly filled with an enormous whirling joy as if the sun had blazed forth laughing and singing along my veins. It was a better feeling than the best spell I had ever cast.

"Could it be that you really are unaware of your own abilities?" said Kitten.

"I never thought I was much good . . ."

She laughed, flung her arms round me, and kissed me on the cheek.

"Well congratulations! Here." She pulled a gold and diamond bracelet off her wrist and balanced it on top of my head. "I now crown you 'The Great Mage.' Oh, look at you!" She shook me gently and the bracelet slid onto the floor. "You're all dazed and amazed. It *is* amazing. Imagine not knowing your own strength all this time."

She laughed.

"You know," she went on, "I remember that story about the little cloth ball you told me. Magic must be instinctive with you. You seem to be at your best when you're not consciously thinking of a spell."

"I suppose I am."

It had never occurred to me that this might not be the same for everyone, but indeed most of the students at the college had not known of their abilities until they had sat the stringent tests that the college ran to find talented youngsters. Every summer the older members of staff traveled the country searching for potential students.

"How can it have happened, that you remained so long unaware of your power?" said Kitten.

In a way it was hard for me to understand too, though at the same time the thought was still so new, I scarcely believed in it. How had it happened? I told Kitten about Michael and his ideas on competition. But even as I spoke I knew there was more to it than that. I began to talk to Kitten about Michael and my upbringing.

It was the first time I had really talked about him to her. In the back of my mind I still looked upon the two of them as natural enemies and so, out of loyalty,

I'd avoided exposing him to her criticism. Now I told her all about our life together, about my feelings after his death, about my certainty that he was disappointed with me. She listened. Her face had its unreadable expression on again. Occasionally she would break in with questions like:

"Why do you think you failed him?"

"He said so. I think. Often he would say . . . I don't know. He adopted me to prove that you could teach women advanced magic. I know he concluded that you couldn't."

Or when I described the sorts of things Michael had said to me and how he'd shaken his head often over my flightiness and my slapdash ways:

"I'm afraid your foster father knew nothing of children. Children are slapdash and flighty."

"But . . ."

"Well are you like that now?"

"I still find magic very tiresome. The little fiddly rituals irritate me. What's that if it's not flightiness?"

"Sounds like sense to me. The difference between children and adults is that adults accept that they must do boring necessary things. It's not that they are suddenly blind to them. Genny's often telling me how repetitious spells can be."

Everything took on a different meaning when brought out and aired under her gaze. Like Michael's constant fussings and warnings against being too proud and too sure and letting it lead me into carelessness or into arousing the envy of men. I'd always assumed he did it because I wasn't any good, but now Kitten pointed out they were just the kinds of things an anxious parent would say to someone who was good in order to make them cautious.

"Your foster father was a very wise man," she said.

"But we all have our limitations. You admit yourself that sometimes he was wrong about things. All your life he told you who you were, like all parents do. You say yourself he was always sparing with praise. The result was that he made you ignorant of your own worth. But no matter what has gone before, it is time now for you to stop taking his estimation as the truth and find out for yourself what you can and can't do. We cannot always be letting people tell us who we are. How can they know the answer when they don't see the world through our eyes?"

Her green eyes were intense.

"When I look at you I don't see someone who is hopelessly flawed. I see a young mage very unsure of herself, but full of potential, unlimited potential. Unlimited because she is untried and nobody can guess at what her limits are. I've seen you cast spells without speaking a word. How many mages do you think can do that?"

Despite myself I was exhilarated by her words. It was as if I'd been afraid to stretch out inside my own skin till now, for fear it would be too small and split under my pressure. Now suddenly I had, and I found it so enormous that I could wave my arms wildly about. I wanted to ask Kitten . . . I'm not sure what I wanted to ask her. I felt a little afraid and wanted her to tell me what to do.

Maria knocked at the door at that moment.

"Madame, I have laid out your blue silk. The carriage will be here in half an hour."

Twilight. We had been talking all afternoon, and suddenly I noticed how dark it was in the room.

"Heavens! Is that the time? Dion, I have to go. Leon hates to be kept waiting." She squeezed my hand. "Thank you again for this afternoon."

She leaped up and rushed into the dressing room. I could hear her and Maria scrambling around. I felt languid and disoriented as if I had woken from a long sleep. I just sat on the sofa. Kitten seemed to understand, for when she bustled out of the dressing room again she said, "Why don't you just sit quietly for a bit? Maria will bring you some more tea. Seems to me you've got a lot to think about."

She patted my head, bade me farewell, and whirled away, with Maria running behind dabbing a last few spots of powder on her back.

Maria did bring me more tea. I sat alone for a long time in that friendly room, till it was completely dark and the only light came from the warm embers in the fireplace.

I cannot describe the turmoil in my mind. My thoughts were singing and whirling. Could it be that I was powerful? I could not believe that I had never realized this before. I remembered the exultation, the exhilaration I felt when magic flowed through me. It was so obvious. So obvious. My head filled with an intoxicating vision of myself, my arms upstretched while power flowed from me and the sky cracked open. Suddenly I felt that there was nothing I could not master. I felt full of strength. And free.

The handkerchief that I must have been pleating and repleating between my hands tore. My muscles were taut with the intensity of my thoughts. I looked down at my hands and laughed. I made the handkerchief whole again in what Michael would have called a wanton waste of magic, jumped up, and threw it up in the air. It would not stay that way once I had forgotten it, but who cared? I wanted to go into the garden and run up and down the paths waving my arms about.

At that moment I heard a noise in Kitten's bedroom.
A loud thud followed by a slow scratching sound.
My hair stood on end.

Maria had long gone, leaving the other rooms in
darkness, and it was quiet except for that sudden
sound. I lit a candle and went reluctantly into the bedroom to look.

The room was still, the velvet curtains like thick
dark shrouds in the candlelight, containing great
holes of shining emptiness that were the mirrors. I
wondered how Kitten could sleep in this room. It was
eerie. Every time I moved, I caught a glimpse of
movement in the corner of my eye from my reflections
in the mirrors.

A box of jewelry had fallen off the dressing table.
It had come open and rings and earrings had fallen
out on the floor. I picked up the box. It was unda-
maged. I put it on the table and began to put fistfuls
of jewelry back into it. Some of the pieces were beautiful, studded with gems that sparkled in the candlelight. I stopped to admire one beautifully wrought
gold and ruby ring in the candlelight.

A huge voice spoke.

"It could be yours."

Demon eyes looked into mine. His face was pressed
up against the glass of the mirror, bare inches from
my own.

I jumped back and squawked.

"Hello, little girl," said Bedazzer. "Not laughing today, are we?"

I could only see his chest and head this time. It
made him enormous. Very close. How had he got
here? I hadn't been thinking of him, had I?

He laughed. "A delightful thought, my dear little
girl. But no. You do not need to think of Bedazzer to

have him near. I watch. I am always watching you."

"Always?" I croaked. My mouth was so dry the words could barely come out. Dignity, Dion, Dignity.

He waved a taloned hand.

"I am always at any gateway. I am always with you. Tonight I showed myself. I felt your little mind running round and round. You needed Bedazzer. I came."

He put one hand on his hard chest. His skin was like tanned hide. I could almost feel it.

I gulped. My heart was going fast. Don't be afraid. He can't get in.

"You are right, there is no need to be afraid. You are in your world. I am in mine. I cannot come through unless you help me. You are perfectly safe."

As a tiger would say before he ate you. What he said must be true, however, for if he were in our world, he would be out plundering our universe for human life. The way demons did.

We stared at each other.

"I felt your thoughts." His voice was enormously deep and husky. It echoed in my bones. It had the compulsive pull of the point of a pin to the fingertip. "You thought you were a god for a minute there, didn't you, little girl. You discovered that which they have been hiding from you. They tried to keep you weak and ignorant. They denied you your birthright."

"They?" But I knew whom he meant. Michael and the tutors at the college. They must have known. Why had they never told me? They were sparing men with praise, of course. And Michael had been afraid for me . . .

"Ha!" yelled the demon. Suddenly he was in every mirror in the room and on the roof. I was surrounded by Bedazzers, all snarling at me with voices like the yowling of cats and the roaring of wolves. Voices like blows.

"He was afraid of you, little girl. Afraid and jealous. How could a mere girl have more power than him? He was outraged. Terrified. He needed to control you, so he kept you ignorant, kept you away from other mages, put you down, made you feel useless all the time, so that you'd never think to yourself, *I did well. I'm good at this.* Why did none of them ever tell you? None of those friends of Michael's? They all knew. They all kept you a fool. Don't you see it was a conspiracy of silence? Because they were all afraid of you. They had to control you. You were too powerful. And, worst of all, you were a woman. And mages despise women."

I was huddled on the cold bed, sweating and shivering. Dazed. It was terrible. It was true. True. Why had they never told me? Could Michael . . . ? Had Michael . . . ? Bitterness against him filled me. Bitterness and a sense of betrayal.

Without a pause the demon's voice dropped and became soft and caressing, almost like a touch.

"That time, the first time I came to the gateway and you resisted me so easily . . . I felt it then. I knew then that you were one of the greatest mages the world has ever seen. You could be a god. You could have anything you wanted. You could rule the world."

I wondered if he knew how empty ruling the world seemed. Especially now.

The room was full of a million penetrating whispers.

"Yes," he hissed. "Ruling the world seems nothing to you now. But soon you will get tired of people always telling you what to do. You will get tired of them treating you like a fool. You will need to prove yourself so that they will honor you for what you are, care what you do. Are you going to be nothing, unnoticed, forever?''

He spread his hands and leaned against the mirrors. His fanged face took on a look of pleasure. He looked like a big friendly dog. My big dog.

''When the time comes for you to be revealed in all your glory, I will be there. To help you. To serve you. I will lead you on journeys through the wonders of many worlds. It will be an alliance between two great powers, those of your world and those of mine. Can you not see it, little girl? It will be a thing of burning greatness.''

He pulled back from the gateway and, behold, there were the swirling stars, no longer hard and cold but hot and glorious, plunging toward me from every side, closer and closer till they filled the world with their blinding, burning brilliance, searing through my mind.

Greatness. I saw myself uplifted, shining, reaching out, encompassing everything. Freedom, release, joy everlasting.

He was above me in the mirror, pressing down against it, eyes half-shut. Ecstatic.

''It would be deep pleasure for me to have a mistress of great power,'' purred that deep voice. The way he said mistress made me tingle between the legs. ''I will always be here for you. Waiting.''

The cold surface of the mirror was hard against my face. I was there pressed against him, up against the ceiling. If only I could reach through and touch . . .

I screamed and pushed away. Fell back on the bed with a bouncing thump.

He grinned toothily and licked his lips and reached out and ran his hand down the mirror.

"Don't let fear deny you pleasure," he purred. Again I wanted more than anything in the world to touch him. I reached out again. The familiarity of the gesture, the memory of how I'd reached out last time broke the spell. I snapped back. Words came to my mind, Words of Power, Words of Dispelling. I gathered all my strength and spoke them.

He reared back, but he was laughing.

"Very well, little girl. I shall go if you desire it. You are a match for Bedazzer." Laughter echoed all around me and was suddenly gone.

I could hear the candle flicker in the silent bedroom.

I got up and ran as fast as I could.

All I wanted was the safety of my mirrorless bedroom, though I knew now that safety was an illusion. I lay on my bed, all the candles in the room lit, weeping from sheer turmoil and fright. Then I thought of what he had told me about Michael, and I wept because it seemed so true. Had it been true? I had always trusted that my foster father had meant the best for me. What if he had actually been seeking to harm me? Far better to believe him mistaken as Kitten had said, than to believe he had lied. But I remembered him telling me I was weak, foolish, capable of being stupid. He had never liked me.

I had forgotten my sense of power. I lay there for hours, sobbing, racked with thoughts, unable to decide one way or the other, until near dawn, when I fell into a feverish sleep full of that blinding light and that soft purring voice.

I awoke still distressed. It was hard to concentrate on the eight o'clock ritual, but the magic helped me think more calmly. I had been so happy before the demon had come. He had robbed me of my moment of pure joy. Was that why he had chosen that moment

to appear? It was a cruel, cruel thing and that seemed
right for a demon. It lied, too. Of course it lied. What
it had said about Michael could not be true, no matter
how well it fit the facts. The very fact that the demon
had said it, made it a lie. I tried to take comfort from
that thought. I could not. Oh I was a fool! Michael
had been right about me. I could not bring myself to
disbelieve the demon. He was too clever. He could
read my mind, play on my fears. I must never let him
speak to me again. I would dispel him immediately.
Next time.

There would be a next time. I was sure of that. Once
again the promptings of good sense told me to go to
the Dean and tell him all of it, but the demon had
sown too much doubt for me to do that. I was more
reluctant than ever to go and reveal my mistake to
them, to trust them and put myself in their power.

# EIGHT

The thought that Michael might purposely have kept me from knowing my own abilities tormented me. He must have known that I was powerful. How could he have not? To leave a mage ignorant of his own power was an act of breathtaking irresponsibility, leaving the mage open to corruption by malign forces. My ignorance had probably attracted the demon to me. I must always have felt that deep down Michael had really cared for me, for now I was shattered by my suspicions. Though I tried to conceal my distress, even Erasmus asked me twice during the next few days, if there was something wrong.

Kitten, too, asked me if something was wrong, but she did so cleverly, catching me at a weak moment so that I burst into tears and told her what I feared about Michael. She listened to my suspicions calmly and then, as was her way, she reinterpreted the situation so that it was made more bearable.

"We may never know now what motivated your

foster father to keep you ignorant. But I cannot believe he was a malicious person," she said. "He could have taken far more advantage of your gifts than he did. From what you have said of him he seems to me merely to have been extraordinarily muddled in his thinking. Perhaps he did not realize the extent of your ignorance. Perhaps he cultivated it because he believed it would protect you. There are lots of reasons for what he did. You must never forget that however badly he did it, he did the greatest thing possible for you. Think if you had been left to grow up in that country inn, not only in poverty but in some wretched half-life."

"That's true," I agreed thoughtfully. "My unused power would have been a curse to me. I would have been easy prey to all kinds of unscrupulous beings."

"He must have cared something for you. Otherwise, why didn't he just send you back to that inn when he'd finished studying you?"

"He used to bring me out and make me do magic for his friends," I muttered. "I was like his performing dog."

"Well then, he must have been proud of you," she said.

This was not the sort of line I had expected her to take. Suddenly everything seemed less black-and-white. I was oddly comforted. Demons *are* liars, I told myself.

I was comforted too by her suggestion that I talk to the Dean of the college about Michael's actions. But while I was still trying to find the courage to approach the Dean, another event cast all thoughts of myself from my mind.

For suddenly, in early summer, Gallia found itself in the grip of a plague, the mysterious and terrible disease that was to become known as "Prostitutes' Sickness," or more commonly as "Whore Sleep."

The sickness first appeared in late spring as the weather became warmer. The first case I saw was a young woman, a laundress and occasional prostitute, who was carried into the clinic by two strapping wharf laborers. They explained with a mixture of embarrassment and ribaldry that one of their friends had hired the woman for the night and awoken in the morning to find her collapsed outside the door.

The woman remained heavily asleep all through our examination.

"This is a most peculiar sickness," said Genny. "I've seen four or five cases already. There doesn't seem to be any actual illness, no fever or inflammation. The patients' skins are pale, there are dark hollows under the eyes, their pulses are slow. They all seem to remain in an almost-unwakable sleep for about twenty hours of the day. It looks like nothing so much as extreme exhaustion, doesn't it? Now take a look through this."

She held out the magic lens she used for looking at patients' life forces. I peered through it. Instead of the golden glow of a healthy person, the young woman was surrounded by the thin brownish shadow usually associated with the dying.

"She's barely alive!"

"Exactly, but where did all her life force go? It can't have just disappeared. If this woman is like the others, there was no sign of her being sick last night." She sighed.

"If you knew the trouble I had yesterday persuading one boy's father that he didn't just need a good beating for being lazy."

Genny's theory was that the sickness was the result

of vampirism. Despite the strong hold of magic on the Peninsula, vampirism was not unknown. Even I had seen victims of it.

"But people bitten by vampires are short of blood, not life force," I protested. "This woman shows no sign of blood loss."

"True," said Genny. "And I've not been able find any bite marks. Nonetheless, I have informed the College of Magic that I suspect there is vampire activity in the city. It seems the most logical explanation for this strange loss of life force. There could easily be forms of vampirism that we've never come across before. If the college searches the city for undead, with any luck they'll be able to find the culprit before there are any more cases."

Unfortunately Genny's hopes proved false. The number of victims we saw increased daily until, just after my second brush with the demon, we realized that we had some kind of plague on our hands. If there were vampires in Gallia, they were amazingly heavy feeders, for in the early weeks of summer we sometimes saw as many as sixty new cases of the illness a week.

At that time most of Gallia was still unaware of what was in its midst. Though Genny took care to inform the palace authorities and the College of Healers, there was little concern over the illness at first. Ours was the main clinic for treating such cases because most of them came from the poorest elements of society. The fee-charging clinics saw very few cases. In those early days people dismissed it as some kind of venereal disease, for many of its victims, though by no means all, were indeed prostitutes of one kind or another. This was the first time I came across the attitude that a sickness that cleansed the city of prostitutes was not an entirely bad thing. Scratch a supposedly easygoing Gallian and like as not underneath was someone as dour and mean-minded as any Morian Burning Light follower. Only the realization that four months before I might well have shared something of that attitude tempered my outrage at this opinion.

Many of the victims were not in fact full-time whores, but fishwives or weavers or such, women and boys who sold themselves on the river docks to get money for some crisis or other. Many of them were brought in by anxious families or friends when they were suddenly unable to be woken in the morning. God knows how many other plague victims had no one, or were dismissed as being drunks, and starved and died unnoticed among the dockside wool bales and warehouses.

No one recovered from the disease; that was its worst aspect. Its victims slept for most of the day and dragged themselves round in an exhausted haze for the few hours they were awake. Their bodies could not seem to replace the life force that had so suddenly disappeared. Since they were often the principal breadwinners of their families, Whore Sleep bought great suffering to the docklands. But it was not the patients with families who were our real problem. They, at least, could be cared for at home. The disease bought out the worst in some people. Some patients were abandoned by their loved ones as soon as a diagnosis had been made. The clinic beds were soon filled with such sad cases. The disease's reputation for being venereal also meant that more than one patient appeared at the clinic bruised and bleeding from a severe beating.

By early summer, my work at the clinic became an

almost–full-time occupation. Summer meant an increase in normal fevers, anyway, and a corresponding increase in work for us. I took as many of the ordinary patients as I could manage, to leave Genny free to work with the plague patients. Apart from brief trips home to perform the protection ritual, I was at the clinic from the very early morning till late at night. Sometimes Genny would even fall asleep at her desk there, and her bodyguard would be faced with the choice of either carrying her home or trying to sleep on the examining table.

Even had I been at home to read to her, Kitten would not have been there. The plague involved her almost as much as us. In early summer much of her time was taken up with rushing around trying to find more beds and solicit money to aid the sick.

It was a thankless task.

"The reputation of this damned sickness makes the milk of human kindness run exceedingly dry. People don't consider prostitutes to be 'deserving poor.' And they worry that they might be damaging their souls by protecting prostitutes from the wages of their sin. Even the honey sisterhood have become strangely stingy. In their case I think it might be superstition. But the healing houses will only give beds to 'decent patients,' and, on top of that, they expect to be paid the going rate for them. And apart from St. Belkis, the religious orders have been chary of giving beds. It's only since I've started pointing out the excellent opportunities nursing offers for redeeming the fallen that I've had any response at all. And being treated as a redeemed sinner is hardly the perfect atmosphere for convalescence. I worry about what I've started there."

It was a grueling time for all three of us, but I found

it inspiring as well. Watching Genny work with the
sick and witnessing her long and tortuous researches
into the illness turned everything I'd ever believed
about healing on its head. For the first time I was
convinced that it was a profession that challenged the
practitioner's intelligence. Suddenly I could see myself dedicating my life to it.

In her effort to discover the nature of the illness, or
at least a cure, she kept detailed notes on each patient
and on every treatment she tried. Her research reminded me of that done by Michael and the other
mages I had known, but the immediate practical ap-
plication of hers was enthralling. Night after night I
sat up with her, helping her go through her notes and
discussing her ideas.

Genny was still convinced that some kind of vampirism was the cause of the illness, but the College of
Magic's search of the city had discovered no undead, and there had been an acrimonious exchange of
letters when they discovered her reasons for asking.
The victims themselves were no help. Not only did
they not have the usual symptoms of vampire attack,
but some of them could actually remember becoming
ill. The victim of a vampire attack usually remembers nothing. It was odd how often the sickness did
correspond with an encounter with a good-looking
client, but the descriptions of the clients, both male
and female, varied so greatly, that it was impossible
that it should all be the same one. While vampires
operated exclusively at night, sometimes these con-
tacts took place in full daylight. Could a host of vampires who sucked the life force out of their victims,
who were undetectable as undead and in every other
way atypical, be working the city of Gallia? Genny

was forced to consider other causes. Perhaps it was some kind of poison in food, or some new kind of sickness.

"Perhaps," said Genny, "it has no symptoms until it has run its course."

She wrote away to Ishtak to see if they'd had any cases of the disease there, but I knew she didn't hold out much hope.

Since she could not find the cause, she began to concentrate on how to help the patients recover. We had already tried the traditional cures for exhaustion, the massive doses of certain herbs and the revitalizing spells, and nobody could say the patients weren't getting enough sleep. Therefore, something completely new was called for.

"If they lack life force," reasoned Genny, "perhaps we should find ways to renew it."

She began feeding the patients on things which could be seen as containing life force. Things like milk, which, after all, was the source of life a mother gave to her children, and fresh fruit, which might be interpreted as being still alive. They were things poor people, who lived almost entirely on oat porridge, and if they were lucky, pickled fish, had never before seen. The patients were so weak they could only eat purees and juices of fruit, but they slowly improved on this diet. Some of the less sick ones were able to go home, to languidly help with light housework or baby watching, although they would never be able to work properly again.

Then one day Genny walked into the clinic carrying a bucket of blood. She'd been to the slaughter yard on her way to the clinic.

"Last night," she explained, "I came to the conclusion that fresh blood must be a good source of life force. That might be why the undead like it. It's a revolting cure, but I think we should try it."

Sure enough, fresh blood, the fresher the better, mixed with milk to make it more palatable, made the patients much better much faster. Fresh raw meat was good, too, though it was hard to get the patients to eat it.

It was only in the late evening when the clinic was finally closed for the day and all the patients were asleep under the guardianship of the nuns, that Genny and I could sit down and look at her notes. This was the best part of the day, when we would drink wine and talk over the treatments and all kinds of other things. Simonetti would often sit in on these talks, an ever-vigilant, but benevolent presence in the corner of the room, while Genny's bodyguard guarded the door. Sometimes Mother Theodosia would join us, too. She took an active interest in the progress of the plague and was one of the few religious leaders to be sympathetic to our efforts.

We were relieved that she was absent the night we realized something very worrying about Prostitutes' Sickness, however. We were talking over why it was that raw fish, which was counted something of a delicacy in Gallia and so was easy to get patients to eat, was not as effective a cure as raw meat, which most of them hated.

"Well, I reckon animal meat works better at restoring life force than fish because animals are more like people," interrupted Simonetti, whose glittering eyes had been following the discussion back and forth. "See, animals are red meat and so are people. Stands to reason they would contain the best kind of life force for people."

Genny and I stared at him. The implications of this dawned on all three of us almost at once.

"But if that's true . . ." I said.

"Human flesh and human blood would be the best cure," Genny finished.

The three of us looked at each other. "St. Belkis," said Genny, "I hope no one else thinks of this."

"I hope the court don't start to get sick. Those bastards'll be eating babies before you know where you're at," said Simonetti.

I was grateful to Kitten for letting me spend so much of my time at the clinic when I was supposed to be protecting her. But she seemed to think it quite reasonable. It was Simonetti who nagged, who would constantly warn me to keep something in reserve, and who would tell me I was getting too tired and it was time to go home. He turned out to be justified.

It annoyed me that though I performed the ritual assiduously every four hours on the hour, it obviously wasn't going to stop the demon popping in for a friendly visit without warning, anytime I happened to be alone with a mirror. There were mirrors all over the house, in the hallway, in the drawing rooms, even one above the stairs. I had spent a wearing couple of days putting protection runes on all of them. I worried about shiny silverware and clean windowpanes, but decided not to do anything about them until it was proved that I should.

I had gained a new insight into the nature of demons. Their magic must run on such completely different principles from human magic, that things like protection spells were simply not relevant to it. The magics Michael had taught me for dealing with demons, runes of protection and distraction, which focused on hiding you from them, were just ordinary magics and obviously not very effective. The only other magic I knew for demons was the Great Chant, the spell by which the United White Colleges had sent Smazor back to his own plane. The chant contained words I had never heard before, and I began to wonder if it was demon magic rather than human magic. The idea of demon magic filled me with curiosity. It would have been so interesting to find out how Bedazzer worked. I recognized this curiosity as the narrow downward path to necromancy, however, and energetically suppressed it.

Then there was Norval. The protection ritual was aimed at him but here, too, it showed annoying limitations. Though Norval couldn't focus on Kitten as the protected person, I'd already realized that he could see me. I was now convinced that it had been him I'd felt watching me when I first came here, and not the demon. One day in early summer, I had an encounter with him that showed up yet another vulnerability in the protection barrier.

It was early morning and I was walking in the garden before leaving for work at the clinic. It was a sultry, blustery day. The sky was that light nowhere grey you get on hot days, a sky that promises a storm, eventually. A hot, gritty wind made the trees surge restlessly. It made the garden seem alive; plants whispered and hissed and made movement continually flicker in the corner of my vision. Once I heard the scratching of little claws behind me and, startled, spun around, but it was only a little cloud of dried leaves blowing across the stone walkway.

What had decided me to walk was the sudden splitting headache I'd got half an hour before. All my nerves ached tightly. I felt as if they were being stretched thin and slowly pulled out through a hole in my forehead. My skin felt feverish. I thought the walk would make me feel better. Instead the garden was beginning to feel unreal under the haziness of the headache.

As I walked through the rustling rosebushes, watching their spiky hands clawing at the sky and their blooms being shattered by the wind and strewn bruised all over the path, I saw a dark figure in a hooded robe standing at the end of the path. I stopped and stared. There was something wrong. A gust of wind shook the roses around me violently, blocking my view for a moment. The figure was gone. With sudden tingling horror, I knew that there had been nothing alive in that robe, that there was no face in darkness beneath the hood.

I turned to run. And there it was standing right behind me, a huge dark figure. It was not standing on the ground. I cried out and stepped back into the rosebushes. The thorns ripped at me, drew blood.

Then suddenly my headache was gone and my vision and my senses cleared.

I thrust out my hand, and spoke the words of dispelling. A bolt of power shot through the robe. Behind the figure a patch of gravel melted into a small puddle. There was laughter from beneath the hood. The figure threw it back and revealed its face and I realized I'd been taken in. The figure was merely a projection. The outlines of its face and hands were fuzzy and translucent and its skin was the wrong color for the daylight garden. The dappled shadows of the firelight of another place flickered on its face.

The projection threw back its head and laughed. I did not at that moment realize who it was, for Kitten had told me that Norval was scarred, and the creature standing in front of me was beautiful. It had the even-featured face of an angel, pale, with blue eyes and ruby lips. There was something inhumanly neat about it. Each dark hair on its head lay neatly in place. Its teeth were like pearls inside its laughing red mouth.

Was this the demon in another guise? I thought with panic. But if it was, what was it doing here in the garden, and why had it sent a projection of itself in such a fair form? My outstretched hand was trembling. Dignity, Dion, I reminded myself, a projection cannot hurt you. I was tempted to dispel it, but I knew that would be foolish. It made better sense to wait and find out what it had to say. I pulled my trembling hand back to my side and stepped out of the rosebushes onto the path.

The projection had stopped laughing and now stood regarding me with mocking amusement.

"Who are you? What do you want?"

The figure bowed.

"Mademoiselle," it said, "I am delighted to make your acquaintance. I'm surprised you don't know me. I am Norval, your enemy. Perhaps I am Norval, your friend."

Here was the reason for my headache. I'd been feeling Norval's sending of a projection through the protection barrier. God and Angels! How had he done it? I hoped he hadn't actually breached it. But it felt intact. Norval was definitely only a projection. I hoped he wasn't projecting at Kitten, too.

"What are you doing here?" I asked. I couldn't help feeling angry. So much for the protection spell. Worse still, Norval couldn't be projecting himself without using considerable magic, black magic which the college claimed couldn't be used on the Peninsula anymore. Somehow he must have got through their guard.

Norval was still amused.

"I know you've been looking for me. A wise plan. It is time we parleyed. We have so much to talk about, so much in common, you and I. We are both mages after all. That makes us more alike under the skin than any mere mortals."

Norval had all the moves and expressions of a courtier. His face had taken on a look of kindly concern. Even though what he was saying held truth, he made my flesh creep with memories of Rosalinda and her betrayal.

"And we are both victims of Kitten Avignon."

"How so?" I was immediately on the defensive.

"My dear young mage, I cannot believe you relish your association with that whore. A waste of your valuable time. A waste of my valuable time. As mages we deserve better than this."

I wished he would go away. His arguments were beginning to sound like those of that stupid Prelate in the carriage.

"The answer to that is simple," I snapped. "Why don't you just forget it all and go away?"

Norval's face took on the most patient look.

"Dion, Dion, don't be like this."

I scowled at him. It was easy to be hostile to a projection.

He clasped his hands together.

"Dion, I'm sure we can work out something mutually satisfactory. Something that will release us both from this tiresome, tiresome situation. But we'll get nowhere if you're like that. I can't just go away. I took a vow to rid the world of Katerina Deserov's poison, and for all our sakes I must carry it out."

"I can't see any reason why I should help a necromancer kill anyone."

"She told you I was a necromancer? Clever bitch. She's poisoning your life, Dion, just as she poisoned mine, just as she poisons the lives of everybody she comes into contact with."

"Then you're not a necromancer?"

"Would I be standing here talking with you now if I were? This is the Oesteradd Peninsula. If I were a necromancer, I would have been caught and put to death several minutes ago. It is true I have occasionally done things which the white mages here do not do. But I am just an ordinary mage like yourself. See. There are no demons whirling around me. Kitty mixes truth and lies so cleverly. You can see it in her life if you care to look. Don't trust her, Dion. She'll betray you like she betrayed me."

He sighed.

"She's probably filled your head with half-truths about me. I'm not a bad man. Vengeful, yes. But if you heard my story, you would understand."

I was torn between curiosity and fear. I didn't want to hear bad things about Kitten, but what if she had lied to me?

"No doubt, you fear to hear bad things about her. You are not the first person to fall under her spell. I was a young nobleman when I first met her. Now I am an exile from my own country, poor, worn-out with trouble . . ."

He stopped as if distressed, shook his head and went on.

"She always was a whore. It is her nature. She has the morals of a bitch in heat. She was younger than you and notorious for her affairs. Rumor has it that she even seduced the Empress, who till then was the most pious of women. You should be especially careful of her seductive powers, my dear young woman.

The shame she brought on her family. They were among the highest in the land and she disgraced them with her whoring. Her poor husband loved her so very dearly, but she is incapable of any feeling, but base rutting lust. In the end his family insisted that he put her aside. He was as kind as he could be, put it about that she was barren, saw that she was provided for. He was a broken man afterward. She does that. She is a destroyer of innocents.

"When I found her, she was on the streets, letting dirty peasants take her up against walls for the sake of pennies. I'd always admired her. I couldn't bear to see her in that degraded state. I rescued her, took her into my own home, cared for her. I realized later that I'd made a mistake, that she needed this low coupling to satisfy her insatiable lusts."

What he was saying fit in with what I had once expected of whores, but I'd lived with Kitten long enough to have realized that the truth was much more complicated. I was sure this insatiably, lustful woman wasn't her.

Norval's voice was low and intense. His face worked, laboring under some strong emotion, blind to his surroundings, seeing only some terrible past.

"I cannot lie. I loved her even though I knew she was unworthy, even when I could smell the sweat of other men upon her, even when she drew me into the most sordid court intrigues, even when she aimed for the very throne. It was all part of her revenge. She wanted the power so she could humble and bring down the Deserovs, punish poor Vassily Deserov for discarding her. That is the kind of monster she is. To that end she seduced a group of us, some of the finest and brightest young men, the flowering of Aramayan nobility. We were all so young and she was so . . . We were her slaves. She enslaved us with her filthy cunt."

He was a man obsessed, his voice bitter and low, his face a mask of mean-minded hatred. It made my flesh creep.

"We quickly found out what kind of monster she is. She overreached herself the way these women always do, and she bought us all down with her. When the Emperor's guards took her, she charmed her way out, fooled them into believing she was the victim. Worse. She sold us all to buy her own freedom. I know this to be true. I was told by one who was there. She betrayed us to the Emperor, named every one of our names in return for her life. We were thrown into prison and tortured. Many were killed. All those fine, strong young men. But Katerina got safe passage to the border."

He was shouting now.

"I made a vow that I would seek her out and revenge us all. Such a monstrous creature deserves to die. A woman who destroyed so many men. Who made me who you see today. Look! Look at me as I really am and shudder!"

The face of the projection changed. The face grew older, harder, the skin pulled tight across the cheekbone so that it looked almost skeletal. A large scar ran down one cheek and pulled the corner of Norval's mouth down. But that was all. The way he'd been talking had made me expect something terrible. It didn't look such a bad disfigurement. Was this the wound that had been the cause of so much hatred? Something Kitten had said about Norval's being vain came back to me.

"You are all that stands between me and my righteous vengeance. I tried to kill her once, but all I did was chase her away. I saved Sopria, but at Gallia's loss. Look into your heart. Can't you see she's up to her old tricks here. The mistress of the Duke. It's only a matter of time before he succumbs to her wiles, and she gets control. Think if he should marry her. What would happen to this poor country then? A woman without morals or restraint poisoning everything. If you love this country, your conscience will tell you what to do. Who is this woman that you should protect her? A depraved slut . . ."

He lowered his voice and began to utter a string of obscenities. Spittle bubbled round his mouth as he hissed out his vitriol. His insubstantial hands clutched at me. Even though they just gripped at air, I leaped back in disgust.

"No!" I cried. For a few moments there I had found myself listening. Some of what Norval said was what respectable people, people like Master John and Michael would have said about Kitten, and it had lulled me. But now he had gone too far. I felt unclean listening to him. The words of the dispelling ritual came to my lips.

"So it's like that," he said. "You, too, have fallen under her spell."

His face changed. It was chilling to see how quickly it changed. The obsession and hatred were gone, replaced again by the mocking cynical mask of the courtier. He was beautiful again, too.

"I wish you joy of your slut mistress. Tell her I look forward to tasting her blood again."

I began the ritual for destroying a projection. He laughed, though he must have felt it. Already his projection was growing hazy.

"Oh I've felt your strength, Powerchild. You have been a great inconvenience to me, you drab little creature. Save your breath. I was going anyway."

And he was gone, leaving no trace but the small puddle of molten gravel cooling on the pathway.

I did not stop to think but ran and ran, into the house, up what suddenly seemed endless flights of stairs and to Kitten's room.

Maria met me on the threshold and grabbed my arm as I tried to rush past.

"Where do you think you're going?"

"Kitten?"

"She's asleep. You can't go rushing in and disturb her."

"Please, I must see her."

Maria looked alarmed.

"What's going on?"

"Please, just go and see if she's all right."

Maria paled.

"You come with me then."

We opened the door of Kitten's room and peered in. I could just make out her body on the bed through the warm, perfumed darkness. I couldn't work out whether the breathing I could hear was hers or ours.

Perhaps I was standing here watching a hollowed-out shell and thinking all the while that everything was all right.

"Please," I whispered to Maria. "Do you think we could wake her up?"

"I'm already awake," said Kitten from the bed. She lifted herself and leaned lazily on her elbow. "What's the problem?"

"Oh, Madame, I am sorry. But Mademoiselle Dion came rushing in here and would insist that something was wrong."

"No! No, Maria! You did right to listen to Dion. You should. You might as well go and open the curtains now you're here."

She lifted the hand lying behind her in the bed. There was a knife in it. She slid it under the pillow. Her face was hard and serious as she did it. Was this the face of Norval's monster? A woman who kept a knife under her pillow? No, that was ridiculous. Norval was obviously crazy.

The room filled with light. It sparkled off her long fair hair and the soft white bedclothes. She looked almost angelic as she reached out her hand to me and said, "What is it, Dion? What's happened?"

It would have been better if I'd not come. Now I would have to tell her what had happened. It would have been better if she had never known.

I went over to the bed and let her take my hand.

"It's Norval. I've just seen him."

She gasped, and her hand clutched mine. If nothing else had, the helpless terror on her face would have persuaded me of Norval's untruth.

"Who? The real Norval?"

"No. No. Just a projection."

"How? Has the protection failed?"

"No. It was only a projection. It couldn't do either of us any harm, so it was able to get through."

"You mean . . ." She put her face in her hands. "Oh God!"

"What?"

"You mean I could wake up one morning and see him . . ."

"No. The spell protects you more then it does me. A mage is supposed to be able to protect himself well enough without . . . It would be very difficult for Norval to focus any kind of spell on you."

She leaned back on the pillows, her arms wrapped around her. She was as pale as the sheets. I'd never seen her look frightened before. It scared me. I wanted to put my arms around her and tell her it would be all right.

"Are you sure of this?"

"Yes," I said, though I was beginning to lose my faith in a protection spell that seemed to have so many failings. I didn't want to frighten her any more. Her hands were trembling.

She took a deep breath. "I'm sorry. That man really scares me. I don't want to wake up one morning and find him here. It would be . . . just the end."

"Guilt," said a little voice in my head. "She is afraid of the guilt she will feel if she sees him."

"Go away, Norval." I told it.

"He scares me too," I said aloud.

"What happened?"

"We talked. He tried to persuade me to give you up to him."

"No doubt he told you I was a whore and deserved to die."

I nodded.

"He always spoke like that about whores. In the old days I didn't count myself in that category." She looked at me. Her face was troubled.

"I didn't listen. He . . . He is a madman."

"He just says what everybody says."

"Kitten." I felt like shaking her. "I didn't believe a word he said."

"I know that. I trust you. Please, don't fail me." She took my hand. "I'd rather you killed me yourself, than let me fall into Norval's hands."

"Kitten! I'm not going to betray you." I realized I meant it. I would never betray Kitten. I cared for her too much to do that. Seeing Norval, seeing the obsessive hatred in his eyes had only strengthened my resolve. His was a hatred capable of anything.

Nobody deserved to be handed over to such a monster.

"I'm sorry, Dion. I do trust you. But . . . I thought a protection spell . . . My faith has been shaken."

I put my arms around her and she leaned against me. She was still trembling. I could have killed Norval in that moment.

"Mademoiselle Dion," said Maria, "there are some gentlemen downstairs to see you."

Kitten straightened up with palpable effort. She wiped her face.

"Madame, are you ill?"

"No, Maria. Who is downstairs?"

"Some mages, Madame. One is an old man—the Dean of the college."

"Dion . . ."

"It's not likely to be anyone else, Kitten. He couldn't get in here."

"No. Of course not. Maria, bring me a brandy. A stiff one. My nerves are getting the better of me and we can't have that."

She pulled back the bedclothes and began to get up.

"I suppose we had better go and see them."

I almost protested. This was mages' business. I suspected we would be discussing facts about the protection spell that she would be better off not knowing. On the other hand an outraged Madame Avignon would be able to make them do exactly what she wanted, where I knew I could not.

So the only protest I made was when she seemed to be about to come down in just her nightdress and robe.

"Kitten, I think you should get dressed."

"What?"

I realized I wanted desperately for her to make a good impression on the Dean and his companions, one of whom was sure to be Master John. I didn't want them thinking of her as a whore. I wanted them to respect her.

"Get dressed. Something respectable. These are mages. Celibate mages. Like monks."

"I don't know. I've known some pretty racy monks."

"Kitten!"

"All right. All right. I take your point. Go down and have your little private talk with them."

I ran downstairs.

The Dean, and, as I had suspected, Master John were waiting in the Blue Drawing Room. Neither man looked comfortable, but while the Dean was standing neatly in the center of the room radiating dignity and solidity, Master John paced up and down the room agitatedly. With them was another mage, a squat young man, who was sprawled in one of the thin-legged chairs nursing a rapidly closing black eye.

"Is Madame Avignon safe?" cried the Dean.

"Yes," I said.

All three men looked visibly relieved. Then Master John's face tightened.

"So where is she? Still in bed no doubt."

The edge of contempt in his voice was hard to take coming on top of Norval's ravings.

"I think you'll find Madame Avignon sleeps no later than the Duke," I said coldly, and then felt silly for saying it. He flushed and stalked away toward the window. I didn't want to make him mad at me, but why was he being like this?

The Dean threw him a searching look.

"What on earth's been going on?" I asked him, trying to keep irritation out of my voice. "A necromancer sent a projection to me here this morning. How could that be?"

"Someone knocked Amadeus on the head." The Dean gestured to the other mage. I remembered Amadeus from the college. He had been in the final class when I had left and had probably become a graduate by now. He'd always been a good-natured soul, and, consequently, there was considerable pathos in his miserable state now.

He let go of the damp rag he was holding over his eye to shake my hand.

"Amadeus here was on watching duty alone, his companion having been taken ill. His relief found him unconscious about twenty minutes ago. The watching bowl showed some traces of black magic activity. A line of power stretching from one of the country districts to this house. Too late to get any kind of a fix on the source, though."

"So he was using black magic." I was pleased. "He told me he wasn't."

Master John snorted. "You ought to know better than to listen to anything a necromancer says."

"Well, a necromancer shouldn't have been here in Gallia," I snapped, stung.

"Dion," said the Dean.

I looked at him resentfully, but refrained from childishly pointing out that Master John had started it. Maybe living with Kitten was having a good effect on me.

To my surprise, the Dean made a face at Master John's back.

"So you spoke to him, then," he said to me.

"Yes."

"That was well done of you, Dion. Did you find out anything useful?"

"I don't know. He tried to persuade me to hand

Madame Avignon over to his vengeance. He has an evil, obsessive nature. How could he send a projection through a protection barrier?"

"A protection barrier doesn't properly cover the protector," snapped Master John. "You're supposed to be able to protect yourself. How was it you didn't realize what was happening and put a stop to it yourself?"

He was right. I should have realized what was happening, instead of just thinking I had a headache, but . . . He was trying to make it all my fault, and it wasn't.

"How could I have expected to come face-to-face with a necromantic projection in this very garden, when the alleged vigilance of the college is supposed to make that kind of thing impossible?"

"Stop trying to put the blame on us."

"Silence both of you. John, what is the matter with you today? I brought you here because I thought you had something useful to add."

"We're mages," snapped Master John. "Do you think I like having to come here and apologize to a . . . to Madame Avignon. Is it really necessary for us to abase ourselves to such a woman?"

"Madame Avignon is a woman to whom we've promised our protection. And now our protection has faltered. Let's overlook the other things for the moment, shall we?"

The Dean turned back to me.

"We've been lucky this time. In fact Norval has shown us where our defenses are weak. If anyone's fallen down on his duties, it is I. I should have put an armed guard over the watchers long ago, when that man tried to kill you, Dion. The problem is that it has been safe here in Gallia too long."

Master John and I both nodded, a little shamefaced.

"But who could have expected Norval to do such a thing," cried the Dean. Now he was striding agitatedly up and down on the royal blue carpet. "He must really be crazy to go to all this trouble. What can he have hoped to achieve? There was no way he could send an actual attack through your protection barrier. Why did he want to waste so much trouble just to send a projection to taunt you? He must have been very sure of his arguments."

"Yes. I think he was."

He dropped his eyes. "I must tell you that I believe the standard sacrifice for putting a projection through a protection barrier is between ten and twenty small children."

There was a horrified silence in the room. I thought of that line of power leading back to that country district.

"What kind of monster is this who wastes the lives of little children? Just so that he can revile his enemy?" whispered Amadeus, distress writ large on his face.

"People trusted us to keep them and theirs safe," said the Dean. "I have sent healers to Jessan. Think of the agony of those people there, what they have lost."

Suddenly Master John spun around. His eyes were blazing.

"And what are we going to tell them? That their sacrifice was worthwhile? That they gave their children to save the life of that useless woman upstairs?"

"John!"

"This necromancer thinks nothing of destroying Gallia to get at that woman. He'll try this again, and when he does, more people will die. Why should Gallia make this sacrifice for this . . . foreigner?"

He dropped his voice.

"This problem can be solved quite simply. He followed her here, and when she leaves, he'll go too."

"So!" said a silky voice from the doorway. "This is the fighting spirit of Gallian magery."

Master John had the decency to look very embarrassed.

All three men bowed awkwardly.

"Master John, how is it every time I come into a room you are saying bad things about me. I shall begin to think you don't like me. I'm sure you wouldn't want that."

She was living up to all his expectations. I pulled a face at her, but she ignored me. She looked grim and dangerous and very beautiful.

"Madame," said Master John resentfully.

"I've no idea whether I'd be prepared to sacrifice myself for the sake of people's children, but I've no intention of sacrificing myself because a pack of allegedly brave men think that my leaving will make their problems just disappear. Do you seriously think Norval would forswear the lush green killing fields of this Peninsula once he'd disposed of me?"

She swept forward. Master John was disconcerted to find himself offering her a chair. She sat regally. It was as daunting as facing the Duke himself.

"Please. Be seated, gentlemen. Dion, who is this fellow?"

"This is Amadeus, Madame." I explained his presence to her.

"I can't imagine why you have dragged this unfortunate man here. What is he? Some kind of sacrificial lamb? All he has done has been to be knocked on the head. Can you not see he's half-dead? Dion, take Monsieur Amadeus to the still room and fix him up with some healing."

Amadeus made for the door rather faster than was dignified.

"Before you leave, Monsieur Amadeus, can you tell anything about the person who attacked you?"

"No, my lady. It was completely without warning."

I was annoyed at being made to leave at such an important moment and took Amadeus down to the still room with bad grace. He, on the other hand, was obviously relieved at being sent away. As I applied the spell for relieving concussion, he became quite chatty and confided in me that Master John had given him the impression he'd probably be executed. As I had guessed, he was newly graduated and had taken on watching duties while he waited for his first position. He was also an accomplished psychic locator and had evidently seen the portrait I'd sent the college.

"There was nothing useful to be found from it, though I expect they've already told you that," he told me. "Hey! Do you think she really posed for it?" he asked as I led him back to the Blue Drawing Room. "She isn't anything like I expected."

What had he hoped for? A whore in a red velvet brothel? I decided he was a stupid fellow.

It was all over when we got back. I'd half expected blood on the walls, but Master John was looking almost happy. The Dean, on the other hand, was looking strained and kept wiping his face with a handkerchief. The three mages left carrying a bag of gold.

Kitten and I stood at the front window and watched them walk away.

"What on earth did you say to Master John?"

"Oh, I've met men like him before. They're easy to manage. A little flattery, a lot of dignity, the tacit acknowledgment that one is indeed a worthless sinner, but a very attractive one despite that."

"You gave them money after they let you down?"

"Don't worry, my love, I put the fear into them. Did you see how tense your Dean looked? The money, that's to cover the healers that are to go out to Jessan to see what can be done there and to send mages to see if they can pick up some kind of trail. It will be money well spent, have no fear. I never waste cash. Anyway, I must go now."

I was glad to see her looking more cheerful and capable. Her earlier fear had shaken me.

"Where?"

"The palace. We decided that His Grace the Duke would be sure to want to put a price on Norval's head, and I must go and make sure that he knows he wants to."

I saw her later going out in one of her plunging-necked dresses. The sight made me feel oddly comforted. If there was anything that could be done about Norval, she could do it.

The Duke had no intention of panicking the general populace by letting them know there was a necromancer on the loose, and, indeed, there was no sign that anybody knew of what had happened at Jessan. The college inmates must have known of the reward, however, for quite suddenly Gallia was very thin of mages. Even the students, who were on summer holidays anyway, had all left. I could imagine with what puppylike enthusiasm many of them were bounding round country Gallia, trying to sniff out the necromancer. I hoped it was someone capable who found him. Secretly I couldn't help feeling that I should have done more to stop Norval earlier and prevent his killing of the children of Jessan. I was glad people were out actively looking for him.

"There is nothing more either of us can do," said Kitten, salving my conscience. "It would be insanity for you to leave the safety of Gallia to go looking for him now. It could even be what he wants. We must just sit tight and wait."

Whore Sleep kept us busy. By the middle of summer it became clear the rich were going to start being exposed to it. The fee-paying clinics began to see more and more patients from the merchant classes. The disease still favored prostitutes, but now they were the professionals who worked in the high-class brothels on Pretty Street. It was usually Genny these houses sent for. She was one of the few healers prepared to come to a brothel. I went with her once. I was curious, and the discovery of my own powerfulness had made me braver and more reckless about such things as my reputation. My ambivalence about Michael had made me likewise ambivalent about everything he'd held dear and suddenly determined to find out things for myself.

The brothel lived up to all my expectations of such places. It was full of tawdry red velvet hangings and chipped gilt. We were met by, to my mind, a typical madam, all blowzy hair and droopy breasts in a stained black satin gown. She was wringing her hands and tears were running down her raddled face, leaving grotesque tracks through the caking of rouge and powder on it. What was she to do, she wept, when so many girls were sick. One or two was bearable. There were enough customers who got a thrill out of having sex with sleeping women for one or two. But

a whole house. She was ruined by God. She was ruined.

I found her amusing until she took us upstairs to
see the girls. In room after grubby little room they lay,
on their backs among the soiled sheets of opulent
beds, little flies collecting in the corners of their
mouths, their shadowed eyes closed or staring blankly
into space. Some of the women had been sick for over
a week. One of them was dead. I was filled with a
bitter anger at the madam and at a world in which
people were treated so.

I never went to one of those places again.

An extraordinarily large number of Burning Light
followers were standing outside the brothel. One of
them came up to Genny and asked her if the house
would have to be closed.

"Yes," she said tiredly. "Everyone here is sick."

The man turned and shouted with joy.

"It's closing."

The group cheered and cried, "Praise be to God!"

A priest began preaching in a loud triumphant
voice, telling passersby about how evil would be punished by God.

I shivered. "Angels!"

"Depressing, isn't it. I see them every time I come
here now. They hover round like vultures."

"Heartless bastards," said Genny's bodyguard.
"These Morians are shits. Duke oughta send the lot
of them back home. Present company excepted, of
course."

He looked at me and blushed.

I couldn't help agreeing with him. I'd always
thought the Duke was insane for letting Burning Light
refugees settle in Gallia. People were frightened by
this plague, and the Burning Light was capitalizing

on it. I couldn't help wondering if the Duke realized what they were capable of. I did, and those nightmare memories disturbed my sleep.

The court had begun to react. The court officials published a circular saying that the healing houses had been thrown open to treat those with the disease. This was a good thing. Overnight it became easy to find beds for those debilitated by the illness. Unfortunately they also published quarantine regulations which only made people panic. There was a mass exodus of those wealthy enough to leave the city. The victims of the sickness were shunned, and were often found lying among piles of garbage or wandering like dazed, exhausted ghosts along the streets. Some of the results of the plague among the well-to-do were even bitterer than among the very poor as jealous spouses murdered their ailing partner and angry parents beat their sick children black-and-blue. Plagues were not uncommon in any big city, but incurable plagues— that was something quite different.

The river trade with Ishtak and Moria began to fall off and caravans of merchants from the Tyronic Duchies began to collect outside the city gates, refusing to enter. Kitten had Mother Theodosia hire a locum from one of the healing houses to run the clinic so that Genny and I could attend plague patients full-time. We mostly went to cases separately now, with only our attendant bodyguards for company. Almost by default I had become a full-fledged healer. I no longer needed Simonetti to remind me to keep some of myself in reserve for Norval, however. I strictly limited the time I worked.

"I wouldn't put it past Norval to have started this plague just to get us off guard," Simonetti said several times.

It was an interesting thought. The mysterious nature of the plague did indeed bear some signs of being magical, but if it was, it was some kind of magic we couldn't fathom. Necromancy was not involved since that would have quickly been detected by the now heavily guarded watchers at the college, and, anyway, if Norval had been the cause of the plague, the plague should have dropped off now, when he must be busily avoiding the eager young mages scouring the countryside for him.

Instead the plague was reaching its zenith. Between ten and twenty new cases were reported every day. At that time, too, Kitten's friend Sateen Giustini fell sick. Since she was an acknowledged member of the honey sisterhood, the great courtesans who only sold themselves to the wealthiest and most important men in the city, her sickness was tantamount to having a case of sickness in the court itself. I was with Genny when the messenger came and went along with her when she went to examine Sateen.

Sateen Giustini's house was in the same area of the city as Kitten's, but it was not as grand as hers. Nor was it as nice inside. It lacked the calm aristocratic air of Kitten's. Sateen evidently liked gilt, and her opulent front hall was full of gilt-edged mirrors and golden cherubs holding lamps. In the sunlight, the effect was hectic.

The door was opened to us not by a servant, but by an expensively dressed woman, a friend who was obviously herself one of the sisterhood. She took Genny by the arm as she led us upstairs and began whispering to her, looking back once or twice at me. The whispering made me curious. I was even more curious when Genny insisted I wait outside while she examined Sateen. I was not alone there.

The anteroom of Sateen's bedchamber was crowded with expensively dressed women and even some well-dressed men. They were silent as Genny pushed through to the bedroom door, but once the door had closed behind her, quiet whispers quickly became an anxious hubbub.

"Look at this tack!" said someone in my ear. I turned. It was Rapunzel, pulling at one of the shiny curtains.

"This isn't silk. If 'Teena got this as silk, she was swindled, and I shall tell her so when she's better."

"Maybe she won't get better," said a woman in a low-cut black gown with a huge gold crucifix at her breast. The hollow-cheeked man beside her nodded soulfully.

Rapunzel scowled at them and, taking my arm, pulled me away through the crowd and into the big bay window at the end of the room.

"So what do ya reckon?"

"What?"

"About Sateen?"

I explained to her that we were getting some good results, but that she might never fully recover.

"Shit." Rapunzel slumped back on the window seat with her elbow on the frame and her head in her hand, looking as if she was going to cry.

"What are all these people doing here?" I asked, hoping to distract her from doing anything so embarrassing.

"Oh them. Friends, acquaintances, some customers. Everybody came as soon as they heard. Everyone wants to know if it is . . . you know"—she lowered her voice to a whisper—"the sickness. They're all afraid of what it might mean."

She stared bleakly out the window.

"Angels, talk about evil days. There they are."

I looked where she was pointing. There was a group of Burning Light people gathering on the roadway outside, their grey robes oddly sinister in the golden summer sun.

A woman near us moaned and turned to hide her head in the bosom of her white-faced companion. I looked at them. Might they be Morians like me? They had the right coloring for it.

"Bastards," hissed Rapunzel. "Bloody pigs."

Everyone was gathered round the window now.

"Can't we send some servants to chase them off?" asked a voice.

"There are no servants," said a woman in a purple-flounced riding habit behind us. "When Nessa came this morning, they'd all run off, taking most of the silver. The only person here was the cook. Dead drunk and with a black eye, waving a candlestick about, saying anyone who was going to rob his lady would have him to deal with."

A brief, unconvincing snigger ran through the crowd, fading quickly into silent dismay.

"You go and chase them off, Binky," said the woman with the crucifix to the hollow-faced man. "You're an official. They'll listen to you."

"No, thank you," said Binky. "Those fellows are mean, and they've got friends in high places."

At that moment a carriage drew up. A carriage with pink twining roses painted on the doorway.

"Yah!" yelled Rapunzel. "It's Pussycat. She'll know what to do."

As if by magic the atmosphere lightened. There was a rustling of silks as people sighed and moved away from the window. Someone darted away to answer the door. Outside Erasmus got out of the carriage and held out his hand to help Kitten out. Her footmen began arguing with the grey-robed group on the street.

When Kitten walked into that room it was as if she filled it. The other courtesans treated her as if she were royalty, gathering around her, almost, but not quite bowing to her. I felt almost proud to be connected with her and had to remind myself that it was an extremely inappropriate emotion.

Kitten took control of the situation in her usual quick, decisive way.

"Has a diagnosis been made?"

"No, Kitten. The healer is still with her."

"Well let us be seated. There's nothing to be done by milling around. Ah! Dion. Have those awful men gone?"

"Yes, Madame." Erasmus had fetched the city watch, and the men in grey were being herded away.

Just at that moment Genny came out of the door. Her normally calm face was troubled.

"Yes, it is the sickness," she said, and there was a sort of muffled wail from the group.

"Dion? Could you come in here a moment? And you too, Madame Avignon?"

Sateen's boudoir was dim and stuffy and huge swaths of red satin made shadows everywhere. The face of the woman in the bed was shadowy too. Or . . . No it wasn't shadowy, it was bruised and puffy. Her lip was split and crusted with dried blood. There was a livid red scratch on her left cheek.

"Aumaz!" cried Kitten.

"Yes. There's something a little unusual about this case." Genny pulled the sheet down to expose the woman's torso. "What do you make of this?"

Her body was covered in deep welts or scratches

and huge swollen bruises. Just looking at her hurt. There was a huge bandage across her torso. Though it was new and white, it was already stained red.

"Someone has stabbed her in the shoulder. Its a funny wound. It looks like she was stabbed several times but only there."

Though her words sounded calm, Genny's voice shook.

"Lord of All!" Kitten covered her mouth.

"It's worse farther down," said Genny, putting back the covers and tucking them neatly around Sateen's chin. "She's been . . . sexually interfered with as well."

"What could have done this? Not vampires surely."

"Maybe a person or group of persons. What do you think, Dion?"

"Me? I don't know."

"I still favor vampires for the sickness but this . . . I never heard of a vampire inflicting such wounds."

"Could it be something to do with Norval? He'd be capable of this," said Kitten.

Genny shrugged. "This kind of torture. It would be very black magic. But we know black magic can be detected. It could just be Norval at play. Or it could be some completely unconnected madman." She sighed.

"Lord of All, I don't know. I don't know about this illness. Has it just occurred as a coincidence, or is it connected with Sateen's injuries. I mean, maybe Norval has brought a new kind of vampire, one we've never seen before, with him." She looked at me inquiringly.

"I've never heard of anything like that. Most necromantic helpers are detectable as necromancy. Only a demon . . ."

"Could it be a demon?" said Kitten intensely.

"I don't think so. Aristo specifically states that demons are messy feeders. No self-control. Surely she wouldn't still be alive if it was a demon."

"Look at this," said a voice from the other side of the bed.

It was the woman who had opened the door. She drew back the bed curtain.

On the wall beside the bed was a sign drawn in blood. The sign of the fiery sun. I knew it well.

It was the sign of the Church of the Burning Light.

I didn't want to hang around in the anteroom while Kitten comforted and tried to reassure the other women. The sight of Sateen's lacerated body and that Burning Light sign . . . It was like being in a haunted house. Even Erasmus couldn't make that better. Suddenly I needed to be outside, where the horrors in that bedroom couldn't get at me. Shivering I ran down the long gilded staircase. The front door was open. There was a man standing in the hallway. He turned and looked up at me. Wild black curls and strange deep dark eyes under heavy eyelids.

Lord Andre Gregorov.

He stood transfixed, one hand resting lightly on his chest, his eyes fixed on my face. Oh, he was a very handsome man. For a long, long moment we stared at each other. It was a very intimate stare. I wanted to look away, but could not.

He was the first to move. He lowered his eyes. For a moment his face took on a sinister look. Then suddenly he smiled. A charming smile, which seemed to make the whole hallway warm. He bowed slightly.

"Mademoiselle."

His voice was like dark velvet.

I nodded my head, too scared to say anything, and wondered about running back upstairs.

He looked around quickly and began to ascend the stairs. He moved eagerly and gracefully, despite the fact that his legs were encased to the thigh in black riding boots. The heels of them came down hard and heavy on the stairs. Spurs jingled.

I wanted to run away, but it looked kind of obvious. Dignity was what was needed here.

He stopped a few steps below me, his head at my chest height. He smelled deliciously of some musky perfume and very faintly of horse. Even at that distance he was almost too close. It felt as if he was touching me. I was tempted to cringe back against the wall.

"Forgive me speaking to you like this, but I feel I must take this opportunity to apologize in person for my crass behavior. I wish I could say that I was drunk at the time. Then it seemed an original way to gain your attention. Now I can only wonder what came over me. Please accept my humble apologies."

I nodded, blushing. I could not meet those warm eyes.

"Forgiven?"

He held out a long elegant hand. For a moment I was tempted to take it. Instead I kept my hands firmly clasped behind my back and just nodded again.

"But not forgotten I see."

He took another two steps toward me. Now he was too close, his shadow touching mine.

"Mademoiselle," he said earnestly, "I would give anything . . ."

"Andre," cried Rapunzel. She stood at the top of the stairs above us. "What are you doing here?"

"I heard Madame Guistini was sick and I came to inquire. How is she?"

"Not so good."

"What's wrong?"

"Come up here and I'll tell you all about it." There was an invitation to more than that in her voice, and he grinned. I felt a momentary regret.

"You're shameless, Rapunzel. Wait there if you're going to be like that. I'll be up in a minute."

"Mademoiselle," he said softly. Somehow he'd managed to take my hand in both of his. They were cool and smooth as silk. "I'm very glad to have had this opportunity to speak with you. Perhaps you will grant me another someday."

"Lord Gregorov," said Kitten from just above us. "How nice to see you." Her voice was smooth and insincere. She thrust her hand between us in a way that couldn't be denied, so that he was forced to let go of mine and kiss hers.

"Madame Avignon. Delightful to see you." He smiled at her in amusement, nodded his head, and continued on up the stairs. My knees felt suddenly weak.

"Come, my love," said Kitten. "Time to leave." She pulled my arm through hers and led me down the stairs.

"What's he doing here?" she said to Erasmus behind us.

"Him! He has lots of friends among the sisterhood."

"Huh!" said Kitten. "He would."

# NINE

Sateen died of her injuries shortly after. Kitten's face was bitter when she heard the news.

"I don't like the Burning Light's chances now," Genny confided later. "Kitten is a powerful enemy."

Kitten began to gather information about the Burning Light. Genny believed that Kitten could have them banished from Gallia in the next few months. Though I couldn't help hoping that she was successful, I also took careful note of this insight into Kitten's character.

It was as if the plague had reached its zenith with Sateen's sickness, however. Suddenly no new cases appeared. Whore Sleep had disappeared as mysteriously as it had come. Though it was late summer before the plague was officially declared over, all at once we had much less to do. Genny went to bed and slept for twenty-four hours. Kitten urged me to entrust my protection duties to another mage and take some rest. I contented myself with spending a few days at home. Kitten made me lie on cushions in the sunny garden

and brought me tea and biscuits with her own hands.
She made me feel like some kind of hero. It was nice
to be able to talk and read to her again.

The day the plague was officially over, Kitten called
the two of us to her room and gave us one of her few
orders.

"The Duke is going to his summer residence in Ishtak at the beginning of August. I will be going and
you two are coming, too."

"Kitten I can't. The patients . . . The clinic . . ."

Kitten poked Genny in the chest with her finger.

"Listen, Madame Appellez, I will not take no for an
answer. I order you to go, and I can get the Duke to
order you to go if that's not enough. You look tired
to death."

Genny still protested, but Kitten had hired Maya,
the healer from the college, to tend the clinic while
she was away, so that she no longer had any excuses
for not going. I myself felt only the tiniest twinge of
guilt at leaving the clinic behind, and that was quickly
overwhelmed by my excitement at going to Ishtak.
Ishtak the golden, Ishtak the wondrous, Ishtak, the
place the Morian Burning Light called the Devil of the
Western Ocean.

"Why doesn't Duke Leon spend more time in Ishtak?"

Genny and I were sitting on the prow of the cargo
barge, wearing big shady hats and leaning against a
pile of luggage. The brown river gurgled under our
prow as we slid slowly along its broad calm waters.
The banks were lush and wooded, soothing to the eye
rather than interesting. Occasionally a neat little town
would appear on the river's edge, or a heron would
rise from the reeds as we passed. Most of the other

passengers on the cargo barge, mostly the private secretaries and personal healers of the very rich, were
sitting under the stuffy awning on the stern. They
were not a very friendly group, and I was glad to be
able to escape from them. It was the first time people
had actually snubbed me for being a courtesan's servant.

"Stuck up creatures," whispered Genny. "They're
always like this. Don't let it worry you. There'll be lots
of other more interesting people to talk to at Ardyne."

Sitting with them would have been like sitting with
the lecturers at the College of Magic. I found I didn't
care about their unspoken hostility and marveled at
my own recklessness. Instead, once we were out of
their earshot, I took the opportunity to ask Genny
about Gallian politics.

"Our Duke is too clever for that," said Genny in
answer to my question. She looked around and
dropped her voice. "Leon Sahr is only Duke of Ishtak
because the merchant families, who really rule it, suffer him to be so. They need someone to act as ruler
so that no one of them becomes preeminent and
they've chosen a foreigner so that he cannot keep too
tight a rein upon them. Their interests would not be
served by having a resident ruler, and he knows it.
They pay him much tribute, and he stays content with
that. I imagine he's taken the lesson of the previous
ruler to heart. Duke Marcus was an Ishtaki, born and
bred, but when he tried to gain power over the merchant-lords, they turned against him. It is said that
the merchants had secretly offered the Dukedom to
Leon before the war. They certainly encouraged and
paid for Leon's campaign against Marcus. When Marcus was killed at Lamia, Leon, as his nephew, naturally came to the throne."

"His own mother's brother," I marveled. "They say he had his uncle, Paul Sahr, murdered, too."

Genny looked around quickly, but the guard was a good way away.

"That is the way it is with these ruling families. Tooth and nail. It's a deadly fight for survival almost from the time they are born. Duke Leon's own mother was plotting with Paul to put Pell on the throne and continue the Regency. Think of it! He was sixteen, and his own mother wanted him dead. Then his older cousin Ferdinand and his own brothers tried to overthrow him when he was eighteen. There's no love lost between him and his sister Matilda, either. You can bet she and his mother would be plotting to overthrow him if it wasn't that they hated his brothers more. You can understand why Leon hasn't hurried to marry and breed a successor. They say it's because of his passion for Kitten, but I could well believe he might have become a little cynical about family life. But I think he will marry soon. That offer of the heiress of Borgen must be very tempting."

"What will happen to Kitten?"

"She thinks she should leave Leon when he marries. Why be another of the poor girl's problems, she says? I told her she'd be less trouble than most of the other mistresses Leon could have."

"Why does everybody hate Lord Dane?"

"The man's a fool, a belligerent fool. He tells everybody that the Peninsula should be united by the sword under Gallian rule. He has alienated both the reformed Church movement and the Ishtakis. I suspect Leon lets him stay at court because while Dane is spouting forth about Gallian military supremacy, nobody notices that our beloved Duke is making more subtle moves in the same direction."

This information threw light on a very disturbing experience I'd had the day before, one which I had taken good care to tell Kitten about. Predictably enough it also concerned Andre Gregorov.

One of the Ducal healers had wanted the cure for Whore Sleep just in case. Naturally they didn't want Genny to bring it in case someone connected her presence with the illness and started some kind of rumor.

On her side, Genny didn't want the Ducal healer, who was no fool, to come to the same kind of conclusion about the blood cure as we had. So she had written out a recipe for a draught made of revitalizing herbs, which was to be mixed with the blood. Both sides agreed that I was a suitable go-between, so off I went.

I was not allowed to take Simonetti into the palace with me. The Duke's father had very sensibly forbidden weapons and bodyguards from entering the palace in order to decrease the possibilities of assassination, and so I had to leave Simonetti at the front gate and submit to being searched for hidden weapons by the mage on duty.

After I had handed over the parchments to Orlando, the healer who had asked for them, I threaded my way back through the maze of corridors toward the palace's entrance. Suddenly, I heard Andre Gregorov's voice just around the corner. I stopped.

". . . lost all interest in assassinating Madame Avignon's little mage," he said.

Who could blame me for staying to listen?

"Damn them to hell! Wishy-washy beggars."

"The girl's just too good. Everybody knows it."

"What else?"

"Lord Pell has a new favorite. The D'Angelo's son has seduced Cora Morfelda. I've seduced her mother. Lord Este is having an affair with . . ."

"Yes, yes! What about the Burning Light?"

"It wasn't easy, but I have made contact with one of the wives. She thinks a meeting could be arranged. But they're maniacs."

"Damn, if only we could get Kitten Avignon out of the way, maybe the Duke would see reason."

"To be quite frank, you're wasting your time. The Duke will never favor a war in Aramaya. He's not even vaguely interested. You'd be better off with Dane."

"Well, get him for us then."

"I think that's something you're going to have to deal with yourself."

"You don't mean to say he's proof against your irresistible attractions."

"No!" Andre snapped angrily. "I mean that if I were to prove to him he could love a man as he loves women, he'd only hate me for it."

There was a rustling of cloth on cloth.

"Andre's voice was silky."

"As you would, Ambassador."

"Keep your hands to yourself!"

Footsteps moved hurriedly away.

"Kindly remember who I am," said the other voice, flustered.

"And you remember who I am, Ambassador. I'm not one of your creatures to be ordered around. I'm merely a helpful fellow countryman."

"If you're not a Soprian spy! I never heard of any Gregorovs from Daznam!"

He slammed the door behind him.

My heart was beating hard. My first urge was to

run away as hard as I could, but I repressed it. I got ready to turn myself invisible even though I knew casting a spell in the palace would set off all kinds of magical alarms.

A hand snaked around the corner and grabbed my wrist.

"Mademoiselle Dion! No, no! There's no point in going invisible. I'm not going to let go."

Andre's grip was like a vise. He pinned my hand to the wall and put his other hand against the wall on my other side so that I was penned in between his arms. I pressed back as hard as I could and turned my head away from his strange dark eyes. One of his shining dark curls hung inches from my cheek.

"What are you doing here, Mademoiselle? A person might think you were listening to things that didn't concern you."

"No!"

He put a finger under my chin.

"Look me in the face and say that. Come. You were spying, weren't you?"

I looked up at him, screwing up my eyes. I just wanted to disappear.

"Hey!" he shook me gently. "Stop that. It's not going to do you any good."

"What?"

"You were going all misty. Didn't you realize?"

I shook my head.

"Now tell me, Mademoiselle. What did you hear?"

"Nothing."

"You're not a very good liar, Mademoiselle. If you heard nothing, why are you so frightened? Look at you, you're trembling all over. Now. Why were you listening?"

"I wasn't."

"Then why were you hiding there?"

"I didn't want to meet . . ."

I stopped confused.

"Who? Me? Avoiding me, are you?"

There was amusement in his voice. That stung. What else was he going to trick me into admitting?

"Tell me, little one . . ."

"I don't have to tell you anything," I yelled, struggling to free my arm. "Let go of me."

"And have you disappear? Oh no!"

I scowled at him.

"I can make you let me go."

He grinned.

"I know that. I know all about you. Do you know what they say about you? That you're the strongest mage on the Peninsula. Does that please you?"

I pulled away from him.

"Oh yes! Krazhan told me all about you. You frightened the silly man. He wanted to go home after meeting you. Made the Ambassador rage. You want to know what he said?"

He leaned over and whispered in my ear.

"So much power and in the hands of a mere girl. Devil save us from the Apocalypse."

I twitched my head away from his tickling breath, turned and found his face level with my own, his mouth only inches from mine. For a moment I was transfixed.

He dropped my arm. I rubbed it and stepped away from him, only to come up against the doorjamb. He leaned lazily against the wall, looking at me from under heavy eyelids.

"There," he said. "You know I can't hurt you. Now, why don't you tell me what you were doing?"

"I was here carrying a message."

"I see. And you heard us talking and didn't want to disturb us."

I nodded.

"And maybe you heard us say something that frightened you, hmm?"

"No, I didn't hear anything."

"Oh, Mademoiselle. You're never going to convince anyone if you can't meet their eyes."

He was too close again. Mind you he'd have been too close even if he was on the other side of the room. He had that kind of physical presence.

"I think I should go," I said turning away angrily. "My bodyguard will be worried about me."

"As you wish. I will escort you."

He moved past me, walked down the hall the way I'd come, and turned and beckoned. "It would be churlish to allow a young lady to walk the palace corridors unescorted. Come."

I followed carefully about five paces behind, going round the corners wide in case he waited and jumped me, but he kept on gracefully striding away, turning his head and smiling back at me every now and again. After six or seven corners and corridors he stopped and waited for me with his hands planted on his hips. I stopped, too, unwilling to pass him even in the wide palace corridors.

"Huh!" he laughed. "Mademoiselle Suspicious."

"Why shouldn't I be?"

"Perhaps you should be. But a word of advice." He moved closer and dropped his voice. "It wouldn't do for Ambassador Deserov to know you overheard us."

"You'll tell him anyway," I said, determined not to back away again.

"Not me. He doesn't own me. I just let him make use of my particular information-gathering skills."

"You're a spy."

"If you like. But I've been a good friend to you. Deserov's been trying to get you killed for some time. He has some special reason of his own for wanting to dispose of your employer. Something to do with land, I think. But I've almost persuaded him it's pointless to try."

"Why?"

"It is pointless. Kitten Avignon is an exile. She'll never return to Aramaya to trouble him. And getting rid of her will avail the Aramayan cause nothing here. Why waste the life of a beautiful and powerful young mage just for Pyotr Deserov's stupid obsession with his sister-in-law?"

I was so shocked. I gasped.

"You know . . ."

"I know lots of things. Tut-tut." He took my arm gently. "You'll have a bruise there I'm afraid. Forgive me."

Before I knew what he was doing, he kissed me quickly on the inside of the wrist.

"Our ways must part here. Ahead of you is the outside door. Fare thee well."

I didn't bid him good-bye. I just went, blushing all over from the kiss. I felt as if his eyes were boring into my back as I went, but I dared not turn around to see if he really was watching.

Now as I sat on the barge with Genny, occasionally rubbing my bruised wrist, it was not the bruises that I rubbed most, but the place on the inside of my wrist where his lips had touched me. It was a good thing I was going to be out of Gallia and away from Lord Andre Gregorov for the next month.

\* \* \*

The sun was sunset red over the great white towers of Ishtak as the barge pulled in among the wooden docks at the mouth of the river. It was the third day of the journey, and I wanted to get off the barge even more than I wanted to see the fleshpots of Ishtak. But once off the barge I forgot how much my underused legs ached. There was an enormous market on the dockside, and, assuming that the group would be a long time unloading, I wandered a few feet away to look at one of the stalls and then a few feet more to look at another. Simonetti had stayed in Gallia, and so he was not there to herd me back to the group. Soon I was entranced by all the wonderful things for sale, the piles of strange-looking fruits, smooth and ruby red or with shaggy tough skins, the little mounds of spices all brown or golden filling the air with their aroma and stall after stall of knickknacks, knives, leather pouches, cups, plates, cloth, gloves, clay pots of scented oil, wood carvings, gaily woven shawls, jewelry, all the things that one could ever desire, and even things like carved ivory back scratchers, that you would never have dreamed of wanting. There was even a tiny little person naked but covered in hair sitting in a cage. I was standing in front of the cage watching a man feed him bananas when Kitten found me.

"There you are. We've been looking for you all over. Don't go wandering off like that. We'd never be able to find you again."

She laughed at my little person in a cage.

"That's a monkey," she said. "He comes from the Sunset Isles."

"That's a monkey?" I'd read about them but never seen one. I was so fascinated by the delicate way he peeled the bananas, that Kitten had to drag me away. She scolded me for wandering off.

"What would Simonetti say? The party went a few minutes ago, and you won't be under their protection anymore. What if someone was watching and waiting? Careless creature . . ."

But she kept breaking off to point out things to me. "That's cardamom from Killara," she'd say, or, "Feel this leather. Isn't it nice. Mmm and it smells so good. Doesn't this green silk feel lovely? Now that would certainly become you, my love."

It was not until we came to the edge of the market and I broke the surface into self-consciousness again that I realized there was something odd about Kitten even being here with me. Usually Kitten traveled amidst the stately splendor of carriages and footmen, but now she'd discarded her usual rich, soft gown and was wearing the same simple brown dress and starched white cap as the market women seemed to be wearing.

"Leon is to dine tonight with the merchant-lords and, thank the Lord, it's gentlemen only," she explained. "I tell you what! I'll send a message to Genny to let her know we're all right. Then let's go sight-seeing, just you and me!"

"Is it safe?"

"Oh safe, safe. Safe is so boring!"

"Kitten?"

She squeezed my arm affectionately. "Well, Simonetti wouldn't approve, but . . . Let's take the risk anyway. I get so tired of always being the aristocrat. I doubt if any of our enemies would have prepared for the possibility of our running round Ishtak alone, and if they have, well, we've got each other, haven't we? Let's go!"

Walking the streets with Kitten was nothing like walking the streets with Genny. It was the difference between daily life and adventure. Not even peasant brown could disguise the fact that Kitten was a very attractive woman. Where the heavy swaths of brocade disguised her jaunty hip-swaying walk, the light peasant cloth emphasized it. She drew stares. Several times men called out to us, and once a drunk outside a tavern yelled, "Come here, hotsie! I've got something good for you."

To which Kitten turned and said with ironic modesty, "Who me, sir? Oh such a tempting offer. How can I bear to refuse?"

The drunk, an enormous, filthy man with flaming red hair, stood up and came at us, but tripped over his feet almost immediately and fell on the greasy cobblestones, to the wild laughter of everyone else in the street.

"Kitten, that was dangerous."

"Oh no. I can run faster than any old drunk." She pinched my cheek. A rare joy seemed to be filling her. I'd only ever seen her like this once before, when she danced with the new bolts of cloth in her boudoir.

"Come on. Let's go down and see the sea."

I followed her through the winding alleyways to the beach. A great wall jutted out into the sea here, making the mouth of the bay narrower. On one side the tide was out and sandbanks showed in the water. On the other lay the deep harbor waters, and in the distance, the docks and the ships. Kitten raced me along the seawall and won easily, for I stopped to marvel at the lazily heaving mass of water dark in the velvety twilight. So much water in one place. It seemed to stretch on forever. And it was strangely alive, like some big sleeping animal. I had never seen the sea before. The whole eastern seaboard of Moria had been turned into a trackless waste by the demon Smazor a hundred years ago, and Morians never went there. Though actually I had seen a sea once before. The ocean of little mouths in my drug dream of the demon. I shivered and made a mental note to put up the relevant runes in my room.

"Cold, my love?" Kitten draped an arm around my shoulder and squeezed me briefly.

I almost confessed everything to her then. How different things would have been if I had.

"Like the sea?"

I nodded.

She laughed and went scampering away along the wall and seemed to jump off the end. I ran quickly after her and found to my relief that there were stairs there.

"Careful, they're slippery," she called, as I scrambled down afterward.

The tide was coming in and waves were lapping at the bottom of the stairs. Kitten had hitched her skirt up over her knees and was paddling in the water along the bottom of the seawall.

"Come on," she said. "Come for a paddle."

I took off my shoes.

Then suddenly I felt something. A kind of frisson. Someone was using magic nearby.

"Kitten!"

She stopped still and turned toward me.

I slipped my shoes back on and ran up the stairs.

A group of men, six of them, were coming down the seawall toward us.

Four of the men carried crossbows.

Kitten came up behind me.

"These men are fools," she whispered. "Don't they know who you are?"

We all stared at one another. The other two men wore cloaks, their hoods drawn down over their faces. I knew that they were mages, probably bonded together to make them more powerful.

The men lifted their crossbows.

"Stop!" yelled a voice. A man came running along the wall. Andre Gregorov.

Then one of the mages turned his head.

"What the hell are you doing?" cried Gregorov.

"His Excellency wants these two dealt with," said the mage.

"That's insane. You can't . . ."

"Fuck off, Gregorov. Fire!"

Andre threw himself sideways against the nearest crossbowman's shoulder so that he staggered into the others. There was a scream. Something smacked into the ground at our feet.

A blast of power drove me back against Kitten. The bonded mages had attacked. Kitten steadied me, pushed me forward.

"Go on! Strike, Dion!"

With her words my fear was gone. I surged forward, cold and heavy with magic. Power began to pour out of my fingers, tingling like shattered ice, pouring out and out in a great sweeping stream, scouring over the seawall. Knocking, blasting the mages, pushing them away, lifting them off the ground so that they hung in the air momentarily jerking and kicking in the blast like little marionettes, and then dumping them off the seawall. They dropped over it like stones. There were two splashes as they hit the water. Laughter. Laughter everywhere. That was me, laughing.

I stopped. Put my arms quickly at my sides. Now everything was stopped. My arms cramped with the effort of it.

I lifted my head again. The seawall was empty except for two shapes sprawled on the stones a few feet away. Three other figures were running away. Had I killed the mages? I ran to the edge of the wall and was relieved to see their heads bobbing in the starlit sea. One yelped and ducked beneath the waves when he saw me. The other, who I recognized from his aura as Lord Krazhan, was gibbering with terror. I could feel it even though I was almost fifty yards away.

"Devil's breath!" said a voice behind me. "And I thought you needed rescuing!" Andre lifted himself up on his elbows.

Somehow I had expected him to be silenced by my display of power. Sort of humiliated.

Instead he laughed.

"Well! Well! So that fool Krazhan was right for once. Is he still alive?"

"Yes."

"Here." He held up his arm.

I went toward him to help him up and suddenly I was filled with fear. My knees went weak.

His face changed then. His eyelids dropped and his smile became sly.

With difficulty I leaned to take his arm.

"And what, may I ask, are you doing here?" said Kitten. She pushed past me, grabbed Andre's arm, and pulled him to his feet.

I was comforted by the warmth and sheer practicality of her.

"I might ask the same of you, Madame Avignon. This seems a very dangerous situation to put yourselves in."

"I had faith in Dion's ability to get us out of trouble. Justified faith. You're not answering my question."

"I overheard Krazhan protesting in the Ambassador's rooms," said Andre. "I followed them here. I didn't realize they were actually going to try and kill you. These family quarrels must be the very devil, Madame Avignon."

He poked the other figure on the ground with his foot. It curled away with a whimper and covered its head with its hands. It was one of the crossbowmen. He wore grey and black, and a Burning Light badge glittered on his coat. A crossbow bolt was stuck through his foot.

"Look at this wretch. Now he's for it, isn't he? I can see I'm going to have to change my allegiance. Assassinating the Ducal favorite indeed! Its no good to be working with a fool. You wind up like this poor bastard."

He bowed toward us.

"May I escort you ladies back to your lodgings?"

"Thank you," said Kitten primly. "But I see the watch is coming. I think we shall be quite secure in their hands."

Andre looked at the lanternlights bobbing toward the other end of the seawall.

"Then I shall just be in the way." He bowed again. "I bid you good-night ladies."

He strode off along the seawall.

Kitten watched him go, hands on her hips.

"He's a very strange man," she said.

She turned to me and sighed. "So, my love, our little adventure ends and I am taught a lesson. Simonetti would tell me I was justly served. But I am sorry that my carelessness put you in such danger."

I shrugged uncomfortably. "You couldn't know."

"I should have guessed. Anyway. Let us see what we can do with this poor wretch."

She meant the wounded man on the stones. She asked me to remove the arrow and close up his wound.

"He's Burning Light," I said.

"Dion!"

"Very well," I said, resigned. "But he won't thank us." The man sat up with his face turned away as I tended to him. I could imagine what revulsion he was feeling. It only showed, however, when I had finished and Kitten leaned over him.

"Perhaps you would like to tell us who hired you?"

His arm shot out. Kitten was knocked off her feet by the blow and tumbled onto me as I knelt on the wall. The man leaped to his feet.

"I ain't telling you nothing, whore!" he hissed. "May Aumaz smite you and your witch dead."

He ran to the end of the wall and threw himself down the steps and into the sea.

The city watch proved easy enough to deal with. The Chief Mage recognized Kitten and was ready to believe anything she told him. They offered to escort us back to the inn. Both of us were subdued by what had happened, and Kitten accepted readily.

It was deep dark when we got back to the inn where our party was lodged and dismissed the city watch. A signboard with a pink rose swung outside the door.

I laughed and pointed at it.

"Look. What a coincidence. Is that why you picked this?"

"Actually, it's not such a coincidence. I own this place. It is called the Inn of the Sweet Rose."

"Given to you by an admirer no doubt."

"Well, actually, Simonetti gave it to me. Lord of All, look at this crowd," said Kitten. "What do you think all this is?"

There was a host of ordinary Ishtakis standing in the street and a smattering of velvet gowns among the everyday brown. The street was bright with the light of their torches and loud with the sound of their laughter.

"What's going on?" Kitten asked a middle-aged man with a huge stomach hanging over his belt.

"We're here to see the Duke's great whore. They say she will appear on that balcony at eight."

"Some say money will be thrown," said his companion, an equally plump woman in a starched white wimple.

"Aye. They say she is the most beautiful woman in the world, with breasts like great milk white melons," continued the man.

The woman elbowed him in the ribs, giggling with embarrassment.

"They say men faint to see her, and that she hears the cries of poor people," he went on more circumspectly.

"Do they?" said Kitten. She winked at me.

"Angels!" she whispered at me as she pulled me away. "Milk white melons indeed! Makes me sound like a cow. Let's try the back door."

I was glad to see that the crowd had cheered her up. I followed her in at the rear door, through the warm kitchens, and into the corridors beyond.

At last she pulled open a door. Golden light and the sound of music streamed out.

"Archimedes, you villain, what have you been telling people?" she demanded. A gust of laughter greeted her.

"Kitten! Where have you been?" cried Genny. "There have been people in and out of here all day. Look at all these petitions."

The table was piled high with scrolls of paper, bouquets of flowers, baskets of fruit, and several boxes of carved or inlaid wood.

"The Scarleones have even sent you a puppy." Genny held up a dark, silky-haired bundle. Kitten stroked it delightedly. Then she turned and surveyed the table.

"Huh! I was never this popular when I actually lived here. Anything special?"

"I've sorted out the interesting ones. There are a few court cases you might like to attend to, and this." Genny pulled a sheaf of greyish paper off the top. "An expedition to find the great south land. They want Ducal funding."

"Mmm yes. Thank you, Genny."

Kitten reached out, took a small round melon out of one of the fruit baskets, and tossed it thoughtfully for a moment. Then a smile crossed her face.

"Archimedes. Come here, you beast!"

"Madame calls and I can but obey." Archimedes bowed mockingly.

She threw the melon at him. He caught it deftly

"Was it you who told people I was going to appear on the balcony at eight? You might have asked me first."

"They wanted a performance. How could I deny them?"

They fell to good-humored wrangling over what dress she was to wear. The room was warm and full of people, actors mostly, from the look of their tawdry clothes, and there was a great hubbub of talk and laughter. In the corner a group of minstrels were playing.

Two days later the Duke and his retinue moved some miles down the bay to the summer château of Ardyne. The official part of the visit was over. The château was away from the heat and smells of summer Ishtak, but still close enough for the Duke to consult frequently with the Council of Twenty who ruled the city-state.

Kitten, overwhelmed with guilt for putting me at risk, had persuaded me to stay in the inn the whole time we were in Ishtak, and I was heartily bored by the time we left.

Ardyne was a very beautiful place—a long white manor house with turrets at either end and a wide, paved terrace in front looking out onto the sea. By the time we reached it, however, Genny and I were not really in the right state of mind to appreciate it. It had been a long, dusty journey in a hooded cart.

The courtyard behind the château was in chaos. It was worse than the beginning of a term at the college. Servants were charging here and there, carrying huge piles of baggage and behaving as if the world would end if the Marquis of such-and-such did not get his clean clothes or Lady so-and-so, her chamomile tea. Considering the reputed tempers of some of their employers, perhaps they were justified.

We gladly left the rest of the baggage to the other servants and, taking our own belongings, wended our way into the château, where we wandered for a time along dark corridors.

"By the Seven! I'm dying for a bath," said Genny.

"My mouth is full of dust. I don't suppose you can do a finding spell, can you?"

"Not without some kind of clue."

"Magic is useless sometimes."

At length we met someone who knew where we were to be. He showed us to a group of rooms at the end of a winding corridor far from the central hall, which had slips of paper with pink roses tacked onto the doors.

"Are you sure these are ours?" I asked anxiously.

"Of course. Who else would have roses of such a frivolous color on the door? Never fear, child. These are our rooms."

They were small rooms containing the simplest furniture—a plain white bed and a hook for clothing. Mine had a table underneath the wide mullioned window. Ivy overhung the window and made the room a little dark, but it was a pleasant, shady kind of darkness.

"Aha," I heard Genny cry from her room. She pulled something out from under the bed. It was a big wooden tub. "Just what I've been wanting."

*A bath would be nice*, I thought.

"But how will we get the water?" I asked. "Everyone else will be wanting one, too."

"Well," said Genny. "Now would be a good time for you to use your magic for something useful."

"You mean . . . ?"

"That's right. Fill the bath with water. Nice hot water. Can you do it?"

"It doesn't seem right."

Even though we'd learned magic in different countries under different teachers, the old lesson that you should never use magic for unnecessary things had been firmly drummed into us both.

"You've got a point," she said.

We stared glumly at the bath. My skin revolted under its layer of grit.

Actually it would be perfectly easy to fill the bath with hot water. I could brings buckets of water up here and heat them up on the way. It just didn't seem right to be using magic for such a purpose. Michael would have . . . Oh hang Michael. I'd love a nice hot bath.

"Is there a tub in my room, do you think?"

"You're going to do it?"

"Yes. Why not?"

Later as I sat in the warm soapy water, I mentally thumbed my nose at Michael and his ilk and pointedly gave myself up to unmagely thoughts, in this case what I was to wear tonight.

I now had quite a wide choice. Kitten had taken advantage of the fact that she now knew my measurements to present me with more dresses. I'd protested because I felt I should, but secretly I was delighted to own such pretty clothing. Really the brown satin with the pattern woven into it was the only one suitable for evening wear, but as well as that I had a lovely dark green dress with a white collar which was too grubby from the journey to wear now, a beautiful peacock blue one and, best of all, a brand-new one in one of the new, and I suspected, expensive prints.

Mine was covered in dark green leaves and small pink rosebuds, and I was inclined to think of it as my livery. Funny how that had become an almost-pleasing thought. I knew more about the court now and had begun to appreciate that being servant to the Duke's mistress, even if she were an acknowledged whore, did give you a certain immunity.

Not enough, however. Two hours later the Chief Protector of the Castle was hauling me across the coals for upsetting his protection spell. If I'd been superstitious, I could have seen it as the righteous ghost of Michael punishing me for thumbing my nose at him. If I had been superstitious.

The Chief Protector was a short grey-haired man with a humorless face, and it seemed he had accounted for my protection spell, but my other activities had completely thrown him out.

"A bath?" he almost shouted. "A bath! You obliterate our Bowl of Seeing for almost ten minutes and pull a month's good spell casting askew and for a bath! By the Seven, the Gallian Dean shall hear of this."

I hung my head. The problem was he was completely in the right. It had been a scandalous waste of magic, and I should have remembered Kitten's instructions to me not to use any more magic than necessary. It's hard to take someone being rude to you when you know it's deserved.

"But, Monsieur Favetti, surely people are using all kinds of magic all the time here," said Kitten mildly. She was all dressed up in one of her off-the-shoulder gowns, which I suspected added to Monsieur Favetti's ire. It seemed the Duke was expecting her, but she'd told me I was too mild-mannered to see a bully like Favetti on my own.

"I thought your protection spells were woven so as to cope with that kind of thing."

"Proper use of magic—yes," snapped Favetti. "Small controlled use of magic—yes. We even make allowances for beauty spells. But this one"—he leveled an outraged finger at me—"this one sprays about great gobbets of power like it was going out of style.

Have you no control, girl? Where did you learn magic? The fish markets?"

"Monsieur Favetti," snapped Kitten. "There is no need to be rude." Her voice took on a low, dangerous tone. "Even I know that the amount of power a mage puts out during a spell is not a sign of lack of control."

Monsieur Favetti took a deep breath, and his face turned puce.

"Believe as you wish, Madame Avignon. But please request your young mage to kindly avoid using her 'powers' within a mile of the castle grounds." He stalked to the door but turned as he opened it.

"Despite what Gallia believes, here in Ishtak the college says women are not fit to learn magic. At this moment I must say I'm proud to be an Ishtaki."

He slammed the door behind him.

"What an unpleasant little man."

"He is right," I said. It was the same depressing old litany again. Frivolity, carelessness, lack of control.

"Oh, my love, you're so stern with yourself. Now come. You made a mistake and have been set right. That is all. Don't worry about it any longer."

I resolved to try not to.

It was quite easy. Genny and I had dinner that evening with Archimedes Brown and his acting troupe, and it was impossible to be gloomy for long in their company.

Unlike the guests, the actors were not lodged in the house, but in a large empty stable building out the back.

I'd thought this rude of the Duke, but Genny told me that this was perfectly usual accommodation for actors. It was in fact quite pleasant; a clean airy building which was always cool even on the hottest days. It was away from the frantic activity of the main stable yard, and the actors had themselves well set up in it with straw pallets in the loft for sleeping on, plenty of piles of straw round the walls for lolling in, and a slow-burning fire under a pot of stew for sitting around. It was there we sat with Archimedes Brown that first night.

Archimedes and Genny knew each other well. "Kitten used to be with his troupe when we were in Ishtak," she told me.

He hugged Genny warmly and, with the flourish of a huge handkerchief, dusted down a pair of stools by the fire. He even fussed over my new dress, wrapping me up in a big white apron lest I get greasy. People brought us hot fresh bread and stew and spiced wine. As usual there was someone strumming a lute, and then there were the stories. Touring disasters, management politics, plays successful, plays failed, and, always, plays comically disrupted. I was looking forward to spending the evening listening to their stories when I went up to my room to do my protection ritual, but when I returned, the camp was the scene of hectic activity. There seemed twice as many people as there had been before and they all seemed to be lacing up each others' gowns, or applying face paint.

"What's happening?" I asked Genny.

"The Duke has sent a message bidding the actors to attend the dancing in the hall. So much for a pleasant evening's talk. Come, shall we walk about or read? It should still be safe enough to walk."

"Safe enough?"

"It's not a good idea to walk in the gardens late at night. You're likely to embarrass yourself by coming upon . . . couples."

She laughed. "The Duke and his friends come here to enjoy themselves after the formality of the court all

year. To enjoy the simple life. Innocent creatures.
They seem to think lovemaking and hunting are the
simple life. Where are the poverty and the hard work,
I ask?"

She caught sight of my face then. "Oh, child! For
goodness' sakes. Don't look so worried."

"Ladies! You must allow me to escort you to the
ball."

Archimedes had come bustling out of the stable. He
had on a magnificent, green velvet tunic with black
lacings.

"Alas," said Genny. "We lack the necessary skills.
Flirting and dancing are not taught at the magic college."

"What do you mean? Will you not even come and
watch? What about Mademoiselle Dion? She would
enjoy it. Mademoiselle, it is a fine spectacle to see the
lords and ladies dance. The clothes are sumptuous,
everybody moves gracefully. You would enjoy it,
Mademoiselle."

"He's right," said Genny. "It is a magnificent sight.
You would like it, Dion. Let's go."

I wanted to see the dancing. But Andre ... After
seeing him at Ishtak, I felt certain he would be here
at Ardyne. He was just the kind of dashing person the
Duke liked.

"There's no need to be shy. Come. You shall sit
quietly in a corner with Madame Genny. Nobody
shall see you."

Archimedes swept us along. Behind us the twenty
or so members of the troupe came dressed in their
stage finery—all airs and graces.

Archimedes had been right. The spectacle was magnificent. The sixty or so dancers moved with grace

through the complicated figures of the dance, the skirts of the women swirling out as they twirled around. Only the youngest and most attractive members of the Duke's circle were here at the summer castle—the handsome, merry gentlemen and beautiful, broad-minded ladies who were his intimates. Jewels sparkled in the brilliant candlelight, silks and satins shone softly, and behind the music the room was filled with the soft susurration of moving cloth and talk.

The Duke sat in a huge chair on a dais at the side of the room. A small gaggle of courtiers surrounded him, informally seated, but on chairs lower than his. Kitten was leaning on the arm of his chair, feeding him sweetmeats and whispering in his ear, often making him laugh. Sometimes the back of his hand stroked her bare arm or he licked her fingers as she fed him. He looked far more benevolent than the last time I had seen him.

There were a number of courtesans of both sexes among the company, several of whom I recognized from Kitten's house. Both the actors and the courtesans were recognizable not only for the loudness of their costumes, but for the air with which they wore them. The aristocrats wore richer clothing and more jewelry, but they did not seem to wear them half so well. Rapunzel, for instance, was resplendent in red velvet gown with black lace, which should have looked thoroughly vulgar but instead looked exotic and dazzling. She flirted outrageously with her partner, slapping him occasionally with her fan and once being slapped on the rump herself, which drew laughter from the company and wicked, twinkling glances from Rapunzel herself.

No one seemed to mind this small intimacy, not

even the handful of quietly dressed healers and secretaries who sat near us in the shadows beneath the Minstrel's Gallery. One or two of them had nodded to us as we came in.

"Be extra careful of the friendly ones," whispered Genny. "Either they or their masters are after something." She stopped short. "By the Seven! What's he doing here? The Duke said . . ."

The hair on the back of my neck prickled. The lean, dark figure of Lord Andre was moving through the crowd. He wore all black tonight except for the white of his shirt, and he moved with his usual feline grace. He was darkly luminous among the gaudy throng. Heads turned as he passed. He stood before the dais and bowed low to the Duke, who smiled warmly and motioned him to sit beside him.

"He just oozes charm. Look at him," whispered Genny.

I was. Every movement he made was silky smooth. I could almost feel the whisper of fabric on fabric as he crossed his thighs. Resolutely I looked away and concentrated on the dancers. The current dance was a whirling, galloping one, exhilarating to watch. The dancers' faces were red, but they laughed with joy as they whirled. Archimedes passed us in the dance and waved, blowing a piece of stray hair out of his face.

"Look out," said Genny. "Kitten's waving at us."

Kitten's face was apologetic as she motioned us to come over. The Duke looked wickedly amused.

"Sometimes I think that man likes making trouble," muttered Genny in my ear.

Lord Andre was a big blind spot at the Duke's side as Genny and I walked over to the dais. I kept my eyes firmly pasted to the ground.

"Ah," said the Duke. "Here are the ladies. Lord Andre was saddened to see two such charming ladies left out of the festivities. We felt sure that you would much prefer to be taking a glass of sparkling wine with us. Come, ladies. Be seated. We are all informal here."

Genny curtsied to Lord Andre and, in a tone just a whisker away from irony, said, "Thank you, my lord. I feel sure there is nothing we should like more."

"Madame Appellez!" said the Duke, amused. "You are such a wholesome creature. Such apt company here in our country retreat. And your little companion, Mademoiselle Dion. So quiet and shy. But not without admirers so I hear."

My face went fiery red. The Duke laughed.

"Do not blush, Mademoiselle. There is no need to be shy. Come, I shall make you both known to the company, then you will have no need of shyness. Ladies and gentlemen! Two eminent practitioners of the magical arts."

No doubt the nobles seated around the Duke were bemused by this whim of their lord, but they gave no sign of it. The women nodded and bowed; the men kissed my hand lightly. Except for Andre. His lips where hard and slightly open against my hand.

"Ah, the chairs. What kept you, man? Over there beside Lord Gregorov. Ladies, pray be seated."

Genny quickly took the chair beside Lord Andre.

A servant thrust cold glasses into our hands. Another filled them.

"A toast," said the Duke. "To the charming mages, Madame Appellez and Mademoiselle Dion."

He drained his glass and turned to Kitten.

"Come, my dear. Let us tread a measure together. Lord Andre, I charge you to take care of the charming ladies."

Kitten raised her eyebrows at us as she was towed away.

The music stopped as the Duke charged onto the floor, but after a slight muddle the couples quickly reformed behind him, and a new dance began.

Genny was busily asking Lord Andre questions about himself. Questions like: "Where are you from, my lord? Do you like Gallia? What is Aramaya like?" She asked them quickly, not leaving him any chance to ask any questions himself. I could hear his deep voice answering, but I could not hear much of the answers above the music. I sipped my wine, kept my eye on the dancers, and tried to look as if I was listening to the conversation of other people sitting nearby.

I felt that he was watching me. I sneaked a glance. He was. I felt a flutter of fright, looked away quickly, and stared at the dancers some more. I could feel his dark eyes boring into the side of my head. Rubbish how could that be? Yet when I looked again, he was still watching. His lips curved, just a little. I looked away.

"Excuse me, Madame." His voice cut through Genny's questions.

"Here, man. Mademoiselle Dion has finished her wine."

A servant came and poured me another glass.

"Thank you," I mumbled.

His smile was caressing.

"Is there anything else you desire?"

"No, thank you."

He nodded and turned to Genny.

"Madame you were saying . . ."

This was stupid. Here I was sitting on this stupid platform with absolutely no business being here, and everybody seeing I had no business being here, and this man was playing some kind of game with me. Well, I wasn't going to play back. It was ridiculous, his acting like he admired me. No doubt he, and probably the Duke, too, were having a joke at my expense.

From then on I stared resolutely at the dancers, sipping my wine and trying to pretend I was relaxed. There was no way I was going to gratify his vanity by looking at him again. Though I could still feel those eyes.

At last, Kitten and the Duke returned in a flurry of courtiers and we were allowed to retire.

"The things I do for you, child," said Genny as we left the ballroom. "My tongue's just about dropping off."

We looked at each other and burst out laughing.

"Are you drunk?" asked Genny. "I know I am."

She slung her arm through mine and we climbed unsteadily up to our rooms.

"I'd lock my door tonight, if I were you," she said as we parted on the landing.

It seemed good advice.

Locked doors are no proof against dreams.

He stood at the bottom of the stairs. He began to come up them. Up and up. My breasts strained at my bodice. There was an enormous aching between my legs. Oh how I wanted him. Faster. It was all right. He was hot with desire. My body was so beautiful.

I stood there naked and he looked at me. His look was like a delicious touch. My breasts ached for his touch. But when he ran his hard hands over them, it wasn't enough. I wanted him all over me. Still he looked. Hungrily. His expert hands moved smoothly and slowly, unbearably slowly over my soft white

skin. Stroking my shoulders, my breasts and nipples
and down my long flanks to my thighs. Up between
my thighs. Cupping the melting wet softness between.
Firmly.

His mouth gripped my breast.

I was on my back on yielding soft sheets. Arching,
thrusting terrifyingly, uncontrollably. To appease the
terrible aching longing between my legs. Huge hard
hands gripped my hips, thrust me up. It was terrible.
Wonderful. So good. Frightening. I can't stop. Don't
stop. I wanted to scream.

Release. Floating lightness and freedom.

I awoke with an arm across me, a hand resting on
my breast. My own hand and arm. I savored the melting feeling of peace. Till I was awake enough to feel
guilty.

On that first morning at Ardyne, the room was
filled with silver early morning light. Had not embarrassment at my dreams driven me out of bed, excitement at the new surroundings surely would have. I
forgot everything as I hung out of the open window,
felt the crisp salt breeze against my face, and saw the
green, tree-filled country below me. Ardyne was built
on a hill above low cliffs, and, in front, terraced gardens stretched down to the cliff edge. On my side of
the château I could see a wooded headland and a path
winding through the garden. I dressed and ran downstairs. The lawn was springy sea grass and the air was
spicy with the scent of sand and salt and ti-tree.

Somewhere below me the sea roared. I found a gate
out onto the headland leading into a forest of short,
spindly trees which creaked and sighed constantly
even in this light wind. It was dark among them. After
a short sloping walk, I climbed up a small hillock

crested by two cypress trees and some rock and there I was. Before me stretched the sea, that magical expanse of lazily moving water shimmering with crystalline light.

My body still felt sticky and drowsy from the night and the sea looked so fresh, deep and morning green, that I pulled off my shoes, ran down the already-warm beach into the cool water, hitched up my skirts, and waded in. It was high tide. The beach sloped steeply and by my third step I was up to my knees in gently heaving water. Then a larger wave took me by surprise and wet my skirt to the waist. I gave in to it. I sat down in the water and let the soothing waves wash over me, roll me back and forward, clean and refresh me. My floating skirt tickled my legs gently. *This must be what it's like to be a mermaid,* I thought. I reclined in the water and let my thoughts run as they would. Inevitably they came to rest on Andre Gregorov.

He was an amazingly attractive man. Everybody said so. I'd heard enough stories of lovelorn women throwing themselves at him. I was beginning to wonder if I wasn't in love with him myself. That would explain the sudden fear I had felt that night in Ishtak. And the dream. My thoughts slid back into the dream of last night. I shook them off quickly. How could I ever look him in the face again, knowing that I'd had such intimate thoughts about him? And what if he found out? The thought was too distressing even to contemplate.

Nobody could claim he was a nice man. A nice man did not send suggestive notes to strange women. What had Erasmus said? "Nobody is that successful with women without being a real bastard."

Perhaps he did find me attractive. That was an exciting idea. No! It was a stupid one. It was ridiculous to think that a man like Lord Andre was going to be attracted to me among all the court beauties and the beautiful courtesans. That kind of thinking was just going to make me vulnerable, and I needed to be careful and strong. The best thing I could do was keep away from him and wait till he lost interest in me.

But how nice it would be if . . . What was it our old housekeeper had said? When a man falls for a woman who is different from his usual love, then you know it is serious.

I sat up and mentally shook myself. Enough of sitting here dreaming. I got out of the water. Now it wasn't so nice. My clothes where heavy with water, and sand had worked its way somehow between my skin and my petticoat in the time-honored way of sand. I wandered up and down the beach, looking at shells and rocks, until I was dry enough to go back to the castle.

It was going to be a hot day, but the garden was cool and shady. I felt wonderful and began to hum and skip a little.

"You are happy this morning, Mademoiselle."

Andre came walking along the path just behind me. He moved quietly, considering he was wearing heavy riding boots—black leather boots that hugged his thighs. I felt as if he'd caught me carving love hearts on the trees.

"A beautiful morning, is it not? And a beautiful place. His Grace has chosen his summer palace well."

"Yes," I said.

"You're up very early."

"Yes."

"This is the best part of the day, don't you think? I do not care to waste it with sleep. So I ride."

I had not put my hair up yet this morning. It hung down my back in a damp braid. He reached out with his riding crop and flicked it gently.

"Have you been swimming, Mademoiselle?"

"I was exploring."

Somehow we began to move along the path again. He sauntered lazily along beside me. The way he moved his hips reminded me . . . I should get away as quickly as possible, but I didn't feel able to move away. Walking with him was like walking on a cliff edge. Exciting and worrying at the same time. I didn't know what to say to him. I did not want to bore him or show myself to be a fool.

"So you are Madame Avignon's personal mage?"

"Yes."

"I am surprised. I did not think anyone but Princes needed personal mages. What is it that you do for her? Or is that an indiscreet question? Perhaps I should ask Madame Avignon herself."

"Yes," I said. Again.

"You're not my idea of a mage. Too young and sweet. Most of the female mages I've met are twice your age and hard as stone. Beautiful of course. All female mages seem to be beautiful."

He smiled at me.

My heart turned over. A diversion. That's what I needed.

"There are other female mages? You have met them?"

"Oh yes. They are common in the West. Surely Madame Avignon has told you that."

"Yes, but not . . . specifically."

"They're not as common as male mages of course, but often much more powerful. But you are the only one I have met here on the Peninsula. Ah! Here is my man. Perhaps you might join me for breakfast. Then you can tell me why women mages are so rare here."

I was almost tempted. His servant had spread a cloth under a shady tree, and fruits were deliciously arrayed upon it. But when I looked into Andre's eyes something in me quailed.

"No, thank you," I said. "I must change my clothes."

"Must you?" he said. "Come, it would be very nice."

"No! I must get back."

"Mademoiselle Dion." He came up close to me, his face suddenly serious. "Mademoiselle . . ." He looked up from under his long dark lashes into my face.

"I once mentioned to the Duke that I should like to be introduced to you. Weeks ago. That is why he had Madame Avignon call you over last night. I could see it was not a fortunate thing. I was discomforted by it, and I think you also. It was not my wish that it happen like that. The Duke though . . . He likes to tease."

He grinned. "You should see the games he plays with his statesmen. Quite wicked. I am sorry if you were made uncomfortable. It truly was not what I had intended."

He bent and kissed my hand lightly.

"Are you sure you will not breakfast with me. No? Then I shall hope to see you later in the day."

He sauntered over to the cloth and threw himself down on it. "Till we meet again, Mademoiselle."

"Good-bye," I said, and went away along the path reluctantly and as quickly as I could without looking hasty.

# TEN

"I don't know if Andre Gregorov put him up to it or not," said Kitten. "He didn't ask Leon to call you over in my hearing. It's quite possible Leon did it to tease us all. Those kinds of things amuse him. He says he comes here for a rest and a change, but he's so much in the habit of playing people off against each other, that he spends most of his time here doing just that and enjoying their discomfiture."

What a pain that must be for her, I thought, though you did not make that kind of criticism of the Duke aloud.

It was midday. Those guests who had awakened were lolling on cushions under billowing white canopies that had been set up on the old terrace to protect delicate complexions from the hot sun. Cold meats, fruits, and iced wine were being offered about by servants. Most of the company looked distinctly bleary-eyed. One or two just lay back limply on the cushions with eyes closed and pained expressions on their faces.

Kitten, Genny, and I sat a little apart.

"I met him in the garden this morning. He said much the same thing as you."

"Did he? What else did he say?"

I felt myself blushing under her suddenly alert gaze.

"He said he was sorry about our being discomforted and that it wasn't his idea. He asked me to have breakfast with him."

"Did you?"

"No," I said. "I thought I should keep out of his way."

"Yes." Kitten was frowning.

"You don't like him."

"I don't trust him. There's something not quite right about him."

"Do you think he's really Aramayan?" asked Genny, handing round the segments of an orange she had peeled.

"Oh yes, I expect so. He looks Aramayan. Gregorov is quite a common name there. He could be just an adventurer. Though, who am I to criticize that? It's just . . ." She pushed her pile of cushions about with her fist as if they had suddenly become uncomfortable. I wondered fleetingly if that not quite rightness consisted of the unbelievableness of his wanting to make up to me and she was too kind to say it.

"Do you think this is some kind of Aramayan plot then?" said Genny.

"If it is, it is a very deep one. It can't be of Pyotr Deserov's making. You know what Andre said that night on the seawall about changing his allegiance? Apparently he went and told Leon about the assassination attempt first thing the next day. So of course, when I told Leon myself, he was put out and asked why I hadn't told him earlier. It took some smoothing over."

"So now you look secretive," said Genny wryly.

"Oh, Dion. It's nice for you to have an admirer, but why did it have to be him? I don't want to see you becoming a pawn in some kind of convoluted Aramayan game. And he's very much one of the court, and they are people to whom lovemaking is a sport like hunting. I suspect that that wouldn't be so for you, Dion."

To my surprise she was blushing.

"I've got no intention of doing anything like that," I muttered.

Genny spread her arms wide in a mocking gesture. "Ladies, allow me to introduce you to a new friend. Madame Kitten Avignon, chaperone and moral guardian."

All at once, the idea of Kitten in such a role struck us as exquisitely funny. We burst out laughing.

"What did the Duke do to the Ambassador?" I asked. "Has he sent him home?"

Kitten pulled a face. "It's a little hard to expel an Ambassador from a big country like Aramaya. They're quick to take offense, and Ishtak has a lot of valuable trade with them. No, the Duke has merely made it clear he is no longer prepared to receive Pyotr Deserov." Something caught her eye. "Well, look who's here. Lord Gregorov, and fresh as a daisy. He was up till four with His Grace, drinking and swapping dirty stories. Sometimes I wonder if he's quite human. Lord Gregorov," she greeted him as he passed us.

"Madame Avignon. Ladies." He nodded to us and

passed along the battlements to where a group of court ladies had been whispering among themselves. He began kissing their hands and laughing with them.

"Do you think he serves Norval?" I asked. "He is Aramayan, after all."

"It's possible, but somehow I doubt it. Norval's an outlaw in Aramaya. They don't like necromancers there either. And if you knew Norval ... Apart from anything else, he's a great prude. Gregorov's bisexual high jinks would upset him no end."

I watched him with the ladies. One of them was feeding him strawberries. I felt unreasonably depressed by the sight. He wouldn't have been having nearly as much fun with us.

"I did wonder if he was some kind of necromancer himself, but if he is, he couldn't practice black magic without the college finding out, could he?"

"Theoretically," I said, remembering Norval and the children of Jessan.

"He has not got a necromancer's nature anyway. Our Andre is quite the bedroom virtuoso. A positive artist in the giving of pleasure, so Rapunzel tells me. Necromancers prefer to give pain."

"An artist in the giving of pleasure. Now there's a recommendation for you," teased Genny.

"Oh shut up, Genny." I smacked her lightly. "I'm not ..."

"Shh, you two!"

A minstrel, one of Archimedes' group, came toward us carrying a beribboned lute. He bowed.

"Lord Gregorov thought you might like some music."

"What a delightful idea!"

Kitten turned and waved at Andre, who smiled and nodded back at us.

"Well and what are you going to play for us?" she asked settling herself comfortably back against the cushions.

The minstrel's lips curved upward in the tiniest smile.

"He suggested love songs," he said.

I loved Ardyne. The rural setting reminded me of the countryside near Mangalore, where I grew up. But now I was free to spend all day walking through the forest at the edge of the sea or in the hills behind the château, secure in the knowledge that there was no Michael waiting angrily at home to berate me for wasting my time. There was no need for me to worry about enemies, either. All that was taken care of by the ten mages under Monsieur Favetti's command, and all I needed to take care of was the special protection I did for Kitten. I could hide all morning in the reeds beside the nearby river, which flowed lazily out to the sea, and watch the waterbirds swimming, if I so desired. I loved the sea, its movement and its sharp coolness. It filled me with a pleasant restless longing.

I missed Kitten's company, however, and began to be alarmed by the thought that she had very little need of me. For the first time in some months I remembered that I was just a servant. Sooner or later Norval would be caught, and I would leave Kitten's house. Then what?

The late breakfast that we had on the castle battlements was the only time during the day that Kitten was able to spend with me, and as that was in public, it was difficult to have a real discussion with her. Other than that she was constantly in the company of the Duke and his friends, and that was no place for me.

The court led a separate life from the rest of the castle's inhabitants. They feasted, danced, gambled, and caroused till dawn and rose in the early afternoon to hunt or bathe in the sea. The servants, on the other hand, rose early, retired late, and tried to remain as invisible as possible. It must have been an exhausting time for them.

Since Genny and I were neither court, nor really servants, we did pretty much as we pleased.

We spent the hotter afternoons sitting around the actors' camp gossiping with them. I loved to go there, although I was too shy to go alone. We would sit on folding stools or sacks of hay sipping cool cider, listening to stories of the previous nights carouse, or just talking listlessly. Throughout the afternoon, the members of the troupe would be rolling out of their bedrolls and staggering down to join our group, often groaning and calling for ale. As well as performing plays after dinner, the actors often kept the nobles company till dawn. And afterward, too. As time went on fewer and fewer of them slept in the stable, until most of them seemed to be spending the nights in the house in the beds of noble admirers. Archimedes had in fact planned for this.

"I always bring young ones with me on these jaunts," he explained. "It pleases the patrons. It's a good opportunity for the children, too. Gives 'em a chance to get a wealthy patron and boosts their careers. They can't all be actors. Some of them would make better whores."

"Why, Archimedes!" said Genny, poking him with her foot. "You immoral old procurer!"

Archimedes wobbled on his folding stool and smacked at her foot.

"Huh! May I remind you, Mesdames, that so-called immoral earnings puts food on your tables?"

"You can't speak like that," I said suddenly angry. "Look at everything Kitten's done for you."

The two of them looked at me sharply.

"Child! He's joking."

I reddened.

"I'm devoted to Kitten," announced Archimedes. "She's the love of my life. My bright and shining star."

"Huh!" snorted Genny. "One of twenty."

She threw a wisp of straw at him, which, of course, fluttered ineffectually to the ground.

"So you admit to pushing sweet young things into the arms of gruesome aristocrats."

"No shame in that." He looked at me earnestly. "There's not much money to be made in acting unless you're very popular. Or a manager like myself. It's especially hard if you're an actress. You've got to buy all your own costumes and your own face paint and there is never enough work. Not many actresses manage it without having a patron of some kind. Those who try usually die paupers. You two are lucky women. You don't need to share anyone's bed to make a crust. That's a rare thing, rarer than you think."

I had never thought of it like that before and was suddenly grateful. I remembered about mages being able to do what they liked. No matter how constrained I felt, I was much freer than other women.

"Anyway, what do you mean by gruesome aristocrats," said Archimedes. "There are none but the best and beautifullest at Ardyne. I wouldn't mind being pushed into the arms of a few of them myself."

"So whose bed did you grace in your meteoric rise to fame and fortune?" laughed Genny.

"We shall draw a veil over that," he said primly.

You learned things hanging around in the stable gossiping, but sometimes they were things you didn't want to know. A few days later I was standing just inside the stable door when I overheard two of the young actresses talking just outside.

"That's not *The Dion*, is it?"

"The very same."

"But she's got no tits. What does the Divine Andre see in her?"

"They say she's a witch. She's probably put a spell on him. What a waste!"

*Well*, I thought bitterly, *so I am the Amazing Titless Woman, am I?* I hoped meanly that these were two women who'd make better whores than actresses.


No matter where Genny and I walked in the afternoons, Andre Gregorov would always ride by and stop and walk with us a little. Sometimes I would meet him in the gardens of a morning, too. If we stood in the shadows of the hall watching the evening's entertainment, a servant would inevitably appear and offer us refreshments, "compliments of Lord Gregorov." He would send musicians to play for us at luncheon or come himself with some little delicacy and sit with us, exchanging slightly wary quips with Kitten. Sometimes late in the evening as I lay dozing on my bed, a minstrel would begin playing a lute beneath my window.

I was embarrassed by these attentions, but part of me enjoyed them. It was sort of fun—like a romantic game, like the behavior of the knight in the *Romance of the Lily* toward his lady.

I was always careful to be on my guard with Andre. I never really felt comfortable with him. No one in a million years would have thought of the man as a chivalrous knight. His nature was obvious, even if the nature of his intentions was not. It was there in the fluid way he walked, in the lazy, confident way he had of looking around a room from under his eyelashes, a look that was secretive, mysterious, and at the same time intimate. He had a way of biting into an apple that made you feel that it was your flesh he was biting into. It never failed to make me blush and look away confused.

Every night I dreamed of him, vivid erotic dreams, the like of which I had never had before. In one I remember I rode naked on a horse, the wind streaming through my hair, the body between my legs moving with mine, up and down, faster and faster, till I was afraid and reached down to grab the horse's mane and found myself not moving astride a horse but Andre, my fingers tangled in his black curls. I could not stop and did not want to.

One morning a week or so after we had come to Ardyne, I was sitting in the water, humming to myself and daydreaming just a little and carefully inexplicitly about Andre Gregorov when I heard him say behind me, "Good morning, Mademoiselle."

I almost jumped out of my skin.

He was lolling on the beach behind me wearing tight black hose and a big white shirt open at the neck. His lean chest and a few curls of hair showed at the opening. I had a moment of groin-tingling memory that wasn't of reality, but of a dream.

I'd started half out of the water when I'd turned, but quickly remembered I was only wearing a thin, wet shift and sat back down again. Way back down.

"What are you doing here?" I snapped.

"I'm bearing you company, Mademoiselle." He was amused by my discomfiture. "It's all part of my plan to endear myself to you. You mean I've worked this hard at it, and you haven't noticed? How depressing."

You were never sure whether to take him seriously or not. He lay stretched out on his stomach beside my clothing, like some great dark cat.

He was so damnably self-confident. I scowled at him.

His manner changed completely.

"Don't be angry at me," he said. "I saw you swimming and I wanted to come down and be with you."

Was he mocking me? I didn't say anything.

He stared at the sand, tracing patterns in it with the tip of his fingers. He had a nice profile. I liked the way his lips rested together so softly. He darted a quick smile at me then and caught me looking.

"You're always looking at me," he said. "Sometimes I'm hopeful that you like me."

"No, I don't . . . I'm not." I stammered. "And how would you know anyway?"

"Because I'm always looking at you. I'm not ashamed of it. I like looking at you. You're beautiful."

He rolled over on his side and smiled at me.

Something inside me turned over. I turned and stared at the horizon. I found I was shivering.

"Perhaps it's time you came out now. You seem to be getting cold, Mademoiselle." He ran his tongue across the word "Mademoiselle" as if it were some delicious sweetmeat.

"I'm fine," I said. There was no way I was going to

go out on the beach with him there waiting like some kind of big cat. And saying those kinds of things.

He was silent for a while. At last, I looked around to see if he was still there.

"Your Madame Avignon. Is she very strict with you? She doesn't seem to like your having an admirer. Does she get angry when I pay attention to you?"

What an odd view of Kitten.

"She's not like that," I said.

"Then she must be very protective of you. Weeks ago I asked her to introduce me to you and she refused point-blank."

This was news to me. And food for thought.

"Yesterday she sent her actor man to me to ask me about my intentions toward you. That Brown character." He grinned crookedly at the sand. "He told me you were too young. Mademoiselle, you should get out. You are shivering."

He was right. I was getting cold and my fingers were going wrinkly. I was trying to think of what magic I could use to prevent him from seeing me without seeming ridiculous. Somehow throwing up a wall of sand between us on the beach seemed a little extreme. It would ruin the beach, too. And upset Monsieur Favetti again.

"Go away first."

"Mademoiselle," he teased, "I've been so looking forward to seeing you get out."

"No doubt," I said. "But I'm not coming out till you go away."

He looked at me speculatively for a moment. I could see he was challenged by that remark and my heart sank.

"Very well," he said. "Your wish is my command." I watched him walk away across the sand, annoying myself by noticing how well made his body was.

As soon as he disappeared, I got quickly out, keeping low, rubbed myself as dry as I could, and put my dress on over my wet shift. Usually I wandered up and down the shoreline looking at the bits and pieces the tide bought in while I waited for my wet shift to dry. Had he seen me in such a moment? How often? It didn't bear thinking about.

He was waiting for me when I came up from the beach, standing in the shadows near one of the big rocks. His face was in shadow.

I felt the distinct urge to stay as far away from him as possible. I was afraid of that familiar yet completely unknown touch of his skin against mine. But he was standing where I would have to pass very close to him as I walked between the rocks. I nodded to him as I passed. He was strangely silent.

Then suddenly his arms were around me hard and very strong, pulling me back against his chest. One hand lay against my hair and his lips were hard against the back of my neck.

"My beautiful little one," he said. "I want so much to be your lover."

I squeaked. Suddenly a burst of power shot out of my fingers and he yelped and dropped me.

"Dammit," he said furiously. "Be like that then."

He turned on his heel and stalked back toward the beach, but after a few steps he stopped and turned. His face was raw. He stood looking at me.

"Dion . . ." he said.

I turned and ran.

I spent the rest of the morning hiding curled up and shivering on the white sheets of my unmade bed. Chaos reigned in my feelings. I was embarrassed by both our behaviors, guilty lest I had misled Andre into behaving in such a way, thrilled that such a man might find me attractive, amazed that I should be wanted by someone so charming, gratified that I had the power to make him behave in such a way, afraid that he might for some perverse reason be playing me for a fool, and terrified by what it might mean if he was indeed serious. As I stuck as close as I could to Genny over the next days, I ran through these feelings again and again, passing through exhilaration and despair and back again over spaces of minutes, quite incapable of concentrated thought. Though several times she asked me if there was something on my mind, I kept the whole thing completely secret, to protect myself lest none of it be real.

For underlying all these feelings was the sense that none of this could possibly be taken seriously. I had not been bought up, like other women of my time, to expect a future vaguely filled with loved ones, with men and children. The only future I had ever foreseen for myself was a solitary one, one full of the dry, reliable monastic joys of lone scholarship and magery. I had dreamed, but they were the kinds of dreams you never expect to come true. I couldn't imagine what the reality would be like. And then what about the physical side of it . . . ?

The only sensible response to Andre was rejection. I regretted this because of the delight his admiration had brought me. I did not think it likely that the pleasant attentions he had showered on me would continue once I had told him no. To my credit I accepted that this should happen. Though the thought of Andre going off to pine for a woman he could never have had a certain romantic appeal all its own, I knew this was unfair. And not at all like Andre.

Over the next two days, however, these chaotic feelings were replaced by depression and a kind of hurt. It seemed that I was not going to be given a chance to reject Andre. He did not look at me at all when we were in company together and no longer sent minstrels or servants to wait on me. I missed all these things at least twice as much as I had feared, although I resolutely told myself it was all for the best. I tried not to watch as he flirted outrageously with various other ladies.

To make it worse, I still dreamed of him, waking up deliciously in the mornings with my head filled with sensuous aching memories and my body curling round the almost-imprint of his strong hands. Once, though, I woke in the middle of the night with a tender throbbing between my legs that I realized, to my distaste, was the result of sexual frustration.

I was not the only one who noticed an absence. On the second day after the confrontation at the beach, Genny poked me in the thigh while we were eating lunch.

"What did you do to get rid of the old tomcat?"

I blushed but shrugged my shoulders.

Genny looked over to where he was sitting laughing with a group of women.

"You're well rid of him. Fickle bastard." She jumped up. "Coming for a walk? Let's go and watch them setting up the field."

"Yes," I said. As I got up to follow her, Kitten caught my hand.

"Don't be upset," she whispered in my ear. "There will be lots of other nicer men."

For once I didn't tell her that I wasn't interested, but somehow what she said helped me. I resolved not to waste any more of my precious time bothering with Andre.

* * *

That night the Duke held a great torchlight ball to celebrate the beginning of the New Year. For several days the woods around the castle had been full of workmen hanging lanterns or planting clumps of white starflowers, the traditional symbol of that Festival, among the trees. They built huge bonfires in the wide, flat field on the landward side of the castle and lay down a great wooden platform for dancing. Kitten had asked some of her New Learning friends to put on one of the new fireworks displays, and she and Archimedes spent most of that afternoon overseeing their setting up. The Duke had invited many of the notables of Ishtak to this particular event. Such an invitation was a great sign of favor, and, as the sun set, a long line of carriages formed before the castle steps.

The sky was full of shooting stars. They shattered into millions of sparkling slivers of light and fell slowly down through the velvety darkness. A great gasp of pleasure rose up from the crowd at every starburst, but here and there people winced or jumped at the loud explosion of the fireworks. Though they filled me with wonder, I stood with my hands over my ears for most of the display, even though the Duke laughed at me, and Kitten slapped me playfully with her fan.

It was traditional to wear new clothes to see in the New Year, and I had been saving my new print dress for the occasion. I had even let Kitten paint the three stars of St. Melchior, St. Balthazar, and St. Kaspar on my forehead and cheeks, and was very pleased with my appearance. But my best dress was nothing to the sartorial splendor of the Ishtaki merchant-princes, whose Holy Stars were painted in rainbow colors or picked out in tiny pieces of gold dust. And their clothes!—great swaths of silk and velvet, beribboned and betasseled and embroidered with layers of jewels and gold leaf—glittered in the torchlight. Even their shoes were covered in bejeweled stars. No wonder previous rulers had passed sumptuary laws to try to prevent the Ishtakis from squandering all their wealth on clothing. It was a far more dazzling crowd than any I had ever seen in Gallia or Moria, and the Gallian courtiers were noticeably drab in comparison. Only Kitten eclipsed the Ishtakis, and she achieved this by wearing a completely plain white dress with only a circlet of small jet stars in her golden hair for decoration.

Once the fireworks were over, I would have been happy just to sit on the dais behind Kitten's chair and watch the magnificent crowd dance. It was not to be, however. Shortly after the dancing began, a servant appeared at my elbow and motioned me toward the Ducal throne.

"Mademoiselle Dion," said the Duke, "this gallant gentleman has requested your hand. In the dance."

Lord Andre Gregorov bowed to me. Unlike the rest of us, his face was not painted with the Holy Stars, but gold thread had been plaited into his black curls in what I supposed was the Aramayan style and star-flowers had been sewn to his jacket.

"He has been such a faithful friend," continued the Duke "that I must beg you to reward him with your favors for my sake."

Kitten closed her ivory fan with an audible snap and looked daggers at the Duke. He merely smirked.

"I . . . I don't know how to dance, Your Grace." I curtsied to the throne. There was something very cruel about the amusement in the Duke's eyes, and hot anger rose in me at the sight of it.

"Mademoiselle, I beg you to try just once." A gentle hand took one of mine. "I feel sure you will find yourself able to dance with me. I am held to be a notable teacher in these matters."

There seemed nothing else to do. I could not refuse the Duke point-blank. I let Lord Andre Gregorov lead me out onto the floor, where a long line of couples was forming.

"Don't look so frightened," he said softly in my ear.

"I really don't know how to dance."

"I suspected as much. That's why I resorted to such an underhand stratagem to get you. Dancing is such a pleasure, and I feel certain that you will like it very much once you have tried it. I will do my best to help you."

And with that he began to explain the steps to me.

They were not actually difficult, and I picked them up quite easily. There were a series of walking steps interspersed with curtsies, and at the end you caught your partner round the waist and twirled around for several beats. Andre's hands, hard on my waist, were disturbing, but the rest of it, precise and in time with the music, was delightful. I found myself smiling.

He smiled back at me. It was ridiculous how happy that smile made me feel. Too soon the music stopped. Andre stopped twirling me around, but he did not let go of me.

"See! I knew if you tried it, you would like it."

The floor was crowded, but he held me closer than necessary and spoke softly in my ear.

"That day I saw you at Madame Avignon's, I recognized a fellow soul in you. Ever since then I have wanted to be your lover. Everything I do now is with that aim in view."

Suddenly I was furious. He spoke as if I was a courtesan. A whore.

"Why don't you just offer me money?" I snapped.

He smiled. "I would if I thought it would do any good."

I could have hit him for that.

"That's it!" I yelled. I wasn't going to listen to his insults. I pushed him away and ran from the dance floor.

Just as I reached the trees an iron-hard hand grabbed my arm, pulled me, swung me round. Oh, he was strong all right, and his chest was hard under my hands as he pulled me tight up against him, almost lifting me off the ground by the wrists.

"No," he cried, "I've waited too long for this. You're not going to . . ."

Suddenly he let go. "Uh! Uh!" he said. "There's no need to zap me, Mademoiselle. Look." He put his hands behind his back and stepped away. I stepped back, too, and came up short against a tree. I found I was panting.

"I'm sorry, Dion," he said, his voice careful and controlled. "It was a bad joke. Please don't go running off now. Talk to me. I've waited three days for this conversation."

"Well nobody would have realized that," I snapped.

"No. I suppose not. I didn't think ignoring you would work. But it was worth a try."

He moved in among the trees. "Dion. Come here. Sit down and talk to me. Look, I'm sitting down."

There was a secluded bench there lit by two candle lanterns. He sat down and leaned back against its back, his hands clasped around one knee. His dark eyes glittered in the lanternlight.

"Come," he said. "We both know I can't do anything to you that you don't like."

I sat down stiffly on the edge of the bench, fists clenched.

"Why does my desire insult you so much?" he asked softly.

"You . . . I'm not some kind of courtesan. I'm a mage. You've got no business thinking about me like that."

"Why not? Are you some kind of nun? Aren't mages human? Don't they have desires? Passions?"

"It's different for us. Virginity is important for a mage."

"Is it? Why?"

He had me there. All Michael had ever said was that virginity had its own power, especially for women. But there weren't actually any spells that used it. Why had Michael gone on about it so?

"I see plenty of mages here in Gallia with families. I can't help wondering . . ."

He was silent for a while.

"You wouldn't be the first mage I've . . . been involved with."

"No doubt!" I said as nastily as I could.

"Hoo hoo." He grinned hugely and slapped his thigh. "She knows my reputation. So she is interested in me after all."

"No, I'm not."

"Aren't you even a bit interested to see if any of those stories are true?"

"How do you know what I've heard?"

"I can imagine. I know what I've done. Gallia's been very good to me. I've found lots of nice playmates for the kinds of games I like to play."

"Well I'm not one of them."

"Yes, I know that. You're too young and soft for that. I want something more with you. I want for us to be lovers. That's something quite different."

"Why?" I cried. "Why me?"

"I've thought about that myself," he said conversationally. "Why when I'm in the middle of this garden of earthly delights, doing all the things I like to do with all sorts of charming people, should I suddenly find my head full of a strange young woman I saw once laughing in a hallway with two courtesans?" He grinned. "Dammit, I must be falling down in my old age. Surely you know how attractive I find you."

"There are lots of attractive women here. More attractive women."

"They aren't you."

"Why me?"

He was silent for a moment.

"You're a very powerful woman, Dion. I wonder sometimes if you realize how powerful. I've met sorceresses before but you . . . You have such an aura of strength. Nobody can tell you what to do. Do you know how rare that is for a woman? Ordinary women have to please. They have no choice. So you always wind up being their master. How can it be otherwise? Pleasing their man is the only strength they have. But you need please nobody. If you don't like me touching you, you sting me. I like that. No, I really do. When I win you, it will be because you want me. And being with you . . . I could never master you. You would have to be my equal, my partner in crime. Like a man only better. I like women better. I like strong women best of all."

He sat staring up at me from under lowered eyelids for such a long time then. I suddenly felt naked. I crossed my hands over my breast. The movement seemed to shake him out of his trance.

"I recognized something else about you that first time I saw you. You're a very sensual woman, Dion. I watched you, and I know the signs. You don't just see the world. You feel it and taste it. You savor its scent. You love the feeling of things against your skin. The wind, the sea, grass, and sand. You love to touch things. Just softly with the tips of your fingers. Makes me wish you would touch me like that. A woman like you would have an immense capacity for pleasure. For passion. I find that very exciting."

His voice had lowered to a velvety purr. It was as if it was caressing my skin. I felt a strange delightful fluttering in the pit of my stomach. That voice even more than those words transfixed me.

"There are ways for you to retain your virginity and still be mine. It need be no impediment to our coming together. And then you and I could really burn."

I felt his hand touch mine. I jumped, and it broke the spell. All the time he'd been talking to me, he'd been moving along the bench toward me, so that now he was beside me, his hand reaching out to me. I jumped quickly off the bench and turned to face him. His smile was rueful, but it was still a smile.

"Well," I said. "That's very interesting. Have you said all you wanted to say?"

He shrugged his shoulders. "Have you?"

"Yes, thank you." I sounded like Genny. I even straightened my cuffs the way she often did. Everything suddenly seemed very easy.

"Well, I must go."

"I suppose this means your answer is no?"

"Yes," I said, beginning to walk away. "I'm sorry, but there's really no other sensible answer."

"I'm not discouraged, you know. You haven't given me the one reason that would discourage me."

That shook me. I stopped and looked back.

He was standing, leaning against a tree his arm around it, his cheek pillowed against its trunk. His smile was soft and very, very affectionate.

"You've never once said you didn't want me," he said.

I turned away. "Well, I don't."

"Look me in the face and say that."

"No."

"Ah, Dion," he said behind me. "If you knew the women I've offended lately by calling them your name in the height of passion."

It seemed like a good time to start running. I did. Again.

As I made my way back through the crowd of revelers toward the château, I looked up at the dais. Kitten's chair was empty and the Duke sat there alone, his face like a thundercloud.

## ELEVEN

W ell," said Kitten. "So it's all on again, then."
It was obvious what she meant. Andre
had taken to sending me minstrels and
sweetmeats again, and last night, when I'd opened up
the door of my bedroom, I had found it full of bouquets of white roses.

"Yes," I said.

It was obvious, too, why Kitten had asked me to
walk in the gardens with her before dinner. I had seen
the brief flash of worry on her face the day before
when the minstrel had come again to play for us at
luncheon. It had been the day after the party, and I
could not even bring myself to look at Andre Gregorov to acknowledge the gift.

Kitten sighed.

"Has he told you why? I mean, has he ever spoken
to you about his intentions?"

"Sort of," I said.

I did not want to tell Kitten what Andre had said.
I was too embarrassed by the way that he had told

me point-blank that he wanted to be my lover; I felt
that if I put what he had said into words, it would in
some magical way come true. Or was I being dishonest with myself? Perhaps I was afraid of what Kitten
would say, afraid that she might in some utterly true
and convincing way expose every word he said as a
lie and show me how ridiculous it would be for a man
like Andre to care about a plain, dull young woman
like me.

"We had a conversation about you when the others
were playing cards last night," said Kitten.

We walked on in silence. She was wearing a magnificent red-and-gold brocade, and it rustled softly as
it brushed the pathway. I wanted to ask her if all was
well between her and the Duke, but could not find
the words to begin. They had seemed on perfectly
good terms yesterday but . . . I didn't want to cause
trouble for Kitten.

She laughed ruefully. "He's so frank. And if he lies,
he's damned good at it. Anyway, I asked him what he
wanted from you. If I were your mother, I'd have
been horrified by some of his answers. And delighted
with the others. Sweet Lord Tansa, I never thought
I'd find myself interviewing prospective suitors like
this."

I spared a moment to wonder what my real mother
would have thought. After all, she had sold me to a
convincing stranger all those years ago. Would Kitten
have done such a thing to a child of hers? It reassured
me that she cared, but at the same time I was annoyed at being discussed behind my back as if I were
a child.

"What did he say?"

"He claims to feel commitment to you, to want to
be with you for some time. I don't know, Dion . . ."

She turned to me and tapped me on the arm imperiously with her fan.

"And you, Mademoiselle?" she said teasingly. "You say nothing. What do you think of all this? Do you want Lord Gregorov for a lover?"

"I'm not interested in that kind of thing," I said quickly. "I told him that."

"And we can see how he's believed you. Now come, Dion. Suppose you changed your mind about him. What then?"

"I really don't know what to do," I said, finding myself close to tears. "I thought I could just keep saying no till he went away."

"Oh, Dion." She put her arm around me and squeezed me against her shoulder. Her scent was nice, familiar and warm.

"Come, we shall sit down. Here."

"What do you think I should do?"

"It's difficult to give advice on matters of the heart. Especially for someone in my position."

We sat for a while.

"You don't like Andre, do you?"

"I don't know, Dion. I suppose I don't. But it's mostly because of you. Otherwise, I'm sure I would think him a charming fellow."

"You don't think he really cares for me."

She was silent a moment.

"Dion, I know you are determined on solitude . . . But you're an attractive young woman with a very loving nature, and I'd always hoped you would meet someone who would persuade you otherwise. Someone who would love you, who would be good to you." She squeezed my shoulder.

"I'm afraid for you with this Andre. There are lots of people in this world whose aim is to find someone to love and be loved by. I think you are one of them. The same kind of person would be the best mate for you. But Andre . . . He's a philanderer, Dion. For someone like him the pleasure of lovemaking is usually in the seduction, not what comes after . . . He should stick to people like Rapunzel and me, who are happy to play that kind of game. Do you understand me?"

"Yes," I said. I thought that I did. She didn't think Andre cared about me. I hoped she was wrong. I was almost sure that she was wrong.

"There's also politics to consider. By his own admission, Andre's been spying for old Pyotr. We only have his word that that is over now. Who knows what kind of intrigues Pyotr may be foolish enough to plan? He seems to want me out of the way very badly. Perhaps Pyotr is even capable of intriguing with Norval. Where does that put Andre then?"

Where indeed? I tried to keep a distrustful frame of mind, but as the month went on it became harder and harder for me to believe Andre didn't care for me. No matter where I went or what I was doing, he could be relied upon to find me alone at least once a day. The few times he did not find me till evening, I missed him and felt miserable.

He would say nice things to me, tell me he liked my dress or show me a nest of blue flowers, which he'd found "because I know such things please you." Once I accused him of following me around. Unabashed, he explained that it was all part of his plan to seduce me.

"If you get used to me," he said, reaching out and touching my wrist, "you won't jump every time I come near you, and that can only be a good thing, can't it."

I scowled at him, but unfortunately his plan was working admirably. Now when he touched my arm or hand, I no longer jumped away. I'd also become used to his propositioning me at least once during every conversation, or his starting sentences with "when we become lovers." In another man it might have been sleazy, but Andre accepted my rejections with good humor. He exerted pressure by assuming that his success was inevitable, and apparently felt no need to push further.

"I just want to let you know that I still want you," he would say.

Did I in fact like his saying these things to me? I knew I shouldn't listen to him, but I was flattered by his devotion.

I grew used to laughing when he told me he wanted me. He accepted it for a while. Then one day he suddenly pulled me against him and said, "Don't get me wrong, Dion. It's not your friend I want to be. I'm deadly serious."

He tried to kiss me, but I pulled away. I was afraid of what might happen if he did. So often in my dreams, a kiss made me lose control.

Being with him was never comfortable. There was always that constant tension, worrying and exhilarating at the same time.

Every night I dreamed of him. It was so peculiar trying to be reserved with a man when you had intensely erotic dream memories of him—when you'd watched him suckle at your breast, felt the firmness of his hands on your skin, watched yourself thrust frenziedly up against him.

I was aware of the real man's body all the time, and

of my own. I was constantly feeling that phantom touch of his hands on me whenever I was with him. I found myself looking secretly at him, noticing his litheness, the hard muscles of his arms and thighs, and the smooth fullness of his mouth.

Sometimes when I looked he would fall silent and return my glance with caressing eyes. I would blush and make some excuse to get away. He never stopped me. I had to keep reminding myself that he had no way of knowing what I dreamed at night.

It was heady stuff.

Slowly over all those days, as we talked he touched upon all my fears. It wasn't his answers that were the persuasive thing; it was the fact that he seemed to understand what went on in my mind—to accept and even to consider such things important.

I quickly confronted him about his being a spy. I was hiding in some bushes early one morning watching the little blue-breasted wrens fluttering in the trees nearby. Suddenly they all rose and flew away.

Lord Andre Gregorov was coming down the pathway. I stayed where I was in the bushes and thought he was going to pass me by, but at the last moment he turned, pulled aside a branch, and smiled crookedly down at me.

"Playing the spy, sweeting?"

I jumped up. My dress was covered in the little prickly leaves of the ti-tree.

"You can talk," I said to hide my embarrassment.

"Look at you. You're covered in leaves." He reached out and began to brush me down. I whirled out of his grasp.

"No, thank you!"

"Why, Dion!" he said with mock hurt. "Anyone would think you didn't trust me."

"And who'd blame me?"

"Why? Because you think I'm a spy?"

I shrugged and walked away up the path. He followed as he always did. A little farther on the trees stopped, and beyond was a patch of low, scrubby bushes overlooking a low cliff. A fresh salt wind whispered in the trees and blew loose strands of my hair around.

"Dion, answer me."

I turned and looked at him. His face was unusually serious.

"Are you afraid because you think of me as a spy?"

I said nothing.

"I'm not precisely that. I've never worked to anyone's command. I just allow people to know the things I know sometimes. I can assure you I have washed my hands of stupid Pyotr Deserov. Dion?"

"How can I know if you're telling the truth? How can I know what motivates you? You might be planning to kill us all, for all I know."

He grinned wolfishly. "Desire is my only motive."

I scowled at him.

"Ask whomever you like about me. I have nothing to hide. Find out about me if you like. I know your Madame Avignon has. Don't look so surprised. You must know she has. Do you think a Duke's favorite stays where she is without having some kind of intelligence network. Not our efficient Madame Avignon. What does she advise you about me? Hey?"

"She doesn't tell me what to do."

"Glad to hear it."

I stared out at sea, angry at him. His voice spoke suddenly from right behind me.

"If I was planning to harm you, what's to stop me now? I could throw you off this cliff."

I tried not to be frightened. "I'd change into a bird. Or a feather."

"So quickly? Well, what if I had a witch manacle and I snapped it on you now? Then I could kill you or kidnap you as I pleased."

I turned quickly and faced him.

"Do you think I haven't had plenty of opportunities to harm you in the past few weeks?"

"The castle's protection . . ."

"But we're outside the range of the protection. We often have been. I could have snapped a witch manacle on you several times had I wanted too."

He spread his empty hands out

"But I haven't even tried, have I? If I had anything to hide, why would I have told you what I was doing that day you caught me with Deserov? Hmm."

The way he talked, the way he looked at me out of his deep, dark eyes was convincing. It always was.

"I don't want to deceive you, Dion. Lies put distance between people. That's not what I want at all."

With difficulty I reminded myself not to believe him, though his words left their usual residue of faith.

I moved away quickly.

"Someone did try to manacle me once. I felt it coming and stopped him."

"Did you now? You're a very good mage, Dion . . ."

The wind muffled the rest of what he said. I turned and looked at him inquiringly.

"I said why do you let the others tell you what to do?"

"What others?"

"Favetti, those old fools at the college."

"They're not old fools."

"But you are greater than all of them. Much greater. Why do you let them take all the glory? Why aren't you Dean of a College of Mages? Why aren't you even considered?"

I shrugged. It could have led to some disturbing thoughts, had my thoughts not already been full of Andre Gregorov.

A few days later I came upon him with Rapunzel in the garden. I remember it was dawn. I had been unable to sleep after the four o'clock incantation because I'd woken up embracing my pillow after a particularly vivid dream about Andre. I was filled with self-disgust. Michael had been right when he had told me blood will out.

It was light, so I dressed and went walking in the damp garden. Down one of the walks I saw Andre and Rapunzel walking arm in arm away from me. She was leaning heavily against him. I turned and walked in the opposite direction as quickly and quietly as possible.

It was as bad as if I'd caught them lying naked together on the grass. I felt as if everything Andre had said to me must be a lie. What a fool I was! I had come so close to believing he cared for me.

I walked blindly for some time. At last I came to myself sitting on an old jetty, staring at the sun on the murky morning waves with my fist clenched, wanting very badly to cry. It was what I had most feared would happen.

Then Andre appeared. I hated him and was as nasty as I could be.

"You're jealous aren't you?" he accused me. "That means you must care for me."

I denied it, and he seized my arm and tried to make me admit it. I was so angry at him I sent a little scratchy bolt of power out of my wrist and burned his hand.

He called me a name and stalked away. I listened to his feet stomp along the wooden jetty. I was horribly confused and ashamed of myself for using my power in that way. I wanted so much for him to come back. Suddenly his footsteps turned and came back down the jetty. He sat quietly down behind me.

"Dion, there's nothing for you to be jealous of. Rapunzel was ill and I was taking her back inside. That's all."

I said nothing.

"Dion, you may not believe it, but I haven't made love to anybody since I've been here."

I wanted desperately to believe him. That seemed a very good reason not to.

"I'm sure I don't care what you do," I said.

"I thought you might. I thought it might ruin my chances with you."

Silence.

"Are you afraid that if you came to me I'd be unfaithful to you? Is that why you keep saying no?"

I didn't know what to say.

"Dion, you know I can't promise I'll never want anybody else. No one can tell what's going to happen in the future. Maybe you'll get tired of me first. I'm not a fool. I know if I have you, I'll have to change my ways. But . . . You're worth that to me. My love."

I was trembling. In the corner of my eye I could see him leaning toward me, looking into my face. I turned my head away. Oddly enough I wanted to cry again. I was suddenly feeling very happy.

"Look at this."

He held his hand out to me. The skin was red and raw. His linen cuff was brown and singed. "If this is what you do when I put my arm round another woman, what'll you do if I actually give you some-

thing to be angry about? I'll have no choice, but to
behave myself."

"I'm sorry. I lost my temper." I felt terribly guilty.
"I can heal it for you."

He pulled his hand away.

"No. I think I'll keep it. Just call me sentimental."
He grinned.

Before I realized it, I was smiling, too.

He was sitting close to me, leaning back against the
pole at the end of the jetty. His hair was tousled. He
was still wearing his red velvet evening coat. I could
smell wine and woodsmoke on him and the faint delicious scent of his sweat. His white linen shirt was
open at the neck showing a few curls of dark hair
against his hard, brown chest.

I remembered vividly dreaming of that hair, soft
against my naked breasts.

He yawned and stretched and looked at me from
under his drooping eyelids. "I'm going to bed," he
said. "Why don't you come, too?"

How would it be if I said yes?

"No, thank you," I said with dignity.

"Fair enough." He sauntered away.

I sat on the end of the jetty and thought about what
he had said for a long time. The cool grey dawn
slowly became a bright and golden morning and I did
not even notice the day had changed color until the
sun began to get in my eyes and the castle clock had
struck 7:30. I had to hurry to get back in time for the
eight o'clock ritual.

Afterward I was still dreamy. I lay down on my
unmade bed. The conversation I'd had with Andre on
the jetty seemed to block out all other thoughts. The
whole scene replayed itself again and again in my
head. The way he called me "my love." The patience

he showed in persuading me out of my jealousy even after I'd burned him, the way he had brought up a subject which I knew now had been worrying me deeply. I couldn't believe I could keep Andre's interest, but he seemed to have no trouble being faithful to me. Or so he said. But it was ridiculous that such a man would be faithful to anybody. He had no need to be. Women—and men—were throwing themselves at him all the time. Why should he resist just for my plain and skinny little self? He was playing me for a fool. And if I gave in to him, he would laugh at me afterward.

This vision was one of such unbearable pain that my eyes filled with tears, but I couldn't maintain it. He'd always been so kind to me. Sure, he'd teased me, but he always said he was sorry. I'd never heard from anybody that he was cruel. Only this morning he'd been helping Rapunzel inside because she was ill. Or had that all been a big lie.

As I lay there with my arm across my body, imagining it was his arm around me, I began to have a sort of vision. I saw myself as if in a picture, seated, dressed all in black. Beside me stood Andre in all his lean grace all in black, too. His hand on my shoulder. My man. My lover.

Our faces had the quiet serious dignity of a king and queen. I saw a greatness in that picture of us together, a strength that came from the special alliance between the two of us. I saw how it might be and the sight of it filled me with powerful joy.

There was a knock at the door.

"Yes." I sat up.

It opened, and Kitten put her head in.

"There you are. Are you all right? You look tired."

"Yes. I didn't sleep well."

She came into the room. She wore a rose pink robe and her hair was tied loosely back. She looked troubled.

"Dion. Rapunzel has been taken ill. We've decided that she must leave Ardyne. Genny is going with her."

"What is it?" I said.

"Genny thinks it's Whore Sleep. She says the symptoms are the same."

"Angels . . . Here? Do you think you're safe?" I asked her.

"I feel fine," she said. "Please, Dion. Genny wanted you to come . . ."

"Of course!"

Rapunzel lay in a huge dark bed hung with sumptuous tapestry curtains. Her face was as white as the crisp linen sheets. Her eyes were closed, the skin around them translucent and bruised-looking. She looked half-alive, just like all those other people.

"Pulse is slow," said Genny. "And her temperature's low. Weak aura, too. It's all the same."

She turned to Kitten.

"Why are you so determined to move her? She's very weak. It would be better if she didn't travel."

Kitten shook her head.

"Leon ordered her moved," she said. "He doesn't want sick people here."

"That's inhuman!" I cried.

"It's Leon," said Kitten. "He's the Duke. He can have whatever he wishes." She leaned against the bedpost. "I begged him to let her stay here, said it only attacked prostitutes, but . . . He doesn't like people to be sick around him. He got angry and said if I hadn't moved her by midday, he'd have the guards do it." She sighed. "It wouldn't matter if it was one of his family or his most trusted adviser. He'd even send me away if I was sick."

"Perhaps Dion could do something to make the trip easier for her," said Genny.

"I'm not powerful enough to fly her to Gallia," I replied.

"There's a nunnery five miles from here," said Kitten.

I saw then that her eyes were full of tears.

"I'll be able to support her in the carriage," I offered quickly. "That should make the journey easier. I can make it as if she never left her bed." I touched Kitten's shoulder.

She put her hand over her eyes and wiped the tears away with a quick, secretive gesture

"Thank you. Thank you. Rap and I, we've been through so much together. I don't want to lose her."

I went and bathed and dressed properly while the two of them got the carriage ready for the journey. I packed the materials for the ritual of protection. I looked up the necessary combination of spells in my books, though it wasn't necessary. I found that my hands were shaking. I was furious with the Duke. How could he be so heartless! But it was pointless to be angry. His word was law, unfortunately.

All my anxieties about Andre seemed trivial now, beside Rapunzel's illness and my duties as a mage.

When it was time, Genny came to fetch me, and together we went down to the carriage. Rapunzel had already been placed inside, and Kitten was crouched on the floor beside her. Rapunzel's head was resting against Kitten's shoulder and she was weeping the usual slow tears of weakness. But when she saw me she screamed, "No, I'm not going with her. Get your little milk pudding face out of here, you bitch."

"Rapunzel?" cried Kitten.

She shook her. Rapunzel took another breath and passed out.

"What in the Angels' name . . . ?" said Genny.

"I'm sorry," said Kitten. "I'm not sure what . . . Dion I'm so sorry."

"It makes no difference," I said, though inwardly I was shaken. "Come, we must start."

"Dion, I think Rapunzel's jealous. Please. Try to forgive her."

I was hurt that Kitten felt it necessary to placate me.

"Just try and keep her quiet while I cast this spell."

It was easy for me to levitate the unconscious Rapunzel off the seat of the coach. Kitten kissed her and got out of the carriage. Genny and I settled ourselves on opposite seats, with Rapunzel floating between us. The coach door closed and we moved off.

It was a rough journey. The carriage was not much better sprung than a cart on wheels, and the route to the convent took us along a heavily rutted road. Genny took Rapunzel's pulse every so often. I just sat back in the corner and concentrated. The coldness of magic was upon me again. It was as if I were watching myself levitate Rapunzel. So I felt nothing but mild interest when Rapunzel woke up and started to call me harsh names and complain about losing Andre to me again. I knew her words would come back to me later, however.

Genny kept looking anxiously at me, afraid, no doubt, that I would become angry and lose my temper. In the end it was she who became angry.

"Shut up. We all know you're a gutter slut. You don't need to talk like one to convince us," she yelled.

Rapunzel cried the same tears of weakness and

swore that Andre was the only man she had ever loved. Finally she fell into another exhausted sleep.

"Oh Dion!" said Genny "I am sorry. I can't put a spell on her. I might kill her."

"She is sick and afraid."

"You're taking all this very calmly. Are you all right?"

"The magic's keeping me calm."

She snorted. "Great! Does it stop you feeling the bumps, too?"

"No," I said. I moved my mind around the spell and found I could widen it to levitate Genny.

She squawked when I lifted her up and then laughed.

"Can you pick yourself up, too?"

I found I could. Soon we were bouncing along the rutted track quite separately from the carriage, feeling no ill effects whatsoever. It was wonderful to actually be using real magic again. I felt as if I were stretching out of a cramped position. It was that same feeling you have when stretching a tired limb, only more intense.

Although I broke the spell when we halted at midday for me to perform the protection ritual, the calmness was replaced by a kind of exhilaration. I found I was not at all tired. Instead I strolled among the roadside trees, listening to the cicadas and watching the wind on the surrounding wheat fields.

Genny called me back to the carriage.

"Keep an eye on Rapunzel for a moment, will you? She shouldn't wake up."

I sat outside the carriage till I heard Rapunzel stir. A little nervously, I put my head round the door of the carriage.

She was tossing her head from side to side as if she was struggling with some thought.

"The sea. So ... Little mouths. Oh God! Little faces!"

She started awake.

"Rapunzel?"

"So thirsty," she moaned.

I tried to give her milk, but she would only take water.

"You must drink the milk," I said. "It'll replenish your life force."

"Where am I?"

I told her about the nunnery.

"Leon threw me out, didn't he?" She began to cry again. "Bastard. Just like him. Last week it was all 'Rapunzel, let's play threesomes' and now ... I'm nothing but spoiled meat. You should have let me die."

I patted her shoulder.

"Kitten was upset," I said. "She ordered all this and she sent us to take care of you."

"Dear old Pussycat, she's the best person I know." Rapunzel began to weep even harder. "I feel so weak."

"Hush," I said. "These strong emotions only make it worse. Try to be calm. Have some more water."

"Dion." Genny's voice was anxious as she peered around the door.

"All is well."

"Well," said Genny. "So you're with us again, Rapunzel. No more words about your broken heart."

Rapunzel seemed puzzled.

"It must have been delirium," said Genny later as we floated along inside the lurching carriage with the sleeping Rapunzel between us. "Perhaps ..." She looked at me as if wondering whether to go on. "Perhaps she was finishing off an argument she had with Lord Andre."

"Perhaps," I said. The calmness of magic was on me again. I was merely interested in her theory.

The calmness stayed with me even after we had arrived at the large white-walled convent which stood amidst the golden wheat fields and I had carried Rapunzel inside and seen her to her bed. It was hard to tell from the demure serious faces of the nuns what they really thought of giving sanctuary to a notorious courtesan and a mage, but I overheard the Mother Superior telling Genny that they were deeply grateful to Madame Avignon for the donations she had given their mother house in Gallia.

One of the nuns led me to a cool, white room, where she said I might rest. Another brought me hot herbal tea. I had not felt tired when I had been in the carriage, but I lay on the fresh straw pallet on the floor and when I next opened my eyes, it was late afternoon and a nun was standing at the door telling me it was almost four o'clock.

It was the first time since I had come to Ardyne that I could not remember dreaming of Andre Gregorov. I scrambled around performing the ritual and then went out into the cloisters.

It was peaceful and soothing there. Somehow the nunnery with the nuns pacing solemnly up and down, heads bent in contemplation, made me think nostalgically of the college. It seemed so safe compared with the emotional upheaval of the last couple of weeks.

I found Genny in the still room telling one of the nuns about her recipe for Prostitutes' Fever. They were discussing ways and means.

"Surely they don't have it here," I asked her.

"There have been some cases in the surrounding villages," she said. "Many of them have died one way or another. The usual depressing catalogue of jealous spouses and angry parents."

"Something to do with the court being here?"

"There might be a link. Every year a crop of bastards is born here about nine months after the court has visited. That points to it being a venereal disease."

I asked her what had been organized for my return to Ardyne.

"The carriage went back to the castle. It'll be back in a couple of days."

I looked at her.

"How important was it really for me to come with you?"

"You have to admit it made the trip considerably easier. I'm sure it helped Rapunzel a great deal."

"So it had nothing to do with wanting to get me out of the castle."

"Kitten and I both thought a break would do you good," said Genny, avoiding my eyes.

I didn't really mind their plotting. The break would give me time to think about Andre. I was coming to a point of no return with him, one in which I was going to have to reject him decisively and take the consequences. Or not reject him.

Rapunzel's words in the carriage had filled me with secret exhilaration, for she had quite independently confirmed what Andre had told me. When she asked to see me the following morning, however, I went with some trepidation, fearing that she would still be angry and abusive.

It was odd to see her so weak. Before she'd always

waved her hands around as she spoke. Now they lay lifelessly before her on the white bedclothes. Her beautiful dark hair hung around her shoulders, echoing the dark hollows under her eyes. She waited till we were alone.

As I had suspected, she did want to talk about what had happened in the carriage.

"Dion," she whispered, "I'm sorry for what I must have said to you yesterday. Genny told me."

"It doesn't matter. You were ill."

"I must have been raving. Seems stupid now. Can't think why I said those things. I may die soon. So why bother with the man?" She was silent for a while.

"Thing is, I remember every word I said to you in that carriage. It's so strange. I don't remember getting sick. I know I had an argument with Andre, but I don't remember the end of it. All I remember is waking up feeling very, very weak, and vaguely I remember Kitten being there. Up until the carriage, it's very hazy. All kinds of strange deliriums . . . But then I've got this crystal clear memory of what I said to you, all those mean things. I thought it was a dream till Genny told me this morning. It was like someone else was saying it all and I was just watching. Still that's no excuse. I want you to know that I'm sorry."

"Don't worry about it."

Her eyes were beginning to droop with tiredness. It was time for me to go.

"Tell me, Rapunzel," I asked, unable to resist the temptation any longer. "Did Lord Gregorov really say . . . ?"

She grinned slightly, a glimpse of the old Rapunzel spirit.

"Aye, he did knock me back for your sake, sweetie. You've made quite a catch there. There've been times I have wanted to scratch your eyes out."

I'd thought that knowing for sure that Rapunzel had spoken the truth would have made my decision easier, but it didn't.

I did not dream as intensely of Andre while I was at the convent, a fact which I put down to the convent's chaste atmosphere. Despite this he was constantly in my mind. I kept seeing that picture of us together as two halves of a whole and remembering the strength and happiness that radiated from that picture. I still woke up in the mornings and lay there half-asleep, fantasizing that he was there with me, holding me close. Secretly I missed the dreams. I came to realize that I liked the idea of his touching me. I did want to have some kind of a relationship with him. When I realized that, I decided to return to the château. I longed for a definitive confrontation and an end to all my worrying.

At the beginning of the third day, I went to Genny and told her I was going to return to the château. She looked at me and sighed.

"Very well," she said. "I think you should stay, and I suspect Kitten does too, but it's your life."

"Why do you think I should stay?" I said.

"Men complicate everything. I'd try to forget him if I were you, and you can't do that at the château."

"I can't make up my mind here," I said.

She shrugged her shoulders.

"Keep a weather eye out for enemies," she said.

It was a humid day. As I walked, the sky became a heavier and heavier grey. Sweat trickled down my face, despite my shady hat. My shoulders under the little bag I was carrying on my back became soaked.

By the time I was halfway back, I began to regret choosing to go home alone. Though I was a good walker, the constant looking out for enemies made me jumpy. I would have enjoyed the shady, tree-lined road much more had I not had to have my witch sight active for those who might hurt me. As it was I saw very few people. Only a few peasants working in the dry, yellow wheat fields.

I was glad when I passed into the range of the château's protection barrier and was able to drop the witch sight for the mile or so through the park, but as I trudged on the air got heavier and heavier. Soon there would be a summer thunderstorm. I wished it would start raining so that the cold rain would wash the dust from my face. At last I came to the bridge over the river. The sight of it winding cool and dark among the reeds proved too much for me.

I had never bathed in it before. It was too dark-looking for me. But now my skin craved the cool, cool water. I climbed down from the bridge and walked along a path through the reeds. I knew the perfect spot, a little shelter with a boat in it and a smooth green patch of grass in front of it on the river's edge. Everywhere else the reeds barred the way to the water.

I took off my robe and plunged in. The water was wonderful. The river bottom was soft and muddy between my toes. The water was as dark brown as tea. I sat there for some time, just letting the slow current wash over me.

After a while I decided it might be fun to walk over to the opposite bank. The river seemed quite harmless. It only came up to my waist, and the current was gentle. I began to walk carefully across the muddy riverbed. Near the farther bank the current increased a little. I took another step, tripped over a hidden rock, staggered, stepped into nothing, and fell. The current knocked me over. I struggled, rolling over and over in the thick dark water and smacking hard against rocks. Water, water swirling, filling my mouth and lungs, whirling, twining petticoats everywhere, tangling my legs and struggling arms.

*Get out, I must get out.* Then a surge ran through me, the water parted, and I thrust into the air, grabbing at it with my fists. I hung there in the heavy air, choking and trying to get my breath, coldly realizing that I'd almost drowned, fool that I was, and would have, too, if my desire to be out of the river had not been enough to get me out. I pushed my wet hair out of my face and that was when I saw him. Andre was standing just below me, thigh deep in the river, looking up at me.

"Are you all right?" he said.

"Fine," I croaked, throat still full of water.

"Dammit, woman! You gave me a fright."

His chest was bare, all hard flat muscles. It was nice to look at. And his upturned face. It was so beautiful. I liked the way he looked up at me, too. I knew coldly that wet petticoats clung and that he had noticed that. I hung in the air regarding him from my detached magic viewpoint. How he attracted me! More than that, I was curious, curious about what would happen if I came down close to him and what would happen next and then next.

"Dion," he said, "come down here." He reached up and caught my hand. And pulled me down toward him.

"I missed you," he said. He kissed my hand, turned it over, and kissed the palm of it. He put out his other arm and slid it round my shoulder, pulling me closer as he did. I could see he had every intention of keeping going until I stopped him. He would kiss my lips soon, I thought. I'd like that.

Suddenly there was a crash of thunder and a great sheet of rain came down. My concentration broke and I found myself suddenly floundering in the river again.

Andre staggered back under the impact of the rain. I could hear his voice, but the downpour was deafening. He leaned toward me to pull me out.

*Angels,* I thought. *What am I doing?*

I jumped up and as quickly as I could ran out of the river and up the bank. I turned to look at him. He was just standing there in the water. As I looked at him, he yelled at me and shook his fists. I ran barefoot down the path through the reeds, arms crossed tight across my chest. The rain was so heavy it stung my neck and arms. My bare feet slipped on the muddy path. I stubbed my toe on a rock and stopped. I suddenly wanted to cry. Here I was in the teeming rain wearing only my petticoat. All my clothes were back at the riverbank. I stood there shivering in the rain for at least ten minutes while I tried to decide whether or not to go back. At last I decided I was being stupid. I had come back to Ardyne to have it out with Andre, and I had better get it over with.

At first I thought he had gone. All my clothes seemed gone, too. Then I saw that he was sitting under the boat shelter. I went closer and stood wondering what to say. Perhaps I should go before . . .

He turned and saw me and beckoned.

I ran in under the shelter. There were two big logs there. My dress was spread out on one of the logs. Andre's shirt and coat hung over the side of the boat. There was a little pile of wood in the center of the shed and beside it a flint and steel, but I could see the wood was too wet to catch. I lit the fire with magic, a homey little spell Genny had taught me.

"Thank you," said Andre. He was leaning against one of the logs. He still wore only his breeches. His wet hair dripped over his bare chest. It fell in even tighter ringlets now. We looked at each other.

"What the hell do you think you were doing out there?" His voice was low and angry.

I stared at my feet.

"First you smile, and you're all willing, and it's like every dream come true. Then suddenly you push me away. What's going on? Are you playing some kind of game with me?"

"It's magic," I said. "It makes you sort of cold and logical. I didn't realize . . ."

I just stood and looked into the fire.

"So, logically you wanted me, but when the spell broke you were too frightened and you ran. Is that what you're saying?"

I didn't say anything.

"Dammit, woman! You're driving me crazy," he yelled. "If you want me, why don't you have me? I'm willing."

"I'm . . ."

"You're what?"

"I lost my nerve," I said, squinting at him as if at a bright light.

"Why are you such a coward? Who brought you up to be so afraid of . . . What are you afraid of? Love-making? Or of me?"

He leaped up and came around the fire at me. I backed off, but the boat and the log were behind me. He was very close. I could smell the delicious scent of his body.

"Look. I can't talk to the top of your head. Sit down here."

I sat down and wrapped my arms about me. He knelt in front of me.

"Dion, look! Everybody's afraid the first time. But I can't believe you . . . After the way you looked at me today, you can't expect me to believe you're not capable of enjoying physical love. You can't go on denying your nature . . . It's going to have to express itself eventually."

He leaned close to me. "You mustn't think that having me as lover means that in ten minutes time you'll be on your back with your legs spread. It'd be a waste. A waste of both of us. I want to go slowly and savor things. Enjoy each moment, each new step. Take the time to get you used to me. It could be weeks before we actually make love. That doesn't worry me. I love you very much," he said softly. "I want you to be happy. I want to be the one to make you happy."

I stared at my hands. I had a lump in my throat.

"Why me?" I said.

"You've asked me that before. Do I need a reason? Do you? Isn't the fact that I want you, that we want each other . . . ? Why isn't that enough reason?"

I was silent.

"Dion, I've not felt this way about anyone for a long time. I find you very beautiful. I could spend days just looking at you. Your neck is so thin and fine and you have the most beautiful eyes. I like the way your back curves. I could go on. But it's more than that. I like you because you're not a fool, because you're strong. You can do things like you did with that fire. You're a powerful woman. That excites me."

"I see. And what would you want me to do with my power?"

"What do you mean?" He looked surprised.

"Perhaps you'd like me to make you rich or powerful."

"I see. You're always afraid I'm going to take advantage of you. Have men been so bad to you in the past? I swear to you all I've ever wanted from you . . . I just want you in my bed. I'm a rich man, and I can talk myself into just about anything. I had a wonderful life until I saw you that day and looked at you and somehow recognized, I don't know . . . some kind of fellow. A partner in crime maybe. I think we could have something together. Something hot."

His voice and his words were transfixing me again. He leaned over me and pressed his lips against my forehead. I didn't move.

"Dion," he whispered.

He put his hand on my cheek softly like a caress and pushed my face upward. He kissed me softly on the mouth. My stomach turned over.

I put my hand on his arm.

He kissed me again. Harder, and with parted lips. I liked it. The place between my legs tightened.

I pushed him away, before things could get too carried away.

"Just let go!" he said with frustration. I stared at the floor, my arms wrapped around myself.

"Dion, look I . . ."

He got up suddenly and went over to the boat and put on his shirt and coat. I sat there watching him doing it out of the corner of my eye. I wanted desperately for him to come and tell me I had to kiss him. That there was no choice. But I was so afraid that if I called him back, I'd regret it.

"Sweetheart," he said, "I want something very simple from you." He knelt down in front of me. "But nothing I say is going to be able to convince you of that. In the end only experience will prove that I'm telling the truth. In the end you're just going to have to take the risk that I'm not lying, just make a jump of faith. Do you understand?"

I nodded.

He sighed. "Look at me. I'm on my knees to you. And is it doing any good? No."

He was silent for a moment. "Would it help you to trust me if we got married?"

Married! God and Angels! It should have occurred to me a long time ago, but never in my wildest dreams had I ever imagined myself as anyone's wife. I was too much the mage. Or maybe I was just a slut like my mother.

"I don't know," I said. "I've never thought about it."

"No, I didn't think you had. I've never thought that kind of thing would be important to you." He sighed and got up. "Well, my love. It's stopped raining. Time to go home." He pulled on his boots.

There was a lump in my throat.

"Andre, I'm sorry."

He turned and looked at me. "I'll live," he said, grinning ruefully.

"If you change your mind, just leave your door un-locked tonight. I'll come in and lie down with you. Good-bye, my love."

He blew me a kiss and went. He didn't look back once.

So much for the great decisive conversation. I trekked slowly up the path to the château. Now I was even more churned up than ever. I was half-afraid, half-hoping that he might be waiting for me in my room, but I didn't see him anywhere around. I wished more than ever that there was some way the decision could be taken out of my hands, that I could be carried away in a moment of passion.

It was good to be back in my shady little room again. I rang for a warm bath and told the servant to inform Kitten of my return. Perhaps I could get Kitten to tell me what to do. If I could bring myself to ask her. But the servant told me Madame Avignon had gone hunting with the rest of the court. I did the late afternoon ritual. Then I locked my door as I bathed and changed. Stupid of course. He'd said the night. After that I lay on the narrow white bed wondering what on earth I was going to do.

To say yes to him seemed to be the right thing to do, but no one but Andre would agree with that. Michael . . . Michael would just shake his head sadly in that I-told-you-so sort of way and tell me I was just like my mother. Perhaps I was. Maybe I should marry Andre. Unimaginable. But then nobody could say I'd done the wrong thing. Fear of what people would say was an awful reason to marry someone. Why did I find it so hard to believe he cared for me? Hadn't he shown his care for me in thousands of ways? He'd been so patient. Was it just that I was a coward? Was it just that I was afraid of that closeness? The naked bodies against each other. I was afraid of that. Everyone was afraid that first time.

I did like it when he touched me. His flesh warm and hard and velvety to touch. I could easily imagine that we might have something special together, as in the dreams. Those ecstatic dreams, each one of which left me feeling like a purring cat, silky soft and satisfied. Would the reality be like that? I remembered my jerking, flailing ecstatic body. Wouldn't he be disgusted as I was disgusted by myself? With such a loss of control, how could I hold my own against him?

And now this offer to come to my room tonight. Nothing could have been worse. I could see myself spending all night getting in and out of bed locking and unlocking the door. I wished it was all over now.

I fell asleep. And dreamed of Andre. It was night and he lay beside me in the bed. His body was all warm and firm. And his hands, too. He undid my dress and stroked my breasts. It was such pleasure. He kissed them with his lips and tongue and sucked the nipples hard. His hands moved along my body . . .

It was so vivid, I was surprised to wake up and find it a dream. And almost disappointed. I remembered I'd locked the door. And, anyway, he'd said night.

*You really are a slut,* I thought, disgusted, as I sat up. Then I felt reckless and didn't care. I would leave the door unlocked and do the worst and then that would be that.

I went downstairs. And changed my mind. Saw Kitten's maid and left a message with her. Changed my mind back. Went to the servants' hall and ate dinner. Changed my mind again. I waited on the supper table and paid my respects to Kitten, but there was no time for more then a few polite words. I wished I could ask her advice, though I knew what it would be. I changed my mind again. Andre was there with them. He looked at me, and I looked back and changed my mind again and smiled and didn't dare look at him again.

The evening ritual was the only peaceful time in the whole evening. I could not change my mind about Andre while doing it. Afterward I sat on my bed for a short time, wondering when he would come and dreading that he would.

This was stupid. It might be four in the morning before the Duke dismissed them. I would go for a walk and try to forget about the whole thing.

The rain had gone, leaving a perfect evening, cool but not cold. The garden smelled wonderfully fresh. At the other end of the gardens was a sort of formal walk, a lane between hedges and statues, with little alcoves all the way along it.

At the end was a round enclosed area with a small tree and a nice little bench around it. I liked to go there in the mornings sometimes and watch the birds play in the trees. You could see the sea if you stood on the bench. I watched the sea turn from blue to black as the sun sank below the horizon. The stars came out in the deep, velvet sky. Everything was peaceful. Once I heard voices, but they went away. The tower clock struck ten. Then I began to think of Andre again. I couldn't remember if I had left my room locked or unlocked. If I wasn't there, would he wait for me? Would he go away discouraged and leave me waiting all night? Would that be a good or bad thing? I got up and hurried up along the path. And stopped.

There was a couple sitting on a bench in one of the alcoves. They were embracing. I could see them quite clearly in the bright moon light. I couldn't tell who they were, but from their rough clothes I thought they must be servants.

As I watched, the man undid the woman's bodice, let out her breasts and, with delectable slowness, began to lick and suckle them. I stood transfixed, listening to their soft moans of pleasure. My own breasts began to ache for that touch. I remembered from the afternoon how good that had felt. There was a tightness between my legs.

I was spying. I could not go past them without their seeing me. I would have to wait until they were gone. I turned and retreated back down the path.

I sat on the bench again. Now I knew they were there I could hear them, too. Little moans of pleasure, and the woman saying yes, yes. My memory was beginning to play back all of this afternoon's dream of Andre. All of it. I could feel those lips upon my breast again. Sucking my nipples. The secret place between my legs was throbbing. I was filled with longing. My hand was on my breast. The nipple hardened. Then, as if in a dream, I lifted my eyes up and there he was, Andre, standing in the shadows at the opening of the hedge. He looked into my eyes, and I knew he could see everything. I stood up. I don't think I meant to leave. In one stride, he was on me, had pulled me against him, was kissing me hard and deep. A few moments later, I was lying pinned beneath him on the ground, my body grinding convulsively desperately up against his. I felt myself opening out. I wanted to scream with agony and pleasure. I would have given him anything. A wave of the most exquisite delight washed over me. I clung to him, laughing and sobbing. He was laughing, too, and kissing my neck.

"Oh, my love, my love. I was beginning to think you didn't want me."

Suddenly I was terribly embarrassed. I sat up. I had acted like some kind of animal. I was still panting. What must he think of me now?

He sat up and put his arms around me from behind.

"So shy, my beautiful one? Or ashamed?"

I nodded.

"Don't be. You've made me very happy. And I you, I hope."

I stared at my lap.

"Come," he said. "What harm have we done? You're still a virgin."

I felt trapped. He had every reason to expect to change that now.

He kissed and nuzzled my neck and my cheeks. One of his hands ran up my bodice and cupped my breast.

"Come I shall spread my cloak in the shadows, and we can lie there and be private."

"I'm not ready . . ."

He pulled me around. Put his fingers on my lips.

"Hush. I know that. Do you think I'm some kind of crude rogerer? Foolish girl. What did I say to you this afternoon? You and I can enjoy each other without my having to enter you. Haven't we just proved that? Come."

He pulled me close to him and kissed me. Then he spread his cloak on the ground and sat down upon it.

"Come," he said. "Trust me. You know I can't do anything to you, that you don't want."

I had never felt so close to another person, so free. He had seen me acting like an animal and was not revolted, but pleased. I went over and lay down beside him, feeling soft and relaxed.

We lay there talking softly for a time. He kissed me and I kissed him back, which delighted him. His hands moved slowly across my body. Every touch delighted me even when he began to undo my clothes.

"Ah. I was right wasn't I? You are a very passionate woman. You should have admitted it earlier. Then it wouldn't have overwhelmed you. But I'm glad it did."

And he began to stroke me and nibble me slowly and silkily, using his fingers and tongue until he bought me to a slow, exquisite climax.

# TWELVE

Suddenly as I lay in his arms dazed with pleasure, I heard the château's clock striking. What hour? Oh my God! What hour? I started up.

I could not see the clock from here, but if I leaped up into the air I could. It was one o'clock. I was an hour late with the protection ritual.

I leaped up, pulling the laces of my bodice back together. I was vaguely aware of Andre shouting something, of his arms pulling me. I was gripped with terrible fear. Before I knew it, I was in the air and flying back toward the château, the top branches of trees tickling my feet as I passed.

I landed clumsily on the windowsill of my room and scrabbled at the mullioned windowpane for a few seconds before I remembered that it was locked. Magically unlocking the catch and scrambling round the pane so that I could climb in, cost me several minutes.

Ten past one. I could feel the spell loosening around me. Was that distant laughter I heard? I scrambled to perform the ritual but was so anxious that I upset the

candle and had to start again. For a horrible moment
I couldn't remember the words. But finally it was
done. It was twenty past one.

I sat at my table. Sometime in the past half hour
some heavy magic had been released in my direction.
My ears were buzzing with it and my head felt as if
someone was driving a spike into it. I had definitely
heard laughter. Thank God, the ritual had held out
for the extra hour. That time must have been built into
the spell. I put my face in my hands. To be late and
for such a reason . . .

The door flew open behind me.

"Dion," cried Kitten. "What happened?"

"What?" I said.

"I heard Norval's voice laughing. What happened?"

"I'm sorry, Kitten. I was late with the ritual."

"How could you be late?" she shouted. "You
know . . ." She stopped. "Dion, why were you late?
You're never late."

I could not begin to tell her. I just said, "I'm sorry"
again.

She came over and brushed the hair away from my
neck.

"You'd better wear a scarf tomorrow," she said.
"You've got love bites on your neck."

I couldn't speak.

"Andre?"

I nodded.

"God, Dion," she said sharply. "You're such a fool
sometimes."

I nodded. "I got distracted."

"Yes, yes. I know this story."

The irritation in her voice made me angry, but I
held back. I knew my anger was just guilt.

"It will never happen again," I said stiffly.

"No," she said after a moment. "I know that."

We stood there in silence. I was trying not to add tears to my other sins.

"Tell me, do you think he distracted you on purpose or was it an accident?"

The same thought had already occurred to me.

"I don't know," I whispered.

"Poor Dion," she said. Her ready sympathy only made me more ashamed. It felt too much like pity. "I was going to say that I'd never trust a man like Andre Gregorov, but when I was nineteen and two years older than you, I did just that. And I was more experienced than you as well. It seems a pity . . . Well, I suppose not. I suppose he was very accomplished."

I nodded. He had seemed to know exactly how to please me. The very thought of it made me blush.

"Come. I shall brush the leaves out of your hair. You must try to sleep." She took my hairbrush from the table and began brushing. Her touch at this moment made me want to shrink away, but I controlled myself. I felt unclean.

"You know," she said, "under any other circumstances I would have been delighted. I'd be itching to know how it was."

I began to cry.

"I'm so ashamed. To be late with the ritual for such a reason. I should never have let him . . ."

She smacked me lightly. "Dion!" she said gently. "Lord Andre is a beautiful and sensuous man. Who could blame you for giving yourself to him? I only wish I trusted his intentions more."

"We didn't . . ."

"No? Well. It hardly matters."

Her hands were shaking. I saw them in the mirror.

"I'm sorry, Kitten. I won't let it happen again."

"It's all right," she said. She sighed and sat down suddenly on the bed behind me and took a big breath. She put her hand up to her eyes. For the second time in a week I watched her wipe back hidden tears. "Norval frightens me so much."

I remembered that moment of fear back in Gallia when she begged me to kill her rather than letting Norval get hold of her.

"I'm so sorry."

"I know you won't let yourself get distracted like that again. God, I need a stiff drink."

"What would you like?"

"Oh! Plum spirit. Why? Have you got some?"

I knew there would be some in the kitchens. I could picture where it was. I made some pour into a glass and bought it to the room.

The glass of plum spirit opening the door and sliding in made her laugh. She caught it in her hand, took a big gulp, and made a face

"Whew! I needed that."

We sat in silence for a while.

"Perhaps I should tell Andre that I don't want to go on with it."

"Why? Because of what happened tonight? Do you think it could happen again? Do you feel that he did distract you on purpose?"

"I just don't think I can be trusted after this. It's not professional. It's not right."

"Dion, you know I'd rather have your full mind on my protection. But do you really think sending Andre away is going to do that? I can see you being just as distracted by wondering what might have been. Why should you be alone just because you have certain duties to perform? Captain Simonetti has a wife whom he loves very much, but he is always an excellent bodyguard. Wouldn't it be better if Andre were permitted to come and visit you in my house? Then I'd know you were safe, and the servants could keep reminding you of the time."

I gaped at her. She made everything seem so ordinary. Ordinary and sordid.

"Dion, if we're anxious about Andre's motives, it seems best to do it that way. You'd be protected in my house. I know it's not very romantic, but love affairs are not all romance."

"No!" I said.

"Dion!"

"I think it would be best to stop it after what has happened. I've got no business carrying on like this. It's . . . It's disgusting."

"Dion. It's not disgusting. There's nothing wrong with having a lover. You're entitled to love and be loved in return."

"Yes, but it doesn't have to mean that."

"Now you are being childish." She put her hand on my arm. "You can't tell me what you feel for Andre isn't very physical."

I knew she was right.

"You've changed your tune," I said bitterly. "Before now it was all 'be careful, Dion.' "

"A person has to suit her advice to the facts." She was silent for a moment. "I know you, Dion. You're quite capable of rejecting Andre just to punish yourself for being late. You're always so hard on yourself. I know neither of us trust his motives. But all love is risky. Tonight you obviously decided the risk was worth it. Don't go and change your mind just because of something that could be the most innocent of accidents."

Perhaps she was right. At the moment I hated myself. What if I had not heard the clock? Kitten would be dead. And where would I be?

I was afraid, too. I'd told myself and told myself that Andre couldn't make me do anything I didn't want to, but tonight out there I'd completely lost control.

"Then you think I should continue with him."

"I don't know, Dion. I wouldn't like to make that decision for you. I don't know what would be best for you. Come let me finish brushing your hair. Then you sleep on it."

Why do people always say that? When you sleep on a thing you can never sleep. I tossed and turned and wept thinking of Andre. But when I thought of how and where I had let him touch me . . . Guilt made me strong in my resolve to put the whole thing off. Surely he would understand. Surely if he cared he would wait. But I had a feeling he wasn't going to understand, that he was going to be very angry.

He came running up the stairs to my room in the middle of the next morning. His tall figure filled the doorway. He had an armful of white roses and a smile which made my heart turn over.

"I understand now why you flew off last night. I expect a protection spell must have a strict schedule."

I told him of my decision.

"No!" he said softly at first.

Then he raised his voice.

"No! You can't do this to me! Not now! Not after last night!"

"Please, Andre. I just want to wait."

"Wait for what?" He grabbed my arms and shook me. "For when? Do you think I'm made of stone?"

"I forgot myself last night. I almost caused a disaster. I don't want that to happen again."

"That's a stupid excuse. You're just punishing yourself for making a mistake. I don't see why you should punish me too. I don't have to put up with that, you straitlaced little cat," he cried.

I got angry then and yelled back.

"Why don't you just leave me alone?"

"All right then. If that's what you want. It's over. I've had it with you. Don't expect me to wait for you to change your mind this time. I can find plenty more appreciative company."

"Yes, why don't you?" I yelled.

"Don't worry. I will." He slammed the door behind him.

A moment later there was shouting in the hallway.

I pulled open my door. Andre was yelling at Kitten.

"... put her up to this, didn't you. Don't think I don't know what you're up to, Madame. I've seen you with Dion, touching her, putting your arms round her."

"Lord Gregorov, watch your tongue."

"Leave her alone!" I said. "She didn't make me do anything."

He turned and saw me.

"No! You really believe that, don't you?" he said. "You trust the Duke's whore. Well, at least I've been honest with you about what I want. I'm not lulling you into my bed like this ... pervert."

"Don't be ridiculous!"

"Ridiculous, is it? You just ask my lady who keeps her warm on nights when the Duke's away. You ask her all about her and her precious Genny. And our good friend Rapunzel."

"Shut your mouth," shouted Kitten. Her face reddened.

"Hah. See that! I'm right, aren't I. Look at that, girl. She's ashamed. I've caught her out. Did you realize that, girl? You're living with a lesbian. And she'll get you eventually."

Kitten slapped him hard across the face.

Andre just looked at her.

"I think you've said quite enough, Lord Gregorov." Kitten's voice was hard as she spat out the words.

Andre turned on his heel and stalked away.

"Oh, Dion," said Kitten beseechingly.

I went into my room, slamming the door and locking it behind me. Then I lay on my bed and cried. I ignored Kitten's knocking at the door. After a short time she went away.

It was dark by the time someone knocked on the door again.

"It's Maria. I've some food for you."

I was hungry. I opened the door.

She spread the food on the worktable with scant respect for the chalk marks and circles.

"Now sit yourself down and eat," she said. I sat. She hovered.

"Madam Avignon was very upset. She wanted to come and talk to you."

I scowled at her.

"Did she send you to plead her case?"

"Yes, that she did. She wanted me to tell you that she thought of you as a friend and nothing more."

"Then what Andre Gregorov said was true."

"That Madame and Genny Appellez were more than just friends, and about Rapunzel. Yes, that's true. Mademoiselle, I've worked for several courtesans. At one time or another, many of them take a woman to their beds. I used to think it was wicked, but now . . . It's just the way of it. Maybe they get sick of men, or maybe it's just that men always mean business to them, or maybe lovemaking just gets to be a habit with them. It's certainly true that plenty of patrons won't have a male rival, but find the idea of women making love quite pleasing. It's no business of yours. It has nothing to do with you."

I stared at the food.

"She and Rapunzel used to appear in erotic tableaux together. That's all. I doubt if it was more than friendly business between them. As for Madame Genny, that was over some time ago, before the Duke even."

"It's wicked," I muttered.

"Foolish girl!" Maria stamped her foot in irritation. "Don't be so judgmental. What do you know of Kitten Avignon? Hasn't she always been good to you? Has she ever given you any reason to fear for your virtue?"

I could think of lots of "perhaps" situations in the past. But no "definites." And yes—she had always been good to me, and I wanted to forget about Andre's words and Kitten's guilty blush. I wanted everything to be as it was between us again, but I suspected that now it never could be. When I saw Kitten in her dressing room the following day, there was constraint between us. There were none of her usual spontaneous hugs or affectionate endearments.

Andre Gregorov went to the Duke almost immediately on leaving me and asked his permission to leave the château that day. It was granted, and he left. It was not known what he had told the Duke, but interested parties did note that a coldness had sprung up between the Duke and his favorite mistress. Interested parties also noted the arrival of another of the

Duke's mistresses, Lady Castille, the following day. She must have been waiting nearby for the Duke to send for her. Now he had.

Archimedes Brown, who was standing with me in the stable yard as I was watching the lady get down from her carriage and who noticed my worried face, said, "Don't worry about the Castille, sweet child. She may be better born, but her charms are no match for Kitten Avignon."

"So you think it will be all right."

"I'm sure of it. Listen, our Kitten didn't get to be top courtesan on looks alone. I've seen her in action. I love that woman. She's magic."

He waggled his hips in a way that gave a certain impression.

"She sort of looks at a fellow like this, see." He pouted his lips and rolled his eyes. He looked more comic than erotic. Despite my heavy heart, I couldn't help giggling as he took a few mincing steps.

"Then if a bit more distraction is needed, she starts to take off her clothes. Or something more imaginative. By the Archangel! It's magnificent to see her in action."

He laughed and spread out his hands, setting the scene. "I'd love to be there tonight. Clash of the Love Goddesses. The Castille will be doing a number on old Leon. Solid workmanlike job, kind of aristocratic, and then our Kitten will appear at the door."

He took a pose, fluttered his eyes, and licked his lips sexily.

"And she'll do her abandoned woman bit. The Castille won't know what hit her. Mind you, if she has the sense to lock the door this time, it could be a problem. But have faith in your mistress, girl. She knows her business."

Kitten's reaction to Lady Castille's arrival was a little different, but no less confident.

"That bloody cow," she said, rubbing rouge savagely off her face. "Now I'll have to put up with her catty remarks and her spiteful slights until Leon decides to forgive me. If he decides to forgive me. And I'll have to act like a bitch in heat the whole time she's here. God! I weary of these court games."

"Maybe you should retire," I said.

"The thought is very appealing today. But Leon would be mortally offended if I didn't fight to get him back. I must play this stupid game for the moment. It used to amuse me, but it's beginning to wear a bit thin. Damn. Pass me that lip salve. No, the black pot."

I couldn't help wondering ungenerously if this was just a rationalization. It would be hard to give up all that money and glory.

She stopped and looked at me in the mirror.

"Maria said she'd spoken to you."

"Yes."

"Dion, I'm not a lesbian despite what people say of courtesans. In fact I've never been much interested in women. Years ago Genny and I happened to fall in love. Now we are just close friends. I've no desire to involve you in that part of my life. Do you believe me?"

"Yes," I said. Knowing as I said it that all I'd done was to suspend judgment till I had further evidence.

She smiled at me. "I'm glad. I'm fond of you, Dion. I don't want us to be on bad terms."

"Did Andre say something to the Duke?"

"It's hard to tell. Lady Castille may be here because of something Andre Gregorov said, or Leon may just be angry at me for opposing him so often lately."

"I'm sorry."

"It's not your fault. I'm just sorry you found all this out this way. And I'm sorry about Andre, too. How do you feel?"

"I'll live," I said. I went away before I began to cry.

It was a uniformly unpleasant next few days.

There was no Genny to distract me, and I was still too shy to visit the actors by myself. The Duke required Kitten's constant attendance as he appeared to struggle over the decision of which mistress he preferred. We received daily messages from Genny telling us that Rapunzel was not improving. Even the weather turned bad, and it became too cool to swim.

Every place I went reminded me of Andre. I tried to persuade myself that it had been for the best, but I began to feel that I had made a big mistake and that Andre had been right about everything, even Kitten. I realized that because I spent so much time with Kitten, I had come to think of our relationship as special. Now I perceived that Kitten and Genny's relationship was the special one, special in a different and much more concrete way. Dimly I felt that I could never be important to Kitten as Genny was. It wasn't that I was jealous. Of course not! It was just that this made it all the worse that I had thrown away my special relationship with Andre. And for her, too. It was in me to resent her sometimes.

I still dreamed about Andre, agonizingly tender and ecstatic dreams. I would awake desolated because I was alone, knowing it didn't have to be like that. I tried not to feel as if I had lost the only person who would ever want me, but I could not see anyone else ever caring for such a stupid person as myself.

Fortunately after five days of this, the Duke left Ardyne to return to the business of state. The summer was officially over.

We left Genny at the convent, and Kitten and I returned to Gallia. We traveled together for the first few days, as Lady Castille was occupying the favored place beside the Duke. Then halfway through the river journey, Kitten received a summons to the Ducal barge, and I spent the rest of the journey on the now-chilly grey river with only a couple of novels for company. This was what the rest of my life will be, I thought. There will come a day when Kitten no longer needs me, and then I will have nothing. I am not really important to her. I'm not really important to anyone. I gave myself over to gloom, which only lifted in the bustle and comfort of arrival home.

Back in Gallia, I returned to my former life of clinic work and reading as if nothing had happened.

Lord Andre Gregorov was also acting as if nothing had happened at Ardyne and with a vengeance. His exploits seemed to have become even more outrageous and there always seemed to be someone bringing us stories of pranks that my lord had played. Had he not persuaded two women, unnamed of course, from two different feuding families to come to bed with him at the same time? Was he not the bold fellow who had seduced a certain young lordling away from the Duke's brother Lord Pell? Lord Pell was reported to be seriously offended by this poaching on his territory, but the Duke, who openly despised his brother, was so much amused by the incident that it seemed Andre was back in favor.

Though some of our visitors looked curiously at me when they visited, Kitten told me that the full extent of what had happened between us at Ardyne did not seem to be known. I was grateful to Andre for this and tried not to show how much his exploits upset me. It didn't grow easier.

I kept busy. Since Genny was still in Ishtak, I took extra work in the clinic helping Maya. When I was alone, however, I was inclined to weep or fall into a maudlin depression.

It was confusing that while I remained a virgin and was therefore technically still pure, I had, in fact, changed. All the sensual feelings that I had barely been aware of before I went to Ardyne were now very much part of my daily life. I felt knowing and slightly besmirched, and the fact that nothing had really happened, that I was still intact, which I think would have comforted my foster father, was no comfort to me at all. The erotic dreams persisted. I had passed a point of no return.

Although I was inclined to avoid Kitten at first, often when I was sad, she seemed to happen upon me. "Are you moping again?" she would say to me in a mock scolding tone, but she would hold me if I was weeping and listen to my woes with seemingly endless patience. I was too miserable to worry myself about the implications of letting her touch me. She said sensible and helpful things and was at pains to provide me with distractions or talk out worries. Once or twice, with uncharacteristic frankness, she even told me of her anxieties over the Duke's continuing coolness. With the typical self-centeredness of the lovelorn, I paid little attention to her problems.

Shortly after we returned from Ardyne, I told Kitten that I still had erotic dreams of Andre every night. She frowned and asked me a few questions about when the dreams had started and how vivid they were. Later that day she came to my room and gave me a magical salve, which she said might help with the dreams if rubbed it on my temples at night.

It had never occurred to me that those dreams had

been set on me. I had always guiltily thought of them as a manifestation of my own evil nature. Not surprisingly, I was entirely ignorant of the existence of such magic. If I had thought about it, I would have assumed that the protection I wove round Kitten and myself would have prevented such things. I was horrified to discover that the salve worked. I still dreamed of Andre, but the dreams were mild and commonplace.

Kitten explained that some noblemen who wished to undertake seductions used dream-sending spells to soften resistance. The sender merely rubbed the spell on his temples and thought the thoughts he wished to send. Dreamers had little resistance to such sendings, and the salve was the best way to combat them.

"It's a low trick," she said.

I was aghast to think that Andre had known all about the dreams I had been having about him and disgusted that he should have manipulated me in such a way. However, I forgave him with surprising ease. It quickly occurred to me that he must still be sending me dreams, and I was filled with hope that all was not over between us. In my heart of hearts, I think I was excited that he was having such thoughts about me. After the first few days, I forgot to apply the salve with extraordinary regularity for someone who was supposed to be disgusted at dreaming lurid dreams.

Although I found Kitten comforting at first, after a while, I became irritated with her. She didn't take my heartbreak seriously enough. She seemed to assume that no matter how sad I was over Andre, I would get over it.

"If at seventeen you have decided that your life has been ruined by one dissolute nobleman, then you are being a great fool. My love—"she took my hand and patted it—"it is terrible while it lasts, and it may last a while, but I have faith that you will live through these terrible feelings and come out the other side older and wiser and go on to be very happy one day."

Naturally, since I wanted a happy ending that included Andre, these sentiments held no appeal for me. And didn't Kitten realize what I had thrown away for her? So I swung between hope and despair and with it between irritation at Kitten, and humble gratitude.

Erasmus Tinctus had finished his painting of Kitten, but he still came to see us several times a week. One would have thought that he and I might have become closer at this time, but in fact Erasmus' state of mind was such that nobody could be close to him. He was in the throes of finally finishing the altarpiece he had been working on for the last two years. It was the pinnacle of his career so far and his tribute to the New Learning and his "dear Madame Avignon."

Erasmus would arrive at the house, all covered in paint, eat a meal or drink tea, and stare into space. Then he would come out with some completely irrelevant philosophical remark about painting and after a passionate and often one-sided discussion would suddenly announce that the rest time he'd allowed himself was over and he must return to work.

He was no help to me in my lovesickness. The few times I got the courage to move around to the topic, he ignored it completely and started to complain instead about how his blue had turned black, or how a false stroke had left his St. Alexandria looking peevish instead of serene.

Unfortunately all his talk was of technique. He did not talk of the altarpiece's subject matter, though he did hint that the Church would be a little unhappy with some of the things he'd done. This failed to set off the appropriate alarm bells in our minds. The genial Gallian Church frequently uttered good-natured protests at the activities of the New Learning followers simply for the sake of form. No one, not even its own clergy, paid much attention to these protests.

Finally Erasmus stopped coming completely, and we did not hear from him until a fortnight later, when we received a letter inviting us to come to the first showing of his altarpiece at the Church of St. Vitalie.

Looking back, it is surprising that the Duke had not ordered an initial private showing of the altarpiece, as was generally his practice. It seems likely that he knew that the work was "daring" and since he was unsure of its reception, he decided to see what the popular reaction would be before he took a stance. Unlike other Gallians, Duke Leon, rat-canny as ever, must have guessed that the presence of a large number of Burning Light believers in the city was going to make a significant difference to the way such examples of the New Learning were going to be received. However, I doubt if even he could have predicted the extent of the catastrophe.

I went to see Erasmus' altarpiece the very first day it was shown to the public. As a result I was one of the few people ever to see it.

Kitten did not go with me, though she had planned to. That morning she had received a summons to the castle, an invitation which could not be refused. I was daunted at the prospect of going to the viewing without her and protested that I knew nothing about art. I could see myself being unable to say anything but "I like it" to Erasmus. He was sure to be disappointed by such inadequate art criticism. And what if I didn't like it?

"One of us must be there," insisted Kitten. She charged me with all sorts of affectionate and apologetic messages to Erasmus and bundled me firmly out of the door.

"If you get stuck, say something about sensitive use of color," she said. "That's always been Ras's strong point."

St. Vitalie, where the altarpiece was on display, was informally known as the parish church of the New Learning. Its priests were very liberal and were even known to hear the confessions of courtesans. The church itself was a tall white building, crowned with a dome overlooking a small, pleasant cobbled square.

When Simonetti and I arrived, this square was full of people scurrying hither and thither. Inside, the long bright nave was crowded and the noise of talking and shouting was deafening. So many art lovers in Gallia? So many of them seemed to be priests and monks. I was disturbed at the number of Burning Light people among the crowd. Looking at the faces of the clergy, I could see that Erasmus had been right. His altarpiece had upset the Church.

Simonetti pushed me through the crowd, toward where I could see the curved top of the altarpiece. He was not very happy to be in such a crowd, but most people gave way when they recognized the garb of a bodyguard.

The crowd was, of course, thickest in front of the altarpiece. Here our view was blocked by two tall courtiers whispering to each other. Then they moved away and we were pushed forward by the crowd behind.

I saw the source of outrage immediately. It stuck

out like a sore on the face of a child. In the center panel Tansa stood, face turned up to heaven, hand outstretched to receive the word of God, which was being handed to him in the shape of a golden rose by the Angel of Annunciation. The face of the Angel was clearly that of Our Lady of Roses, Kitten Avignon. It was common enough for altarpiece painters to use the faces of respectable nobles as models for Tansa's attendant saints. But to use a fallen woman like Kitten Avignon, and in such an important role . . . You might as well have put horns and a tail on Tansa himself.

"Blasphemy," shouted a voice somewhere beside us.

Simonetti mouthed a curse.

"Come on. We'd better get out of here before there's trouble."

A man had pulled free of the crowd and was standing beside the altarpiece. His pointing finger punched the air.

"Behold," he cried, "the Holy Church held to ransom by the Whore of Babylon. Behold the putrid child of this foul New Learning heresy."

He swung around to face us.

It was Ryart Dashalle, his lean fanatic's face suffused with self-righteous anger.

"See where the seductions of this pernicious learning lead. They would have it that we worship filthy whores. Well, I say righteous Tansites must rise up against such blasphemy. Rise up and stone the devils who have soiled the Holy Church."

Ryart Dashalle! An escaped prisoner like him would be very foolish to be standing here so openly. Unless he felt very sure of his safety.

Simonetti grabbed my arm. If Dashalle saw me

now, things could get unpleasant. We fought back through the crowd, but it had become much bigger and it was hard to make any headway.

Then from deep inside the church, came the chanting of hymns. The sound chilled my blood. It was "Cleanse the Unrighteous," the battle hymn of the fundamentalist Church of the Burning Light, a song all moderate Morians had learned to fear.

And so had everyone else.

Panic seized the crowd. People began to scream and rush for the door. The inside of the church became a great whirlpool of human beings. In the rush I was pulled away from Simonetti. Behind me I heard a crash. The altarpiece had disappeared into the crowd. I struggled for the door, not daring to push too hard lest I fall and be trampled, unable to put my feet down or gain my balance because of the momentum of the people around me. Behind us voices were chanting. I heard the words, "death to the blasphemer" shouted in Morian.

It took me a few moments of panic before I thought to cast a spell. I didn't want to do anything that would make me too obvious, so I cast a spell which allowed me to walk unseen among the crowd. Immediately everyone turned shadowy and distant, the way they always do with such a spell. Unfortunately their feet and elbows remained unpleasantly substantial. Someone slammed painfully down on my foot and then I was elbowed in the eye. Then suddenly I was out of the door like a cork out of a bottle and tumbling down the stairs. I managed to cast a protection spell on myself to avoid being trampled and saw a man who was not so lucky go down among the forest of legs charging down the stairs. I couldn't reach him to help him.

People were fleeing out of the church square like

ants out of a flooded anthill. Some men in the black-and-grey garb of the Burning Light were building a pyre and defending it with cudgels and fists from a few hardy townspeople. I walked silently past the shadowy brawlers, hearing the sickening thud of fists upon flesh. A woman tried to stop two of them carrying off her flower cart. They pushed her to the ground, yelling that God hated the despoilers of the land.

It was good to be under a spell at that moment. I knew I was horrified by the sight of the big stake in the middle of the pile of wood, but I felt nothing of it. I saw Simonetti valiantly trying to get back into the church and, knowing logically that I should prevent him, I drifted up to him and took him by the shoulder. This broke the spell and suddenly I was blinking at the brightness of the world and filled with confused and frightened emotions.

Simonetti grabbed my arm and pulled me off the steps and into an alleyway leading off the square.

"Come on," he said. "Let's get out of here."

"No!" I said. "Wait!"

"Listen, girl," he hissed, shaking me fiercely. "You know your duty. Protecting Kitten. I'm not going to let you put yourself in danger."

Just then a huge crowd of shouting, singing people burst from the church and streamed down the steps. They were the supporters of the Burning Light, Morians, all dressed in black and grey, and a sprinkling of Gallians noticeable for their more ordinary clothing. Every Burning Light person in Gallia must have been there. Those people were frighteningly organized, marching and chanting and shaking their fists. Their faces were full of the repulsive self-righteousness that I'd seen so often before. It always filled me with sick hatred.

Some huge wooden object was being carried above the heads of the crowd. It was the altarpiece. As we watched, it disappeared into the crowd like water down a drainhole, and we heard sounds of splintering wood. Huge pieces of it were flung up out of the swirling crowd and onto the pile of wood around the stake.

The crowd was not satisfied with the altarpiece. They stayed in the square shouting, milling angrily around. They were waiting for someone. Someone to be burned at that stake?

Bitter memories of Moria flooded back. I remembered that time Michael and I had hidden among the chimneys of Mangalore. I remembered the less lucky mages; Peter, Michael's apprentice Mordred . . . All lined up in witch manacles and being led out to the fire. The screams, the smell . . .

Tears were running down my face now as I watched. Some poor creature was going to . . . Erasmus. Oh Erasmus. Would it be you?

Several people had advised us to get away as they'd run past us standing in the alleyway. Now the flight of people from the square had stopped.

"These people hate you mages," Simonetti whispered. "Come on. Or do you want to wind up on that pyre?" He grabbed me round the waist and started hauling me away.

"No," I said. "What about Erasmus? We've got to find him. Help him."

He hesitated for a moment. Then he said, "Girl, I'm not paid to protect him. There's nothing we can do for him now. He'll have to take his chances. The city militia will be here soon."

I struggled with him and then quite coldly I decided I must get away from him. I couldn't stand by and let anyone go through this horrible death, especially if it was going to be Erasmus.

"Very well," I said wearily. "Let me go."

He put me down, and, as he did, I made myself disappear.

"You fool!" yelled Simonetti behind me.

I crawled quickly away on my hands and knees to avoid Simonetti, who was swinging his arms through the air above my head, trying to catch and hold me. I slipped out of the alleyway, round the edge of the square, and into another alleyway. There I let myself become visible. I would have preferred to be invisible to such people as were on the square, and I could certainly have used the coldness of magic at that moment, but I was afraid that remaining invisible would exhaust me, use up strength that I might soon need.

I pulled my cloak around me and slipped into the crowd, hoping desperately that the militia would come.

Suddenly the crowd roared. A group of black-and-grey-garbed priests appeared in the church door. They dragged out a prisoner and threw him on the church porch near the top of the steps. Ryart Dashalle stood astride the inert body and began to harangue the crowd. In his right hand he held a great golden staff topped with a sun disc. In his left he waved an unlit torch.

I knew the body, even at that distance. It was Erasmus.

I was trembling with fright. I told myself firmly that Dashalle could not see me in all this crowd. It was small comfort. This was a crowd who hated any kind of magic not associated with the Church. Dashalle was screaming frenziedly at them, his upraised fist punching the air while they yelled violently in response.

In Moria, Burning Light priests were always armed with iron rings and protective spells to keep my kind out of their minds and witch manacles to make us helpless before them. In Moria there would be a priest standing among those on the steps now, called a witch hunter, using magic that would show up any other magic being used. If they'd known I was there . . . The thought didn't bear thinking on.

I had no idea what I was going to do. Oh Angels. I prayed that the militia get here before I had to do anything.

"Burn the blasphemer!" screamed Dashalle.

The crowd roared its approval. The priests grabbed Erasmus and dragged him between them down the steps. I saw him being hauled, feet dragging, through the crowd, who were kicking and punching at him. He was dripping wet. They'd taken the trouble to bring him around for the burning so that he could be aware of his purification.

He was moving his head a little, but mercifully he seemed dazed. His pleasant face and curly brown hair were covered in blood. I couldn't get close to him in the crowd. Their frenzy was too great. The priests and their henchmen had to beat them back with cudgels in order to get him to the stake.

Oh Angels, where were those soldiers? I did know one very strong spell that would carry us a short distance through space and time and out of danger. But it was an exhausting spell. It needed enormous power, and I dared not take us too far lest I suddenly find myself exhausted and powerless and only halfway there. I had to think of somewhere safe to go.

Somewhere close by. There'd be no second chance of avoiding the crowd if they came out of the square looking for us. I struggled through the crush toward the pyre where Erasmus had been bound. Only with rope, thank God. There were no witch manacles today.

The crowd were pushing forward, the faithful wanting to be as close to the burning pyre as possible. Men with cudgels were still heaving them back. I got as close as I could. Then I let myself drop to the ground. Unnoticed in the thrashing mass of legs, I slipped into invisibility. Feet trod all over me as I struggled to rise again and get to the front. My cloak was torn away from me. I tried to keep moving, to keep down lest somebody notice that they couldn't actually see me.

At last I was out in the empty space and slithering over the greasy cobblestones to the pyre. I dodged around the guards. I was most likely to be caught here, where if anyone accidentally touched me, they could see that their hand was being stopped by thin air.

The pyre was already smouldering. It stank of pitch. It would burn quickly when it went. I had to be fast. I swallowed and dived for the pyre.

I climbed as fast as I could across the smouldering logs. They began to move and collapse under my feet, pushing me away from Erasmus. Desperately I threw myself at the stake. Any fool would know I was there now. I yelped as my skin connected with the hot logs. The acrid smell of burning smoke stank in my nostrils and the sparks were like little hot needles.

I grasped Erasmus in my arms and felt my invisibility slipping away. Oh, Angels! Let me be anywhere but here! Let me be at ... the charity clinic of St.

Belkis. At my back the crowd began to scream.
"Witchcraft!" I let the spell out.

A huge gut-wrenching blast of power, a great shudder through my bones, and we tumbled onto a rough
wooden floor. I lay there gasping, gasping for breath
while power ripped out of me. My whole body was
jarred, like an elbow is when you knock it. My nostrils
were full of the smell of smouldering cloth. The ceiling whirled, and, for a moment, I could neither move
nor speak and Erasmus lay across my legs like a dead,
dead weight.

# THIRTEEN

Someone screamed and suddenly there were nuns everywhere, all fluttering black-and-white robes and voices calling my name. Hands pulled me up off the floor and patted me to see if I was whole. I leaned limply against the end of a bed, feeling winded. A startled woman sitting up in the bed opposite stared at me with her mouth agape. The tiny red-faced baby in her arms let out a wail and she blinked and pushed her nipple back in its mouth.

"Praise God!" cried someone from among the nuns crouching on the floor around Erasmus. "He's still alive, poor lamb."

"Quickly! Get him into the clinic." It was Sister Bertrida. "Dion, are you well?"

I was fine. I really was fine. For a few moments I'd felt winded, but now I was beginning to feel . . . good. Great! It was like falling into freezing cold water. At first you gasp from shock and then when you get out, your skin tingles, energy surges through you, you feel fabulous!

I took a deep breath and looked into Sister Bertrida's concerned eyes.

"Yes. I'm good. There is a riot at St. Vitalie. The Burning Light are burning Erasmus' altarpiece. You should barricade the doors. There are violent people about."

I stood up and strode after the nuns carrying Erasmus.

"Put him on the table. I shall heal him now. Call Mother Theodosia."

Maya was in the clinic, but I brushed off her offers of help for me and drew her to Erasmus.

I felt such an amazing calm. It was as if for a moment I could control the world. It can only have been the coldness of magic.

The nuns pulled Erasmus' clothing off and washed him down. We examined him. He was hardly burned at all, but he was concussed and two ribs and several fingers were broken. His ankle was shattered, and it was hard for us to get it back together properly. By the time we had finished, I knew he would paint again, but it was likely he would always walk with a limp. He would live, though, and the magic with which we set his bones meant they had already begun to knit.

The healing kept me calm. It was only when the nuns had carried Erasmus away to bed that it left me. My knees began to tremble and the scorches on my hands and legs began to sting. I sat down on a stool and put my head between my legs. What had I done! Suddenly I was terrified. I could have been caught and be burning now alongside Erasmus.

"Dion, my child."

Mother Theodosia was standing over me, offering me a cup of wine. I took a gulp of it, choking a little on sharp herbs that had been steeped in it.

"What's happening? There are people gathering outside."

I could hear them. There was muffled chanting coming from the street outside. Could the mob . . . It was only a few blocks from here to St. Vitalie. Could they have discovered where I had gone? If they had witch hunters among them, it wouldn't have been hard. Oh no! What had I brought upon us all?

"Have you locked the doors?" I asked quickly.

"Yes," said Maya. She was standing on a table peering out of the high window. "They look nasty. Lots of Burning Light. What's going on?"

I should have thought of this. I put my head in my hands. Now I had put everybody in danger. Oh stupid, stupid Dion!

I told them briefly about the riot in the church and how I had rescued Erasmus. Outside the muttering of the crowd grew.

"You pulled him off the pyre?" said Maya, climbing down from the table and coming toward me. "And bought him all the way here? Through space and time? My God, Dion! I'm surprised you're still conscious."

"Sweet Lord Tansa," said Mother Theodosia. "You brave, brave child." She hugged me to her.

"I'm so sorry, Mother. I . . ."

Smash. There was glass everywhere as a huge cobblestone came crashing through the window. It smashed onto the table where, a moment ago, Maya had been standing.

The screams of "Witch! Burn the witch!" were suddenly much louder.

"Quickly. Let's get everyone out of here."

Mother Theodosia ran into the other room, shouting orders at the nuns in the hospice as she went.

Maya was pulling jars off the shelves into a basket. "Dion, grab that Calgrin."

I grabbed the bottle and pulled an armful of bandages out of a drawer.

Another cobblestone came smashing through the window. A third slammed into the shelf beside us, shattering glass bottles everywhere.

"Come ON, Maya!"

I grabbed her arm and pulled her from the room and down the corridor into the clinic. The screams of "Witch! Burn the witch!" from the street were muffled as I slammed the door behind us.

The clinic and hospital were flimsy wooden buildings, built against the convent wall. A door had been cut into the wall of the convent behind so that the nuns could come through without having to enter the outside world. Now they were hustling all the patients through that door.

The door between the clinic and the hospital room had no bolt. I could hear the smashing of wood and glass behind it. I pressed a little spell into the doorframe, stumbling over its unfamiliar words. The door and the frame melted together to form a single piece of wood. I pressed my ear against the door. Were those voices I could hear in the corridor beyond?

"Dion, come on. Everyone's out now. We can go," said Maya tugging my arm.

I turned and saw the hospital was empty. Maya and I ran to the convent door. Behind us blows began falling on the hospital door.

The door in the wall of the convent was strong, thick, and bound with iron. It had heavy iron bolts and a thick iron bar. Mother Theodosia had evidently been looking to the time when the clinic might be moved from that place, and the wall might have to be closed again. The iron would slow the Burning Light priests for a short time at least. It would give time for the patients, some of whom were very slow or being carried on stretchers by the nuns, to get to safety.

The convent itself had a ten-foot-high stone wall around it. I did not feel so confident that that would hold back an angry Burning Light. I tried to tell myself that I was being too afraid of them. This was not Moria. This was Gallia. The authorities would come and break things up before they went too far. Though, trying to burn Erasmus at the stake and breaking into St. Belkis charity clinic . . . That was already going pretty far.

As if to echo my thoughts, Mother Theodosia muttered, "Where on earth are the militia?"

On the other side of the wall was a lawn. The long line of patients and attendant nuns was moving across it, into an old stone building with high arched windows and a squat tower at one end.

"That's the old chapel," said Mother Theodosia. "The nuns hid here last century when Yustine Sahr captured Gallia. It's built like a fortress."

There was a shout from behind us. We turned to see a couple of men standing on the roof of the hospital. Luckily it was too high for them to jump into the convent grounds, but they were shouting and hurling rocks ineffectually in our direction.

"Fools!" snorted Maya. "But how is it they got here so quickly? That's what I wonder. It's as if they could follow you here."

"They did," I said guiltily. "There will be experienced witch hunters among them. They will have picked up some kind of trail from the magic I used to get here. Oh Mother, I am so sorry. I have put us all in danger. I didn't think. Perhaps if I left . . ."

"Oh, hush," she chided me. "Don't be so foolish. Do you think I would have preferred you out there facing that mob on your own with a wounded man on your hands? You did right to come here. A convent is also a place of sanctuary."

Inside the chapel, the patients had been arrayed against the far wall and among the pews. A baby was crying. The nuns were sitting in neat rows on the pews. On the altar steps sat a little group of novices. Some of them were only little girls. Erasmus lay tidily on a stretcher beside the wall with several other unconscious patients. The sight of so many helpless and innocent people, the thought of them breaking under the violence of the mob from the cathedral close . . .

"I should go away from here now," I cried. "Using magic. There's a good chance they'd follow me away, a very good chance. At least some of them."

"You might be better to stay here, Dion, and protect us," said Mother Theodosia. She put her arm round my shoulders and squeezed me. "We shall do our best, but if there are priest-mages in that mob, we shall be hard-pressed to keep them out. And they will still be wanting to get Erasmus."

I wished very much for Captain Simonetti then. I was terrified of being trapped in the convent. I remembered too clearly that time in Moria when we narrowly escaped a similar mob, climbing away over roofs, and how people had been burned behind us. My hands were trembling; my first impulse was to run, to get away. I feared that it might just be cowardice on my part. Or was it wisdom? Simonetti would have known which it was. He would have known whether it was wisest to go or stay. I wished

I hadn't had to leave him back in the church square. I hoped he was safe now.

Mother Theodosia was right, I decided. Who else was to defend them if I didn't?

At that moment one of the little novices, who had climbed onto the sill of one of the high arched windows and was peering out through an unstained pane, let out a cry.

"There's a man climbing over the wall."

Mother Theodosia crossed herself.

"How many are there, child?"

"Only one. Oh no! There's more." She squeaked with excitement. "They're chasing him. Oh run! Run!" Then she screamed. "They're shooting at him. Look out! Oh quickly, quickly run!"

"Open the door," cried someone.

Maybe it was Simonetti! I ran to the door as it opened and stepped out, tensed and ready to fight.

A tall, dark man came sprinting across the grass. It was too tall for Simonetti. Lord of All! It was Andre Gregorov. He was way ahead of the six or eight men pursuing him, but a couple had knelt down to shoot arrows at him.

With an edge of panic, I bespelled the arrows backward even before they had left the bows and both men tumbled back head over heels.

"Dion!" cried Andre. He was laughing! Laughing with exhilaration. At the chapel doorway he reached out and swung me into his arms, pulling me back into the doorway.

"Dion! Dion!" he cried, hugging me so fiercely I thought I'd be crushed. "You're safe. Oh my darling, you're safe." He kissed my face. "I had to get in here. I had to know that you were all right."

It was as if all those angry words had never been

spoken between us. It was as if we were back in that walled garden again. I just stood there clinging to him and letting him kiss and fondle me. I hardly noticed the door slamming shut behind us and the fists that banged briefly upon it afterward. Andre was so tender. He began telling me that he was sorry, that he'd been impatient and unreasonable, that his life was meaningless without me.

Then suddenly I became aware that the little novices were giggling. I pulled away from him. Everyone in the chapel was regarding us with intense interest, some benignly and some with displeasure. A few of the nuns had their faces averted.

"Mother Theodosia, this is Lord Andre Gregorov."

I tried to be unaware of the fact that Andre still had one arm draped around my waist.

"Sir," she cried. "Have you any news of the militia?"

He bowed low to her. It was odd to see him being respectful to a nun. He seemed different here. Less sensual. Less . . . something.

"Alas, Reverend Mother, I know no more than you. I have been following the mob since St. Vitalie. I was there in time to see Erasmus Tinctus disappear from the pyre in Mademoiselle Dion's arms. I had come to St. Vitalie to get Mademoiselle. Something has happened at the palace."

"What?"

"A priest of the Burning Light attempted to shoot the Duke as he rode through the crowd. Madame Avignon pushed him out of the way and took the arrow herself."

"God and Angels!" I felt as if my heart had stopped.

"Is she hurt? Is she dead? Oh Andre! What has happened?"

"She was not dead when I left, but, yes, very badly wounded. I came to tell you. Perhaps to take you to her. Perhaps to protect you if the worst happened. I know what she was . . . is to you. But I was too late. Now we are stuck here."

Mother Theodosia had covered her mouth with her hands in horror.

"Perhaps this is why the militia are slow to come today," said Andre. "They may be held up at the palace."

"I would that we could offer prayers for the poor woman," said the nun. "She has done great good in this city. But we cannot. We must pray for our own safety."

Just then the little girl in the window squeaked.

"There's more men coming over the wall. Lots and lots."

A crossbow bolt hit the stained glass window with a smack and the little girl jumped back in fright and almost tumbled down from the windowsill.

"Come down from there now, Berengaria," cried one of the nuns, reaching up to help her down.

A rain of crossbow bolts, arrows, and rocks began smacking against the windows. The glass, though old, was thick and strongly anchored in its frames and for the moment it held.

I stood still, stunned and filled with cold horror. I wanted to go to Kitten now. Immediately. I wondered for a moment if I could jump though space and time to her in the palace, but it was over two miles away. I'd never heard of anyone doing such a jump. I would probably become unconscious during it, maybe even

kill myself from exhaustion by doing it. Tears came
to my eyes.

Mother Theodosia put her arms around me.

"My dear, we must concentrate now on keeping
ourselves alive so that we may be of use to her later.
Will you hold them off now, while we pray to
strengthen the defenses? If you go up into the bell
tower, you will be able to see properly."

Her words strengthened me. She was right. We
must all get safely through this time. There was something I could do for Kitten, too.

"Has anyone any chalk?" I cried.

At that moment a bolt shattered one of the small
stained glass panes. Fists were pounding on the door.

"Dion!" cried Andre. He took my hand. "Come.
Let's see what we can do to chase them off."

"In a moment!" I cried. Several of the nuns had
produced chalk from their capacious pockets. I took
a piece and followed him up the bell tower steps. Behind me the nuns formed into rows in front of the
chapel door, bowing their heads in prayer. Some of
the patients joined them. Mother Theodosia stood before them. They would channel the energy of their
faith in God through her, briefly giving her the power
to strengthen the doors of the chapel and bind them
together more strongly in defense.

It seemed that the Burning Light priests had not
been much troubled by the iron door in the convent
wall. Now people were streaming through the doorway and an angry crowd had collected beneath us,
shouting, waving their fists, hurling stones at the windows, and pounding against the door. It was as if the
walls of the chapel had began to melt and the chapel
was now surrounded by a puddle of angry stones,

each stone a screaming head. I could not help shuddering at how many of them there were. There must have been a couple hundred people down there. I wondered briefly how many of them would be priests or priest-mages and hoped it was not as many as it looked to be.

Up in the bell tower, I put my hand against the bricks of the wall and sent a surge of power through the walls of the chapel to hold the glass, wood, and bricks together so that they would not shatter under the weight of the missiles. The building creaked like a fighter stretching his muscles.

Then I crouched on the wooden floor and began to draw the characters necessary for the protection ritual.

"What are you doing?" cried Andre.

"The protection ritual. I will weave some healing spells into it. Perhaps it will help."

"Do you really think that is wise at this moment?"

"Shut up!" I snapped at him. "I know full well you never liked her, Andre."

He turned away and withdrew to the other side of the tower. I continued with the ritual.

Doing it calmed me and when I had finished, I apologized to him.

He answered without turning. "There's no need. I know you are frightened. I know what she is to you."

His voice was calm, but cold.

"I do not know when I will get another chance," I said. "And perhaps it may help her."

"Yes."

The parapet of the bell tower was low. Andre was kneeling before it looking over the top. I saw that I had offended him. *I must do something,* I thought. *Otherwise I will always be alone.* I went and crouched beside him.

"I'm sorry," I said.

He shrugged but did not look at me.

"I know what she is to you."

"It's not like that," I snapped.

All that delight at the chapel door—was that now going to disappear again, leaving me as bereft as ever? Had I thrown away my one chance at happiness? Again!

"I don't know why I came," he snapped.

"Well, why did you? You've been having such a lot of fun lately. What could you possibly want with me?"

"It doesn't matter what I do anymore. I always wind up thinking of you. When she fell from that horse all I could think of was how you would feel. All I could think was to get to you to comfort you. It was useless, wasn't it?"

"Oh, no, Andre. It wasn't useless." I touched his arm.

He seized my wrist and kissed it so savagely that I thought he was going to bite it.

"I don't know why I thought we were equal. You have me completely at your command. Witch!"

He pulled me against him.

At that moment the whole chapel shuddered. I felt something jar through me.

Below us a space had cleared around the chapel door and a man was leaning against it. Even from up in the bell tower I could see his lips moving in a spell. He was surrounded by six or seven men kneeling in much the same way as the nuns had been kneeling together inside the chapel.

What a fool I was! I'd let them get themselves organized into prayer positions, and now they would be much stronger.

"You are such a distraction to me," I muttered to Andre.

"I'm glad to hear you say that," he purred, leaning against me.

I sent a prickly surge of power down through the wall. The man cried out in pain and pulled his hands away and his spell was disrupted. He whirled, looking up, and saw me.

"Witch!" he screamed. Others took up the cry and there was a flurry of missiles. We had to duck as a couple of arrows whizzed over our heads and a few stray rocks thumped down behind us.

The next moment, there was a kind of loud *crump*.

"Look out!" cried Andre. "Fireball!"

I had never seen one before. It took more power to put one together than most single mages could manage. The man below us had the powers of his companions to draw on. His fireball rose from a tiny light in his hands and ascended through the air toward us, growing and growing in a great whirl of orange flame, until it blocked out everything else, rearing over us in a huge wave of searing heat.

I threw up my hand and willed it back. In my panic I forgot to speak the Words of Extinction that we are trained to use against such things.

It slowed, stopped and then rolled away from us like a broken wave rolls back into the sea, scorching quickly down the wall of the tower and rolling savagely away across the crowd. There were screams and people running everywhere. I thought then about the Words of Extinction, but it was too late.

"Well-done!" cried Andre.

I turned away, sickened by the smell of singeing flesh and hair that rose up to us.

He put his head against mine.

"They would have killed you in a minute, little mage. I for one am pleased to see them burned around the edges. Come now. They are forming up for another attempt. You must do something to stop them. Can you make a fireball of your own?"

I thought I probably could, but even in this situation I was reluctant to hurt too many people. It seemed better just to keep them out until the militia came and to concentrate on hurting their leaders instead. Anyway in truth the fireball had done little to disperse the crowd. If anything it had just made them more determined, and they were clustering back around the door of the chapel, shouting with renewed frenzy and throwing plenty of missiles our way so that we had to keep ducking behind the parapet. The group of mages had moved away from the door and seemed to be working at breaking through the less protected wall. If I leaned out over the parapet a little, I could still see them. I focused on their leader.

"Look out!" cried Andre pulling me back as a crossbow bolt whizzed past my face.

"Curse you!" he shouted, scooping a rock from the floor of the tower and hitting the crossbowman expertly on the head with it.

"Damn! If only I had a bow. Go on, Dion! I'll keep watch."

I leaned out over the parapet again and focused on the central mage. I could feel the power moving through him into the wall. A few moments later, though, he dropped to the ground unconscious.

Andre cheered.

"Have you killed the villain?"

"No. Just sent him to sleep."

"Oh, Dion, you're too kind. They'll wake him."

I could feel them trying. *Let them try!* I thought.

"No, they won't. I'm holding him asleep."

"You should have killed him. You're too gentle. Couldn't you have stopped his heart?"

"That's a necromancy spell," I said, a little shocked.

He shrugged and turned away to peer over the parapet again.

"Look, we've got friends," he said a moment later.

Someone was firing arrows into the crowd through the big wrought-iron gates in the front of the convent and a few stones were flying over the wall. Farther out in the street beyond the wall, a group of wharf workers were brawling bare-fisted with some Burning Light men.

The mages had moved even farther down the wall of the chapel. No doubt they were re-forming, but it would take them time to attune themselves to another focus. I sat back down against the parapet and tried to shut out the shouting below. The coldness of magic left me. I found myself worrying about Kitten.

"There is some wider plan behind all this," said Andre beside me. "Have you thought upon that? The Burning Light is hardly big enough to stage an uprising, yet here they are, causing mayhem and sending someone to assassinate the Duke."

*And Kitten Avignon,* I thought unwillingly. I tried to focus on what he was saying.

"You mean this is all a plot?"

"You have to wonder."

"That conversation I overheard in the palace."

"Mmm, I remember that well, little mage. The first time I ever kissed you."

He reached out for me, but I pushed his hands off.

"Ambassador Deserov. He was seeking an alliance with the Burning Light, wasn't he?"

"Seeking? He'd got one. I got it for him. It seems I

have reason to regret those pleasant moments. I wonder if he has promised them something."

"He wanted Lord Dane, too. You fell out over that."

"That's right. Interesting, isn't it? If the Duke is assassinated, who is his logical successor but Lord Dane? He favors an Aramayan alliance, you know. Yet he could hardly publicly countenance his own brother's assassination. The Duke is very popular. I wonder if the idea was for Dane to put down this uprising and be placed on the throne by grateful and relieved nobles. Deserov might just be ruthless enough to organize that. I wonder if this scenario has occurred to the Burning Light."

A voice rose stridently from the crowd below.

"We shall have victory and drive out the defilers. The Angel of God has promised us victory. We call upon Him to smite the witch and to give us victory!"

We peered cautiously over the parapet.

"Look, there's Dashalle," cried Andre. "Now surely you can bring yourself to kill him."

The crowd was fraying at the edges, restive perhaps at the lack of result. Ryart Dashalle was rallying them. His voice, strengthened with magic, echoed off the convent walls, raging. People had gathered round him, shouting in response to his words, jabbing their fists in the air, but a trickle of people were wending their way back toward the door in the wall.

Dashalle's words left me in no doubt of the fiery fate that awaited me, but somehow it was the least of my worries. How was Kitten? I had begun to worry about Simonetti, too. If Andre could guess where I was, so could Simonetti.

"Perhaps he has gone to the palace," suggested Andre. "Or perhaps he is simply out there awaiting his chances."

I tried to believe him. I forced my mind to focus on Ryart Dashalle, to deal with him as I had with the other priest, but worry disrupted my concentration and my anger and hatred of him came out of me like a blow and hit at him. He swayed at little on the piece of stone he was standing on, but he was well protected from such magic.

"That's right, Dion," whispered Andre. "Hurt him. Think of what he has done to you and yours. Think of what he plans to do to you. Gentleness is wasted on him. He will always be a destroyer. Get him before he gets you."

His hands squeezed my shoulders.

He was right. It was good to have Andre at my back. It was good to be fighting with him. I concentrated on hitting out at Ryart Dashalle with all the bitter force of my hatred.

Suddenly there was a flash. A burst of blue wizard's fire smashed through the front gate. The next moment forty or so horsemen were charging out of the exhaust smoke, riding into the crowd, swords slashing right and left. The crowd scattered before them. A phalanx of mages came striding though the smoke behind them. My concentration was disrupted and by the time I'd stopped cheering, Ryart Dashalle had disappeared. It didn't much matter.

The militia had finally come.

The chapel doors were open and the nuns were crowding out onto the steps. A few horsemen were still riding around the convent grounds chasing a last few stragglers and trying to get a couple of men out of a nearby tree. Most of the horsemen had gone back out of the gate and were pursuing the Burning Light rioters in the streets. The phalanx of mages had gone with them.

The militia captain trotted over to the chapel steps. He bowed his head to Mother Theodosia.

"Holy Mother, I apologize for our late arrival. I think we have chased most of them away, but there may be stragglers, and there is much fighting in the streets. I'd keep everyone in the chapel for the time being."

"Sir," cried Mother Theodosia, "is it true what they say about the Duke?"

"That these fiends made an attempt on his life? Yes, but it failed, thank God! Yow!"

The last exclamation came as the horse reared.

"What of Madame . . ." I cried.

But the captain had been too busy steadying his horse to hear me. Then there was a blast of mage's fire from beyond the clinic, and he spurred away, shouting his farewells behind him.

Perhaps he would have mentioned it if she had died, I thought. Or would it be too unimportant?

I wished there was some way that I could find out. I wished . . .

"Dion." Andre's hand was hot against the small of my back. He cupped my face with his hands and pressed his lips lingeringly against my brow. "Poor Dion! You are beside yourself with worry. Come. Let me take you to her."

I clung to him.

"Oh God, Andre, what if she's dead?"

He squeezed my shoulders.

"Then I shall be there to protect you. Come."

I could hear the tiny voice of Simonetti telling me not to put myself in danger, but it was being drowned out by the voices that clamored after Kitten Avignon. I had to know that she was safe.

"Let me do this thing for you, Dion," said Andre.

He drew me toward the convent gate.

"Dion," cried a voice behind us. Sister Bertrida came running after us. Maya was close on her heels. "You can't go out there. It's not safe. There's sure to be more fighting."

"You can't rely on magic," said Maya. "You must need time to rest."

She lowered her voice.

"This man. Can you really trust him? He's a foreigner, isn't he?"

I looked at her, startled. That thought had hardly entered my mind. I wanted to tell her not to be ridiculous. Andre had returned to me, and I wasn't going to upset things by expressing such foolish doubts. For a moment I wondered if she was in collusion with Genny. No. That was ridiculous. She meant well, but she didn't really understand. I had to get to the palace. How better to go there than with Andre, alone? It would cement the "specialness" of our relationship.

"I have to find out about Kitten," I told her. "I have to know if she's safe."

"Then let me come with you," said Maya.

Andre caught my eye and raised his eyebrows before turning to Maya.

"Madame," he said, bowing very respectfully, "fewer is better in this case. The wisest course might even be to let Dion go alone. But I could not bear to let her do that." He lifted a white hand and tenderly pushed a piece of hair off my face. "But two companions whom she might have to protect . . . I urge you to stay here, Madame Healer."

"Yes," said Mother Theodosia, who had joined the

group. "Stay here with us, Maya. We have need of
you. Dion, I urge you to stay, too. You would be much
safer here. But," she said, as I opened my mouth to
protest, "I understand how you feel and after what I
have seen you do today, I would be very surprised if
you did not arrive at the castle safely. But just to
please me and further protect yourself, please wear
this habit." She thrust a bundle of black cloth into my
arms. "If people see you as a nun, they will be less
inclined to trouble you."

The street outside the convent was empty, but lit-
tered with stones and bits of wood. The houses across
the way where shuttered and silent. The city itself was
strangely quiet, yet full of distant noise. The effect was
sinister. Behind us back toward St. Vitalie, we could
hear shouts and screams and the occasional roar of
mage's fire.

Andre and I crossed into the streets beyond, stop-
ping only for Andre to pick up a stout-looking cudgel
that had been thrown in the gutter. Our feet clattered
loudly in the watchful silence of those little streets. I
moved at a quick pace half-jogging, half-walking. Andre kept pace with me, easily striding along with his
typical catlike grace. I couldn't help feeling happy at
his closeness, but the happiness was quickly sub-
merged in dark and troubled thoughts.

The area between the convent and the Church of St.
Vitalie was quite affluent, but beyond the convent a
much more humble area began. Here the streets were
narrow, full of tall shabby houses huddled shoulder
to shoulder, most with a little open-air shop on the
ground floor. All of the shops were shut today, tightly
shuttered. Some of these shutters were smashed.

There were signs of some of the houses being broken open or attacked.

"It would be best if you did not speak more than necessary," said Andre. "I have a feeling Morians are not popular in this city today."

These houses. Of course! A chill went down my spine. Many Morian refugees lived in this area. Most of them were not Burning Light. Surely people must be able to tell the difference. Then again that mob at the convent; how much distinction would they have made between me and the nuns?

My mind was too full of Kitten to give it much thought. I was full of cold fear at what might have happened to her. If Kitten were dead, would I have been able to feel it in the protection spell? I dared not use this for hope. I didn't know. There was so much I didn't know. I tried to comfort myself that she would be in good hands at the palace, but I couldn't help remembering what she had told me about the Duke's coolness toward her. What was it again? Oh, Dion, you heartless self-centered wretch. You didn't even listen when she was asking for help, after all she's done for you.

If the Duke no longer cared if she lived or died, what might happen to her now that she was injured? The Duke did not like sick people. Maybe he would ignore her or send her away out into the violent streets. No, surely not. Surely he would call healers for her. These were silly thoughts. She would be fine. The palace was not enemy territory. She was an experienced courtier. But what if she were lying unconscious? All alone. This was silly. She did have her bodyguard. But he would have to wait outside. And who was he anyway to let her take an arrow? Perhaps Norval had bribed him. What if . . . ? She would be all alone. No Genny! No Simonetti! Oh, God and Angels! I did not even want to think where Simonetti might be!

"Dion, I think we should go another . . ."

We had entered a square, but Andre had turned and was pushing back the way we came. Too late. I saw what he was trying to stop me from seeing. Some sort of official building stood in the square. It had a long high balcony and from that balcony ten or so bodies hung by their necks like macabre fruits. Only some of them wore black and grey.

I gasped, sickened. Even from several feet away we could smell the stench of shit and death coming from them. There was not a flicker of life left in one of them.

"I'm sorry," said Andre. "I didn't want you to see this."

He pulled me against him then and hugged me tightly. Despite everything my hands savored the strength of his hard back. We were together and alive. That was good.

Simonetti would have cursed me, I reflected, as a few moments later we made our way across the square. I had no idea how we had got to this square. I wasn't really sure where we were. I must pay attention to what was going on instead of getting caught up in my anxieties.

We turned the corner and ran full tilt into another two bodies, hanging from an inn sign. Despite myself I let out a cry.

They, too, were quite dead. I had almost trodden on a bundle of rags at the woman's feet, before I realized it was a tiny baby, its neck broken. There was nothing I could do for any of them. Tears prickled in my eyes.

These people were not Burning Light. They wore

the distinct gaudy clothes of Wanderers, embroidered with their holy symbols. They were a strange sect of pre-Tansite animists, descended from the original inhabitants of the Peninsula, and because of this, and because most of them had magical powers of one sort or another, they were as much persecuted by the Burning Light as mages.

"Yes," said Andre quietly at my side. "A bad day to be Morian."

A fat man in a greasy shirt appeared in the doorway with a stool.

"Out of the way then," he said. "Don't want these Burning Light scum hanging here, putting off customers! Try and assassinate our Duke, will they?" He poked the dead man's belly savagely.

I opened my mouth to dispute with him, but Andre grabbed me by the arm and hauled me quickly away.

"I told you keep your mouth shut," he hissed. "Your accent could get us killed."

"But they weren't Burning Light," I hissed in return. I found I was crying.

"Mobs don't make fine distinctions. And Dion, don't go off trying to rescue anyone either. Even you wouldn't be able to hold out against a whole mob."

"I know. I know!" I strode angrily away from him, more than anything to hide my tears.

When he caught up with me at the next corner, his touch was gentle.

"I'm sorry," I whispered to him.

"It's nothing," he said.

I thought for a moment he was angry and darted a quick glance at him.

His face was tender.

"You've forgiven me for far more than you'll ever need me to forgive you for," he said softly.

I don't know exactly what made me do it. It must have been his softness after all that danger and those poor dead people. I flung my arms around him. His mouth came down hard on mine and suddenly nothing else mattered. I kissed him savagely in a frenzy of lips and tongue and teeth. His hand slid down my spine pushing me against him.

Suddenly there was shouting. A stream of people erupted into the other end of the street. They wore black and grey. They ran full tilt toward us.

"Devils!" swore Andre. He pulled me back around the corner.

"Quickly, down here."

There was a small alley on our left. We dived into it running and kept running, over the slippery refuse-strewn cobbles. Another alley appeared on our right. Andre swerved into it, ducking under a line of washing. I followed and kept on following as he turned, darted down the next alley and the next, following a twisting, turning path. After a time we slowed to a jog, then stopped, panting and leaning against a wall.

There was no sound of pursuit. There were only the sounds of normal life coming out of the surrounding houses; the sound of a loom clacking, people talking, and a baby crying somewhere nearby. The alley itself was deserted.

I pressed a hand to my hot face.

"Lord of All, what was I thinking of back there?"

"I know what I was thinking of," said Andre, reaching toward me.

I evaded his hands, smiling.

"I think it might be better to keep our minds on getting to the palace."

Andre grinned wickedly.

"I'll do my best, though it isn't easy. I love that nun's costume."

"Andre," I warned, though his words filled me with pleasure.

I looked around. More tall, narrow houses. I had no idea where we were.

"Are we lost? Do you know which direction to go?"

"Dion! You doubt me. I'm shattered."

"So you know where we are?"

He grinned ruefully.

"Well, not exactly, but I can get us back to a main street. I think if we go down this alley we can work our way along in the right direction. Come."

He reached out to take my hand, but the wicked twinkle in his eyes stopped me.

"I think I'll just follow you. We have to get to the palace."

"True." He sighed. "Oh, Dion! You are such a distraction to me. Come on then. This way."

I followed him through a series of narrow and twisting little streets, marveling at his sense of direction. Quite quickly we came out onto a main street. It was much the same kind of area as we had left when we'd run away from the mob. Tall, thin houses with little shops at their feet. Andre looked carefully up and down the street, before we stepped out onto it.

"Ah. We're here," he said. "Good. I know where we are now."

It was more than I did. We were now in a completely unfamiliar part of the city.

"Have we come much out of our way?" I asked anxiously.

"Only a little. We seem to have gone in pretty much the right direction. The palace is this way."

He set off confidently. Then, as we turned our third corner, he cursed.

His hand gripped my arm.

"No, don't stop. They've seen us now. We'll just continue along here as if we're innocent. Remember, you look like a nun."

It was a broad street with an ornate fountain in the center, almost a square. A large group of men in Burning Light garb were gathered round the fountain. A pair of burly-looking fellows were standing as if on guard at either end of the street. The first pair stared at us with unfriendly eyes as we passed, but did nothing to stop us. I walked quickly along at Andre's side, head bowed, heart pounding.

We had almost reached the other end of the street, when someone shouted behind us.

"Hey you! Stop! Stop them!"

I thought I knew that voice, but I was not stupid enough to turn round.

As the two guards moved to intercept us it cried, "Witch! She's the witch! Stop her!"

"Run!" shouted Andre. He swung his fist and caught the first guard squarely on the jaw. I hitched up my skirts and took to my heels, darting through the grasping hands of the other guard and hearing thuds and grunts behind me. I dashed down the street out of the square. Behind came shouting and sounds of pursuit. Andre sprinted past me on long legs.

"Next left!" he hissed in my ear as he passed. He was into the street before me, and, as I turned, he waved his hand to the right and darted down that street.

I pelted after him. He was running down the side of the street bouncing off the front doors of the little shops. Suddenly he turned.

"Here! Great! In here!"

He half pushed me, half pulled me into a dark, open doorway, slamming the door behind us.

It was dark inside the building, and there was something very unpleasant about the atmosphere in the room. Had Andre not been pushing me, I think I might have balked despite the danger.

Light came through the slatted shutters at the front. Andre was leaning over, peering out of them onto the street.

"Whew! That was close. How'd he recognize you?"

"Did you see his face?"

"It was Ryart Dashalle. He must have a sixth sense."

"I thought I recognized the voice."

"We'd better hope . . . Here they come."

We stood silently in the darkness. I hoped the men would go past, but instead they began to search up and down the street, trying doors and shutters. There were a lot of them, at least twenty, maybe more.

Someone tried our door, but Andre had barred it and he moved on.

"Keep trying. She's in here somewhere," said a voice. I craned my head around. It was he. Ryart Dashalle. I could just see him through the chinks in the shutters, standing near the end of the street.

"Curse it," breathed Andre. "Looks like we're stuck here now."

As my eyes adjusted to the light coming through the shutters, I saw the reason for the uncomfortable atmosphere. This was a toolmaker's shop. All around the walls hung wrenches, pliers, and hammers, all of them made out of iron. No doubt there was a smithy filled with iron ingots out the back. Cold, cruel iron.

I shivered.

Andre put his arm round me.

"Don't worry! I won't let them take you."

I didn't see any point in telling him the real reason why I was shivering. The searching men were bad enough.

"I'll go see if there's a back way out of this place. We might have to use it. Don't want to get trapped. You'd better stay here, Dion, and slow them down if they try to come in the front."

I crouched at the window, trying to stay far enough away from the shutters to be hidden and close enough to keep an eye on Dashalle. The wall between us seemed so thin.

Two men in the robes of priests were crouched in the center of the street casting the Bowl of Seeing spell on a mirror so that they could search for magical traces. Much good it would do them. I hadn't done any magic since the convent . . . How long ago had that been anyway?

Even as I watched one of them got up and came past the front of the shop.

"Ryart, there's no sign of her. Are you sure about this?"

"The Angel Exultate spoke to me just before telling me it was her. And it was. He said she would be hiding in this street. He bade me capture her. We must do his bidding. It is the only way to victory."

"Ryart, this Angel . . ."

I moved closer to the front of the shop straining to hear what the other man was saying.

And then suddenly . . .

Snap.

Burning cold iron came down around my neck.

I screamed and twisted around.

In the darkness behind me was a black shadow,

huge and craggy, filling the tiny shop, towering shockingly over me. Cruel red eyes burned holes in the darkness.

I screamed and pushed away from him, choking in that burning cold circle around my neck. My fingers stubbed bluntly against hot scaly flesh. And it was only then that I realized. This was not a person. It was . . . Oh God and Angels. It was a demon! It was Bedazzer!

Real substantial flesh, as real as I was. My nostrils filled with his burning sulfurous stench. He was here with me in this world. I was suddenly like an ant. I cried out mindlessly for help. All my power, all my will to get away from him was sapped by the iron, my blows falling on him with no more force than the tiny pathetic pats of a child. I panicked, struggled, kicked, and tore at him. It was like wrestling with a tree. He took each of my arms as calmly and reasonably as if I'd been a rag doll and put iron wrist manacles round them.

I bit him. He tasted foul, and his scaly flesh burned my mouth.

"Where is Andre, fiend? What have you done to him?"

Bedazzer smiled, showing his fangs, and there, before my eyes, he changed.

He became Andre, tall and dark and beautiful. He pulled me into his arms and I was engulfed by the sweet musky scent of his body, a scent as familiar as my own. It was Andre. He smiled his sexy little smile.

"There is no Andre, little mage," he said. "There was only ever Bedazzer."

There was a crash on the door behind us. Bedazzer laughed and shouted something in his thunderous voice. The door flew open on faces and figures, and suddenly I was being thrown toward it, through it, out of it. I hit the ground painfully and rolled there winded, unable to get up, though I had the will and mind to do it. There were men standing over me.

I tried to scream for help, but couldn't get the breath.

Someone grabbed me, pulled off my wimple, and gripped my hair.

"Witch!" screamed a huge face pushed against mine, spittle flying.

"No!" I howled. "Help me! It's a d . . ."

The front of the shop burst open, splinters of wood flying everywhere.

"Run!" I screamed. "Run!"

I got a savage backhand across the face for my trouble.

They were not running. They were kneeling, hands clasped in supplication.

Through the shattered front of the shop strode not a demon, but a beautiful creature, all luminous white skin and golden hair, with huge white wings on his broad square shoulders.

"Oh! Angel Exultate!" cried Dashalle. "We praise and worship you and thank you most humbly for this sign of your power. Who can now doubt the certainty of the victory that you promised us?"

The Angel threw back its head to laugh. Its laughter was like beautiful music.

It was music that rose and changed and cracked until it became the screech of a bow on the strings of a broken viol. The creature before us changed, too, spreading out its suddenly scaly arms as its pure white wings changed to black bat's leather. Its beautiful face was suddenly a fanged demonic snout. Red eyes flashed.

"Fools!" he shouted in a voice like triumphant thunder. "There is no Angel Exultate. There is only ever Bedazzer."

He seized Ryart Dashalle by the throat, lifted the man, goggling and wriggling like a spider stuck on a pin, up and, with a great snap, bit into his head as if it were a gooey egg and sucked out the juices.

There was a frenzy of screaming, wailing, and running as Burning Light men scattered pointlessly before him like barnyard fowl before the butcher. Bedazzer strode among them, scooping up struggling creatures, biting down and laughing, laughing like a child in a sweetshop. Even his gaze, turned intensely upon them, was enough to fell them so that they lay in pathetic, crumpled heaps like dead leaves scattered over the street, all life sucked out of them, not dead, but as good as. Whore Sleep!

I staggered up off the ground.

*Get away! Get away!* my mind screamed. The weight of the chains was so heavy I could not straighten up. I struggled along with appalling slowness, bowed down under this weight, cringing, flesh crawling, expecting any moment the smashing blow, the sharp fangs knifing into my tender flesh. Behind me men screamed and fell on and on. Would the screaming never end? I staggered and struggled along, till I slipped and almost fell. Gentle hands caught me and lifted me up. I looked up into a handsome scarred face.

"My dear little Dion," said Norval. His face was smug. "Be careful. You might damage yourself. And we couldn't have that."

# FOURTEEN

Norval's face was still smug some time later. He towered over me as I crouched in the greasy straw. The chain that joined me to the wall was too short to let me sit, so I had to crouch or kneel in order not to choke myself. My legs were too shaky with fright and shock to stand up.

"That's right," he purred. "Humiliating, isn't it? Think about it. I knew every nasty private thing you did. I was party to all those grubby little dreams you reveled in."

I screamed and lunged at him, tearing the air in front of me with my useless hands. In that moment all I wanted was to rip him limb from limb. I hated him. But the chain stuck tight in the wall. The iron collar choked me agonizingly, and the room blurred for a moment. I fell back against the stone wall and half drooped, half hung there. My breath came in uncontrolled gasps. I wanted to laugh and cry and scream at the same time.

"You trusted the wrong man, didn't you, even after

I showed you how suspect he was. Betrayed by your emotions. Ha! A typical woman's weakness. What a fool you've been, little Dion."

He rolled the words across his tongue like a creamy sweetmeat, his face full of rich, sensuous contempt.

I began to weep from sheer humiliation and despair. I felt as if all my clothes had been taken away from me, no, worse, as if even my skin had been peeled off and Norval was laughing at my naked, vulnerable bones.

"That's right. Weep, you pathetic creature."

He heaved a contented little sigh.

"You know it was a perfect moment when those stupid fanatics knew they had been betrayed. There is such genuine pleasure in seeing people like that. But it was all over so soon. This though. Now this really is perfect. Gloating may just be the most exquisite pleasure known to man. And you know the best thing of all. There's nothing wrong with Kitten Avignon. Yet. She was never the slightest bit hurt by the assassin, and she waits now at the Ducal Palace, hoping that you are still safe and hiding behind one of the Duke's pathetic little mages. Oh, Katerina, are you in for a big shock."

"No!" I screamed. "No!"

"Oh, yes."

He waved a languid hand.

"Bring me a chair, slave. A chair that won't collapse or harm me in any other way."

Bedazzer reached out and literally pulled a chair through the wall. Just as he had pulled me through the wall when he'd brought me to this room. Such power was beyond belief. Or it showed that demons bore little relation to the laws of this world.

He set the chair down neatly in front of the big

wooden table that stood in the middle of the room and became as motionless as a statue beside it, arms by his side, staring at the floor.

The worst of it was that he still wore Andre's form, although his hands were Bedazzer's, great scaly hands with long talons.

Norval stretched out in the chair, elegantly crossing his long legs. With sudden clarity I realized that Andre's body was just like his own—long, lean, and elegant.

He must have ordered the demon to take on such a form.

Norval's smile was oddly avuncular.

"Now I've destroyed you, I'm feeling generous, so I'll gratify you by telling you that you've been quite a thorn in my side. Do you know, you might be the most powerful mage I have ever met? Even with the aid of Bedazzer, I could not break through your protection barrier. Ah, but in wits—in wits I far outmatched you. I had the genius to recognize how the special seductive powers of a demon could be used against you where force had failed. I guessed early on your weakness, you see. Your exploitable weakness. Poor little girl. So love starved. The man who brought you up was a great fool. He made you an easy target for the Prince of Passion here."

"You said you'd feed me when I brought the woman," snarled Bedazzer.

His eyes glowed red. His expression was sullen and animalistic.

"Now, now, my Prince. Patience. Patience," said Norval. "You'll get fed when it suits me and not before. I had the cunning to carry my plan through," he continued. "To move my slave in ways which caused you to trust him. Oh, Bedazzer's words were all his own, as were those disgusting dreams he sent you. I did not soil my hands with the base mechanics of the thing. But the way dear Andre protected you from Deserov's hopeless little plots and the outburst of that whore Rapunzel in the carriage. That was all my work. And you were completely taken in by it. Just as Ryart Dashalle was taken in by the Angel Exultate. Mmm, yes, that was a master stroke. Even though those stupid creatures failed to kill Duke Leon, Bedazzer and I got what we wanted. With a few juicy extras. And there'll be plenty of pickings for the Prince here in the next few days. Ah! What a consummate puppet master I am."

He reached behind him and took a razor and a long leather belt off the table.

"A demon slave is so useful, if you're cunning enough to control him properly. You were the one who led me to him. Yes, your very self. Doesn't it make you squirm to know that I would never have had this exquisite tool if it hadn't been for you and your little secret sin? I watched you protecting yourself against him and realized my little milk white mage had a demon playmate. Tsk. Tsk. Your foster father must be just whirling in his grave. Dabbling in black magic. What dangerous taste in fun you have."

I huddled against the wall, put my hands over my ears, and tried to stop sobbing. The hateful voice still came through in my mind. He could do that now. He could enter my mind if he wanted to. He had stripped away every vestige of my power.

"I hunger!" growled Bedazzer thunderously. I would never have believed that elegant Andre could look so animal.

"Oh, stop complaining," snapped Norval. "You've done very well today."

He rolled up his sleeve, put the belt around his slender white arm, and tightened it. His forearm was covered with little scars.

"Demons and their needs. Feeding is the be-all and end-all of their existence, and sometimes it makes them very tiresome. They cannot be allowed to feed at will. They are so greedy and indiscreet about finding food. Look what happened when I had to loosen my control on him earlier this summer. Can you guess? The plague in Gallia. That's right, the Whore Sleep. An expert in demonology might have recognized it for the feeding of a bound demon. But no one in Gallia did, because they've never seen such a thing before. Safe, cretinous little Peninsula. Lucky Bedazzer. Of course I had to stop him. He would have betrayed us both through his hunger eventually. He cannot control himself."

He smiled at me. "Just like you, slut."

He opened the razor carefully, bought it down on a vein and dug it in. Blood trickled from the cut.

Bedazzer watched with intense drooling hunger, but he did not move.

Norval watched him out of the corner of his eye. "Look at him. Disgusting. You're filth," he told Bedazzer, "Call me Master."

"Master," moaned Bedazzer. "Let me feed, Master."

Norval smiled sweetly. "I have complete control over him. I know his secret name. I could even send him away hungry if it pleased me."

He flexed his arm and the blood spurted. Bedazzer could scarcely contain himself.

"Now be nice, Bedazzer. Show me what a good little Prince you can be."

Bedazzer sucked back his drool and dropped to his

knees. His face took on a humble fawning expression. "I am your slave, Master. Have mercy on me."

"Yes, you are my slave. Here, filth."

Andre seized Norval's arm with Bedazzer's great horny hands and guzzled at the cut, noisily licking and sucking.

"A minor demon; but nonetheless a demon, and now mine to play with. Do you know how I finally got him? An old necromancer's trick. I searched among the demons communicating with this plane for one who might have a grudge against him. It was easy to find one. All demons hate each other. This one knew Bedazzer's secret name, which availed him nothing, but which he was delighted to tell me for the pleasure of seeing our Prince enslaved. It seems you had once served him a similar turn, my Prince."

Bedazzer lifted his head momentarily and hissed like some huge cat.

"Ha. He doesn't like to know his own enslavement. Let me tell you something else about the nature of demons. That way you will be able to appreciate your fate so much the more. No matter how much human scum you feed them, demons will fade from this plane unless you regularly feed them some of your own substance. Blood or breast milk or sexual juices. The last is, of course, the most preferable way of giving. Demons can make themselves into the most beautiful women in the world. They are most proficient at giving pleasure. They read your mind and become exactly the thing you desire. As I'm sure you know by now, little whore."

He laughed at my blush. I would have laughed, too. Embarrassment was a stupid emotion in this situation.

"But sex with demons is very unwise. Very, very

unwise. They're cunning. They tend to take advantage of . . . the situation to sneak more than their fair share. Don't they, turd?'' He slapped Bedazzer on the back of the head. The demon raised his bloody muzzle, grunted "yes, Master" and dived his head back to his slurping.

"That's why I feed him like this. That's why I could never let him actually make love to you. There was too much danger that he would find some way of stealing the power out of you, and you would notice. They find the life force of mages almost nourishing. It's full of the right kind of power, you see. Which makes you, of course, a very juicy little person. Which is why I'm going to use you to feed him." He leaned his head back against the chair, closed his eyes, and heaved a sigh.

"Feeding him has always been so unpleasant and tiring. But I can bind us together magically, make us one, and tap your power to feed him in my place. It's an old, old necromancer's trick. In you, I have a safe supply of his very favorite food. Like the paralyzed caterpillar a wasp lays its eggs on to feed its young. What a delicious parallel."

He was silent for a moment. I heard ragged sobbing breathing somewhere far away over the obscene slurping of Bedazzer and realized it was my own.

"Your stupid foster father took all that trouble to enslave you to him with fear and love and ignorance and then he didn't use your power. What is it with you white mages? What is the virtue in unused power? If you'd been my apprentice . . ." He smiled. "Well, you'd have turned out much prettier for a start. But if you'd been my apprentice, I wouldn't need the Prince here. I wouldn't have had to feed him. So it's fitting that you will feed him for me. Here. Get off me, filth." He heaved Bedazzer away from him. The demon fell on the floor, hissing.

"You've had enough!" shouted Norval.

He stood up and wrapped a pure white bandage round his arm.

Somewhere through the open door a clock began to strike. The last protection ritual which I had done in the convent tower would be wearing out. It would unravel all the more quickly now I was manacled.

"Ah!" said Norval. "The time draws on."

"More!" growled Bedazzer. His face was covered in blood.

"Stop whining, slave. I'll leave you with your new little plaything. You can do what you like with her now. But you may not permanently damage her or consume more than one tenth of her essence."

"One tenth is not very much!"

Norval spoke some words in a harsh-sounding language I could not understand. Bedazzer scowled at him.

"I must obey you, Master."

Norval turned to go. Bedazzer/Andre crouched in the straw, staring at me with burning coal eyes. Suddenly I wished Norval would stay. I didn't want to be left alone with the demon.

"Don't worry. He can't kill unless I give him specific permission to do so. Consider yourself lucky that I have a use for you. Though I'm sure the next little while will be sufficiently unpleasant. Oh and, slave, you must keep the manacle on her at all times. You must not set her free."

He used the strange words again. This time I tried to remember them.

He waved at me. "Good-bye, Dion Michaeline. Try

to cultivate the mentality of a plate of food. That's all you are now."

I heard his footsteps going away up the stairs.

As soon as he was gone, Bedazzer stood up, took a white handkerchief out of Andre's pocket, and wiped his mouth with it. His demeanor changed so much that he was scarcely believable as the creature that had crouched subhumanly in the straw a moment before. He turned and looked at me.

Though his eyes glowed demon red in the dark, he still wore the shape of my erstwhile lover. He smiled Andre's wicked smile at me. Despite myself, my heart turned over. He laughed softly and swaggered toward me. I shrank back against the wall. He stood over me, long arms crossed, face amused.

"What a passionate creature you are, little mage. You should have known all that pushed-down passion would be your downfall. Didn't Bedazzer warn you?"

Suddenly he grabbed me by my hair and dragged me to my feet. He thrust his glaring, blazing face into mine and screamed, "Hey, bitch! What business did you have in Bedazzer's country? If you had listened to Bedazzer, I would not be enslaved. This is all your fault."

"No!" I screamed.

His claws raked my face.

"Oh, yes. You made the link, you marked Bedazzer so that Norval could find him. And Norval came looking for Bedazzer—didn't he—and he made me a slave. He plotted with Bedazzer's enemies and used the Words of Power and now I must humble myself for Norval's pleasure."

He pulled me close to him and said softly, "So now you are Norval's slave, too."

He threw me back against the wall, picked me up, smashed me against the wall again and held me there.

"So now Norval will give you to Bedazzer for his consumption."

He smiled and delicately licked the blood off my cheek with his long, obscenely purple tongue. His breath was sulfurous.

Horrible visions filled my mind. Visions of rape, dismemberment, torture. I was sobbing with terror. I could not help it.

"Yes, all interesting," purred the demon. "I could enjoy your essence in all kinds of ways. Slow like a worm in a flower. Remember the sickness of the whores of Gallia. Remember the death of Sateen Guistini."

He licked my cheek again. I screamed and thrust out my hand, to push his face away. I could think of nothing except fear.

"Please!" I wept. "Please!"

But he had tired of me for the moment. He walked away, still with Andre's elegant walk, and threw himself down on the chair just as Norval had done. He crossed his ankles and stretched out with lazy elegance, his hands behind his head. Just like Norval. Just like Andre. Except for the glowing red eyes and the claws.

His face was strangely mild.

"I'm not of a mind to feed just now. Be calm. You have no reason to be afraid at this moment. Look at you. You are mindless with fear. It is pathetic to see one of your power in such a state."

He knew me, this demon. He knew the power scolding had over me.

I straightened up. Took some deep breaths. Tried to be calm.

"Yes," whispered Bedazzer. "That is well. Show a little pride. A little dignity. You are one of the great ones, little girl. Bedazzer knows that. Bedazzer saw that from the start. That is why he followed you. That is why he offered you an alliance. Offered you what Norval took by force. But you were stupid, and now we are both slaves."

His soft voice was indefinably soothing, like a cool, winding pathway on a summer's day. Astonishingly, I felt myself relaxing to it.

"It was not my wish to deceive you in so cruel a fashion. It is not my wish to torment you now. It is our Master who decrees that I should wear this guise so that you might be ever reminded of your defeat. It is our Master who calls you slut and whore and tells you to be ashamed. It is not Bedazzer. Bedazzer sought only our mutual pleasure."

He was placating me. He wanted something.

"Yes. Be hopeful. We can still be allies. Slaves allied against the Master."

He leaned forward. His face took on a vicious look.

"Why should such as we be slaves to such a worm? Norval is a nothing against you. Or me. He has little power of his own. He is weak from feeding me. You could annihilate him with a flick of your finger if you chose. If you were free, I could offer you the world. I tried it once before. Remember that night when you had just discovered your power. In your mistress's chamber. He'd enslaved me by then, but I slipped in without his knowing. Think of it. I could have touched you then, but I was forbidden to reveal myself to you. But if you had accepted my offer, you could have saved us both. You could have set me free. We could . . ."

He stopped and seemed to listen.

Suddenly he leaped out of the chair. Dived toward me. His claws stung my throat as he dragged me up. Suddenly his maw gaped, enormous sulfurous foulness, row upon row of pointed, blackened fangs, lunging at my throat.

I screamed as he bit down. His jaws closed with a snap on empty air. I sobbed with terror and found that he was holding me up, that I was leaning against him shivering. His scaly fingers stroked my hair tenderly.

He was listening. "Ah," he said. "It is well. Norval was beginning to wonder why it was so quiet. Now he is content."

He shook me.

"Stop that. Listen. Quickly. Soon he will call me away to fetch your friend for him. Perhaps I can set you free. Then you could kill Norval and escape. How would that be?"

"Stop tormenting me," I shrieked. My eyes streamed with tears.

"I'm not tormenting you," he said. "I will make a pact with you. If I undo your chains, you will kill Norval for me."

Kill Norval! If I were to kill Norval, Bedazzer would be free, free to range across the earth, to go where he pleased, to feed where he pleased. A sickening vision of the great Wasteland of Moria rose in my mind. I saw the helpless scrambling terror of the Burning Light men in that little street again, multiplied millions of times over, their injuries millions of times more savage, inflicted on millions more bodies till it left me with such a vision of destruction that I shook my head to chase it away.

"Precisely," said Bedazzer. "But do you have any choice?"

Did I have a choice? To be a meal for Bedazzer or to set him free in the larder to feed as he wished.

I stared at him. *No*, my mind shouted, but my lips could not utter that hopeless word. Possibilities were beginning to unfurl.

Bedazzer smiled Andre's crooked smile.

"I will tell you now that if you have any ideas of escaping without killing Norval, I will know about it the minute the thought enters your head, and I will stop you. I've no intention of losing the advantages I get from your capture unless I get greater advantages in return. You have no hope of escape unless you cooperate with me." Then he stopped again and listened.

"He calls," said the demon. "I go." He ran his hand down the chain that attached me to the wall, and suddenly it was longer. "Rest now. Marshal your strength."

With an elegant wave of his taloned hand, he disappeared.

Although Bedazzer had lengthened the chain so that I could lie down, no matter how I lay, the cold iron manacle was tight around my throat. I tried to think things through calmly. It wasn't easy. I wanted nothing more than to curl up and weep, to give in to hopelessness and the appalling sense of my own stupidity.

I had betrayed Kitten. Soon she would be living through the kind of hell a man like Norval could devise for her. Oh, Angels! I had been such a fool.

But cold-clawed anger was growing in me. An anger so strong that it was beginning to make me shiver. Killing Norval was no longer a problem. I imagined the amused victorious thoughts that must have gone through Norval's mind every time the demon had touched or kissed me. By God, I wanted to kill Norval now. I would get that bastard back. I would scourge and destroy and crush him.

But how to get out? How to save Kitten and myself? I had no doubts that the demon spoke the truth when it said it would stop me if I tried to escape without killing Norval. Killing Norval was the simplest, even the most desirable solution. But it would mean setting the demon free, and I could not set such a being free!

I must get free without him!

Desperately I began pulling at the manacle, prying at the links of the chain, and even trying to pull it over my head, ripping my neck and pulling out great lumps of hair in my frenzy. I could find no gaps. The iron was strong and the manacle well-made. The staple that held the chain to the wall was stamped firm into solid concrete. I strained and strained, but it wouldn't give. I had never been so weak. Always before there had been magic. God damn Norval! Damn his stinking rotten soul to hell! I screamed at the wall and slammed it with my fist. I would help the demon. Anything to get that lying scum Norval. Anything!

Slowly the black tearing anger faded and turned into a feverish dream as I leaned exhausted against the wall. In it I saw again the street and the men of the Burning Light scattering before Bedazzer, only to be consumed without even being caught. And this was only a bound demon! If he were free? It would be the reality of all those visions of hell on earth that the old writers had described so well—people with the flesh sucked from their living bones, entrails scattered red upon the burned grass, the wind still screaming with the cries of the already dead, trees bled white and great brown dust clouds blowing across a desert that had once been Gallia. I heard again the sound of flesh as it tore and bones as they cracked and crunched. I had already seen the work of my so-called ally. He was not some kind of big friendly dog, but a demon and a destroyer. And if he were released . . .

I was being tricked again.

The demon must know how much I hated Norval. He had even fed that hatred. No doubt he counted on that filling my mind and blinding me to the truth.

Bedazzer was the real enemy. We were just walking food to such a creature, like so many sheep. He was cunning. He read our minds, Norval's and mine, and used our thoughts and feelings against us. He had played a slavish and bestial role for Norval that I had found unrecognizable. My Bedazzer would probably be just as unrecognizable to Norval. Norval was just a pawn in a losing game with Bedazzer, in reality no better off than I. Knowing that made it easier for me to think clearly about Bedazzer. I could not set Bedazzer free.

Bedazzer. Andre.

There had been so much that had fascinated me about Andre that in the end must have been really Bedazzer. Andre's pleasure-loving amorality and his dizzying freedom of action were probably demonic qualities. Andre had made me feel understood. He'd known my nature and felt admiration for it. No! No, no, no! Don't be a fool!

Andre had never existed and Bedazzer . . . Did Bedazzer feel anything, but hunger? Even in the persona of Andre, the demon had merely told me what I wanted, no, needed, to hear in order to manipulate me. He told an irresistible mixture of truth and lies. He knew that a mixture of admiration and scolding worked on me. In these ways he had bound me to him as surely as if he had been the loving Andre he had claimed to be.

Could I really defeat Norval? Why otherwise would Bedazzer have set me on to kill him? I suspected I could best Norval in a battle of power, for if Bedazzer freed me and Norval killed me, both of them would lose a great deal. No. Norval was not the problem.

Concentrate on Bedazzer. Could I ever beat Bedazzer in a battle of power? Bleakly, I remembered again Bedazzer and the Burning Light men. Could I do anything against even the small power he showed then? Calm, Dion! Think.

Bedazzer must know that I must turn and try to destroy him when Norval was dead. Or did he count on my not knowing how to? It was possible he was right. I knew how to take my part in the Great Chant. But to destroy a demon by myself. How did I do that?

I remembered the words of the Dean the day we had spoken of demons. He'd spoken of how the Great Chant worked, of how the mages could destroy a demon on this plane by containing it, cutting it off from its own plane and the roots of its power there. Surely a single mage could also attempt the same thing. Perhaps I could. Then I remembered what else the Dean had said.

"Never, never imagine you could ever be a match for a demon." I could not fight Bedazzer alone and hope to win. He was simply too powerful.

And if I set the demon free? Oh, Angel of Mercy! I couldn't make this decision. I was frightened. I wished someone was here to talk to. I wished Kitten could be here to tell me what to do.

Then I remembered.

Kitten probably was here. Now. And what would

Norval be doing to her? Oh, God. I was sorry. I was so sorry. Oh Kitten, it was all my fault.

I was crying again, my body shuddering with sobs. *Calm down!* I told myself. You have to atone for your stupidity now. No more weakness. You have to make this up to Kitten if it kills you. *Think, woman! Think!*

When Bedazzer set me free maybe I could just take Kitten and run for it. Jump through space and time again. Bedazzer had said he would stop me, but maybe if I was quick . . . Maybe I could get us to Gallia. Even if Bedazzer came after me I could draw on the help of the college there. We might be saved. But he would see my intention the minute it entered my mind. And Bedazzer was so powerful he could easily stop me. Couldn't he?

I lay in the straw, picking thoughtfully at pieces of it. Strange that Norval had never sent Bedazzer to fight me before. Could it be that I was capable of beating him? No! That was a stupid thought! I could not even hope to perform the feats I'd seen Bedazzer do. Maybe the protection . . . Defense did put you at an advantage. Yes, that was it. Perhaps it had been too difficult for the demon to break through a defensive barrier. That didn't mean I could beat him in an open battle.

Suppose the demon were free a few hours.

I had a sudden vision of those rows and rows of blackened, pointed teeth. Of an ecstasy of crunching bone and all around a carrion wasteland of bloody dismembered limbs. Even a few blood-soaked hours would turn Gallia into this nightmare. All those innocent people as good as killed by me. Because I trusted wrongly. Because I couldn't control my own filthy lusts. How could I live with that?

No.

As I lay there in that dim clammy room, I tried and tried again to find a sure way through this puzzle. As I grew more tired and confused, submitting to Norval's plans for me began to seem the most reasonable choice. I had failed to protect Kitten, and her death would be forever on my conscience, but better one innocent life than the hundreds who would die as a demon raged across Gallia. And God knew *I* deserved to die for my blundering.

I fell into weak, maudlin weeping. This was my state of mind when the demon came back for me.

He came as Andre, all graceful limbs and long dark hair. His loose white shirt was spattered with bright blood.

He grabbed me, pulled me to my feet roughly, and shook me.

"Full of despair, are we? Silly girl." His tone was affectionate rather than cruel.

"Norval has your friend now. He plays with her. And he wants you fetched to come and watch. Do you think you can bear that?"

His taunting made me angry.

"Better that than to set you free."

"Ah, so this is your choice, is it?" He leaned toward me. I tried to keep my mind empty so he could not see how I planned to escape. Once again I smelled the beloved scent of Andre's body. I smelled blood, too.

"Look at this." He pulled at his bloody shirt. "This is the blood of your beloved friend. Norval had me rape her. Yes. Rape her." He repeated the words slowly. "In demon form. You know what that means, don't you."

I remembered the first time that I'd seen him. That huge spiky phallus. I shuddered.

"No!"

"Yes. It was agony for her. She will die of those wounds soon. If Norval lets her. Come. Enough of this," he said. He held out his hand and something ripped through the wall. It was another witch manacle. An identical one.

He opened it and came toward me.

"I will not help you."

"Indeed!" he said politely. He snapped the second manacle round my neck.

"I will help you if you bind yourself to me."

"Now there's a very brave proposal," he said amused.

He opened the second set of wrist manacles. "But I think not. Why exchange one master for another?"

"I will help you if you tell me your name."

"My name is Bedazzer," he said. "Or do you prefer Andre, sweetheart?"

"Damn you!" I screamed. "I will not set you free."

"No?" he said unperturbed. "Well, I'm not going to tell you my true name, so we're even. It's your loss. And Kitten Avignon's. Norval won't just kill you. And I'm not merciful. It won't be quick or clean for either of you."

He finished snapping the second set of manacles around my wrist. I had to stretch my neck to accommodate the two sets of neck manacles.

"But just in case you change your mind."

He reached out and flicked each of the locks of the first manacle with the tip of a delicate white finger. The padlocks opened. He heaved a sigh of satisfaction, turned his back on me, and walked away.

"What?!"

"Well, come on. Take it off. We haven't got all day."

I stared at him suspiciously.

"What's going on?"

"Take it off, stupid."

I pulled the heavy manacle off my neck. It was as if my blood had started to run again. Gone was the drained feeling. Instead I was filled with exhilaration, with a bright and shining strength. Although it looked exactly like a witch manacle, whatever that second manacle was made of, it wasn't iron.

"Happy now? Better?"

I stared at him amazed. How could he do this if he were a slave?

"This is how it is with us. Even when we are slaves, we can do anything we are not specifically told not to do. A clever demon such as I lulls his master into thinking he is slavish and bestial so that he becomes careless in his orders. As Norval has. If he had been more exact in his orders, if he had specified which manacle to leave on or if he had specified an iron one, all would have been lost. But he merely told me not to take the manacle off. He said nothing about unlocking it."

"That's ridiculous!"

He shrugged. "That is how it works. That is why so few enslave us and survive."

He took the end of the leading chain in his hand. "Just keep in mind, sweetheart, I will stop you if you try to rescue Kitten without killing Norval. And remember, too, my master must not notice too early that you are free. He will be much closer to Kitten Avignon than you are."

Then he put his arms round me. Like Andre.

"You can beat him," he said. "It will be easy for you." He kissed me softly on the cheek.

I couldn't help feeling comforted.


She was strapped to the great stone table. Her face and her torn shift were covered in blood, and she lay in a great pool of blood which seemed to be seeping from between her legs. I tried to rush toward her, but the demon jerked warningly on the chain and pulled me back.

*Be strong*, I thought. *You must not give in to Bedazzer. He wants you to get upset.*

"Ah, Dion," purred Norval. He was wearing a white, blood-spattered butcher's apron and heavy white gloves. Burning black candles were arranged neatly around the room. On a bench beside the table where Kitten lay were arranged tools, the violent shattering tools that belong on a carpenter's bench and the small wicked tools of the torturer.

"A chair for our guest, Bedazzer. Behold! You see now your failure is complete. Now I am free to punish this whore as she should be punished. Hey, whore"—he shook Kitten's bloodied face—"wake up and see your betrayer."

"I'm sorry, Kitten. I'm so sorry."

Tears had begun to run down my face. It was terrible to see her like this. I could hardly bear it. I must be strong. I was going to see her die.

She moaned and muttered something.

"Slave! Bring me unpoisoned wine that will not make me sick and that I will like the taste of."

A goblet appeared out of the air beside him. He took it and sipped from it.

"Katerina," he called softly. "Katerina. Wake up, darling, wake up and take your medicine."

And suddenly he dashed wine over her. She cried out as its bitterness stung the wounds on her face. I winced for her. Her head rolled, and she opened bleary green eyes.

"Now where were we? A little anatomy lesson for my charming friends."

He spread out the palm of her hand and laid it neatly by her side.

"In the palm of the hand we have the . . ." He began to name the bones. He reached behind him and brought out a steel-headed hammer.

Still talking, he lifted it above his head.

It was the last thing he ever did.

I screamed and lunged forward. Norval's face was so full of smug pleasure. I hated him so much I could not bear it. My hatred surged uncontrollably forward. A bolt of flame ripped out of my hands, streamed across the room, smashed him against the wall, engulfed him. Destroy. Destroy. My anger poured out of me in that mindless cleansing fire and kept pouring uncontrolled—out and out, though Norval was now just a small pile of smoking ash beside the wall.

Then, in that moment I thought of the demon.

Bedazzer. The real enemy. I pulled back and felt the ends of my fingertips sizzle as I reined all that power in too hard.

My arms cramped agonizingly.

I spun round and saw Bedazzer stretching out. He looked freed. He looked bigger and somehow brighter.

*I must stop him*, I thought.

I reached out toward him and let all that power loose again. This time I had to push it out. A great blast of fire hit him.

He stood calmly in the midst of the flames, Andre's

long dark hair blowing back in the blast of heat. Then he threw back his head and let out such a great howl of laughter that the room trembled with it. He began to change. His skin became scaly and thorny, his limbs, great, grey, sinewy logs, and his face, under a great, horned head, the toothy snout of the demon I had first seen, with row upon row of sharp blackened teeth in that open, laughing mouth. He threw open his arms, stretched them to the clawed fingertips, and began to grow, his body thrusting itself up and out, slamming against the roof and bursting through it with a great, joyful, destructive smash. His laughter grew with him so that it began to shake not only the building, but the surrounding countryside.

I watched him with horror. How could you engulf a being who just kept growing and growing? Then I realized that by growing so enormous he was betraying himself. It would be no time before someone saw him, if they had not already seen him, and went for help. Then the college would come. They would dispel him, they would finish him. All I had to do was keep him busy till them. I was filled with a great rush of hope, and with it I began myself to grow, my limbs and torso stretching, a wonderful stretching as if all my limbs had been constricted and had suddenly uncramped.

He looked down and stopped laughing. A scowl moved like a thunderous cloud across his giant face. "So," he hissed. He had felt my thoughts. My hope had betrayed me. But the coldness of magic was on me and I felt no dismay. I felt only a wild reckless exhilaration at feeling my power unfurl within me and at the thought of pushing it finally to the limits. I would grow big enough to throw myself upon him like a blanket over a fire and smother him. It didn't matter whether I could or not. The trying was all. I wanted that exhilarating struggle. My fear of him had disappeared as the magic took hold.

He slashed at me with a great scything fist. My skin was granite, invulnerable, and the blow sent out sparks as it hit me but did not hurt me, though its force was enough to make me stagger backward.

Then reality cycled backward with a sickening jolt, and suddenly I was looking down on the demon again as he stood before me the size of an ordinary man wearing Andre's body. For a moment we stared at each other.

"If you were not such a fool, you would fear me," he said in a great voice of a thousand voices.

*Yes, I suppose I would*, I thought through the unreality that was magic. I wondered whether to hit at him or not. Perhaps from this height I could squash him if I stamped on him.

Then he did a thing I would never have expected.

He turned and, like a bolt of lightning, dived for the wall.

"Follow!" I screamed. I hurled myself down into my normal size, diving after him. "Catch!"

He was as a magnet to the me who was now filled with whirling magic. I caught his ankle as he dived through the wall. The wall slammed toward me. I must go through it. Could go through it, did go through it. My habit ripped as I passed through the rough stone.

Bedazzer shot into the air, which sizzled from the heat of his body. My clothes were smouldering from that heat, but I was invulnerable to fire.

*Must hold on tight. Must engulf him. Must cut him off.*

He hissed and twisted in my grasp, but I held on, held on and more. I grabbed his leg with my other hand, heaved myself up, and suddenly had my legs and arms twined around his leg, in a position so ridiculous that I actually laughed out loud. The wind wailed in my ears as we streaked dizzyingly across the sky.

Below us a cluster of buildings shot into view—a farm, no, a small village. Bedazzer swooped like a great carrion crow, howling a thunderous battle roar. I thought of the protection barrier that had kept him away from Kitten for so long and thrust out my hand. I simply did it. I cast a bubble of protection over the village. It was as easy as yawning. The demon dived, his maw gaping wide, toward the village. People were turning in the main street, screaming up into the sky, dropping things, running.

Thump. Bedazzer hit the invisible wall of protection and his teeth screeched shatteringly over it. He yowled in a madness of bitter, bitter disappointment. He turned in the air and scratched down at me with such savagery that it ripped momentarily through my invulnerability and broke my skin. Still I hung on for dear life.

We hung still for a moment in midair and then suddenly he writhed in my arms, boiled, and changed.

Now I was holding on to something smooth and green and slimy, the tail of a thick slippery serpent. He flicked his tail and turned back on himself. His flat head darted at me hissing, his tongue flicking out. I yelped with shock, loosened my grip, and began to slide down the greasy surface. I scrabbled to regain hold. He hissed again, spattering burning poison from his fangs.

Fangs! That was it! I grew fangs and claws, pushing them out and biting into the serpent's slimy skin, digging my claws into its flesh till the scales began to part.

The snake disappeared.

A glistening drop of water lay in the palm of my clawed hand. Astonished I watched him slip through my fingers and fall slowly at first, but then faster and faster, to earth. I threw myself after him, pushing myself downward till the air rushed up past me. Water. Glass. I became glass.

I stretched out my glass arms and joined my hands. He fell into them. Quickly I circled and joined myself. Suddenly the demon was contained in a perfect glass sphere of me.

I had engulfed him! I could feel him seething in my glass belly, his substance sliding on my walls. It tickled. I hung there in midair, feeling my crystalline purity, glorying in the wonderful feeling of the sun as it passed through me.

Smash! A great surging fire ripped through me. Smash! I burst open and shattered into a thousand pieces. A dizzying moment of utter pain. The darkness of unbeing.

I was plunging uncontrollably toward the ground. I was myself again, nerves and skin screaming with agony as pieces of me smacked back together again.

Bedazzer? Where was he?

He streaked through the sky below, a ball of molten fire. Part of my shattered self had stuck with him. Now it drew me to him like a magnet. I fell into him, becoming fire, too, melding with his substance. Even unconscious and shattered I had not let him go.

Together we contended in midair like twin comets in mortal combat. No matter how he strove, no matter how he twisted and turned, still I would not let Bedazzer go. He changed his shape. He changed with dizzying speed, and I changed with him. We flickered through forms and beings so quickly that I became mindless instinct, half-conscious, barely aware of anything but the need to push my tortured body through changes after him.

If he became a lion with burning wings and great raking claws, still I held on, though his breath burned me and his claws ripped through all protection and shredded my skin. If his hide dripped acid, I became stone and kept with him though my rocky skin boiled where he touched. Once he became a gnat, I grew a sticky frog's tongue and tried to swallow him.

I remember little else of that midair battle. It is a kaleidoscope of shapes and pain. But I clung to him and did not let him go, through shift after shift.

At last I began to feel myself tiring. Staying in the air was taking too much effort. In the air he was too fast for me to engulf again. That time was past now. It was time to even the odds. It was time to return to my own milieu. To earth.

I turned myself to stone. A hundred tons of stone. I was too heavy for him. I pulled him with me and, together, we plummeted to earth.

As we fell Bedazzer changed into a dragon and a giant spider. But though he writhed and wriggled, I held on with all my power. He could not get away from me. Could it be that we were evenly matched, that I was as strong as that? As strong as a demon?

The magic was surging inside me, flowing smoothly and easily, like milk and honey. All the time we had struggled, I had not needed a single spell. Despite the pain of changing my body, it was exhilarating.

We crashed through the broken roof of Norval's

house and came down with a spine-shattering smack on the hard, hard stone floor. My heavy stone body gouged the floor and protected me from hurt.

We were back where we started. Norval's torture room had changed little, though pieces of the roof now lay scattered around the floor. Some of the black candles still burned. But Kitten no longer lay on the table. I wondered vaguely where she was. Had she crawled away? Died? I knew I would be very worried about her when the magic passed, but there was no time for that now. Bedazzer still struggled in my arms.

We wrestled together in a hollow in the floor. Suddenly he stopped and before my very eyes became Andre again. His soft, dark hair tickled my face.

I realized that we did indeed lie together entwined like lovers, my legs and arms around him and him on top of me. The beast with two backs.

He began to move against me as a lover would. I felt his hardness against me, and I knew that this must be giving me great pleasure. It was lucky that the coldness of magic prevented me from feeling it, for otherwise it would have been almost impossible to resist him. Even now as I looked at his face and body and his wicked little smile and saw how beautiful he was, it seemed so sad that our love could never be.

"Oh, but it can," he purred. "You know it can. You could be my Mistress in all ways. What exquisite pleasure you would know. Think on it. Dion and her demon lover."

Clearly he did not know the coldness of magic. I knew how much I wanted it to be true.

"Let us make the first consummation," he murmured. His head came down to nuzzle my neck. I heard his mouth open. The picture of Andre kneeling before Norval and drinking his blood was vivid in my mind.

I lifted my rock fist and smashed him on the side of the head.

He yowled.

"My love!" he sobbed. "Why do you hurt me so?"

"You are not Andre. You are Bedazzer."

He snarled and reared up above me. Andre's face split open and suddenly a huge sulfurous, black-fanged maw gaped above me. It plunged down at my face.

"No." I shoved my fist into his mouth. Jagged teeth stabbed into it and broke off. Even though my flesh was stone, the pain was searing. Molten grey stone seeped from the wounds. But the demon could get no nourishment from stone.

"Get back to your own place," I screamed. "I am too strong for you. You cannot win."

"You are merely my equal," he hissed. He heaved and rolled me over, but he could not break free. "I never saw so strong a mortal before. That is why you could walk on my beach and live. That is why I followed you to this plane and courted you. I wanted to consume all that strength. And I will. You are still just a mortal. Your strength is limited. I can keep fighting like this forever. Can you?"

I hit his head with my stone fist and heaved. He yelped, and we rolled.

Thump.

I was underneath him again. Engulfing him was easier from underneath. My hands and feet grew together across his back and I began to stretch my power so that it, too, would grow up his sides and across his back. He seemed to have a lot of energy. Something was making it very difficult, but I must keep trying. Soon he would be magically enveloped inside a parcel of flesh and magic that had been me. Then he would be contained, cut off from the self in the other plane, the source of all his power, and he would die. Or help would come and destroy him.

He went limp within my arms.

Then he threw back his head and laughed Andre's sensuous laugh.

"You deny it, but see. Even now you seek to have me inside you. Perverse creature. I am happy to submit."

And he began to nestle himself into me, nuzzling at my neck like a tiny baby.

His flesh became sticky. He was beginning to melt. I could feel his legs disappearing, his substance seeping through my clothes, coating my legs with a kind of oily film. And worse. I could feel my skin beginning to absorb the oil.

I screamed and stopped engulfing him, made myself impervious to him.

Andre's handsome face was amused.

"You'll have to make up your mind," he said. "Do you want me inside or out? You can't have it both ways."

Again I struggled to engulf him. Again I could feel him melting into me. Again I stopped and made myself impervious. I tried again but with the same result. He had me. I could not beat him without engulfing him and I could not seem to engulf him without his being able to make my body absorb him.

"No," he moaned softly. "Don't stop it. It is meant to be. We shall become one. One flesh. I will lose my self for you, melt and become part of you. Our beings will mingle, become a single greater being. A marriage of body and soul, a true marriage. Indivisible.

That is the wondrous fate that awaits you. That is what I offer you. Come let yourself partake of my substance and my power."

Only his head retained its shape. The rest of him lay on me like a pool of sweet oil, seeping through my clothes and caressing my skin. Even through the coldness of magic I was losing control of my feelings. I wanted what he offered me. I loved him so. Yet the thought of him inside of me, befouling me, a living chaotic cancer . . . He would always be there. I could never let go, for he would be waiting . . .

"No, no, sweetheart. If we become one, we would be a new being together. Bedazzer would be lost forever."

And so would Dion, I realized.

"We would be something new and wonderful together. Do you not realize that your good would balance my evil? Your power would join with my hunger. Together we would be mighty."

My good! What good was this? I was like all humans, a mixture of both good and evil. He was lying to me. And yet I wanted so much to give in to him. How could I bear to lose Andre? To be one with him was all I could wish for. This wondrous marriage. My mind was filled with the singing glory of it. To be one being for always.

No! I must not . . . Somehow he was drawing me in. His thoughts were entering my mind. I was losing myself to him. Oh, God and Angels, where was the college? Where was the help? I needed it! Now.

"Help me!" I screamed aloud.

Then beneath the panic, coldness. That's right. Cling to that coldness of magic. Win it back. You have a plan. What is it? Perhaps there is hope. Perhaps you can trick him. Take him into you for now. Lull him.

When they come, those college mages, they will dispel him then. Then you will be free and everyone will be saved. Do it! You can have the pleasure of union with-out the consequences.

I relaxed. I felt my substance open to his, felt us begin to meld. I let myself slip out of control as I had once before in his arms.

"Yes," he whispered. "Yes!"

And in that moment of becoming one, I glimpsed his mind and saw the triumph there, saw the future. We could never be divided. The college would be forced to kill us both as one. We would be one at war with itself. Bedazzer planned to win that war. And feed. And feed.

I screamed. With all my strength, I expelled him from me. Pushed him away so hard, that the sinews of my hands, grown together over his neck parted and almost broke.

He snarled. Foul words came from his mouth. He struggled in my arms again. We wrestled as we had before, rolling over and over, smashing each other against the stone floor.

And now I felt myself fraying. Exhaustion was coming. Though I was struggling to contain him, I could not seem to manage it. Soon I was going to lose hold. I could not go on much longer. I gripped him, pulled my magic around him, and prayed for help.

And then suddenly, it came.

A figure rose up behind us, all broken and bloody in a torn white petticoat. It swayed over us.

There was a knife in its hand.

"Kitten," I screamed, "get away from here. For God's sake get help."

She lifted the knife between her palms as if she were praying.

"No! You cannot kill him." I said. "Don't! Get away! Get help!"

Though Bedazzer lay on top of me, his back exposed to her knife, he knew she was there.

"She cannot do it, your friend," he hissed urgently. "When she stabs me my flesh will fry her. Tell her not to. She is too close to death already. Or do you want to hear her sizzle?"

His head was blocking my view.

"No! Kitten! Don't!"

There was a thump. Bedazzer screamed, a terrible earth-shattering scream.

Suddenly my magic slid around him, as smoothly and easily as silk. To my amazement, I had completely engulfed him.

For a moment I heard him shrieking and howling, but it was as if it was a long way off. Then suddenly he was still. I felt an absence inside the envelope as if he was no longer there, though I could see his body through my arms. I knew it was over. I let go.

Bang. He burst out of my arms and, screeching, flew across room and smacked hard against the wall. The impact threw him off the wall and he plunged, still screeching, into the opposite wall.

It was like watching a balloon losing all its air. He smashed from wall to wall, howling a terrible undead howl. But every moment he was growing weaker.

I flung my arms around Kitten. She was still alive and she fell on top of me. I heard her broken bones crunch. She cried out. I wrapped my arms around her as gently as I could, gave her what power I had left.

The demon kept screaming. Screaming and screaming like the hounds of hell. Now he was thrashing on the ground. Bits of him were coming away and melting into the floor, making the stone bubble. He crawled toward us, lunged for us. Bits of his acid body splattered over us. Andre's face fell toward us. I smacked out with my naked hand. The blow threw what was left of him across the room. He splattered damply against the wall and fell as dry ash on the very pile that had been Norval.

The knife stood upright in that pile of ash.

It was Norval's magic knife covered in runes of dark power. Kitten couldn't have hit the demon with anything better.

She lay in my arms. I had stopped her from bleeding, but she was as white as death.

"Oh, God, Kitten." I wept. "I'm so sorry."

"That man had a hole in the back of his neck," she murmured. "It seemed a good thing to stick a knife in it."

She fainted.

The air began to tingle with magic as everywhere around us the mages of the White College appeared in the room.

# FIFTEEN

The hooves of the restless packhorses clattered on the cobblestones. Golden sunlight dappled their coats as a sharp autumn breeze blew the leaves of the spreading trees above. Simonetti and I stood waiting for the ostler to bring my horse round from the inn stables. I was leaving Gallia, leaving Kitten Avignon and her welcoming household to take up a position as healer in a small district near the Morian border.

The district was so small and far away that they had been for almost a year without a qualified healer and had been glad to accept me without qualifications. It was not a very glorious position. Had I wanted something better, had I wanted to stay in Gallia for instance, something much more elevated would surely have been found for me. For I was a heroine in Gallia now that I had defeated a demon.

When the mages of the White College found us in the ruins of Norval's house, their initial reaction to my explanation of what had happened was so disbelieving that had I had the strength, I think I would have thought up some kind of lie. When the Dean arrived, however, he ordered them to stop ridiculing me. He had seen some of the fight in the Bowl of Seeing, and he recognized the remains of Andre's body for what they were. He, it seemed, had no doubts. Had I not been so tired, I should have enjoyed the gaping astonishment and inadequate mumbled apologies that followed. As it was I was happy merely to accept the congratulations of the Dean for my achievement and to be placed on a cart beside Kitten to be transported magically back to the city.

The mages cheered as the cart flew away.

I could not find it in my heart to blame those mages for their incredulity. Even I was astonished at what had happened. How could Kitten and I alone have defeated such a powerful being as a demon? Was I really so very powerful? And what about Kitten? How could the driving of Norval's magic knife into the back of Bedazzer's neck by one who did not even possess the supposed protecting power of virginity have hurt him so? Was it the runes on the knife? The metal of the knife? Had Kitten merely been lucky enough to drive the knife into the right place to sever the connection between Bedazzer and his own world?

For days after the battle the nerves in my body sang and tingled as a result of the rapid changes I had gone through. My limbs were so filled with pins and needles that I could not feel the things I touched. I was weak from exhaustion, and my body seemed to be unsure of its shape. For almost a week someone had to watch me when I slept, for whenever I was unconscious, my body would metamorphose. The first time I fell asleep after the battle, I managed to set the bedclothes alight after having a dream about fire.

The Dean visited me every day to oversee my recovery. He was full of speculation over what had actually happened. Kitten's sexual status bothered him a great deal. The magical books placed great emphasis on the importance of a woman's honor in protecting her against creatures of darkness. Could it be, suggested the Dean finally, that Kitten's act was largely irrelevant, that it had merely had the effect of distracting the demon long enough for me to get the upper hand?

"No!" I said firmly. "By the time Kitten stabbed Bedazzer, the demon and I had reached a stalemate. We were too evenly matched for either of us to win, and soon I would have exhausted my power and been overcome. Kitten's act was pivotal. As she struck him, I felt the strength go out of him. Her blow severed him from his source. I could never have won without her."

The Dean's face was troubled as he left.

Master John, however, had a different explanation for our victory. He called late in my convalescence to congratulate me.

"Even defeating such a minor demon is quite a feat," he said.

He managed to imply that Bedazzer had been a pretty weak demon several times during the following conversation. I did not let his opinion bother me. A demon was a demon, a terrible and chaotic force in our world, no matter how weak he was on his own plane. Most mages recognized this and saw me as a heroine.

Any mage who had any vague acquaintance with me called to express his admiration. Amadeus, for instance, came to see me. He chattered on for some time about how he and some other novice mages had spent most of the night after my battle crawling round the floor of Norval's house, scraping up bits of what they hoped was demon slime to take back to the college to be studied. The college had decided it needed to increase its knowledge of demons and demonology and was in the process of selecting mages to send to the Western empires to study the subject.

"The chaps at the college are green with envy at my knowing you," he said. "And look at this." He pulled out a small card. On it was printed a very flattering portrait of me.

"Garthan Redon did it. I thought you might like a copy. They're very popular at the moment. Garthan had dozens printed and is making a fortune from selling them. Even pictures of Madame Avignon are popular although, mind you, they always were. I wonder if you would sign my own copy of your picture. You would? Thank you very much!"

Even though I had defeated a demon, however, I was not going to be selected for the journey to the Western empires. The Dean told me, though he had the decency to look uncomfortable as he did so, that such a voyage in the company of a group of male mages had been deemed too dangerous and difficult for a young woman. But would I like a stipend from the college to support me while I studied the necromantic texts the Dean had locked in his study?

I told him I would think about it. In truth I did not much care. Though the mages and people of Gallia might flock to show their admiration at my victory, and though the Duke might hold a feast in my honor, decorate me with a medal, and reward me with money and land, I was filled with a sense of overwhelming failure and depression. Though my victory had been a glorious one, for me it was entirely overshadowed by the ignominious betrayal and defeat that had come before it.

I felt this most bitterly during my daily visits to Kitten Avignon's sickbed.

Kitten was recovering well. Genny told me that in a few months there would be no physical signs left of the tortures she had suffered at Norval's hands. But I knew that no matter how her body healed, the memory of that torture and rape would live forever behind those bright green eyes.

"How can you bear those memories?" I asked her once, when she spoke to me of what had happened. I knew it was hard for her to recall that time, and that she was only doing so because she sensed my distress and wanted to help me with it. To help me, always to help me.

"My love," she said, and the kindness in her voice made me weep though I tried to hide it by turning away. "My remembrance of that pain always ends with the memory of the moment when I knew Norval was dead. I saw you kill Norval, finally free me of him at last. My feelings toward you are all of gratitude and joy to you for that moment. I came through the nightmare and realized all my dreams of freedom."

Was she lying? It was just that her screams had woken me often in the night, though sometimes I was not sure if the screams came from her nightmares or mine. Strange how after all this, I was still suspecting her veracity. I no longer suspected her motives, however. I knew they were kind. They had always been kind.

"Dion," she had said to me, "when I lay on that table and Norval . . . Dion, I cursed you. I hated you for failing me. But I forgave you everything the moment Norval died. You must forgive yourself. It is over now."

I was more in sympathy with the Duke's attitude. Though he was fulsome in his praise for me in public, when I met him at Kitten's house, I could sense his displeasure. I thought I knew the reason. In the end I had simply failed to protect Kitten Avignon, and that was the task he had set me.

Other people felt the Ducal displeasure in those weeks following the outbreak of the demon.

The days after the Church of the Burning Light's assassination attempt on the Duke had been a bloodbath for Burning Light members and for many other quite innocent Morian refugees. Gangs of ordinary Gallians roamed the streets exacting summary justice on any Morian they could catch. It had been two days before the Ducal troops moved languidly out from their barracks to break up the mobs, and by then every post on the main thoroughfare of Gallia was decorated with the grisly remains of Morians, hanged or beheaded, and the roads outside the town were crowded with Morians who were once again refugees.

Though the Patriarch protested this savage slaughter, he did not do so very vigorously. The link between the deceased Necromancer Norval and the Gallian Church of the Burning Light was well-known by now, and the Patriarch was not about to support any group with a necromantic taint. The Church of the Burning Light would probably never exist in Gallia again.

Lord Dane was now lodged in the Fortress for his part in the assassination attempt. Though his links with the Burning Light were tenuous, nobody doubted his complicity. Then there was his well-known friendship with Ambassador Deserov.

Deserov had left Gallia under a considerable cloud. The Duke had no qualms now about expelling him. He had written to the Emperor expressing gravest suspicions concerning his involvement with a mysterious Aramayan adventurer called Andre Gregorov, who was himself almost certainly linked with a certain scar-faced exile turned necromancer called Norval. It was rumored that Andre Gregorov was in the Fortress being put to excruciating tortures by the Duke's inquisitors if indeed he had not already died as a result of those tortures. If anyone asked me about him, and there were those who did, I replied that I did not know—as I had been instructed to by the Duke's agents. Andre Gregorov had been close to many powerful Gallians, including the Duke, and apparently it was deemed better that his actual nature be known to as few people as possible.

The Ducal inquisitors were less lucky with Erasmus Tinctus, who had been spirited out of Gallia under the very nose of the Ducal militia and was later heard of in Borgen, where his studio became a center of the New Learning. There were calls from the Gallian Orthodox Church for him to be tried for blasphemy, so it was unlikely that he would ever return. It was good that he was spreading the New Learning in another state, for he had done it little good in Gallia. The Reform Church movement had taken the Altarpiece Scandal as an opportunity to gain greater control of the Gallian Orthodox Church and had begun to discipline all clergy who took a lenient view of the New Learning.

If the Duke did not persecute the New Learning, he did let it be known that he had begun to question the wisdom of the movement. The most obvious sign of this was his dismissal of Madame Kitten Avignon as his mistress. It was sufficiently unclear whether or not she had urged Erasmus to put her face on that altarpiece for her to continue to enjoy his favor in the face of Church anger.

Yet although Viscountess Clemence had already taken her place in the Ducal bed, the Duke visited Kitten Avignon's house almost daily and let it be seen that he did so. When taken to task for this by Dowager Countess Matilda, who suggested arrest for blasphemy might be a more appropriate fate for Madame Avignon, he replied sharply, "The woman pulled me out of the way of an assassin's arrow. She saved my life. Though I may not agree with her ideas, that must qualify her forever to be treated as my friend. To do otherwise would indelibly stain my honor."

After all I had seen of him, his cold heart must have held considerable tenderness for Kitten, for he thus saved her from the ignominious ruin that has been the lot of discarded favorites throughout time.

For myself, Kitten's loss of favor was just another stick to beat my guilty back. In hindsight it was so obvious what Andre had been.

"Don't feel bad about trusting him," said Simonetti. "Look what happened to me."

Running through the alleyways following the crowd to St. Vitalie, Simonetti had met up with Andre Gregorov. The two of them had agreed to team up to try and find me. A few minutes later, Andre had handed Simonetti over to a group of Burning Light followers, who had beaten him senseless and left him tied up on a street corner for later attention. He was lucky to be alive. He was even luckier that Andre had not bothered to deal with him himself. Whore Sleep was still incurable.

I found little if any consolation in Simonetti's story.

My thoughts churned round and round even more stormily than they had after Michael's death. If only I had listened to Maya that moment outside the convent. If only I had listened to Simonetti back in the square; if only I had been less trusting; if only I had gone to the Dean that first time I had seen Bedazzer, or even the second; if only . . . I had called up a demon, I had loved him, and I failed the best person I knew because of that love.

The worst thing of all, and the thing which I did not confess to anybody, was that in that moment when Bedazzer sought to become one with me, my longing for him had almost overcome the coldness of magic. I had felt a fellowship between myself and the demon, and I very much feared that this said something terrible about me.

I wanted to be by myself until my internal tumult died down, to have something both straightforward and absorbing to do till I sorted myself out. That was why I sought out the post of healer in the borderlands.

Kitten and Genny had been horrified when I told them.

"You can't do this," cried Genny. "You're wasting yourself. You're the greatest mage on the Peninsula! How can you just throw yourself away as a healer? For God's sake, girl, grab the opportunities your victory has bought you!"

She actually seized me and shook me.

"I won't let you be so stupid!"

I understood the logic of what she was saying, but being a great mage had no more appeal for me than Bedazzer's offers of ruling the world had had.

"Genny!" said Kitten. Even though she lay weakly

in her bed, hers was still the voice of authority.

"Dion, come here." She took my face gently between her hands. "If you don't want to be a mage anymore, you could still stay with us. We would like you to stay with us, wouldn't we, Genny?"

"I don't understand you, Dion," said Genny almost in tears. "No woman ever had such opportunities as you do. How can you throw them away?"

"I think I understand," said Kitten. "Our Dion has always been the powerful mage. She seeks a period of ordinariness."

I saw the understanding in her green eyes. She always seemed to understand.

"Don't encourage her. She will never be ordinary," cried Genny. "Your power will always find you out, Dion. You cannot just let go of magic."

"Genny is right, you know. You can never really be ordinary. But I think she will not believe this till she finds it out for herself, Genny."

"I need to do this," I said.

"I've never seen you so sure," said Kitten. "But must you really leave us? Don't punish yourself in this way."

"Yes, if you are seeking atonement, then make it up to Kitten by facing up to life and being successful at it. That's what she would really like, isn't it, Kitten?"

"Genny is right," said Kitten quietly.

"I just don't feel I should stay here. I made such a terrible mistake with Andre. Because I was afraid of being alone. Because I was so innocent. I cannot let these weaknesses remain. You always took such good care of me, Kitten, but I need to go out alone and learn to look after myself. It seems to me this healing position would be a good place to learn."

"Yes," said Kitten. "I see what you mean. We must

try to accept Dion's decision, Genny. She knows what is best for her."

I was not so sure of that as I waited now in the sunlit inn yard. How could I leave the only real home I had ever known, the only people in the world I really thought of as friends?

The ostler had finally brought round my horse. Simonetti helped me mount and checked that my baggage was properly stowed.

"Be careful," he said. "Keep your wits about you. Always have some kind of defensive spell in your mind when you're passing through a forest. These pack trains sometimes get attacked."

Soon he would not be there to nag. Despite myself, my eyes filled with tears. It was a good thing I had said farewell to Kitten at the house. Had she been here, the temptation to cast myself into her arms, weeping and begging to stay, would have been unbearable. Only Simonetti's taciturn reserve stopped me from doing it to him.

He took my hand.

"Kit told me to tell you . . . if you ever needed anything, anything at all, if you were even a bit lonely, just to call and she would come. She meant it, too. You see that you do."

"Please tell her thank you," I said. "Thank you for everything." It seemed such an inadequate thing to say, but I couldn't think of anything better.

We shook hands and Simonetti moved back from the horse. I maneuvered it into place in the column of packhorses.

The chink of bridles reminded me suddenly, vividly, of Andre.

What of Andre/Bedazzer? Would I also call to him when I was lonely the way I probably had that first time I saw him on the beach of bones? His going had filled me with a terrible sense of loss. Part of me still longed for him, though I knew that to do so was dangerous and might even call him up again. I dreamed of him often at night, both as Bedazzer and as Andre, and I could not tell which one I longed for most. I could not stop myself, even after the terrible things I had seen him do. I truly had loved Andre, and the connection was still there. I knew that the demon would always be a part of me, and that I must learn to live with that.

But if I felt a connection with him, there was no answering pull from his side. I had no sense of his presence watching me, trying to break through the runes of distraction that had surrounded me at Kitten's house. That was as it should be. I knew that no matter how much I longed for Bedazzer, I would place those runes all around me wherever I went, so that he could never find me again.

The leader of the pack train called out the signal to start. The horses moved slowly forward.

# OTHER WORLDS, OTHER LANDS
*by Jane Routley*

Basically I write because I'm nosy. I'm fascinated by people. I want to know what it's like to be them. In a small way, writing—making my own people who strut and fret on my own stage—is one way of doing it. Travel, my other passion, is another. I love nosing around in other countries, watching the people in cafes or on the streets and imagining their lives. For a new world person, being able to live in the old world is true pleasure. It's wonderful fuel for the fantasy writer too!

On one of my first journeys I went to Verona with a friend. We stayed in the youth hotel, a beautiful white villa on the hill where the sun came golden at the open windows in the morning. My friend had heard of this special garden, and after we'd seen Juliet's house and all the proper touristy things, we bought some wine, cheese and bread and set off to find it. The Guisitini gardens were a jewel hidden behind high shabby walls—a formal renaissance garden of hedges and neat flowerbeds, yet designed to give a sense of the unknown lurking somewhere further back. As we wandered along the quiet sunlit paths, I could almost hear the flirtatious chatter of Renaissance ladies and the shush of their velvet gowns. Almost. That garden was the ancestor of Kitten Avignon's garden in *Mage Heart* and the gardens at Arden where Andre courted Dion.

*Aramaya*, on the other hand, was inspired by a later trip to St. Petersburg. St. Petersburg was a smack in the eye—so big, so overstated, so extravagant, full of enormous old Czarist palaces stuffed with art treasures and churches with onion domes covered in fine gold leaf. The subway stations, palaces of the workers, were filled with marble and chandeliers. You could almost smell the past, the snowy troika rides and the wild caviar and champagne parties that once happened here, and understand too why it all had to end. Even the city's decay was extravagant. Roads and houses crumbling from neglect, it was mouldering away into something rich and strange beneath its peculiar white summer sky.